CHANGE OF LEADS

BOOK THREE

DANGEROUS GAMES

THE NAVARRE LINK CHRONICLES

CHANGE OF LEADS

BOOK THREE
DANGEROUS GAMES

A. K. BRAUNEIS

First Printing: 2021
Second Printing 2022
Printed and bound in the USA
ISBN: 978-1-7335920-4-8

Two Blazes Artworks
710 Terry Lane
Selah WA 98942
USA

www.twoblazesartworks.com

Cover art, interior illustrations and design by A. K. Brauneis.

Dedication

To my husband, Paul. Though often shaking his head at my chaotic creativity, he has always been there with his love and support throughout this whole process. Love you, Babe. You're the best thing to come into my life.

To Peter Deuel. Though gone from this Earth for many years, he was, back then and still is now, my creative inspiration.

Acknowledgments

Where would I be without the westerns! Movies, TV, books, they were all my sanctuary, my private world where I could go anytime and disappear into a world filled with fun and adventure.

Jimmy Stewart, Audie Murphy, and Ben Johnston, to name only a few who kept my eyes glued to the screen. Wagon Train, Wanted Dead or Alive, High Chaparral, Lancer, and my all-time forever favorite, Alias Smith and Jones. Westerns were abundant when I was growing up, and I'm sure I watched every single movie and most of the TV series that were out there.

Charlie Russell! Oh my, what an influence he had, and still has, on my creative endeavors. Attending the Out West Art Show in Great Falls, Montana has become one of the highlights of my year.

Max Brand was my favorite western author, and though I read books by others, his were the ones that kept me coming back.

Today, I watch most of the new western movies that hit the silver screen, giving my support to a genre that has lost its way but is struggling to make a comeback. At the very least, these more recent westerns have been entertaining, but there are a few that stand out as gems: Butch Cassidy and the Sundance Kid, Tombstone, Silverado, Dances With Wolves, Appaloosa, and yes, I did enjoy Cowboys and Aliens!

I thank all these creations, and the many people that helped in their production for giving me a love that has lasted a lifetime. Now, here I am, writing my own western series, and enjoying every minute of it.

For those people in my life now who have helped me along the way I would like to thank:

Lisa Baird for the many hours she dedicated to proofreading this manuscript. And for her knowledge of legal proceedings and terminology.

Bob Schrader for his invaluable assistance in accurately depicting the courtroom scenes. With some leeway for creative license, of course. Any and all errors are completely of my own doing.

Renee Slider, curator at the Wyoming Territorial Prison National Park, for all of her assistance in tracking down the details.

S. Whyment for her support and contributions toward character development.

Stephanie Haenicke for the many hours she dedicated to proof-reading all the various versions of this manuscript.

Eric Hotz for his technical support. For someone, like myself, who is computer illiterate, his advice and assistance has been invaluable.

Also, to the various online writing sites that offered me a safe place to get my literary feet wet and for helping me realize when it was time to move on.

And, of course, my writing critique group. This group has shown me so much support and encouragement, both in fine tuning my manuscripts, and in weathering the stormy waters of self-publication. You're a great group of ladies!

Thank you!

Also available on Amazon

ICE: Prelude to the Navarre Link Chronicles
ISBN 987-1-7335920-3-1

CHANGE OF LEADS: THE LOST SHOE
ISBN 13:978-1-7335920-0-0

CHANGE OF LEADS: AFTERSHOCK
ISBN 978-1-7335920-1-7

Prelude

Jack faces his own trial. With long-buried evidence brought up against him, he tries to prepare himself for a deadly outcome, but at the last moment, Governor Warren comes through with the pardon.

Jack's friends celebrate the positive outcome, but Jack cannot join in on the festivity. His hurt and anger over Leon's fate drives him into a depression. With drugs and alcohol as his crutches, his actions and changed behavior cause some friends to doubt his sincerity. When he finally hits the bottom, he turns to David for help and thus begins his recovery.

Leon struggles to adjust to life in prison. Warden Mitchel and the senior guard, Floyd Carson, are determined to break the spirit of the charismatic outlaw.

Still, Leon persists. He finds a new friend in Walter Palin, the prison's doctor, and reunites with an old friend, Dr. Mariam Soames who runs the local orphanage and offers sermons at the prison. He also finds an ally in Kenny Reece, another senior guard who disapproves of his superiors' treatment of prisoners and does what he can to buffer the effects.

Reviews

I see these series of novels as historical fiction, where we learn about things we've never known--like the prison system of the time, the politics of governors changing, the beginnings of medicine, the beginning of psychiatry, what it was really like living in an Old West town, living on a ranch. I keep reading it over and over. I don't get bored. I'm fascinated by it all.

Jennifer Kelly, Author: *The Higher the Tide the Warmer the Water.*

His best friend and nephew, Jack Kiefer, has been pardoned, but Napoleon Nash feels like he's wasting away in prison.

Prison life is harsh and it's all Napoleon can do to keep himself out of trouble.

Jack Kiefer may be free, but it isn't the kind of freedom he values, riddled with guilt that he's free but Napoleon's life seems doomed.

The Marsham family stands behind their friends, Jack and Napoleon, and their daughters are actively working toward getting Napoleon pardoned, but it's a lonesome, uphill, struggle.

Brauneis writes westerns with authority. Her scenes are vivid, dynamic plots are exciting, and her characters appealing and realistic.

The books are a continuing series with the plot carried forward in subsequent volumes.

Mary Trimble, Author: *Sailing with Impunity*

This story certainly fits the title. Leon and Jack did everything they were supposed to do to get a pardon but Leon still ends up in prison.

He had to be a strong, confident man to lead an outlaw gang, but here he has to suppress that to survive.

Jack struggles with his friend/uncle being in prison and unable, so far, to make any headway to get him released.

There are many things in play here, and so much can go wrong. Jack has a right to worry.

Can they get Leon out in time?

Gin Pope

Table of Contents

CHAPTER ONE
ONWARD

Arvada, Colorado,
Spring 1886

"David! David, wake up."

The first thing the good doctor became aware of was Tricia calling his name. The second thing was the throbbing pain radiating from the back of his head. He groaned and started to sit up, rubbing the lump that was developing where he had whacked himself against the wall. Tricia had him by the arm, trying to help him. Worry was in her eyes, but overwhelming relief was in her voice.

"David. Oh, thank goodness. What happened?"

David groaned again, rubbing his neck as he looked around. The bed was in disarray and his chair knocked over. Two cups lay desolate upon a floor puddled with coffee, but fortunately the kerosene lamp was still upright upon the table, so this, at least, was a good thing.

"Jack remembered that night, that's what happened," David mumbled.

"Oh dear." Tricia helped her husband stand up and then got him sitting on the edge of the bed. "It doesn't appear to have gone well."

David barked a laugh and then closed his eyes against the throbbing this caused. "Where is he?"

"I don't know. I heard all this crashing and yelling and came to see if you were all right. The front door was wide open, then I found you lying on the floor in here.

She sat on the bed beside David, still holding his arm and rubbing his back, reassuring herself that he was going to be okay. For a woman who could handle just about any crisis concerning her husband's patients, when it came to her own husband, she was just as worried and protective of him as any newlywed would be.

"Oh no," David moaned. "I've got to find him."

"No David. Wait—" Tricia tugged him back down when he attempted to stand up. "You were unconscious. Just wait a bit. It's still dark outside anyway. Just wait until it gets light. Please."

David sat for a moment, his head pounding, as his stomach did a nauseating turn. He knew he should rest, but . . .

"I'm all right Tricia. Just a headache. I'll take some laudanum, enough to take the edge off. I'll be all right."

He got to his feet and walked slowly down to his office to do just that. Tricia sighed with resignation and began to clean up the guest room just to have something to do.

By the time David was dressed, Tricia was in the kitchen, hugging her own cup of coffee and looking distressed.

He smiled at her, some of the color having returned to his face, then he gave her a big hug and a kiss on the cheek.

"I won't go far. If he stayed in town, he'll be easy to find since all he's wearing are his long johns. I'll let Carl know he's run off again. If he's not in town, well, as soon as it gets light, hopefully we can track him down. He can't go far without his boots."

"Yes, all right," Tricia relented. "But if you start feeling dizzy, you get back here."

"Yes, Mother."

He smiled and gave his wife another kiss on the cheek, then left the house, bundling his coat around him against the early morning chill. One good thing was that dawn was not far off, and once it got light, everything would be a lot easier to handle.

The town was quiet as David walked along the boardwalk toward the saloon and then to the sheriff's office. The "late-nighters" had all gone home to sleep it off, and the "rise and shiners" weren't quite ready to rise and shine yet. Not a soul could be seen, and not a dog was barking. That was disappointing.

David knocked on the door of the sheriff's office and then walked in, waking up the night deputy where he slept perched on a chair with his legs up on the desk.

"Oh, Doc! Jeez, ah . . . I'm sorry," the deputy looked frazzled. Getting caught sleeping on duty wasn't a good thing.

David smiled. "Don't worry about it, Robbie," he assured the young man. "When does Sheriff Jacobs usually get in?"

"Oh, gee ahh," the deputy rubbed his eyes and took out his pocket watch, "Not for another hour or so. Can I help ya, Doc?"

"I just wanted to let him know that Kiefer's run off again."

"Oh," came the worried response. "Does he have his gun with him?"

"No."

"Oh good. I don't want to have to go through that again."

"He doesn't have too much else with him either," David said. "Including his boots and a coat. I'm hoping he won't be hard to find."

"Oh yeah. Well, I could go get the sheriff if you want, but if Kiefer's not in town it'll be kinda hard to track him down before it gets light."

"Yes, I agree. Just let Sheriff Jacobs know what's happened when he gets in. I'll take a walk around town and see if I can find him. If I can't, I'll come back when it's light, and we'll go from there."

"Yeah, okay Doc."

An hour and a half later, David had had no luck finding his wayward patient. Finally, he decided to go home for some breakfast and assure his wife that he was not only still coherent, but alert and feeling fine.

Some more coffee and something to eat completed his recovery and he was eager to return to the sheriff's office and get something going.

Approaching the office, David smiled to see three horses, his own little chestnut, Rudy, included, all tacked up and waiting for the posse to get organized. David was just mounting the steps and wondering how many lawmen it took to make a posse, when Carl Jacobs and Ben Palin came out and greeted him.

"Hey there, Doc," said Jacobs, "you're just in time. Figured you'd want to come along."

"Yes. Definitely."

"Okay, let's mount up. Ben here is a pretty good tracker and the ground is still damp from the rain we've had. I don't think he's gonna be too hard to find."

The three men got on board and turned their horses toward David's house. The fact that Kiefer hadn't been found in town would strongly suggest that he had headed out the other way, toward the back country, so that seemed like the best place to start.

"You sayin' he's not wearin' any boots?" Jacobs asked the doctor.

"That's right. No boots, no hat, no coat. Just his long johns."

"He's gonna be dang cold when we find him. Good thing we got some blankets with us. Don't worry, Doc; he won't have gone far without boots."

"Yeah."

Sure enough, not too far beyond David's house, Ben spotted man-size footprints in the soft dirt along the side of the road. It looked like he was running and heading toward open country, in the general direction of the Rocking M. It was highly doubtful a man could get that far on foot, even with boots, and though they were all aware of Kiefer's past and experience, they were still hopeful of finding him quickly.

Three miles out of town, Ben pulled up and dismounted. He squatted down to take a closer look at the foot print, then straightened up and looked at the doc.

"There's blood here," he pointed at the print to prove it. "Lots of rocks along this trail; he's probably cut up his feet some."

"Boy, oh boy," Jacobs shook his head. "He was doin' real well there too, Doc. What in the world set him off this time?"

"Oh well, he had a bad night," David sighed, resting his hands on the saddle horn. "Bad dreams, you know. He got upset. He probably regrets it now. I wouldn't be surprised if we were to meet him coming back toward town."

Jacobs laughed. "That would certainly make things easier, wouldn't it?" He nudged his horse, and the group picked up the trot.

Turns out, David was close to being right. A couple of more miles down the road and the small posse spotted the fugitive sitting on a rock, hugging his knees and shivering. As they rode closer, Jack looked up and sent them an embarrassed smile.

"About time you fellas showed up," he commented. "I'm freezin'."

David smiled and, dismounting, he untied the blanket from behind his saddle and approached his friend.

"Good morning, Jack. How are you?"

"Like I said, I'm freezin'," Jack repeated, looking downtrodden, "and I can't walk—I've cut up my feet."

"Yes, I know," David told him as he draped the blanket

across his shoulders. "If we help you, do you think you can get up on my horse?"

Jack sent a despondent look over to the animal.

"I donno, David. I'll try."

Ben had dismounted and led the doctor's horse closer to them. Both men grabbed an arm and helped Jack get to his feet. Jack tried to take a step and almost went down, sucking his teeth with the pain. But Ben and David held him up and basically carried him over to the horse.

Jack grabbed hold of the saddle horn and they heaved him up and into the saddle.

David mounted behind him, made sure Jack was snuggled into the blanket, and then they turned back toward town.

"Oh, Carl," David began, "do you think Ben here could ride out to the Rocking M to let them know what's happened? I don't think Jack is going to be up to working out there for a while."

"Sure," Jacobs agreed. "Ben . . . off ya go."

"Yes sir, Sheriff," Ben answered. "I'll see ya back in town in a couple of hours." He turned his horse again and headed off at a gallop toward the Rocking M.

***

Jacobs helped David get Jack settled onto his bed, while Tricia hovered around, trying to be helpful.

"Would you like some coffee, Jack?"

"No thanks."

"Do you want anything to eat?"

"No thanks."

"How about you, Carl? Would you like some coffee?"

"No thank you, ma'am," he answered her. "I best be gettin' back to the office for now." He sent a quick look to Jack. "So, young fella, think you're gonna stay put for a while now?"

"Yeah, Sheriff. I'm not goin' anywhere," then added the mumble, "even if I could." He mustered up a smile and met Jacobs' eye. "I'm sorry for the trouble I caused ya, Sheriff. It won't happen again."

***

Shortly after Carl left, David returned to Jack's room with a wash basin filled with warm medicated water.

"Here, Jack," he said, setting it down on the floor, "soak your feet in this for a while, then I'll look at them and see what kind of damage you've done."

"Yeah. Ouch."

"Yes, I know. Just ease them in gradually. It's going to hurt at first, but you can't blame me for that; this time it was all your own doing."

"I know." He dipped his toes into the water then bit his lower lip as he forced the rest of his feet into the warm liquid. "I'm sorry. I seem to recall pushing you. Did I hurt you?"

David was about to shrug it off when Tricia's voice came in from the kitchen.

"You knocked him out."

Jack groaned. "Aww, jeez. I'm sorry." He stared at his feet, ashamed of himself. "This seems ta be gettin' worse and worse. As soon as I think I'm doin' better, somethin' else comes out of the blue ta knock me flat. How many more revelations am I gonna have before I'm done with this?"

"I think you've run the gauntlet now." David sat down on the chair again. "This is the one I was waiting for, in any case."

Jack looked at him, feeling slightly defensive. "You knew this was gonna happen?"

"Well—yeah," David admitted. "Cameron and I knew what had happened in Cheyenne, and I knew you would remember it eventually, although I didn't foresee you knocking me out and dashing down the street with no clothes on."

Jack groaned again. "Oh, no wonder Cameron was so . . ." he sighed, his shoulders slumping. "I couldn't figure out why he didn't trust me. I thought maybe it was because of what came out at the trial, but he seemed all right at the dinner party. But that look he gave me when we were on the train, headin' home . . ." Jack hung his head. "I guess I don't blame him now."

"Cameron doesn't hold that against you anymore, Jack," David assured him. "It was hard on him at first, but he's come to realize there were a lot of other factors in play there. Your behavior in Cheyenne was very much out of character for you."

Jack didn't respond. He felt low and wondered how he was going to be able to face his friends again, knowing what they knew about him.

David put a consolatory hand on his shoulder.

"Give it time, Jack. It'll be all right. Here, let me change the water, it's getting rather bloody."

***

A few days later, Jack hobbled his way outside to sit on the front porch and soak up some of the sunny warmth in the hope that it would help him feel better. He couldn't seem to lift himself out of this slump. The bout of depression wasn't as acute as the first one, but it still lingered, and he began to wonder if he was ever going to be truly happy again.

He sat back, nursing a cup of coffee as his bandaged feet rested upon a pillow on a stool. He was feeling downright sorry for himself, when he noticed a familiar team of horses coming toward him. As the buckboard came closer, he soon recognized Sam at the lines and then Jean sitting on the bench beside him.

Jack groaned, feeling a tingle of dread go through him. He wasn't ready to face any of his friends just yet.

David had constantly assured him he didn't have anything to worry about in that quarter, but Jack himself felt so ashamed of his actions that he couldn't imagine anyone else feeling anything different.

How can I face Jean? There's no point in tryin' to pretend that all is well; she'll see right through any kind of a ruse I might try to put forth. Ha. Yeah. Jean can see right into my heart and soul, and now, knowing what truly lurks there, she ain't likely ta have any affection left for me.

She must be coming to tell me, to my face, ta stay away from Penny. That must be it. That's what any wise woman would do; protect her children from the monster who had been pretending all this time to be a decent man. How could she even consider me now as being part of her family, as being a husband to Penny? That's over.

He thought he would be relieved with that door slamming in his face. This way, it wouldn't have to be Jack breaking Penny's heart; her own parents were going to end it all for him. He could just ride away and not be bothered with it anymore.

But he didn't feel relieved at all; he felt hurt and

disappointed.

I'm gonna miss Penny. Damn, I'm gonna miss all of 'em. Little Elijah's growin' so fast; I was kinda lookin' forward ta seein' 'im take his first steps, hearing 'im speak his first words. He sighed with regret. That ain't gonna happen now.

The buckboard stopped right in front of David's house and Sam stepped down to help Jean disembark from the vehicle.

"Mornin', Mr. Kiefer," Sam greeted him.

Jack nodded his reply. He felt his throat tighten with shame, and the anticipation of unveiled disapproval from this woman whom he had come to love and respect, as he would have his own mother.

Jean smiled at him as she climbed the steps onto the porch.

Jack shifted uncomfortably in his chair. *What's this all about? Is she tryin' ta soften the blow? Why bother? Make the cut quick and clean—get it over with.*

"Good morning, Mathew," she greeted him. "How are you feeling today?"

Jack didn't answer her. He felt so ashamed, and the knot in his gut tightened along with the knot in his throat. He was vaguely aware of Sam returning to the buckboard and driving away. *Why don't he just wait for Jean to say her piece and then let her leave? Why force her to stay and prolong the agony?*

Jean sighed when Jack looked away from her. She was carrying a basket filled with freshly baked scones; he could smell them and it took him back. Back to that day, almost a year ago, when he and Leon came for a visit and had enjoyed Jean's wonderful meals and fresh baked goods.

She's deliberately torturing me.

"I'll just take these in to Tricia," Jean told him. "Perhaps she'll put on some tea for us while we visit. How does that sound?"

Like a set-up, was Jack's first thought, but again, he didn't say anything.

Jean went into the house to greet her hostess and present her with the baking. Though he couldn't make out what they were saying, he could hear the two women talking and laughing together. *What—are they laughing at me? Do they think this is funny? I didn't think Jean was that cruel. Well, just goes to show ya.*

After a few minutes of the two ladies visiting, Jean came back onto the porch and, pulling up one of the other chairs, she sat down beside her friend and gave him a gentle touch on his hand. He felt like he wanted to pull it away from her, but he didn't. He didn't look at her either.

"Tricia's going to put some tea on for us," Jean said. "She says that you haven't had any breakfast yet, so she'll bring out some of the scones I brought, with some preserves. Does that sound good?"

No outward response.

Why is she torturing me like this? Why does she persist in pretending that this is a friendly social call? Why can't she just say her piece and leave?

"Mathew? Won't you look at me?" A sadness lingered in her voice. "Won't you wish me a good morning?"

Jack felt his throat and eyes start to burn and he turned even further away from her. *Oh no. I'm not going to start crying again, am I? I haven't cried this much since I was eight years old. And what good would it do anyway? What was the point? Ah no—*

He felt the sobs gathering strength, and a tear spilled out to roll down his cheek.

No, not again.

He couldn't believe how weak he was—what a baby. First in front of David, now in front of Jean. This was getting ridiculous.

"Mathew. It's all right," Jean whispered to him. "My dear, sweet Mathew. It's all right."

Then Jean was crying too, and Jack couldn't believe it. Why would she be crying for him? It hurt him that he was hurting her, and he wanted to take her pain away. She shouldn't be crying for him—he wasn't worth it.

But she was crying, and he felt her tears become his. Their eyes met for an instant, but then he dropped his gaze as his anguish overtook him.

She touched his face, then pulled him into her heart and rocked him like a child, while his sobs came forth again, ran their course and then, finally, quieted.

Trish came out with a tray full of tea and scones, but she did an abrupt about face and left the two friends alone for a little while longer. She could keep the snacks warm on the stove for a while yet and give Jack time to compose himself. She smiled. David had been right again, in suggesting that Jean come by to speak with their patient. Her husband knew that Jean had a special relationship with the two ex-outlaws. Jack had totally shut down and retreated within himself, refusing to speak to anyone about anything.

But David had told Tricia that Napoleon had bared his soul to Jean on the day of his arrest, and David hoped that maybe Jack would now do the same. It looked as though the strategy just might be paying off.

After a time, Jack pulled away from Jean. Sitting back in his chair, he took a deep breath and, rubbing his eyes, he swallowed down the last dregs of his emotions.

Jean smiled.

"Feeling better now?" she asked him.

"Hmm."

"How about some tea?"

"Yeah."

She patted his hand, then stood and disappeared into the house, only to return a few minutes later, laden with the tray and goodies. Trish followed closely behind, bringing some preserves and utensils, then left them alone once more.

Jean poured the tea, then settled into her chair while they both enjoyed the first few sips in silence.

"I thought you hated me," Jack mumbled. "I thought you were coming to tell me to leave and never come back."

"No, Mathew, I don't hate you. Not at all."

"I did a terrible thing."

"Yes, you did," she saw her words cut him. "But you're sorry for it and that's what matters now."

Jack nodded and took another sip of tea.

"How can you forgive me?"

Jean sighed and thought about this for a moment.

"If you showed no remorse over it, then I would have realized that I had been wrong about you. But the very fact that you are suffering so from the guilt of it only serves to support my opinion of what kind of man you are." She leaned toward him and put a hand on his arm. "You are a good man, Mathew; please don't lose sight of that."

"I donno," he said, shaking his head. "The things I've done—not just that night in Cheyenne, but before—before I was even twenty years old, I'd done some terrible things."

"You've gone through a lot in your life," Jean said. "More than anyone should have to. And the worst of it was before you were even old enough to understand what was going on. Those events couldn't help but cause damage. I agree, you have done some terrible things: things that would have destroyed a less courageous heart; things that could have turned you into just as cruel and vicious a man as the men who attacked your farm. But it didn't. Instead you learned compassion, and you felt remorse. The fates have given you a second chance, Mathew—don't throw it away."

"I don't know how," Jack admitted. "I'm tryin'. I wanna help Leon, but I can't do that when I'm like this. But I don't know how to change it."

"This has been an incredibly traumatic year—for all of us," Jean smiled and gave his hand a squeeze. "You've been through a lot of changes and a lot of growth."

Jack snorted at this.

"No, you'll see," Jean insisted. "Right now, you're still suffering the growing pains, but you're going to come out of all this a better, stronger man. Of that, I have no doubt.

"You have been forced to look back on your life and face up to the things you have done and been battered down by. That would be hard on anyone. But it's time to stop looking backwards now, Mathew. Time to put away regrets and wishing that things could be changed, because they can't be. All you can do is take away with you the lessons you've learned and move onward."

She shook his arm until he turned to face her. "It's time to move forward now. It's time to become the man you were meant to be; the man your mother knew you would be. The man she saw in you when she looked into her little boy's eyes."

***

Laramie, Wyoming,
Spring 1886

Jack limped into the processing room, his left hand clutching a cane, while keeping his right hand available for any trouble that might come his way. This precaution was completely an instinct now, since he always had to leave his holster and gun with one of the guards when coming to visit a prisoner. Some habits refuse to go away.

He painfully made his way to the table and sat down, meeting Leon's furrowed brow and concerned look.

Jack smiled, sheepishly. "I injured my feet."

"Yeah, David said you went for a run around the block without any boots on," Leon sat back and cocked a brow. "I thought he was joking, but . . . what were you trying to accomplish with that?"

Jack sighed. He knew this was going to be awkward. His uncle could be just as bad as David when it came to pushing a point.

"I know, it was stupid," he admitted. "I had a bad dream, is all."

"Hmm."

"Oh, there you go again," Jack complained.

"What?"

"Actin' like ya know more than you're lettin' on," Jack snapped. "I suppose David told ya all about it."

"No. He figured if you wanted me to know, you would tell me yourself."

The atmosphere became laden with an awkward, expectant silence.

"Okay," Leon relented with an air of injured feelings, "if you can tell David, but you can't tell me—that's fine."

"Naw, Leon, that ain't it. It's just, well . . . David already knew; he was just waitin' for me ta figure it out. And it's . . . shameful, what I done. I even blubbered like a baby in front of Jean—jeez, that was embarrassin'."

"Yeah." Leon remembered his own breakdown with her. "She seems to have that effect on people. So, Jean knows too?"

"Yeah." Jack shrugged. "And Cameron, and Taggard. It seems that everyone but me knew what happened that night."

"And me."

"Leon—"

"Well . . . I just . . ." Leon shrugged, feeling defensive. "Why can't you tell me? We're partners, aren't we?"

"Yeah, a 'course."

"Well?"

"Well . . ."

Silence.

An eternity ticked by.

Leon sighed. "How was your Easter?" He decided it was better to change the subject than waste the whole hour waiting for Jack to tell him something he didn't want to tell him. The man could be so stubborn sometimes.

"Good," Jack brightened, relieved that they were on to something else. "Steven came up from Denver, and the Marshams all came into town for services on Good Friday. We got together at David and Tricia's place for lunch afterward, so it was quite the gatherin'."

"Yeah, I bet."

Jack grinned. "You should 'a seen Eli. He was squirmin' all over the place—didn't wanna sit still. He's crawlin' everywhere now and poor Jean is at her wits end, tryin' ta keep track of 'im."

***

Arvada, Colorado,
Good Friday

Everyone sat around the kitchen table enjoying after-lunch tea and Jean's freshly baked pie. Eli would not sit still and was starting to exasperate his mother, which says a lot, considering Jean's endless well of patience.

"Oh, Mama," Penny said, "let me take him outside for a while. I'll play with him on the front porch."

"Ah, Penny, you're a dear."

Penny came around the table and, taking her little brother in her arms, headed out the front door with him screaming and complaining the whole way.

But Penny must have done something right, because within five minutes the screaming had ceased and was replaced with excited little boy laughter. Everyone inside the house breathed a sigh of relief.

"What a handful." Jean sighed, pushing a loose strand of graying hair from her brow. "The girls were easy compared to this one."

Cameron smiled. "At least we have the girls to help with him—well, Penny, anyway, since Caroline will be leaving us." He glanced at Steven. "How is your office coming along? Will you be open for business soon?"

Steven swallowed a mouthful of pie. "Oh yes. Actually, I'm open for business now. I even have a few clients on the books. There is already plenty for Caroline to do once she gets settled in." The young couple in question smiled at each other.

"Good," said Cameron. "Would hate to see her go all the way to Denver and not have a job waiting for her."

"Oh, Papa." Caroline rolled her eyes, knowing she was being teased.

Jean sat quietly, drinking her tea.

"Anymore headway with Leon's case?" Jack asked once there was an opening.

"Yes," Steven said, though he looked confused. "I got an anonymous tip from someone, that Governor Warren is into some dirty business dealings, and that I should start doing some digging into certain companies out this way. But, I'm not quite sure what to make of it all. If the tip isn't legitimate, there could be accusations of slander for one thing, and at the least, a big waste of my time. Still, I'll look into it and see where it goes."

Jack sat up straighter in his chair, suddenly very interested in this information.

"Do you know where the tip came from?" he asked, though he figured he already had a good idea.

"No, not really," Steven admitted. "Certainly not from anywhere around here. Maybe back east or maybe even up north. But how would anyone in those areas know what the Governor of Wyoming was doing?"

"Oh, you'd be surprised," Jack commented. "Especially if this tip is comin' from who I think it's comin' from."

"Who do you think it's coming from?"

"Well, let's just say it might be a friend from way back. A very resourceful friend from way back."

***

Laramie, Wyoming

"You think it was Gabriella?" Leon asked.

"That's what I'm thinkin'," Jack admitted. "I take it you heard from her?"

"Yeah," Leon sighed. "She wrote me a letter about a month ago. She said she was going to try and help."

"Uh huh. She sent me a letter around the same time sayin' much the same thing. If she's been able ta dig up some dirt on

Warren, well, I don't think she's beyond a little bit 'a blackmail."

He cringed and darted a glance at the guard. Murray was standing so quietly that it was easy to forget the man was there.

Leon just shrugged and shook his head, suggesting that Jack shouldn't worry too much about it. As far as Leon was concerned, the lower end guards weren't all that bright anyway, and Murray probably didn't even know who Warren was.

"Yeah, okay," Jack relaxed. "Anyway, that's all there is on that for now, so Steven is lookin' into it."

Leon nodded, then moved on. "I got a letter from Josey last week saying that Caroline got moved in at the boarding house right after Easter. She said she was a little homesick the first few nights but settled in after that. She's getting along just fine, now."

"Yeah," Jack agreed. "Cameron took her into Denver on the Monday followin' Easter and helped ta get her moved in. He said she was all excited to be off on this 'new adventure' and couldn't wait for him ta head back home, so she could get on with bein' an 'independent adult'."

"Uh huh," Leon smiled. "How did Jean take it?"

Jack shrugged. "Well, accordin' ta Penny, she put on a brave face at first, but as soon as the buckboard had driven outta the yard she started cryin'. I suppose it must be hard on a mother, watchin' her first-born leave the nest."

"I suppose," Leon contemplated this. "Never really thought about it before. It's one of those things that just . . . happens."

"I suppose," Jack echoed. Then it was his turn to change the subject. "How about you? Was there anything special here for Easter?"

"Naw," Leon sneered. "Just the usual service on Sunday. The only difference was the sermon was aimed more toward the significance of Easter and all that. It was kind of interesting, but," Leon shrugged, "not really my cup of tea."

"Yeah, I know."

"Oh, but Mariam came by for a visit again, right after that," Leon brightened. "That was nice. She brought me another book."

"Oh? Which one?"

"The Four Guardsmen by Alexandre Dumas."

"Oh. Have ya read it before?"

"Not that one, no."

"Well, that's good. Anyone else been comin' to see ya?"

"Yeah, actually," Leon admitted, with a confused frown. "Frank came by."

"Frank?"

"Yeah."

"We know a couple 'a Franks, Leon. Which one?"

"Carlyle."

"Carlyle?"

"Yeah."

***

The previous week

Leon sat in the processing room, shackled hand and foot as usual, waiting with some curiosity for whomever it was coming to visit him.

Well, it's not likely to be Jack, because he was just here last week. Of course, something might have come up that was worth a second visit, so, maybe. Hmm, let's see. It could be Taggard. That would be nice. I haven't seen him since I was sick. A couple of letters, telling me to eat more. He smirked. *Nothing new there. That's it, I think. Who else would come visit? David or Cameron? Hmm, not likely. They're both busy. Oh! Maybe it's Steven with some news.*

He sat up a tad straighter as the door opened, but then his jaw dropped.

The dark-haired, weaselly-looking man in the black suit and fedora stepped into the room, all puffed up as though he owned the place. But with his first look at his old "friend" sitting at the table, he stopped and stared.

Leon sighed with frustration. There it was again; that look of shock and pity that seemed to flash across everyone's face the first time they saw him as a convict.

Do I really look that different? It's bad enough getting it from Jack and Taggard, but Frank Carlyle? Having this bastard feeling sorry for me is downright degrading.

Usually a master at keeping his thoughts hidden behind his beady eyes, on this occasion, Frank Carlyle showed his surprise openly, making no effort to conceal it. At least Leon's other visitors had quickly hidden their shock away and then come forward to greet their friend in as normal a manner as possible. But Frank stood there, frowning and chewing his lip, until Leon finally smiled at him and brought him out of his trance.

"Hi ya Frank. What brings you calling?"

Frank's black eyes shifted to meet Leon's brown ones. Everything about Frank was black: his eyes, his short-cropped hair, his moustache, and his brows that were knotted together in consternation. Even his clothing was black. A tall, slim, arrow-straight man, always in black. And he wondered why people looked at him askance.

If anyone could have scared Caroline away from her previous intention of becoming an undercover agent, Frank was it. Fortunately, as far as Leon was concerned, Steven had come along and accomplished much the same change of heart.

Frank's eyes narrowed as he took in Leon's situation. Realizing he was expected to respond to the greeting, he forced a smile onto his rigid face and came forward, stepping nimbly around the table.

"Nash," he greeted the convict. "It's been a long time."

He extended a hand for shaking, then quickly withdrew it when he noted that Leon was shackled. This fact surprised him. Though he knew the lot of a convict; he had seen it before, but he had never prepared himself to see Nash in that situation.

Like so many people before him, Frank couldn't help but be affected by the outlaw's charisma, though he never allowed it to show through. He was a government agent, assigned to keep Nash and Kiefer in line, and he couldn't, nor had he ever, allowed Leon's natural magnetism to overwhelm that relationship.

Still, there was a grudging respect between the two men, so now, seeing Leon like this, wearing prison garb, with shaved head and shackled hand and foot, it didn't seem right. For some reason, if he had even thought of it at all, Frank assumed Leon's normal command over any given situation would allow him to avoid being controlled in this manner.

Frank expected to see Leon as he'd always been, cocky, almost to the point of arrogance, and very much in charge. It now seemed that Napoleon Nash had finally met his match in the Auburn Prison System.

Then, before Frank could process all this new information, Officer Pearson stepped between the two men, his rifle up and blocking the Wells Fargo man from getting any closer to the prisoner. Apparently, the fact that Frank was a law officer of sorts held very little credence with the officials at this institution.

"No physical contact with the prisoner," Pearson reminded him. "Please be seated on the other side of the table and remain there."

A dangerous glint came through the narrowed eyes, but then Frank released an indignant puff and backed off.

He sat down opposite Leon and whispered to the inmate, "A little touchy, ain't they?"

Pearson returned to his corner, but he sent a scowl toward the detective and kept a wary eye on him.

"Don't worry about it, Frank," Leon commented. "They're always like that. I guess they're afraid you're going to slip me a lock pick or something. Imagine, someone actually wanting to break out of this place."

Frank snorted. "If I was plannin' on breaking you outta here, it wouldn't be some lame-brain idea like that."

"Hmm." Leon sighed. "So . . . what brings ya here, Frank?"

"Oh, well, I was just delivering some documents to our office in Cheyenne and thought I'd take this opportunity to check up on you."

"Ah," Leon nodded. "Still with Wells Fargo, are you?"

"Yes. Why wouldn't I be? I'm one of their top agents, and they know it. There are certain assignments that only I can handle."

"Uh huh. Like delivering documents."

"I know." Frank sniffed, his eyes narrowing with suspicion. "Lately, they have been noticeably cautious of me."

"Right." Leon smiled. "Keeping an agent like you busy delivering documents. You think your boss is trying to shuffle you out of the way? I know you were out of the country at the time of our arrests, but didn't anybody let you know what had happened?"

Frank's demeanor hardened as he had to acknowledge his deliberate exclusion.

"No," he stated, his lip curling with irritation. "I didn't know anything about it until I was back home, then it was too late. Otherwise, I would have been right there for you, and you know it. Which is why, I suppose, the Governor's Office kept me abroad."

"And why all you're doing now is delivering documents."

More irritation etched the angular face.

"I've delivered documents before," Frank pointed out, trying to reconcile, in his own mind, the reasons for his apparent demotion. "They're highly confidential and can't be trusted to anyone other than their most reliable agents. I will remain optimistic that this has nothing to do with my relationship with you fellas. Still, if I had been made aware of your situation, I would have returned to the States, and offered my testimony."

"And done what, Frank?" Leon asked him. "Expose the governor for the lying, double-crossing opportunist that he is? Things would have come up, Frank; things that you've done that weren't quite legal. Things that we helped you 'straighten out' on the side. You wouldn't have done us any good, and you most likely would have lost your job."

"Well . . . I donno," Frank mumbled. "It's not unusual for an agent to step over the line in order to get a job done, you know that. Anything you helped me with was always toward that end."

"Yeah, I know," Leon conceded, "but, given the circumstances, if you had come forward, the Governor's office would have used some of our shadier tactics against you. You would have been railroaded out of your job. Perhaps it was best that you were kept in the dark."

Frank's jaw tightened. He didn't like the fact that Leon knew things about him that could get him into trouble if they came to light. But he also acknowledged that he knew things about Nash and Kiefer that would have vetoed their pardon deal anyway. He wisely decided to change the subject. "How's Kiefer?"

"He's good," Leon informed him. "He's staying with friends in Colorado and they are all working at getting that pardon for me. So, who knows, maybe I'll be outta here before next Christmas."

"Good Nash. That's good." His squinty eyes squinted further "Kiefer's in Colorado, you say?"

"Yeah. Near Denver. A little town called Arvada. If you want to get in touch with him, that's the place."

"Yeah, yeah sure." Frank's manner became blustery now that past deeds were left behind. "I already sent a telegram to that lawyer fella, but never heard back from him. I have a feeling your partner's keeping me at bay. He never did trust me much."

Leon allowed a crooked smile. "Yeah, well, we didn't exactly start out on the best of terms, did we? You damn near killed me the first time we met, and that didn't set well with him. Then pistol-whipping me and pulling a gun on him only added to his ire. Jack Kiefer is not a man you can push, Frank. You know that."

Frank snorted. "That's the sign of a successful interrogation, if the subject thinks he's gonna die. I kept tellin' ya it would be easier on you if you'd simply give us the information we wanted."

Leon's jaw set, the resentment of that first meeting fighting it's way to the surface. He made no comment.

"As for that second time, you were getting too mouthy, thinkin' you were runnin' the show." Frank continued. "My job was ta keep my eye on you two, make sure you stayed on track. You just needed reminding, that's all. Kiefer would have come at me if I hadn't pulled my gun on him. You think I'm stupid?"

"No," Leon shook his head. "When I first met you, you scared the bejeesus outta me, and you're anything but stupid, Frank. Maybe a little awkward, socially, but . . ."

Frank scowled. "It ain't my job to be social. Your partner needs to figure that out. How long is he gonna hold a grudge?"

Leon dropped his eyes, a heavy sadness hitting his heart. "It's not just that, Frank. There is that other incident . . ."

Frank sighed. "That was unfortunate."

Leon met his eye with this understatement.

Frank held it. "You seem to have gotten past it."

"Jack wasn't there, I was," Leon mumbled. "I know what happened. Jack doesn't forget things like that. He actually treats you well, considering."

"Humph. What's done is done. Time he got past it."

Leon simply nodded. *How does someone get past something like that?*

Silence settled between them, then Frank pushed himself away from the table, ending the conversation.

"Time ta go. I'll keep in touch, at least with Kiefer." He then frowned, realizing that more should be said at this parting. "We'll get ya outta here, Nash. Just you hang in there—we'll get ya out. And eat something, will ya? You're lookin' a little peaked."

Leon rolled his eyes. "Yeah, Frank."

"And you be careful in here; prison can be a very dangerous place, lots of unsavory people around."

Leon hesitated. He could never be sure if Frank was being serious with some of the remarks he blurted out.

"Yeah Frank, I know. Thanks for coming by."

And then Frank was gone.
Leon heard Pearson snort behind him, and he sighed.
"Yeah."

CHAPTER TWO
MIXED FEELINGS

"That was weird," Jack stated.

"Yeah," Leon agreed. "Did you ever hear from him?"

"Steven did mention hearing from him a while back," Jack admitted. "I guess we never did follow through on it. Didn't really see the point."

"Hmm," Leon nodded. "I can understand that. Still, as much as I hate to admit it, he has helped us out in the past. You might consider getting hold of him. Wouldn't be a problem for either of you now, since you have your pardon."

"Yeah, I know," Jack agreed. "I just don't know what he could do, and I still prefer not to be around 'im. But yeah, I'll think about it."

"Okay." Then Leon smiled. "How's Penny?"

Much to Leon's surprise, Jack forgot to get defensive and he brightened up and smiled back at his friend.

"She's good. She showed up at David's place a little while after Easter, all eager to go for a ride . . ."

***

Arvada, Colorado

. . . "Jack, you've got company," Tricia called to him from the kitchen.

Jack hobbled out from his bedroom and, at a gesture from Tricia, carried through to the front door. Stepping onto the porch, he was met by a very pretty picture.

Penny, with her long blonde hair done up in a nice neat bun

at the nape of her neck, was wearing that very fetching riding habit, and sitting aboard a bright-eyed and energetic Karma.

Penny grinned as her friend came outside.

"C'mon Mathew," she invited him. "It's a beautiful day for a ride. Let's go shake off the cobwebs."

Jack chuckled. "You rode all the way into town just ta invite me out for a ride?"

"Yes, of course. Go get ready. I'll ride down to the livery and have Midnight saddled up for you."

"Well, all right," Jack agreed, still grinning. "Let's do it."

***

Twenty minutes later, Penny returned, leading both horses. She stood waiting outside the Gibson residence for Jack to appear.

Jack was busy pulling on a few more layers of socks over his still bandaged feet. He then, very carefully, slid them into a larger pair of David's lace-up boots, hoping that would be enough to protect the injuries from any more abuse. If he didn't get off his horse to walk around, he ought to be all right.

While he was busy putting together his coat, hat and newly re-acquired holster and gun, Tricia stepped outside and went down the steps to greet their visitor.

"Good morning, Penny. How is your mother?"

"She's fine, Mrs. Gibson. Still kind of missing Caroline." She rolled her eyes, "but other than that, she's all right. Is Dr. Gibson at home?"

"No, he's doing his rounds," Tricia answered, then approached Karma and gave the dark liver mare a pat on the face. "So, this is Karma, is it? This is the first time I've seen her up close, but I sure have heard quite a few tales about her."

"Oh yes. Isn't she beautiful?" Penny beamed with pleasure. "Papa has found the perfect stallion to breed her to, and we're all so excited about it."

"Really?" Tricia tweaked a brow. "You're not going to breed her to Gambler? I thought having your own stallion would save paying a fee to someone else."

"Normally, that's true," Penny admitted, "but Papa wants to bring a whole new blood line into our breeding program, so that means having to find two horses who are not already a part of it.

Since Karma is such a lovely mare, Papa is hoping that with the right stallion, we'll get a top-quality colt to be our new foundation sire. Gambler is getting pretty long in the tooth, so—oh, hi Mathew. Are you ready to go?"

Tricia turned to see Jack gingerly making his way across the porch and down the steps, using the hand railing for support. His pain was evident.

"Oh, Jack," Tricia frowned with concern, "you just wait there, and I'll bring Midnight over to you,"

"Yeah, good idea," Jack mumbled, though he felt silly having two women assisting him to mount his own horse.

Still, it did make all the difference when Tricia brought Midnight alongside the steps and Jack was able to simply grab the saddle horn, step into the stirrup and swing aboard. It still hurt, but nothing like having to haul himself up from ground level.

Penny turned back to the mare, and even though Karma was a tall horse for such a little lady, Penny had no trouble at all getting her foot in the stirrup and swinging into the saddle. Then, with a wave to Tricia, they turned the horses to the street and headed out of town at a gentle trot.

***

Once they got to more open countryside, they let the horses have their heads and soon the two four-legged friends were racing each other across the landscape.

Jack discovered that having his feet in the stirrups was not a good idea, so soon slid out of them and galloped on, enjoying the view ahead of him, this being the backside of Penny. She sat comfortably in the saddle, her hips moving in rhythm with Karma's stride and being no end of a distraction for the man riding along behind her.

Five miles later, the horses slowed of their own accord, and soon they had settled into a comfortable jog trot. Jack drew Midnight up alongside Karma, so he and his companion could talk together. Her face was flushed with excitement, and a few strands of her hair had come loose from the bun and floated around her face in an enticing manner.

Jack smiled at her but tried to keep his natural response to her femininity under control. He knew from past experience that becoming aroused while riding a horse was not only uncomfortable but had the potential for outright embarrassment. He took his hat off, ran his hand through his curls and then plunked the hat down onto his lap and made sure it stayed there, just in case.

Penny was oblivious.

"That was fun." Her eyes sparkled with excitement as Jack came up beside her. "Now that the weather is more accommodating, we'll have to get out for rides like this more often."

"Yeah, uh huh."

"Do you know when you're going to be moving back out to our ranch?" Penny asked, hope taking over her countenance.

"No, not really. Once my feet heal up, I may head over to Medicine Bow to do some work for my friend, Sheriff Murphy."

"Oh," came the disappointed response.

"And I think Max Coburn has some jobs for me to do, as well."

"Oh, that Mr. Coburn," Penny laughed, "he was such a funny old bear."

"Yeah," Jack commented skeptically. "That's Max all right: a funny old bear." *Until he started to growl, then maybe not so much.*

"Still, you know Papa has work for you at the ranch," she gently pushed.

"Yeah, I know. I gotta find a way ta make a livin' now, stand on my own two feet. I don't wanna be relyin' on the charity of others—that ain't right."

"It's not charity," Penny was quick to point out. "Papa needs help, especially through the summer. Sam can't do it all. Besides," she mumbled, almost under her breath, "I think Sam is planning on getting married later in the summer, so he may not be around much after that."

"He still needs to have a job, especially if he gets married," Jack pointed out. "I know he wants ta buy that little house the Randolphs have for sale. It's still close enough for him ta continue workin' at your place. Besides, Sam ain't your father's only employee. He has a number of fellas workin' up at the line cabin. Not ta mention all them others tendin' to the timber. He ain't short 'a help."

"Hmm."

Jack smiled. Obviously, Penny had hoped Jack wouldn't think of that, so then she would be able to convince him that, with

Sam possibly leaving, he had to come back to the Rocking M in order to take over. This strategy was quickly shot down.

"Let's wait and see what happens," Jack suggested. "David thinks it's gonna be awhile before I can get back to any physical work anyway. So, we'll see."

Penny brightened. "Okay."

Jack chuckled softly. "Besides," he added, "we've still got to get Leon outta prison. How are you comin' with them fliers?"

"Great. Caroline took a whole bunch of them with her when she went to Denver and is going to be handing them out there again. Plus, Steven is sending more out to the other territories. Wyoming, of course, and Montana too, I think."

"Good," Jack nodded. "In the meanwhile, Taggard is still pestering the governor, and Steven is doin' some diggin' where that gentleman is concerned. So . . . onward!"

"How is Peter?" Penny asked, concern taking over her features. "I miss him so much. I want to go visit him, but Papa won't let me."

"No, he's right, Penny," Jack confirmed Cameron's decree. "Not only is that prison no place for a young lady, but I don't think Leon would want you to see him like that."

"But I wouldn't mind. It wouldn't bother me," she insisted. "He must be so lonely and maybe I could help him to feel better and know that we all still care about him."

"He knows," Jack assured her. "Your letters mean a lot to him. You keep on writin' 'em and you'll be helpin' him in more ways than you can imagine."

"Yes, I suppose," Penny conceded, but she didn't look happy about it.

"Tell ya what," Jack offered, "next time I see 'im, I'll ask if he's okay with you comin' for a visit. If he says it's okay, then maybe we can convince your pa ta let ya go."

Penny smiled brightly. "All right." Then she stood up in her stirrups and pointed. "Oh look. There's the perfect place for us to have a little picnic. There's a nice big tree we can sit under, and the creek is right there. I brought us lunch, you know."

"Did you," Jack commented, feeling like he'd been set up. "I donno, Penny. Once I get off Midnight, I may not be able to get back on again."

"Of course, you'll be able to. I'll just lead him into the creek and you can use the bank to mount up—just like you did with the Gibson's porch steps."

Jack was not comfortable with this situation at all—it was too much like his dream, and he did not need to be reminded of that. Still, he could see no reasonable way out of it, and before he knew it, they were at the tree and Penny had already dismounted.

Jack gave a resigned sigh and then, slowly bringing his right leg over the horn of the saddle, he then used the pommel to hold onto while he carefully lowered himself to the ground. He gingerly put weight on his feet, then hobbled over to the tree and sat down with a "humph".

Penny pulled the lunches out of her saddlebags, then taking a couple of long lines from the saddle, she tethered the two horses and turned them out to graze. She returned to the tree and settled in beside her friend, and laid out the sandwiches and some of her mother's ever-present cookies.

Jack sat against the tree trunk and closed his eyes for a moment. It was a very pleasant afternoon; the sun shone with a subtle spring breeze rustling through the grasses and leaves. He listened quietly to the water in the creek, to the birds in the tree above them, and to the occasional contented snort from the horses. For the first time in a long time, he felt relaxed.

Yeah, life was pretty good right now. There was still a lot that needed to be done; indeed, they were just getting started. But Jack knew he was on the mend. He'd been through hell and high water, physically and emotionally, but he was seeing his way through it now; he was ready to start forging ahead.

He opened his eyes to see Penny watching him, a calm and gentle expression on her face. She smiled. He felt an almost overpowering desire to take her in his arms and kiss her—almost. He knew he couldn't do that; it was too soon after all the turmoil they'd been through, and with all that was still yet to be done—he just couldn't go down that road yet, if ever.

He didn't know if what he felt for Penny now was real, or simply a response to the knowledge that she wanted him. There was something enticing and erotic, knowing that a young and beautiful woman wanted you and only you, but that response was lust, not love.

Jack didn't know which emotion he felt, and until he did know, he would have to keep his desire in check.

He smiled at her and settled into eating lunch.

Penny sighed in disappointment.

***

Laramie, Wyoming

"Then what happened?"

"Nothin," said Jack. "We ate our lunch, got back on the horses and returned to town."

"Well, that was anticlimactic," Leon complained.

"Yeah. It was meant ta be, Leon. And that's the way it's gonna stay—at least for now. There's too much goin' on with everything else for me ta know what's right in that area. So, for now, we'll just leave it be."

"Yeah." Leon reflected, "if Penny lets you."

"I'm just gonna have to be strong."

"Uh huh."

Jack sent his partner a look of irritation, then decided it was time to change the subject.

"So, have you been behavin' yourself? You been stayin' outta trouble?"

"I don't know," Leon frowned with honest concern.

"What do ya mean, ya don't know?" Jack questioned. "How could you not know?"

"I don't know. Kind of a strange thing happened earlier this week."

***

Earlier that week

"Convict. Follow me."

Leon looked up from the stack of cigars he'd been packaging, then brushed the excess tobacco off his hands before following Murray out of the warehouse.

Much to Leon's surprise and confusion, he was taken to the community room on the second floor and stopped outside the guards' room. Murray stepped inside, snatched up a set of irons and shackled him, hand and foot.

This, in itself, was not unusual treatment, but it was a weekday and there were no visitors allowed in the prison during the week. Yet, Murray stuck to protocol and led Leon down the stairs to the main floor. He unlocked the barred door exiting the cell block and motioned Leon through.

As expected, they headed down the hallway toward the barred door on the right that opened onto the entrance hallway, and Leon felt his heart rate quicken. So close to the outside world, but no way to get to it. The only time he had stepped through that hallway was when he first arrived at the prison. Since then, any approach to the processing room, or the warden's office, was through side doors that opened onto the back hall that they now walked along.

Apparently, there was a visitor here to see him, since they headed right for the processing room. Then Murray caught him by surprise when he pulled Leon up short and knocked on the first door that led into the warden's office.

Leon was also familiar with this room and hoped never to step into it again.

"Yes, what is it?" came the response from inside the office.

Leon's heart sank even more. Just hearing that voice sent dread down his spine.

Well, maybe this is a good thing, Maybe the governor has decided to grant me a pardon.

But even as he thought this, his natural cynicism knew it wasn't true. Something was up, and Leon already knew he wasn't going to like it.

Murray opened the door and mumbled some words to his boss, then turned and indicated for Leon to enter the office.

Murray followed him.

Warden Mitchell sat at his large oak desk, going over some papers, but as soon as the prisoner was presented to him, he sat back in his chair and scrutinized the man standing before him.

"Thank you, Officer," he dismissed Murray, "you may wait outside. Please close the door behind you."

"Yes sir."

Murray left, leaving Leon standing alone in the center of the office floor. His heart sank a little more when he saw that Taggard wasn't there. He knew he wouldn't be, but that little thread of hope had remained—until now. No, it was just Leon and the warden.

The warden continued to scrutinize him.

Leon remembered the lessons from his first day at the prison. He didn't move from where he had been put. He kept his eyes down, didn't shift position and certainly didn't sigh with boredom. He stood still—quiet—waiting.

Finally, Mitchell smiled. "Well, it's good to see you have learned the rules. But I hear you're an intelligent man, so I had no doubt that you would."

Leon discerned that there was no direct question in amongst that statement, so he did not respond, nor did he look up. He continued to wait.

"I understand you have been working in the infirmary and the laundry room these past few months," Mitchell said. "It is unusual for a convict who has only been here for less than a year to be trusted with those duties. I hope you appreciate the privilege."

No comment.

"Do you appreciate the privilege, Convict?"

"Yes sir, Warden."

"Good. I'm sure you are also aware of the fact that privileges once given, can also be taken away."

Oh, here it comes. There was never something for nothing, there was going to be a price to pay. Leon waited for the ax to fall.

"As I have already noted, you are a very intelligent man, Mr. Nash. You're also a very cautious one. You pay attention to what is going on around you; you keep tabs on what everyone is doing, guards and other inmates alike."

Leon continued to stand quietly. He really did not like the way this audience was going.

"All I ask is that you continue to do what you have already been doing," Mitchell clarified. "The only difference is that from now on, you will be doing it for me."

Leon remained quiet, his eyes down but his mind spinning. The full import of what Warden Mitchell expected was not lost on him, and if he agreed to it, it would be a very dangerous game.

"You may speak freely," the warden informed the inmate.

The change in Leon's demeanor was instantaneous. The quiet, submissive convict was immediately replaced by the charismatic, but totally cynical outlaw. His lip pulled up in a subtle sneer and he locked Mitchell down in a dark accusing stare.

The warden had to remind himself not to squirm, and then he felt angry that a lowly convict could have that effect upon him.

Warden Mitchell was the one in control here.

"In other words," Leon stated, "you want me to be a spy within a pack of wolves."

"Oh, 'spy' is such an insidious term," Mitchell regained his composure and returned the convict's stare with his own intimidation. "Perhaps you should think of it as simply, 'gathering information'. It's not like I'm asking you to sneak into their cells and rummage through their belongings."

Mitchell sent Leon a cold smile which held a double-edged sword.

Leon mimicked the expression and threw it right back at him. "And if I refuse, I'll lose my privileges."

"Let's just say, I could make your stay with us very uncomfortable."

Leon snorted.

"Oh, I know," the warden continued. "It's already uncomfortable as far as you're concerned. But believe me, what you have now will seem like a night in a luxury hotel compared to what I can put you through."

Leon sighed and weighed his options. "So, if I do agree to help you out, then I can expect to retain my privileges. Is that the arrangement we're talking about here?"

"Oh, I can do more than that, Mr. Nash." Mitchell's smile was smooth. "If I'm satisfied with the job you do, in a year or two I just might be willing to recommend that pardon your friends are so adamant you deserve."

Leon felt his anger rising, but he clamped his jaws down tight on the scornful laughter that fought to burst forth. The offer was absurd. Did Mitchell think he was a fool? This was just another false promise—like all the other false promises. Just another carrot dangling in front of his nose. If Leon did a good job as an informant, why would Mitchel be willing to set him free and lose that valuable contact?

Mitchell sat back and folded his arms. The cynicism in the man standing before him was so heavy it dripped, and the hard, brown eyes boring into the official spoke volumes more than any words could have done.

"Well, any way you choose to look at this, Mr. Nash, you would be wise to consider the offer. I have you under my thumb for the next twenty—no, excuse me, for the next nineteen and a half years. All I need to do is add a little pressure and I can crush you like a beetle under my shoe." The warden sat back, steepling his fingers under his chin. "I'll let you think on that for a while, how's that? Guard!"

Leon dropped his eyes and became the subservient convict again, just as Murray stepped into the office.

"Escort Mr. Nash back to the warehouse, so he may continue with his duties."

"Yes sir, Warden."

Murray took hold of Leon's arm and shuffled him out of the office and back into the prison proper.

***

Leon never would have thought it possible for the sound of those heavy doors shutting and locking behind him would ever bring with them a sense of relief. Even if it was short-lived.

That night, he lay on his cot, staring up at a ceiling he couldn't see and tried to think himself out of the corner he had been backed into.

Life was hard at the prison, but even at that, Leon knew he had it better than most of the inmates here. He had people; friends and family on the outside, who supported him. He had visitors almost every weekend, and letters enough to fill in the gaps between books and medical journals. The quick glances of resentment from the other inmates were not lost on him. The fact that he had been given privileges that most of them could never hope to attain did not help with his popularity.

And it's not like it matters to me how popular I am in here. Ha. I've done everything I could to discourage any kind of presumption of camaraderie. But to turn informant, well, that's just asking to get my throat cut. But if I don't, then I'll lose those privileges, and they sure have become a lifeline for me.

The warden's threat was not lost on Napoleon Nash.

I know exactly what would happen to me if I lose my days in the laundry room and even more so, the infirmary. If I lose my reading privileges, maybe even my visitor rights, I would go mad.

A shiver attacked his spine. He had seen other inmates go that way; even in the short time Leon had been there, he had seen others lose their grasp on reason.

It was always the ones who had no one to turn to. No one coming to visit, no one writing letters, no one to talk to. Even though the incident involving Hicks had happened before Leon had been incarcerated, he'd learned through the silent grapevine what had happened, and he knew why.

That convict, who had turned on the guard and plunged the pencil into his throat, hadn't done it out of any personal vendetta; there had been no malicious intent, no rhyme or reason. The inmate's mind simply snapped, and insanity had run amok.

The contacts he had with the outside world, and that one day a week with Dr. Palin, being able to speak with him one on one, like a human being, were precious to him. *Those are the things that hold me together, and now they are being threatened. How can I walk that fine line and keep myself both safe and sane?*

He sighed, and rolling onto his side, hugged his knees and stared into the abyss.

C'mon, brain, we have to work this out.

***

"I donno, Leon. That sounds like trouble ta me," Jack said.

"Yeah. I still don't know what I'm going to do." He sent a quick glance back toward the guard and lowered his voice. "Just try and play both sides of the fence for now, I suppose."

"Maybe I could tell Taggard about this, or Steven," Jack suggested. "Steven's a lawyer; maybe he could block the warden, or somethin'."

"No, I don't think that's a good idea. Mitchell's the one in control here. If anybody from the outside tried to put pressure on him, he'd just back off until they were gone and then crucify me."

"Yeah, I suppose."

"Aw, don't worry about it, Jack. I'll think of something; I always do. You know that."

"I know. But this sounds like it could get dangerous. Jeez, we thought livin' on the run was bad, but this is insane."

"Yeah." Leon sighed. "Don't worry; I'll watch my back."

"Hmm."

The two men sat in silence for a few moments, each lost in their own thoughts.

For the first time since he'd started coming to visit his

partner, Jack felt real fear for Leon's safety. Just as Leon had felt frustrated at not being there for his partner during his life and death struggles, Jack felt the impotency of not being here to watch Leon's back. It was what he was used to doing. That was one of his roles in their partnership, but now, he was prevented from performing that role just at a time when Leon needed his protection the most.

As for Leon, seeing the fear and frustration on Jack's countenance made him regret telling him about the situation in the first place. It was just going to cause him to worry and fret over something he couldn't do anything about. Leon would figure it out; he had every confidence in himself that he would. He had to. It was just going to take some thinking and some pacing, but he would figure it out.

"I beat up a prostitute," Jack stated, out of the blue.

"What?" Leon was startled out of his reverie. *Did I hear that right?*

Their eyes locked for an instant, then Jack turned away.

"That last night in Cheyenne. I went to the saloon after everyone else had gone to bed, I hired a girl for the night, and I . . . hit her."

"Oh."

Jack sat silently, staring at his hands that rested on the table in front of him. He couldn't bring himself to look into Leon's eyes.

"I . . . umm . . ." Jack coughed, trying to clear his throat. Deep sigh. "It was everything we have always despised . . . always looked down on and, I . . . I hurt her real bad, Uncle Leon."

"Why?" he asked gently, quietly. He could see the hurt in Jack's eyes; he could hear it in his voice. This was no longer a joke or a tease; this was painful.

Jack shrugged silently, still not able to look up. "David said it was because I had been on that morphine for too long. That I had become . . . ahh . . . dependent on it. Then, between what happened to you, and then me, comin' off that drug . . . well . . . it made me crazy." Jack slumped and looked defeated. "I donno. David explains it better. Maybe you should just ask him."

"Yeah. Yeah, I could. But I'm still glad you told me."

Jack gave a mild snort, but still wouldn't look up; in fact, he was doing everything he could to avoid meeting his uncle's eyes.

"Is she all right?" Leon finally asked.

"I suppose," came the weak response. "The Madam didn't

lay charges in any case, so long as I didn't go back to that saloon again. I was just . . . I was passed out . . . I don't remember anything after that. Apparently, David and Cameron made sure I was on the train the next morning, 'cause that's where I woke up."

"Hmm." Leon nodded. "So, when you ran out of David's house with no boots on, that was . . . what?"

"That was when I remembered . . . what I had done. I'd had a bad dream . . . and when I described it to David, that was when I remembered." Jack stopped and ran a hand over his eyes, then he sighed, and his jaw tightened with the pain he felt. "Oh God, Leon. It was awful. I just . . . I know I hurt her bad. I broke her nose and split her lip. I left her black and blue. I know . . . I know I made her bleed. Oh God . . ." Jack nearly gagged, struggling to prevent his stomach from turning over.

Leon leaned forward, trying to raise his hands, trying to bring some comfort to his friend. But he was shackled. He couldn't do it, and he resented it more at that moment than at any other. To be denied the ability to offer the most basic of physical contacts at a time when it was so sorely needed, was one of the cruelest injustices of Leon's predicament. All he could do was offer Jack his company and support and hope that would be enough.

The two friends sat in companionable silence until Jack could bring himself under control again. He gave another deep sigh and finally raised his eyes to meet his friend's gaze.

The pain Leon saw there was enough to break his heart. "Have you been able to talk to David about it?"

"No. Not like this. And like I said, all I did with Jean was blubber like a baby."

"Well, I'm glad you saved that part for her," Leon said. "I don't think I could've handled it."

Jack laughed a little. "Yeah. Women like that kinda stuff."

"Hmm," Leon nodded. Silence prevailed again, while Leon watched his friend still struggling with his inner demons. "You're still my partner, you know. We're still family. This doesn't change anything."

Jack smiled and nodded acceptance, obviously relieved.

"Yeah, thanks, Leon." Then taking deep breath, Jack straightened up and sent his friend another weak smile.

Leon smiled back. "You all right now?"

"Yeah, I think so."

"Good. Because I still need you to get me outta here."

Jack smiled back, brighter this time. "Yeah."

Then Murray gave a quiet cough. "Ahh, you fellas have had an hour and a half now, so let's wrap it up."

"Oh." Leon sent Jack a sheepish smile. "I guess we've kinda gone over time."

"Yeah." Jack stood up. He sent a quick glance to the guard, on the verg of thanking him for the extra time, but not sure if that was acceptable etiquette. "I guess I better go."

Murray stepped over and, taking Leon's arm, motioned him to his feet.

Leon kept his eyes on his partner. "Okay, Jack. You sure you're all right now?"

"Yeah, Leon. I'm fine. You?"

"Yeah. Don't worry; I'll figure something out."

"Okay. Take care of yourself. I'll see ya next month."

CHAPTER THREE
LINES IN THE DIRT

Jack hobbled out to the hallway after Leon was gone. He glanced at the closed door of the warden's office and felt his hackles rise. He sensed that the office was empty though, so Jack didn't mind staying where he was to await the return of his belongings. He'd done this enough times now to know the routine. The guard would be back soon enough.

Not surprisingly, his mind was on the conversation he'd just had with Leon. He had been anxious about confessing the details of his shameful behavior, afraid that after all the other things his partner had recently discovered about him, this episode would be the final straw.

Now, of course, after having told Leon about it, a huge weight was off his shoulders. That had been the last thing; the last secret that needed to be divulged, admitted to, owned up to, faced and accepted. Now it was done, and Leon knew the worst. He had not turned away in revulsion and anger, but had come forward with compassion and support, and far from breaking their partnership, he had re-affirmed it.

Jack felt a mixture of emotions as he leaned against the wall. Relief over his own confession was now marred with the worry over Leon's new predicament. Who would have thought that being in a prison could be so dangerous? Surviving inside really was a complex game of strategy and covertness. Jack could only hope Leon's natural intelligence and deviousness would enable him to not only survive it but to come out on top.

"Mr. Kiefer."

Jack came out of his musings and was surprised by the appearance of a much older man than the stoic Mr. Murray. It was the intelligent gray eyes that gave him away, not that Leon had ever mentioned the eye color. But this man needed no introduction.

"My name is Ken Reece," the guard said, as he handed Jack's coat and holster over to him.

"Oh, yeah. Mr. Reece," Jack accepted his belongings, and then the forthcoming handshake. "Leon has mentioned you. He told me that you're one of the good guards."

"Really?" Kenny cocked a brow, surprised. "That's good to know. I've had to be tough with him sometimes." He smiled. "Your friend can be difficult to handle."

Jack snorted. "Good ta know that prison ain't changed 'im."

Kenny nodded but made no comment about that observation. He was on another errand.

"Warden Mitchell has requested you join him for a few minutes. He asked me to ensure that you did not get away from him." The guard smiled at Jack's raised brow. "Sorry. Poor choice of words. He asked me to keep an eye out for you. He had a business lunch at his house but should be along any moment." He glanced at Jack's cane. "Would you like to have a seat and wait for him in his office?"

Jack considered the offer but decided that sitting alone in that room would be more uncomfortable than standing on his sore feet.

"Nah, that's okay, Mr. Reece. I think I'm fine right here. Any idea what this is about?"

"No, not really," Kenny admitted. "Perhaps it is just to introduce himself. You are a regular visitor here, after all."

"Yeah," came the skeptical reply.

"In fact, I was hoping to get the opportunity to do just that myself." Kenny glanced around, ensuring they were alone. "Of course, I am aware of your shared history with Mr. Nash; that you are not only partners and friends, but also family. I hoped I could get your contact information, someplace where I can get in touch with you if the need were to arise."

"I suppose," Jack agreed, though he was confused. "I thought that information was already on file here. The warden knows how ta get in touch with Sheriff Murphy. Both Taggard Murphy and Governor Warren know where I am."

"Yes, well . . ." Kenny hesitated, "there may come a time when I might need to get hold of you quickly, but at the same time avoid official channels—if you understand my meaning."

Jack was beginning to. He sent a quizzical look to the guard.

"Yeah, uh huh. The best way ta get hold 'a me directly is ta send atelegram to Arvada in Colorado. The telegrapher knows who I am, and somebody from the ranch checks for messages whenever there's a trip ta town."

"Thank you." Kenny nodded. "I thought this would be the case, but I wanted to be sure."

"Uh huh." Jack couldn't quite decide if Kenny really was a friend, or if he was just playing the game to gain their confidence. Still, Leon recommended him as a contact, and Leon usually could read people well. Still, Jack was hesitant to trust any official at the prison.

Then Kenny offered his hand for shaking, and the two men locked eyes.

There was something about the expression that met Jack straight on, and in that instant, he mind was made up. He accepted Kenny's hand and held that intense gaze.

"Watch his back for me, will ya?" Jack asked him.

"Already am, Mr. Kiefer. Already am."

***

"Ah, Mr. Kiefer. Good of you to wait."

Warden Mitchell entered the building and offered his hand to the visitor.

Jack felt his skin crawl but found a way to accept the offering, and the two men shook hands.

"Uh huh. What can I do for ya?"

"Well, come into my office and let's discuss it. Thank you, Officer Reece, you may return to your duties."

"Yessir. Good day, Mr. Kiefer."

Jack and Kenny exchanged a quick glance, each knowing they hadn't concluded their business yet.

"Yeah, you too." Then Jack followed the warden into his office.

The room he found himself in was not quite as opulent as the governor's office, but it still conveyed authority and a position of power. It was designed with the purpose of intimidating the uninitiated.

Fortunately, the more times Jack found himself in offices such as these, the less intimidated he was by them, and by the type of men who generally occupied them.

As soon as the door closed, Warden Mitchell gestured to a comfortable armchair

"Please, Mr. Kiefer, have a seat."

"Thank you," Jack answered as he casually assessed this new reptile. He then sank into the plush leather-covered chair and waited for the next round.

A trustee entered the office, carrying with him the inevitable tray laden with two glasses of some dark amber liquid. He placed one on the side table by Jack and the other on the desk beside the warden. He then discreetly left.

"Please, Mr. Kiefer, try the sherry," Warden Mitchell suggested. "It is most definitely top shelf, and I'm sure you'll enjoy it."

"Thank you, Mr. Mitchell," Jack eyed the liquid. He would have preferred a beer, if truth be known. Still, he took the glass and tried it, playing the game until he got a gist of where this was all going. He had to admit, it was different, but not bad.

"Well," Mitchell began after taking a sip himself, "I have to admit, I always expected to eventually meet you, Mr. Kiefer. It's a pleasure to have it happen under such different circumstances from what I had imagined.

"Uh huh. Likewise."

Mitchell smiled. "Yes."

There was a moment of silence while Warden Mitchell took his turn to assess the man sitting across from him, and Jack patiently waited, knowing he was being scrutinized.

Jack already had a good idea of what he was dealing with here.

"I suggested a meeting with you today, simply to introduce myself. Also, to let you know that if you have any concerns at all about your friend's situation, you may feel free to bring them to my attention at any time."

"Oh yeah?" Jack responded. "That's good of ya, Warden. I'll be sure ta keep that in mind."

"I know you come to visit Mr. Nash on a regular basis," Mitchell continued, "and that you speak together on a variety of topics. Considering that you were partners, and that—"

"Ahh, are partners," Jack corrected him.

"Yes. Of course. Are partners. And that your opinion obviously matters a great deal to him."

"Yeah." Jack's caution rose. He was getting a pretty good feel for where this was going.

"Of course, he has told you of our little arrangement to assist me in keeping our prison running smoothly."

Jack was hardly surprised that the warden was aware of the conversation between himself and Leon, since there was always a guard present during their meetings. But he was surprised at how quickly the information had reached the top. He was also a little resentful of Mitchell's assumption that Leon was going to agree to their little arrangement.

"He mentioned it. Didn't say he was gonna do it though."

"Yes, I'm aware of that." A smarmy smile appeared. "There's not too much goes on in this prison that I'm not aware of, Mr. Kiefer. But still, having someone right in the midst of the action, so to speak, would be invaluable to me. And Mr. Nash is the perfect candidate."

"Why?"

"Why?" Mitchell repeated.

"Yes, Warden. Why?"

"I would have thought that to you—his partner—it would be blatantly obvious."

Unbeknownst to himself, Jack had indeed grown over the last six months. Instead of feeling insecure and intimidated by Mitchell's attempt at condescension, he recognized it immediately as a ploy to manipulate. He smiled inwardly at how ridiculous it all was.

"Is that a fact?" Jack asked. "Well, since it ain't blatantly obvious, perhaps you should explain it to me; just ta be sure we're both on the same page, ya understand."

"Of course. Well," Mitchell collected his thoughts, "I have noticed that Mr. Nash does not play into the political games of the other prisoners, or of the guards, for that matter. He tends to keep himself apart, and other than his rather unlikely friendship with the prison doctor, he has formed no alliances with anyone here."

Again, Jack noted to himself that Mitchell was unaware of Leon's regard for Kenny. It was also apparent that the guard himself had been careful to not show any signs of favoritism.

"Mr. Nash is quick-witted and constantly aware of what's

going on around him," Mitchell continued, oblivious to Jack's observation, "all of which tends to make him a perfect candidate for what I need to help me stay informed as to the atmosphere inside the prison proper."

Jack nodded, expressing interest. To all intents and purposes, he appeared to be considering the warden's offer.

"And, if Leon agrees ta help you out with this?"

"I'm aware of your endeavors to arrange a pardon for your friend," Mitchell commented with a touch of grease. "I can make that pardon happen with the tip of my feathered quill. As I have already told Mr. Nash, if he agrees, well, after a couple of years, I just might see fit to submit a recommendation for his release. And believe me, I influence those decisions all the time."

"Why?"

Mitchell sighed. "Again with the 'why', Mr. Kiefer? Why is my offer so difficult for you to understand?"

"Because it don't make no sense," Jack shot back at him. "You finally get yourself a reliable informant and then you're gonna turn 'im loose? I find it kinda hard ta put much faith in that, Mr. Mitchell."

"You doubt my word, Mr. Kiefer?" Mitchell asked with some indignation.

Jack's ire rose. "I have lost count as ta how many government officials and upstandin' businessmen have given us their word, only ta turn their backs and walk away when it came time to pay up.

"Considerin' the odds, I think I have every right ta doubt your word. And I think it's safe ta say that Leon ain't got too much confidence in it, either."

"I strongly suggest that you endeavor to change his mind," Mitchell shot back, his patience wearing thin. "I assure you, Mr. Kiefer, it would be in your partner's best interests if you cooperate with me in convincing him to accept the offer."

Jack sat back and forced himself to come down off his anger. He was tempted to challenge the warden on this but realized that doing so would be pointless. Leon was right about one thing; Mitchell was in charge here, and he could make Leon's life a misery if he chose to do so.

"What if I try and he refuses?" Jack asked quickly, now that his temper was under control.

"I think you already know the answer to that, Mr. Kiefer, or you wouldn't be relenting so easily. Might I suggest you put this to him in such a way that he does not refuse."

The two men sat and stared at one another, neither one willing to relax their stance.

"You both have until your next visit, Mr. Kiefer," Mitchell granted him, "then I'll expect an answer."

"Right." Jack pushed himself to his feet, knowing the discussion had come to an end. "Good day, Mr. Mitchell."

"Mr. Kiefer." The warden did not stand to see his guest out.

***

Hobbling to the front door, Jack was deep in thought. This was going to take some handling, but again, he didn't have a clue how to do it. Despite his hurting feet, and Leon's protest, he decided it was time to extend his journey and head to Medicine Bow for a face-to-face discussion with his friend. Taggard might not be able to get Leon out of here, but he might have some suggestions on how to best deal with this situation.

Why does life have to get so dang complicated?

***

Medicine Bow, Wyoming

"What the hell happened to you?"

"Aww, Taggard. Nothin'," Jack grumbled. "I'm surprised David didn't write ya a ten-page letter, tellin' ya all about it."

"No, he didn't say anything about you gettin' hurt," Taggard assured his friend. "He did send a short note to let me know you had a breakthrough though, and that you should be on the mend now."

"More like a breakdown."

"What?"

"Nothin'." Jack sighed, then smiled at the sheriff. "It's okay Taggard, I just kinda overreacted to rememberin' some 'a that stuff, is all. I cut my feet some. They're healin' up. Another couple 'a weeks and I'll be ready ta dance on the Fourth of July."

"Uh huh. Well, sit down, Jack. Do ya want a whiskey?"

"Yeah, sure."

Taggard poured them a couple of shots and returned to his desk.

"So, what brings ya here? Have ya seen Leon?"

"Yeah. That's kinda what does bring me here."

"Is that hardhead starvin' himself, again?"

"No, no. He's fine," Jack waved this concern away. "It's somethin' else."

Taggard sent him a quizzical look.

Jack hesitated, trying to think how best to describe the situation.

"It seems the warden wants Leon ta kinda become an informant for 'im, and he's made it real clear what'll happen if Leon don't."

"Oh brother," Taggard sighed and leaned back in his chair. "That's not good. What does Leon say?"

Jack shrugged. "Try and play both sides of the fence and watch his back. I donno, Taggard, I'm just lettin' ya know in case you have any ideas."

Taggard downed his whiskey, then sat and thought about it for a few minutes.

"No, there's not really much we can do," he said. "Unfortunately, in a prison, the warden runs the show. How he deals with discipline is up to him, so long as he doesn't stray too far away from what the federal prison system dictates. Using prisoners to spy on other prisoners is not a new ploy, nor is it considered unethical. If something were ta happen to the informant, well, that's the chance ya take. It's just a convict after all."

"Damn," Jack mumbled. "We were safer up in Elk Mountain."

"Hmm." Then Taggard sent Jack a suspicious look. "You don't mean nothin' by that do ya? Like in headin' back up there?"

"Oh. No," Jack assured him. "No, I'm not."

"Good. I don't wanna have ta shoot ya."

Another moment of silence, then . . .

"Anything new with the governor?" Jack asked.

"No." And this was followed by an irritated scowl. "It's like he's gone to ground. He's not taking any appointments right now, and certainly not with me."

"Ya mean he's gone inta hidin'?"

"Yeah, that's how it seems."

"Why would he be doin' that?"

"Well, those rumors of dirty business dealings have sorta become more than just rumors. Apparently, President Cleveland isn't too happy about what's goin' on and there may be some sparks flyin'."

"Oh." Jack's shoulders slumped in disappointment.

"What?" Taggard asked, confused. "That could be in our favor. If Governor Warren gets booted outta office, maybe the next governor will be more accommodatin'."

"Yeah. It's just that we already had wind of somethin' along those lines, and friends were doin' some diggin', in hopes that we could find something to . . . ah . . ." Jack stopped, suddenly remembering who he was talking to.

"I hope you weren't about to say 'blackmail'," Taggard growled at him. "Cause last I heard, blackmailin' a government official is against the law, and if that's what you had in mind 'a doin'—"

"Oh no, Taggard," Jack backstepped. "Persuade . . . that's all I was meanin'."

"Uh huh."

Jack was lying. Taggard knew Jack was lying, and Jack knew Taggard knew he was lying.

"Well, it's a moot point anyway," Taggard continued. "Cause it just might be gettin' ready ta blow up in his face officially, so there may not be anything left to 'persuade' 'im with."

Jack finished his whiskey, then, folding his arms, he sat back with a sigh.

"We gotta get him outta there, Taggard. He's doin' okay now, but . . ."

"I know, Jack." Taggard recalled Leon's quiet plea when Taggard had gone to see him in the prison infirmary. "We're all tryin'. Leon is just gonna have ta play it close, watch his back . . . and stay outta trouble."

"Yeah, I guess."

"Ya hungry?"

"Yeah, gettin' there."

"Well, c'mon. Let's get some supper at the café, and then you can stay the night at my place. Head back ta Colorado on the morning train."

"Yeah, okay. Thanks."

***

Laramie, Wyoming

Leon needed time to think.

When the weather was accommodating, and time allowed, he preferred to do his thinking outdoors, since pacing was an intricate part of his problem-solving process. So much so, that when he was finally left to finish up an afternoon on his own, he headed outdoors, so he could think and pace and think some more.

Jack really has been going through a hard time, just like Taggard said, and I had sneered at it. 'What hard times could Jack possibly be going through that would even come close to what I'm experiencing, being initiated into the prison?' He gave a snort. *Well, now I know, and now, I agree; Jack has been going through a hard time.*

I can't imagine how he has kept that all bottled up and out of sight. Three killings in his youth, and now, having to acknowledge committing an act that could not honestly be called anything other than rape.

Leon frowned, then sighed with all these revelations. At least the killings he could understand. Those weren't meaningless. It might not have been right, what Jack had done, but it sure was understandable. And Leon meant it when he'd said that if he hadn't blocked out the worst of what those men had done, he might very well have helped Jack with that vendetta.

Of course, Jack, being Jack, would feel guilt and regret about it. And it did explain why Jack was always so concerned about people. He'd driven Leon nuts over the edge sometimes with his insistence on helping people, especially women. Leon always thought he was just trying to impress them, but apparently he was being sincere.

I shouldn't have teased him so much about it

But now, what happened in Cheyenne . . . Again, Leon frowned and shook his head over this surprising event. *I gotta admit, I never would have thought it possible for Jack to behave like that. It isn't in his nature. This doesn't make sense.*

Leon groaned and rubbed his eyes. This heavy thinking gave him a headache. He absently walked along the fence line, head down and eyes to the ground, as his musings took over.

It must have been devastating for Jack to come face to face with that memory. No wonder he had taken off at a run, out the door, without any boots on, and kept on running until his cut feet forced him to finally stop. And Jack shrugs it off as "just over-reacting a little". Again, Leon snorted.

He recalled reading something about drug dependency and addiction in the journals Doc Palin had loaned him, but he'd never realized how powerful an effect it could have on a person's character. Until now.

Yeah, not until my closest friend admitted to committing a horrendous act, mostly due to his dependency on a drug that had been initially administered to help him. How quickly a friend could become an enemy, without you even knowing.

Leon sighed with his inner musings. Originally, he figured all he really had to do was read the books, learn some of the hands-on techniques from Dr. Palin, and he'd be ready to open his own practice, if he wanted to. Now, he was beginning to realize that there was a lot more to being a doctor than just the book learning and a little bit of practical experience. There was so much more to the human condition. What his nephew was going through and having to deal with, made that very clear.

Still, Leon cocked a brow. *I have no doubt Jack will come through this all right; it's just going to take some time. But he's already dealing with it, isn't he? Dealing with it and moving ahead. On top of that, he's had help. The same friends who are trying to help me are out there already helping Jack. Hmm, I wonder how we're ever going to repay them . . ..*

I'll write to David and ask him more about this addiction stuff. I'll ask Palin about it too.

But as much as Leon liked the prison doctor, even he could see the difference between a sawbones and an artist. Yes, he would definitely be writing David a letter. The more Leon knew about what Jack was going through, and why, the better a partner and friend he could be to him, and that was more important than anything else, right now.

Then Leon's thoughts went over to his own current problem.

Ohh, what to do about that?

Even with staying alert and keeping track of what was going on around him, he'd never really gotten wind of anything covert.

Indeed, all those little power plays swirling around the prison were anything but covert; they were blatantly obvious to anyone who cared to pay attention.

Now the warden wants me to come up with information? About what? And if word gets around that I've had been singled out like this, my life would have no more worth than a rabbit in a lion's den.

I can't do it. Suddenly, it just came to him; he couldn't be a snitch. *Isn't that the main reason I'm here in the first place? Because I wouldn't betray a confidence, because I couldn't turn others in just to save my own skin? What the warden is asking me to do is simply another example of betraying my fellows just to protect my own situation. None of these inmates are my friends, none of them really matter to me, but that's beside the point.*

The warden is asking me to betray my own moral conscience, just like DeFord tried to do. And I do have a moral conscience, despite DeFord's insinuations. Snort. *Well, he found out, didn't he? And now the warden is putting me to the same test. Well, he'll find out just like DeFord did. I'll stay true to my path despite what consequences may come of it.*

The sun was going down; it would be suppertime soon. Once his conundrum had been quieted, Leon could feel that the ever-present Wyoming wind was developing a chill, despite the energized walking he had been doing around and around the yard. It was time to head indoors.

He sighed deeply, releasing the stress that had been building up with this new dilemma, but now that he had come to his decision, he felt the weight of it leave his shoulders. He smiled to himself and looked up from his inner musings to take one last survey of the yard around him.

He felt a chill go through him, and he froze.

Anger rose inside him, anger at himself for being so stupid.

Dammit! All that talk about being observant and aware of my surroundings, and yet, again, I got distracted. Stupid! I should have returned to my cell.

I should have gone to my cot and stared at the ceiling and done my thinking that way—that would have worked just as well. I can't think and watch my back at the same time, I know that. That's what Jack is for. How could I be so stupid?

Over by the far wall was Hank Boeman, and standing beside

him, as though in some sort of silent conference with one another, was the new inmate, Carl Harris. Leon had been relieved when the new alpha had arrived. He had smiled smugly to himself, watching the two of them circling each other like opposing stallions, each trying to get in the first kick. But now, instead of being kept busy challenging one another for the top wolf position, they had somehow come to the agreement to join forces. At least temporarily, at least until their main adversary had been taken care of.

Leon had looked up to find both men staring directly at him.

CHAPTER FOUR
A FALSE START

Laramie. Spring 1886

Leon sat quietly in the processing room. He had no idea who was coming to see him, but in a way, that was kind of fun, too. Like being presented with a gift and you had to wait before you were allowed to open it. He smiled a little in anticipation. He doubted it was Jack again; he wasn't due for another couple of weeks. Wouldn't be Frank, he'd already put in his token visit and probably wouldn't come back. Might be Dr. Mariam. Hmm. Well, whoever it was, Leon wished they'd hurry up, as he was starting to get a little antsy.

Finally, the door opened and oh, it was Taggard.

Leon smiled broadly, pleased to see his friend, but the smile quickly dropped from his face when Taggard was followed into the room by Steven Granger.

The lawyer?

Oh no. Did Jack go ahead and tell them what the warden had said? This was what comes of letting Jack out on his own.

"Howdy Taggard," Leon greeted his friend.

"Hey, Leon."

"Mr. Granger."

"Afternoon, Mr. Nash."

"You're lookin' better than the last time I saw ya," Taggard commented. "You could still stand ta put on a few more pounds though. We don't need ya gettin' sick again, come winter."

Leon smiled. "Yes, mother."

Taggard sent him a nasty look. Then he and Steven glanced at the guard standing by the rear door.

"Guard," Steven addressed him, "would you please give us some privacy?"

Murray pushed himself off the wall and, with a glance at the inmate, turned to leave.

"I'll be right outside the door if you need anything," he assured the two men.

"As long as you're not right up against it," Steven cautioned him.

Murray sent him a smirk, then left the three men alone.

Leon looked confused, then impressed.

"How did you do that? Every time I tell them to go away, I get rapped with the billy club."

Steven smiled as he and Taggard sat down at the table.

"Being an official of the court does have its advantages," Steven explained. "I sent the warden a telegram, stating we were planning to appeal your sentence, and I requested some time with you to discuss that issue. Legally, he is obligated to grant you time to discuss your case with your lawyer—in private. So, here we are."

"Oh." Leon's features morphed into his broad smile again. "Are we going to be appealing my sentence?"

"We are in the process, Mr. Nash," Steven assured him. "But all of this takes time and Governor Warren is fighting other fires right now, and isn't too interested in seeing us."

"Ah," Leon accepted that, but disappointment settled over him again. "So, what do I owe this visit to then? Not that I'm not happy to see you Taggard, but it seems an awful lot of trouble to go through just to say 'hello'."

"Jack told me about the little arrangement the warden is trying to make with you," Taggard said. "I thought it would be a good idea for you to inform your lawyer about that, just so we all know what's going on."

"Ah," Leon commented again. "I asked Jack not to tell you. I guess I'm going to have to watch what I say to him from now on."

"C'mon, Leon. Don't be so cynical," Taggard snapped at him. "Jack only has your best interests at heart, you know that. I, for one, am glad he told me. We're all on the same side here; it'd help if you would remember that."

Leon had the good grace to look contrite. There he was, mouthin' off again, and allowing the frustrations he felt over his predicament to be dumped onto the very people who were trying to help him.

"Yeah, you're right, Taggard, I'm sorry. It's just that I don't see what you can do from the outside. Like I told Jack, you put pressure on Mitchell, the next thing you know, you'll be getting a telegram informing you that Napoleon Nash was shot while trying to escape."

"You're quite right, Mr. Nash," Steven put in. "It would be safer for the moment if Warden Mitchell doesn't know that we discussed this. As far as he is concerned, all we talked about was your possible appeal. But I believe it is important that we know exactly what Mitchell wants you to do, and just how far you intend to go with it."

"Well, again, like I told Jack. Mitchell wants me to spy on the guards and the other inmates, and then report back to him with anything suspicious I might become privy to. If I agree to do this, then I can not only expect to retain my current privileges, but he will also be more open to recommending me for a pardon in a year or two, if he's happy with the job I do for him."

"And if you don't agree?" Steven asked.

"Then he will make my life a living hell." Leon sneered. "As though it weren't that already."

"Yes," Steven nodded. "And how optimistic do you feel about the warden considering you for a pardon?"

Leon snorted, then sent a bitter smile to Taggard. "What is it with these government officials? Why are they always trying to wheel and deal and then slime their way out from under? Mitchell is no more likely to recommend me for a pardon than Warren is in granting it. I'm beginning to think that politics is a bigger racket than robbing trains."

"They're not all dishonest, Mr. Nash," Steven assured him. "Most of them are just trying to watch their backs, like everybody else."

Leon snorted again. He wasn't convinced.

"So, what are your intentions?" Steven continued. "Have you decided what answer you are going to give the warden with respect to his offer?"

"I'm not going to do it," Leon's tone was firm. "I'm not going to turn snitch for anybody."

Steven nodded then sighed. "I'm not surprised at that.

Considering your history, I pretty much expected this to be your answer. But, might I suggest that you play along for now? Simply agree to carry on with what you have always done in watching your own back and if, by chance, you hear of anything you consider is worth bringing to his attention, you will do so."

"I donno, Mr. Granger," Leon looked skeptical. "Some of the other inmates already know I tried to make peace with the law. If they even get a whiff of me leaning that way again, I could easily wake up one morning to find my throat slit. It's a dangerous game."

"Yes, I realize that," Steven agreed. "But if you refuse the warden outright, then he could do just as much, and you're right, there really is nothing we can do to stop him. Using prisoners to spy on other prisoners is not anything new, and any punishment he doles out to you can easily be made to took legitimate. Do you have any friends in here at all?"

"Ah, yeah," Leon considered. "Ah, there's Dr. Soames, but she's not at the prison all the time. I suppose one of the senior guards, Kenny Reece, watches my back, but not so much as anybody else would notice. Then the Doc, over in the infirmary. We get along all right."

Steven glanced at Taggard. "Do you know any of these men?"

"Yeah. I met both of them when Leon was sick. Reece seemed like a solid enough fellow, but that doctor struck me as a bit of a drunk."

"Aww, Palin's all right," Leon defended the doctor. "Just don't let him offer you a drink, that's all."

Taggard smiled, then continued. "Kiefer said that Reece was willin' ta get in touch 'unofficially' if he felt that Leon was in any danger, or if anything suspicious happens, so it sounds like he'll be a good contact."

"Really?" Leon cocked a brow. "I didn't know that Jack and Reece had spoken at all. Hmm, that's interesting."

"Yes," Steven agreed. "It does seem you have friends all around you. Do try to keep that in mind when things get tough. And please, consider what I said about how to deal with Warden Mitchell, and we'll do what we can about pursuing an appeal for you. If we're lucky, the Territory of Wyoming just might have a new governor by Christmas—perhaps one who isn't quite so gun shy."

"Yeah, all right, Mr. Granger. Thanks," Leon agreed. Then

he smiled. "How is Caroline?"

Steven brightened up considerably.

"She's great. She's picking up the routine at the office very quickly and already knows more about some of my cases than I do. I think she's going to work out just fine."

"Yeah, in more ways than one, I hear," Leon commented with a grin.

Steven suddenly turned shy, but he smiled with pleasure anyway.

"Yes, I certainly hope so."

"How are things goin' otherwise, Leon?" Taggard asked him, letting Steven get off the hook. "You sure you're eatin' enough?"

"Yeah Taggard. Stop pesterin', will ya?" Leon showed some irritation. "And aside from the bed bugs, no heat, cold coffee, lumpy oatmeal, guards trying to get me to slip up so they can beat me to a pulp, and other prisoners trying to knife me in the back, everything's fine!"

Taggard sighed. "Yeah, okay Leon. I'm sorry."

Leon slumped with instant regret. "No Taggard, it's not you. It's just this place. Some days are harder to handle than others."

"I know," Taggard assured him. "We'll keep on tryin' at our end and you keep on playin' your cards close in here, okay?"

"Yeah, okay. Thanks for coming."

"All right, Mr. Nash," said Steven as he stood up. "I will keep in touch."

"Yeah."

Steven walked around to the door and opened it to summon the guard, and Murray came into the room.

"Thank you," Steven told him. "We're done for now."

"Fine," Murray answered, then walked to the prisoner. "C'mon Nash, let's go."

He took the inmate by the arm and pulled him to his feet.

In that instant, before Murray shuffled him toward the door and back into the prison proper, Leon locked eyes with Taggard. All the regrets and frustrations of their present predicament flashed between the two friends. Then Leon was gone, back into the miserable existence that had become his reality.

Taggard and Steven made their own exit, neither one of them feeling that much had been accomplished.

***

Once Leon was released from his bindings and allowed a certain measure of freedom, he decided to return to his cell to read and think. It was a pleasant spring day, but he wanted to be able to let his mind wander and not have to worry so much about his back. Having learned his lesson from the previous incident, off to his cell he went.

As soon as he stepped across the threshold, he knew something was amiss. He couldn't quite put his finger on it, just a feeling, but he knew there'd been an intrusion. Someone had been in here.

He did a scan of the area, not too difficult considering the size of the shoebox. Nothing was out of place, and yet, something was wrong. He stepped in further and looked closer. His books were all in place, his cot had not been disturbed, and the box under his table, which held his letters, did not appear to have been moved. Then a sudden and terrible thought came to him. He grabbed the box and started to rummage through it.

He flipped through the letters, becoming more and more distressed as he got deeper into the pile and wasn't finding the one he sought.

Don't panic yet, he told himself, you might have just missed it. Look again, slow down, it must be here!

But a second run-through still did not produce what he was searching for. A chill of dread went through him and then the heat of rising anger; Gabriella's letter was gone.

He turned and looked into the aisle, his lips tightening with indignant hostility. He didn't stop to think why he was angry over the disappearance of that letter; he'd been set to throw it out himself. But angry he was.

In an instant, he was out of his cell and heading down the stairs toward the outer door. He knew who he was looking for and he knew exactly what he was going to do once he found him.

Even through his anger, a little voice in the back of his mind nagged at him, trying to make the rest of his body see reason.

Don't do this. You know what you'll get for fighting. Do you want to spend two days in the dark cell? Do you? Do you want to lose your privileges, hmm? It's not important—you've read that letter so many times, you know it word for word, you don't need the actual letter, you've got it stored in your head. C'mon Napoleon, don't do this.

But his legs and his heart didn't listen to his brain, and he burst out the door and into the yard, fuming and ready for a fight. He gave a quick look around the enclosure, and then he saw them, Boeman and Harris over by the far wall. He headed straight toward them at a fast walk, his eyes locked onto Boeman like a cougar stalking its prey. His intent was obvious.

Boeman saw him coming and with a sneering smile of anticipation, he straightened up and squared off. Finally, he'd found something that would rattle Leon out of his lofty indifference to the natural order of things.

Carson saw the two adversaries heading for a confrontation and, holding his rifle at ease, he crossed his arms and settled back to watch the two bucks lock horns.

Then, dammit. Where did he come from?

Kenny was in Leon's face, blocking his bead on Boeman. The guard grabbed him by his shirt front and shook him, but Leon was so focused on his goal, that he walked right through Kenny. The guard did not relent. He dug in his heels and, leaning his weight into the convict, he slapped him across the face.

Just for an instant, guard and inmate stared at each other, challenging the dictate. Then something akin to reason came back into Leon's eyes and, dropping his gaze, he backed off and submitted.

The charged atmosphere in the yard came down a notch in disappointment. The other, lesser wolves in the pack had their appetites whetted for blood, and they circled hungrily to watch the two dominates rip each other apart. Now, it appeared it wasn't going to happen.

"Convict, follow me." Kenny turned and walked toward the door back into the prison proper.

Leon seethed, but he was too conditioned to follow that particular order to ignore it. Nonetheless, he still turned to look at Boeman, and in that one quick glance, the two men reached an understanding. A confrontation was coming—this wasn't over yet. Leon turned eyes forward and followed Kenny inside, much to the grumbling of the most senior guard, and the other inmates in the yard.

Leon felt his anger subside, but he still trembled with the

adrenaline rush that had built up and then, suddenly, had nowhere to go. He kept his eyes focused on Kenny's back, but his mind was racing. Now that he was calmer, he realized he couldn't even be sure it was Boeman who had taken the letter. It could have been Harris, it could even have been Carson, hoping to set up the confrontation. But Boeman hadn't been surprised by Leon's challenge, indeed, he seemed to be expecting it, so . . .

Damn. Maybe all three of them were in on it together; wouldn't that be a treat.

The two men arrived back at the scene of the crime and Kenny ushered Leon into his cell. The guard slid the door closed and locked it manually.

"You stay in here for the rest of the afternoon, Nash," Kenny told him. "Take some time to calm down."

Then Kenny was gone, leaving Leon standing with his back to the aisle and thinking that maybe, he just might take the warden up on his offer after all—and mean it.

***

After a time of silent ranting, Leon sighed and sat down on his cot. Pushing himself into the corner, he mumbled and cursed and gave himself time to start thinking reasonably.

That was a stupid thing to do—again. I seem to be doing a lot of stupid things, lately. I'm not thinking clearly anymore. What has happened to my quick wit? My devious mind? What happened to being covert? That was stupid, charging down there to attack Boeman in plain sight of everyone—of course I'd be punished for that. And Gabi certainly wouldn't have been impressed. I can hear her in my head. How did she get in there again? Admonishing me in her lyrical French accent, telling me what an idiot I am. Yes, she was good at that. I don't know how I ever put up with her.

Leon groaned audibly and ran his hands over his scalp, there being no hair left for the purpose of abusing. He hadn't done himself any favors with his overreaction, that's for sure.

Kenny's mad at me, I can tell. The last thing I want to do is try the patience of that particular guard. Carson could send me to the dark cell, but Kenny, by withdrawing his support, could send me to the insane asylum.

Then another thought came to Leon's mind. He frowned and

turned still as stone while the thought took hold and spread out, slowly becoming a plan. It was a dangerous plan as he would very likely be hurt and almost certainly spend time in the dark cell.

This likely eventuality sent fear shivering through him, and he almost abandoned the whole idea. But it wouldn't go away, and he knew that he just might have to accept that punishment if he was going to play games with the warden and the other inmates, and still manage to keep himself alive.

Yes, the plan took hold, and the more Leon thought about it, the more he was convinced that it just might work.

It was safe to say that anyone who knew Napoleon Nash well, would have shivered at the smile that played about his lips.

***

Two weeks later, Jack showed up for his usual visit, and Leon could tell right off that his nephew was concerned about what Leon was going to do about the warden's offer. Jack didn't know about Taggard and Steven's visit and what was discussed, so he still wasn't sure how Leon was going to respond.

They didn't jump into it right away, but sat across from each other as usual, and started the visit off with the typical small talk.

"How ya doin', Leon? You stayin' outta trouble?"

"Yes. Sort of."

"Sorta? What does that mean?"

"Almost got into a fight a while back, but Kenny stopped it in time."

"Oh. Well, that's good. What was it about?"

"Someone went into my cell and stole Gabi's letter."

"Oh." Jack was surprised. "Who would do that?"

"I don't know," Leon shrugged. "I thought I knew at the time, but the more I think about it, the more I don't know."

"Well, why would somebody do that?"

"I told you about that one inmate who keeps trying to push me into a fight," Leon explained. "At first, I thought it was him, but then I thought, maybe it was," he stopped, remembering that Murray was standing right behind him, ". . . well—somebody else trying to set up a confrontation between us."

Jack let out his breath. "Damn, you really do have to watch your back in here."

"Hmm."

"That's a shame about Gabi's letter," Jack commented. "I know it's hard hearin' from her again, but—

"Oh, I got it back."

"Ya did? How?"

Leon shrugged. "Whoever took it, put it back the next day."

"Oh brother." Jack rolled his eyes. "Somebody's playin' games with ya, Leon."

"Uh huh."

"Speakin' a which," Jack began, quietly, "you made up your mind about that other thing yet?"

"Yeah, uh huh," Leon answered, then cocked his head ever so slightly and rolled his eyes toward the guard standing behind him.

Jack didn't follow Leon's look, didn't change his expression at all, but he still got the message; what Leon was going to say next was for the guard's ears and was to be taken with a very big grain of salt.

"I think I'm going to take the warden up on his offer," Leon commented. "It sounds like a fair arrangement and I think he will stand by his word."

"Yeah," Jack agreed. "I got the impression that he was an honorable man. It certainly won't hurt ya to be on good terms with 'im."

"Hmm. That's what I thought." Leon smiled and changed the subject. "I see you don't have the cane anymore. Your feet healed up?"

Jack returned the smile, the mood lightening. "Yeah, they're good. I'm back workin' for Cameron again—oh, and I took Karma over to meet her new boyfriend. We're all hopin' that magic will be made."

"Ahh." Leon's smile broadened. "The diva's going to be a mother, is she?"

"Well, we're hopin'," Jack repeated. "It was quite a trip. I had ta stay in the boxcar with her the whole way, and she was squealin' and carryin' on like she always does when she's in season, so hopefully, this time it will amount to something. I'll be goin' to get her again in a couple of weeks, and if she don't come inta season again next month, then I guess we can figure she took."

Leon nodded. His smile dropped, and he turned serious again. "Yeah, that's good. I hope Cameron gets a good colt out of her. He deserves some payback for all we've put him through."

"That's for sure," Jack agreed. "That bothers me sometimes. I feel like I owe 'im, but I don't know what to do about it. Damn. He's still helpin' me out; lettin' me stay at the ranch and givin' me work. I donno, part of me feels I should move on, start makin' my own way. Sometimes I think it might be better all-around if'n I just disappeared for a while."

"Why?" Leon asked. "Do you get the feeling they want you to leave?"

"No. No, not at all. But . . . well, Jean said that what Penny was feelin' for me is just a teenage crush. If I give it some time, she'll probably get over it."

"Yeah."

"Yeah, but she's not gettin' over it, Leon," Jack pointed out, a little louder than he'd intended. "Just the opposite. It's kinda awkward."

"Maybe it's not a teenage crush; maybe she's really in love."

Jack sent Leon a look suggesting that this comment wasn't even remotely funny.

Leon did his best to stifle a smile; it wasn't very often he saw Jack at a loss about how to deal with a young lady's affections.

"Yeah, okay," Leon acknowledged the look. "So, as you stated last month, you'll just have to be strong. What's the problem?"

"The problem is, she can be very, well . . . you know . . . she can be really . . . well . . .."

"What?" Leon enjoyed this; he didn't get much entertainment these days.

"Enticin'. That's what," Jack yelled at him, looking embarrassed and frustrated all at the same time. "I'm worried that one a these times, I might just . . . well . . . you know. And then, jeez, oh man. Cameron would skin me alive. So, I'm thinkin', maybe it would be better if I just left. Give her a chance ta meet some young fella closer to her own age."

Leon nodded, considering the options. "So, why don't you then? You could always head over to Red Sands and work for Max for a while."

"Yeah, I know. But another part of me likes bein' at the Marshams' place. I got friends there—and family, I guess, so it's hard ta leave. Besides, if I head over ta Texas, well then, I wouldn't be able to get in ta see you. That don't feel right."

"Yeah, I can understand that. But jeez, Jack, you've got your own life now; you have a chance to build something for yourself. Don't go throwing it away on a lost cause."

"What do ya mean 'a lost cause'?" Jack threw back at him. "I know damn well that Steven is workin' on an appeal for you. We're gonna get you outta here. And don't you even think for one minute that I'm gonna turn my back on you and walk away. That ain't gonna happen, Leon."

"Okay, okay." If Leon's hands hadn't been shackled, he would have thrown them up in his own defense. "I'm just saying, I wouldn't be mad at you if you decided to—"

"No," Jack was adamant. "It ain't gonna happen."

Leon nodded, silently relieved, but still feeling that he had to put the offer out there anyway, just in case.

"So, you think Cameron is just keeping you on out of the goodness of his heart? Is there really no work for you there?"

"No, that ain't the case at all. Just the opposite. Sam bought a small place just outside Arvada, and he's gonna be gettin' married next month, so he won't be around as much. He'll still be workin' the ranch, but a course, once he has a wife, he'll be goin' home at night." Jack grinned as another thought struck him. "I think his ma is gonna be sellin' her place and movin' in with 'em. Hope that don't end the marriage before it rightly gets started!"

"Hmm," was Leon's only comment.

Jack sent Leon a frustrated look. "Yeah, I know," he said, "you're not really interested in what Sam is doin'. I'm just explainin' why Cameron kinda wants me ta stick around some. I thought about takin' Rick Layton up on his offer ta go and work his spread for a while, but Taggard don't think it's a good idea for me to go back to Wyoming, permanent. Too many people here don't agree with how my trial ended. He figures I should give it a few years, let things calm down."

"Yeah, that makes sense," Leon agreed. "Don't want you getting shot in the back."

"No," Jack agreed. "And besides, Morrison's home base is in that town close to Rick's place so . . . I don't really wanna be runnin' inta him, if ya know what I mean."

Leon's brows went up and he nodded in complete agreement. He sat quietly for a moment, considering Jack's options.

"So," he continued, with a shrug, "you may as well just stay on at the Marshams' for now and stop worrying about it. You've got a job there, and friends, like you say, plus Mr. Granger is handy, now that he's in Denver. Who knows, maybe that appeal will come to something and I could be out of here by Christmas."

Jack smiled. "That'd be great. "I just don't feel right about strikin' out on my own, not until all this nonsense is cleared up. So, yeah, I think you're right, and I'll stay put for now. I'll just have ta be real careful where Penny is concerned."

"I got faith in you, Jack." Then, "How's your shoulder coming along? Think you can hit the side of a barn yet?"

"Yeah Leon. I can hit the side of a barn. Not too good with the smaller stuff yet though." He turned serious. "Still kinda slow too. I think Jean could outdraw me now."

"What does David say about that?"

Jack shrugged, looking heartbroken. "Just ta keep at it. Ta keep on with the stretchin' every day and keep practicin'. It'll improve."

"Well, that's good, isn't it?"

"Yeah, but I asked David how long I have ta keep on with the stretchin' and he said probably for the rest of my life!"

"Oh."

"Yeah. He says that if I stop stretchin' out them muscles, they'll seize up on me and get stiff again, and I'll never get my speed back. And even at that, he figures I'll never be as fast as I was." Jack's voice caught a little on the last bit.

"I'm sorry, Jack," Leon sympathized, knowing how hard that would be for his nephew to accept.

Jack nodded, then forcing himself to brighten up, he smiled. "Still, David also said that the one time he saw me draw my gun, I was so drunk I could barely stand up, and he couldn't believe the speed of it. So, if I keep workin' at it, then maybe I'll be able to get some 'a that speed back again, even when I'm not lubricated with alcohol."

Leon chuckled. "There ya go. I always knew drinking was good for something."

***

Not surprisingly, shortly after Jack left the prison, Leon

found himself, once more, standing in the middle of the warden's office.

Mitchell sat back in his comfortable chair behind his desk, his arms folded, while he scrutinized the inmate.

Leon stood quietly, waiting for Mitchell to get done with his little attempt at intimidation so they could get down to business. Ho hum.

"So, did you and your partner have a chance to discuss our little arrangement?"

"Yes sir, Warden," was Leon's only response. He knew damn well that Mitchell was already aware of what he and Jack had discussed. This little game was getting old.

"Would you care to elaborate?"

Leon took this as permission to speak freely.

"I thought about it, Warden, and I figured that, well . . . I haven't got any friends in here anyway, and all you're asking me to do is just carry on doing what I've already been doing . . . so, I don't see any harm in it. So long as I can keep my current privileges."

Mitchell's smile was so self-satisfied, it almost made Leon give up the game and throw the warden's offer in his face. Fortunately, he was beginning to regain his devious mindset and remained subservient and accommodating.

"Of course, of course," Mitchell agreed. "And, like I said; I can do even more than that for you if I'm pleased with your efforts. I'll arrange for you to see me once a month, or if something urgent comes up, well, you just let Officer Murray know and he'll bring you here. How's that?"

"Yes sir, Warden."

"Good. Guard!"

***

That night, Leon lay on his cot staring at a ceiling he couldn't see and thought about the lion's den he had allowed himself to be walked into. Finally, he groaned and pushed those thoughts away. His brain was just going in circles, so he wasn't accomplishing anything anyway.

I need to get some sleep. He closed his eyes. *Busy day tomorrow, yup. Important work to be done.* Heavy sigh. *I wonder what Gabriella is going to do. That lady always was full of surprises*. He saw them then; her green eyes flashing in his mind, as clearly as though she were laying here beside him. *I can smell her; that wonderful scent. I'd forgotten about that. My goodness, but she's beautiful.*

He snapped his eyes open. Urges grew inside him again, the kind of urges he didn't want to deal with in here.

I have to stop thinking about that stuff. I have to stay focused on what's going on around me, now more than ever. I can't allow myself to daydream; that could be fatal. I have to stay alert now, and watch for any signs at all.

I can't make my move until Boeman does, and when he does, I have to react instantly and explosively. For my plan to work, for it to be believable, I have to send myself back to the dark cell.

CHAPTER FIVE
THE FIGHT

Laramie, Wyoming

The following weeks in the warehouse were stressful. Leon kept reminding himself that he had to appear relaxed, and to simply carry on with his duties, while ignoring everyone else. The way things were now, everybody was watching everybody, so nobody was making a move. Boeman wasn't that stupid; he knew Leon was watching for him and he wasn't going to try anything while his opponent's suspicions were up.

And it wasn't just the other inmates watching the pack in anticipation of entertainment. Reece had cautioned the other guards that there was bad blood brewing between the two inmates and not to let them get too close to one another. It wasn't the time for either of the adversaries to initiate a confrontation, and the tension grew.

Leon knew he had to relax.

***

The first day in the infirmary after the near fight in the yard, Kenny made it clear to Leon what he thought about the inmate's behavior. As the guard walked him over to begin his day helping Palin, Leon found himself being verbally reprimanded in such a way as to remind him of his days at Blessed Heart. The fact that Leon had once been the most successful leader of that infamous outlaw band, "The Elk Mountain Gang" didn't seem to impress Kenny Reece one little bit.

"I don't know what the hell you thought you were doing, Nash," Kenny went on. "I thought you were supposed to be smart. It's bad enough you were launching sneak attacks on the other inmates just because they ticked you off—and don't even think about denying it, because I know that's what you were doing."

Leon had no intention of denying it. There were no direct questions in this onslaught anyway, so how was he supposed to deny it even if he had been contemplating doing so?

"You seem to be taking your privileges for granted these days," Kenny continued, "but believe me, you can lose them just as quickly as you got them, so I suggest you smarten up and start toeing the line. You think you're so high and mighty just because you have friends looking out for you and a lawyer coming to see you. You think that means you can get away with starting a fight with another inmate?

"Believe me, it doesn't. You start doing stupid things like that and you are going to end up in real trouble.

"Then what in the hell am I supposed to tell your nephew? He thinks I'm in here looking out for you. But if you are going to insist on being stupid, well then you will be on your own, because even I can't stop you from being punished for fighting. I hope you're listening to me, Nash. I hope you hear what I'm saying."

Oh God, Leon was in misery. *Kind of hard not to hear you. Thank goodness, here we are at the infirmary.*

"Here ya go, Doc," Kenny announced as they walked in. "I hope he doesn't give you any trouble today."

Then Kenny was gone, back to the warehouse to continue with his day. Leon stood in the middle of the infirmary; his expression sheepish.

Palin sent him a speculative look.

"Just can't stay outta trouble, can ya, Nash?"

Leon sighed and rolled his eyes. If this is the chewing he was getting hit with for some minor indiscretion, what was going to be the fallout when he deliberately goes out of his way to create an incident?

"Yeah, I know, Doc," Leon admitted, playing the game. "It was stupid."

"Hmm," came the response. "Just don't let it happen again. I need you over here."

Aww jeez, here comes the guilt trip.

So, not only was Kenny ticked off at him, but once things really light up, ole' Doc Palin was going to be pretty pissed at him as well. He hoped he wasn't cutting his own throat with his scheming.

***

Three weeks after Jack's last visit, things in the warehouse and the prison proper had settled down to the usual routine. Almost everyone had forgotten about the confrontation in the yard, and Leon had begun to relax his stance.

Maybe Boeman wasn't going to make a move. Maybe he was waiting for Leon to show his hand first. Well, that wasn't going to happen. Sooner or later, Boeman was going to start something and Leon knew it. All he had to do was be ready for it.

Then, when it finally did happen, it wasn't Boeman making the move, but Harris. And the intent wasn't just to battle it out for dominance; it was to commit murder.

It was laundry day for Leon, and he was on the third level, distributing prison garb and other materials back to their respective owners. Officer Davis was armed and perched in the third level lookout, keeping a casual eye on the assembly of inmates below him, as they came in through the yard door on their way from the warehouse to the common room for lunch. It was the regular routine, and aside from the scuffling of feet on the ground level, all was quiet.

Leon had just dropped off his final pile of clean laundry to a cell and headed for the stairway to go down and have lunch along with everyone else. He got halfway to the stairs when a sudden movement in the cell to his right, caught his eye. He didn't even have time to recognize it as a threat, when he felt himself propelled over to the railing and then a hand grasped his left ankle and hoisted him up and over.

Leon let out a yell of shock and instant terror when he saw the ground floor, three levels down, come spinning up toward him as he went over the railing head first.

Leon's insistence that he could move like a rattlesnake at the first sign of trouble, fortunately, was not an exaggeration. His left hand made a frantic grab for the hand rail just as his torso went over and down, quickly followed by his hips and then his legs. But his grip on the railing held, and the momentum of his fall carried him around, his swing continuing with his right-hand grabbing hold and carrying him on through the arc. He catapulted himself up and over the railing again, to land gracefully, very close to his take-off point.

It happened in a flash, and once he was upright again, all he got was a fleeting impression of Harris's face, and a pair of eyes filled with fear and surprise at the failure of his assault. Then he was gone and running toward the stairs and the lower levels. Leon took off after him. His blood was up, and he was ready for a fight.

Davis was startled out of his complacency by Leon's sudden yell. Instantly switching his attention, he brought his rifle around, but it all happened so fast, the barrel of the weapon got caught up in the bars of the lookout. By the time the flustered guard got his rifle organized again, it was too late for him to get a shot off without possibly hitting his own co-workers.

The inmates and guards, down on the ground level, had all glanced up at the sound of Leon's yell and now the whole area was in an uproar as every convict started yelling encouragement to their own favored combatant.

The guards were on the move. Armed only with the billy clubs, some attempted to get the assembly under control, while others ran toward the stairway to intercept the two antagonists and prevent a brawl.

Leon didn't even hear the uproar coming from the floor beneath him or acknowledge the orders from the guards to stand down. Any game plan he had worked out and intended on following, was gone from his mind. Harris had tried to kill him, and Leon had every intention of reciprocating.

Harris reached the first stairway and ran down them three at a time, but Leon got there right behind him and didn't bother with the steps at all. He leaped from a flat-out run and landed squarely on Harris's back. He grabbed hold, pulling them both over and tumbling down the last few steps to the second-floor landing. They both felt the air knocked out of their lungs, but they were too far gone to care.

Harris twisted around and plowed the heel of his right hand into Leon's nose. Leon grunted, his eyes watering. He fell back against the wall, losing his grip. Harris was up and sent a kick toward his adversary, but Leon dodged it and grabbed hold of the foot, intent on bringing his quarry down. Harris twisted away again and pulled free, leaving Leon holding onto an empty shoe.

Then the chase was on again. By this time, Officers Murray and Pearson were on their way up the first flight of stairs, their billy clubs out and ready for action. Harris saw them coming, and grabbing the hand rail, he leapt over the railing and landed hard amongst the other inmates.

They were more than happy to grab him and send him on his way. Leon instantly followed and was given the same reception as soon as he hit ground level. The inmates cheered them on, giving them running room and doing their best to block the guards and prevent them from interfering.

Murray and Pearson turned on their heels and came charging back down the stairs again, their clubs swinging to clear themselves a path. By this time, Reece had joined Carson on the floor, trying to restore order, but the mob mentality had taken hold and it was turning into a free-for-all.

The alarm klaxon screamed out its warning, but it came too late to lock down the prison proper and secure the inmates within its confines. Harris made a dash out the exit and ran for all he was worth, across the open yard toward the warehouse. Leon was right on his heels and he was closely followed by the cheering mob.

Rifle shots from the watchtowers were ignored by all concerned. And those guards didn't dare aim to shoot into the pack for fear of hitting their own men. Containing this riot was going to be up to the guards on the ground, armed only with billy clubs.

Every officer, except those guarding the main gates, made a dash for the warehouse. All firearms were instantly locked up to prevent an inmate from overpowering an armed guard and getting hold of a weapon. Many of the inmates, as they entered the warehouse, grabbed wooden broom handles and other convenient pieces of equipment, preparing to meet the onslaught of the guards coming up behind them, and the riot was in full swing.

In the meantime, Harris and Leon were oblivious to any other battle going on aside from their own. Harris ran like mad through the work area, knocking over benches and worktables in an effort to trip Leon up. But Leon leapt over all the obstacles and kept coming. Harris twisted in his run and threw tools at him, but Leon just dodged any projectiles that came his way, and he kept coming.

Two more strides and Leon was on him, grabbing the back of his shirt. Harris scrambled, then got hold of a broom handle and, twisting again, he bellowed his war cry and swung the handle around, aiming for Leon's head.

Leon brought his arm up just in time, blocking the blow, and he didn't even feel the wood breaking against his elbow. He was seeing red as he lunged at Harris and got his hands around his adversary's throat. The two men went down with a crash, and Leon started to squeeze, his lips drawn back in an savage snarl.

Harris found himself fighting for his life. He twisted and squirmed, punched and kicked, but no matter what he tried, he couldn't get his assailant off him.

Then, out of nowhere, Leon felt an arm come around his throat from behind. The tables were turned, and Leon was the one fighting for life. His hold on Harris loosened and that convict pulled away from Leon's grip and scrambled to his feet, gasping for air.

Leon pushed himself up off the floor, desperately reaching behind him, trying to get a hold of whomever it was choking the life out of him. He dug his heels in and pushed backwards, sending himself and his assailant tumbling over an upended work table. The hold on his throat loosened, and he twisted around to come face to face with Boeman.

Leon's rage rose another notch and, as both men found their footing, he sent a right-handed punch straight into Boeman's face, breaking his nose. But all that did was enrage his adversary even more. Boeman retaliated with a powerful blow to Leon's gut, followed by a sharp upper cut to his jaw.

Leon staggered backward, right into the waiting arms of Harris.

Harris took the advantage and, grabbing hold of Leon, he held his arms back in a vice-like grip, and Boeman came forward to begin an assault with his fists. Leon kicked out at him, but whatever blows he was able to land, did nothing to slow Boeman down. He came on with his attack until Leon tasted blood and mucus, and he knew he was on the edge of passing out.

Meanwhile, the scuffle between the guards and other inmates was violent but short-lived. The guards were well trained in the techniques of quashing an uprising, and the thin broom handles were no match for the disciplined and effective onslaught of the billy clubs.

It didn't take long for the main insurgents to be beaten into submission, and then the rest of the rioters were quickly subdued and pushed, prodded and cajoled back to their cells.

At the same time as the group was being handled, Carson, Reece and Pearson came at a run to the three combatants who each seemed determined to demolish the work floor in their battle for supremacy.

Each guard grabbed in inmate and pulled them apart, but all three convicts were blinded by their battle rage and fought everything and anyone who came within reach.

Pearson managed to drag Harris away, and as that prisoner bit and kicked just for the sake of fighting, Pearson cold-cocked him with the club and put him onto the floor. With that inmate semi-conscious, Pearson dragged him over to the stairs and back to his cell. One less to worry about.

But Reece and Carson still had their hands full. Once Leon felt himself freed from Harris, he head-butted Reece and lunged at the subdued Boeman, again going for the throat. Carson, Boeman and Leon all went down in a heap and then Boeman was free from Carson, and he and Leon were at each other again, fighting for the upper hand.

Carson was getting trampled by the two convicts and when Reece ran in to grab Leon, he got nailed again with a staggering blow from Boeman who had been aiming for Leon's face and missed. All four men sprawled on the floor, while Kenny, shaking his head from the blow, tried to get back on his knees and bring his club into play. Boeman was sandwiched in between, with Carson underneath him, and Leon on top; he was frantic to get himself out of this vulnerable position and into the clear.

He swung again at Leon, this time hitting him squarely on the side of his head, knocking him over. Then Boeman rolled clear of Carson and was attempting to get to his feet when Leon grabbed him again. Boeman twisted, kicking out, but Leon caught his leg, pulling him off balance and then making another rush. This time, Leon got a hold on Boeman's throat that wasn't going to break loose. Boeman lashed out, boxing Leon on the ears, trying to kick at him, but nothing worked, and he was again fighting for his life.

Reece was on his feet and hit Leon behind his knees with the club, bringing him down, but all that happened was Leon took Boeman down with him. Carson and Reece both had hold of their respective inmates, trying to break Leon's stranglehold on his adversary.

"Nash!" Reece yelled at him. "Let him go!"

But Leon only squeezed harder. His lids were closed to slits and his eyes had rolled back so that only white shone through; he was in a bloodlust, hearing and feeling nothing.

Boeman was turning blue.

"God dammit, Nash. Let him go. I swear, I'll break your arm. Let him go!"

Nothing short of brute force was going to end this. Reece got himself into the clear and, raising the billy club, he brought it down in a crushing blow to Leon's left forearm. There was a resounding crack as the bone broke in two, and Leon's left arm loosened its hold and dropped to his side. He was still hanging on with his right, but Carson grabbed his wrist and squeezed it until the fingers started to release. Boeman suddenly gasped in a lungful of air.

He tried to scramble away from his assailant, but then Leon's lids opened wide and his eyes rolled down. The rage that was in them was feral and beyond reason. He tried to lunge forward again, to re-claim his hold on Boeman's throat with his right hand, ignoring the pain coming from his left. But Reece had too strong a lock on him, and he couldn't quite reach his goal.

Still, Leon wouldn't let up. He kept fighting against Reece while Carson got in between Leon and Boeman. He tried using his club to punch Leon in the ribs, but it was cramped quarters and Carson couldn't get any oomph into it. Leon didn't even feel it.

Kenny had a quick choice to make. Did he maintain his lock on Nash, or take the chance of releasing him to bring the club into play? He hadn't wanted to take things this far. He'd hoped that a broken arm would be enough of a shock to bring Nash out of it and begin to see reason, but that wasn't happening. The inmate only became more enraged. This had to end, and end now.

Kenny released his hold and, as he expected, Nash immediately took advantage and lunged at Boeman, who dropped to his knees to avoid the attack. But Kenny was lightning fast, and that billy club came down on the back of Leon's head with a sickening thud, and the battle was over.

Leon sank the rest of the way to the floor and lay there, unconscious, his arm broken, his rib cage battered and bruised. Blood covered his face to the point where he was unrecognizable.

The two guards breathed sighs of relief. They stood, hands on knees, gasping air into their burning lungs, and giving the adrenaline time to settle down.

Boeman, crumpled on the floor, dragged himself away from his opponent and then lay on his back, mouth open, gulping in air with a hand to his throat. Like Leon, he was bleeding from his nose, his mouth and his ears, not to mention the numerous cuts and bruises obtained during the wild rampage through the workstations. He emitted the occasional groan.

Finally, Carson got his breath back.

"Punishment for three of 'em," he stated between gasps. "Nash can spend two days in the dark cell, beginning now! As for Harris and Boeman, they can haul around the Oregon Boot for a couple 'a days. See how they like that. Nash can have the privilege of seeing the doctor when his punishment is done!"

Reece was in no mood to argue.

***

When Leon awoke, he was hit with a wave of panic, thinking he had gone blind. He tried to scramble to his feet and experienced nauseating pain as his left arm collapsed under him, and his head started to spin. He lay there for a few moments, still as stone, giving himself a chance to stop trembling while he listened to his racing heart gradually slow down to normal.

As he lay there, staring into the darkness, his mind became rational again and he realized he wasn't actually blind, but simply in the dark cell. At least that part of his plan had worked out. As for the rest of it, he closed his eyes and groaned. That had not been part of the plan; he had known he was probably going to get hurt to some degree, but this had been way over the top—he wasn't a masochist, after all.

He knew damn well that Boeman was behind the attack. His antagonism toward Leon had reached new levels. Yet, Boeman was smart enough to know he couldn't get away with killing Leon, so the next best thing was to convince someone else to do it for him. Obviously, Harris was just the right combination of aggressive and stupid to allow himself to be manipulated into doing it. Or at least trying to.

The only good thing about the viciousness of the battle was that now, hopefully, both Boeman and Harris would leave him alone. Just because Leon had, on the most part, been avoiding a fight, it didn't mean he couldn't hold his own if the fight was forced on him. He only hoped that Kenny wasn't going to hold too big of a grudge.

Leon sighed and pushed himself up into a sitting position. He gingerly cradled his left arm and thought miserably that there wasn't one square inch on his body that didn't hurt. Even his head pounded. He leaned back against the wall and closed his eyes, trying to relax. He thought ruefully that the one good thing about the situation was that he was so exhausted and beaten down, he didn't have the energy to conjure up the dark terrors that generally assaulted him in this cell.

He was wrong.

He wasn't aware of the passage of time, but eventually he slipped into unconsciousness again, and when he woke up the second time, he was hot and feverish. He had the shakes. He wished he had his warm blanket to wrap around himself, but not having it, he simply curled into a ball, partly for warmth and partly to protect his hurting body.

Then the nightmares started, and the hallucinations took hold so that even in waking, the darkness still held the creatures of his imagination. He pushed himself into a corner and screamed out his terror to a world that couldn't hear him and didn't care. He prayed for death to take him, so this misery that was his life could be over and done with, and he could find peace again.

But life went on despite his ravings. By the time his punishment was over, and they opened the cell to release him, he was only semi-conscious, and he had to be dragged out into the light. He was carried to the infirmary and left in the good care of Doctors Palin and Mariam.

Between the two of them, they got him bathed and patched up. Palin set the arm and administered quinine for the fever and to help him sleep. The doctor got him settled on one of the cots and left him to recover.

Mariam stayed by his side through most of the duration, to help him through his fever. She also tended to the other two inmates who were there to recover from their various injuries, but as fair with her time as she tried to be, she still tended to spend most of it at the bedside of her friend.

She sat beside him, applying cool compresses to his forehead as she listened to his quiet ramblings, mostly about Jack. But some were about his sister, or about someone named Caroline, then it would be someone named Ella. Then other musings that made no sense and would gradually peter out to nothing.

She worried about her friend, not only about his chances for long-term survival in this awful place, but also about the sanctity of his soul.

Of course, she knew that neither he nor Jack were church-going men, not many single men in this hard land were. It often took a wife and family to bring a man to the church. Then, once she learned of her friends' true identities, it made even more sense that they had neglected the spiritual part of their lives. Therefore, she had been pleased to learn that Napoleon, at least, had been attending chapel here at the prison and would perhaps find a new path for himself

But as time went on, she realized he had slowly but surely decreased his attendance to Sunday services, preferring instead to remain alone in his cell, reading his books or writing letters. And now, after seeing the result of his allowing the dark part of his soul, the dark part that we all carry within us, to burst forth and wreak such havoc, she couldn't help but feel worried and disappointed. She wanted to help him find his way back, and she only hoped he would let her.

Of course, she was completely unaware of the complex game Leon was playing, or of the strategy involved with setting up his persona as a dangerous inmate. Despite the events having gotten out of hand in the extreme, it all still played in with what Leon was trying to accomplish. Hopefully he had made his stance clear to the other inmates now and would never have to set himself up to accept such abuses again. Guards and inmates alike would look at him and see trouble, and hopefully, the last thing they'd see was snitch.

***

Arvada, Colorado,
Summer 1886

Jack had gone into town with Sam to help with supplies on the morning when he received a very unusual telegram. He stood on the steps of the telegraph office, not quite believing what he was reading.

J.K. (stop) Don't come (stop) NN privileges revoked one month (stop) Started riot (stop) K.R.

Jack stood there and read the message a couple of times

before shaking his head and mumbling to himself. *He started a riot? What the hell was he thinkin'?*

He sighed and, turning around, went straight back into the office to send a reply.

K.R. (stop) Coming to see you (stop) When and where? (stop) J.K.

The next day, Jack got his reply.

J.K. (stop) This Sat. 8:00 pm (stop) Jail Breakers Saloon (stop) K.R.

***

Jack arrived at the saloon on Saturday evening at 7:45, ordered himself a beer and sat down at one of the tables to wait. He deliberately chose one that was in the far corner where he could not only keep watch on the front door, but it would also give them some measure of privacy once they got talking.

Shortly after he settled, Kenny arrived. He went to the bar, ordered himself a beer, then turned and casually surveyed the room looking for his contact.

Jack spotted him when he entered but didn't recognize him at first. He had only met the guard once before, and tonight, Kenny was off duty and wearing civilian clothes, so he didn't stand out as anyone special. But as he approached the bar, Jack picked up on the body language and, meeting his eyes, he nodded to him in recognition.

Kenny responded and, picking up his beer, headed to the table.

Jack stood and they shook hands in greeting.

"Mr. Reece. Thank you for meetin' with me."

"You know, you may as well call me Kenny," the guard said as he sat down. "I get the feeling we're going to be chatting a lot as time goes by."

"Yeah, good point. Name's Jack." Jack frowned, taking note of the black eye Kenny sported.

Kenny gave a small, knowing smile. "Not 'Kid'?" he asked.

"Naw. Only people who knew me as an outlaw call me 'Kid'.

I never did like it much, but you know how these things get started. I'm hopin' ta leave that life behind me."

"Hmm, those changes come to us all." Kenny took a swig of beer.

"Yeah, I suppose so." Then Jack got down to business. "So, what's all this about Leon startin' a riot?"

Kenny swallowed his beer and rolled his eyes. "That was crazy. I don't know what the hell has gotten into your partner. As I mentioned to you before, he has always been a bit hard to handle, but this past month it's almost as though he's deliberately asking for trouble."

"Well, what started it?" Jack asked. "What set 'im off?"

"He and another inmate, Boeman, have been circling each other like wolves ever since Nash came to us. Now, it's normal when a new prisoner comes in for things to get stirred up a bit. Just a shuffling of the pecking order, you know. Everybody has to find their footing again. Generally, things get sorted out with just a look or a bit of gesturing, and it's fine. But not between those two." Kenny shook his head and sighed. "I guess what really stuck in Boeman's craw is the fact that he was sending out challenges to Nash, but Nash was simply ignoring him. Kind of an insult, I guess."

"Yup," Jack commented. "Leon is good at insultin' people without even openin' his mouth." He smiled. "Even better at it when he does open his mouth."

"Uh huh," Kenny agreed. "Then something happened about a month ago: Nash came out to the yard and made a beeline straight for Boeman and was looking for a fight. Fortunately, I defused it that time, but trouble was brewing. We could all feel it, we all knew it was coming. I tried to reason with him, get him to stand down, to think about what he was risking by starting trouble, but I knew he wasn't listening." Kenny paused, took another drink from his beer, then blew out a sigh. "Jeez, what a mad house. I don't know for sure what set it off. One of the guards who was on the floor at the time, said another inmate by the name of Harris tried to throw Nash off the third level walkway."

"Ohh," Jack groaned.

"Yeah," Kenny agreed. "He failed, obviously. But Nash just went crazy. It ended up across the yard, in the warehouse, and had the three of them, Nash, Boeman, and Harris, going for blood. Of course, that got the other inmates all worked up and the next thing you know, we had a riot on our hands."

Jack shook his head and the two men sat in silence.

"How is he?" Jack finally asked. "Was he badly hurt?"

"Yup."

Jack closed his eyes and groaned.

Kenny nodded. "Aside from the damage the three men did to each other, I had to get rough on Nash myself—again—just to stop him from killing Boeman. He wouldn't back off. I guess one of the reasons I was willing to meet you here is that I hoped you would have some insight into why your partner is behaving like this. He was always very careful before, making sure he didn't get caught breaking the rules. Now, suddenly, it's like he doesn't care anymore."

"Yeah," Jack mumbled. He looked into Kenny's grey eyes and saw honest concern there. Jack ran his hands through his hair and then, for better or worse, came to a decision. He was going to trust Kenny implicitly, until the guard proved himself unworthy of it. Jack hoped he was right in his instincts about the man, because if he wasn't, it could become even more dangerous for Leon inside that prison.

But Jack also knew that Leon needed someone to watch his back in there, and since Jack wasn't available to do that, he had to hope Kenny was true to his word and was already doing it. That being the case, the more Kenny knew of the true situation, the better he'd be able to watch out for Jack's partner.

Jack sighed and took the plunge.

"Do you know anything about the deal Warden Mitchell made with Leon?"

"No. What deal?"

"Mitchell recruited Leon to do some spyin' for him. Just . . . you know . . . keep on doin' what he's always been doin' in watchin' his own back, only now, he's ta report anything 'suspicious' to the warden. In return, the warden assured him he could keep his privileges and maybe even be pardoned in a year or two."

Kenny snorted. "That's a hoot. I can't remember the last time Warden Michell pardoned a lifer. That's not going to happen."

"Yeah, we already figured that. But the warden also made it very clear what direction Leon's life would go in if he refused the offer. So, Leon decided to play along with the warden, pretend to agree and then heavily censor whatever information he passed on to him."

Kenny slowly let out his breath. "Ohh, that's very risky."

"Yup," Jack agreed. "But we couldn't think of any other way out of it."

"So . . ." Kenny speculated, thinking it through and then putting it into words. "All this sudden tendency toward aggression is really just a ruse on Nash's part to make it appear that he's a dangerous criminal. Therefore, he would be the last person anyone, guards and inmates alike, would suspect of being in cahoots with the warden. When in fact, he really isn't in cahoots with the warden, but makes it appear to that gentleman that he is."

"Yup, that's pretty much it."

"That's smart, and devious." Then Kenny smiled. "And just the type of behavior I've come to expect from him." He turned serious again, and looked Jack in the eye. "But like I said, very risky. He's walking a fine line."

"Yup. So, I'm hopin' you'll watch his back, and maybe cut 'im some slack on the punishment end 'a things."

"I'll do what I can," Kenny offered, "but Carson is senior to me and has the last say on that. Still, I'll watch out for him." He hesitated and frowned. "That still doesn't really explain the ferociousness of this last confrontation. There is no doubt in my mind that Nash was going to kill Boeman. Just how was that supposed to help his situation?

"Ahh, I have a feelin' that weren't part of the plan," Jack admitted. "Leon suspected Boeman of takin' somethin' that was real important to him, and when everything came to a head, well, I think he kinda lost control."

"Yeah. Just a bit," Kenny emphasized with raised eyebrows. "You should a seen the carnage left behind."

Jack chuckled. "Yeah, okay." Then he sent the guard a hopeful glance. "Sure there's no chance a gettin' in ta see 'im tomorrow?"

Kenny sent him a frustrated look. "I had a feeling you were going to ask me that."

Jack smiled and threw an inquisitive look back at him.

"Well," Kenny took another swig of beer while he considered. "Nash will be in the infirmary for another day or two, just to make sure the fever is gone." He stopped and thought about the pros and cons. Jack waited it out. "Carson's not working tomorrow, so . . . maybe I can sneak you in."

Jack grinned.

"Maybe," Kenny reiterated. "And not for long."

"Sure."

Kenny sighed again. What was he getting himself into? "Okay, come up to the prison tomorrow after breakfast and do what you normally do when you're coming to visit. When the guard informs you that Nash can't come to visit, get angry and ask to speak with me. We'll take it from there."

"Thanks. I really appreciate it."

"Yeah," Kenny shook his head, frowning. "What is it about you two? You always manage to get what you want."

Jack simply smiled.

***

Following Kenny down the hall, into South Block, set Jack Kiefer on edge. Even knowing he was a visitor and could turn around and leave this place at any time, he still felt the oppressive atmosphere weighing him down. That weight became heavier and more suffocating as they entered the prison proper and strode past the row of cells. It truly was a cold and daunting place. Jack had to constantly remind himself to just keep putting one foot in front of the other, and not to panic.

Having taken Jack the long way around to avoid unwanted scrutiny, Kenny opened a door and ushered Jack into the infirmary. The first things Jack noticed were the three cots lined up along the far wall and even a dentist chair at the far end.

Two of the beds were occupied. If that wasn't enough to give it away, the place just smelled like a hospital; sterile and sickly all at the same time. At least it was light and airy, but still obviously, a prison.

Kenny touched Jack's arm and nodded to the far cot where a pale and dejected inmate sat with his left arm in a sling. He was staring off into space with a haunted and distant look in his eye.

All the other times Jack had come to see his partner, Leon had known he was having a visitor, so he had adopted a demeanor to match the occasion. But now, Jack caught him off guard without his mask on. Seeing that expression coming from his friend sent chills through Jack's chest. He had to remind himself to keep breathing. It was terrifying; as though little by little, breath by breath, Leon's soul was dying.

Something caught Leon's attention, some little movement by the far door that brought him back to the present and caused him to glance over that way. The last person Leon expected to see walking into the infirmary was his nephew, so when their eyes met, the change in the inmate's countenance was instantaneous. His face lit up with a smile that brought the sparkle back into his eyes and the bedeviling return to his persona.

Jack grinned back.

"Hey, Kid!" Leon teased him as he got up off the cot. "What are you doing here? I didn't think I was getting any visitors for a month."

"Yeah, well, Kenny snuck me in the back way," Jack informed him, "so I could see how you were doin'."

"Aww, great." Leon was thrilled and threw his right arm around Jack's shoulder in a big friendship hug that had been a long time coming.

Jack returned it and couldn't help but think how skinny Leon felt underneath the coarse prison garb, but he decided it would be best not to mention it right then.

Leon sent a quick, apprehensive glance to Kenny who was busy talking with Dr. Palin. Obviously, the inmate was expecting to get reprimanded for the physical contact, but when no reprimand was forthcoming, he relaxed and smiled again. He slapped Jack on the back and then rested his hand on his nephew's shoulder, not wanting to break the contact.

"How ya doin', Leon?" Jack asked him, concern in his eyes. "Ya look like you've been through the wars, here. And what's with that bump on the back 'a your head?"

"No, no, nothin. I'm fine," Leon insisted, as he led Jack back to his cot and indicated a chair for him to pull up and use. "I just had a little trouble with the locals, you know."

"Uh huh," came the skeptical response. "Kinda went a little over the top though, didn't ya? It's one thing ta convince the other inmates you're a bad egg, but another to get yourself killed doin' it." Jack's blue eyes filled with concern. "What is it with you these days? What is this, the third or fourth time you've totally lost it? You used to be the cool-headed planner, and I was the one with the explosive temper, remember?"

Leon sent another quick glance to the guard, then lowered his voice.

"Yeah, I know. I guess it's just being cooped up like this. I don't know. I just . . . I'm trying to adjust to it, but it seems like things bother me a lot more now, and once my temper flares up, I don't seem to be able to bring it back down again." He put a hand on Jack's arm and sent him one of his impish smiles. "I know I did kind of lose control there for a bit, but it worked though, didn't it? Nobody's going to suspect anything now."

"Uh huh," Jack commented again. "I hope you're right. But even Kenny thinks it's a dangerous game you're playin'."

"You told Kenny?" Leon frowned, his tone skeptical.

"Yeah."

"Oh."

"C'mon Leon," Jack assured him quietly, hearing the doubt in his friend's voice, "you said yourself we could trust 'im, and I needed ta have someone in here watchin' your back."

"Yeah, I suppose."

Jack put a hand on Leon's right arm and gave him a gentle shake. Leon looked up from his brooding and met those blue eyes.

"You need someone in here watchin' your back," Jack reiterated. "Kenny's the best bet we got."

Leon smiled, bringing himself out of his doubting thoughts and letting Jack take the lead on this one.

"Yeah, you're right. Of course. It's good." He brightened and gave Jack a gentle punch on the arm. It was as though he was looking for any excuse to indulge in the physical touch while he could. "How's my favorite girl? Is she in the 'delicate' way?"

Jack snorted. "Your brain is addled, Leon. There ain't nothin' delicate about her 'way'." Then he smiled. "But yeah, Cameron's pretty sure she is."

"Ha, ha!" Leon was all excited, grinning from ear to ear. "Now you'll have to keep me up to date with this, right Jack? Keep me informed as to how she's doing and all."

"Yeah, 'a course. And you can bet Penny will be writin' ya letters all full of what Karma is up to and who knows, ya might even be home in time for the new arrival. It takes eleven months, ya know."

"Eleven months?"

"Yeah."

"That long?"

"Yeah."

"Oh." Leon became thoughtful. "Well, maybe."

"Mathew!"

Jack looked up, startled, and then a huge smile broke across his face.

"Mariam," he greeted the familiar face. "Ho, ho. Leon told me you were helpin' out here." He gave her a big hug and a kiss on the cheek. "How are ya?"

"I'm fine, Mathew. Oh, I'm sorry, I mean Jack. My, that is going to take some getting used to."

"That's all right. Either one will do."

She smiled with pleasure, happy to see him. "I'm so glad things have worked out for you. You deserve it."

"Well, I don't know about that, ma'am—"

"Don't you get going on that stuff again, Jack," Leon interrupted him. "Just be happy with what the fates gave you. Besides, like I said before, I need you out there to help me get out of here."

Jack looked repentant and smiled. "Yeah, you're right." His smile brightened. "I'll try ta be more appreciative of the luck of the Irish."

"Yeah!"

***

On the other side of the room, Kenny stood quietly leaning against the counter, watching the three friends bantering back and forth. He'd known Nash for almost a year now and had never heard him laugh before—at least, not like this, not without the bitter and sardonic undertone to it. It made him wonder, and not for the first time, at the legitimacy of the penal system that he worked in these days.

It was one thing to lock people up in prison. If they had broken the laws of the land, or were dangerous to the citizenry of the country, then of course they had to be dealt with. But the strict rules of no talking and no physical contact by the prisoners with members of their family, or of close friends, didn't seem right somehow. He wondered at the long-term psychological effect those rules might have on an individual, since it seemed to him that it was completely contradictory to basic human nature.

Seeing Nash come alive when Jack walked into the room, seeing his face light up with a smile, seeing him reaching out for the physical contact that is normally denied the inmates, brought all these musings back to Kenny with a vengeance.

The Napoleon Nash whom Kenny had come to know was stoic and unpredictable; some might even say dangerous. But there was intelligence there, and a thinking, logical mind. Kenny also knew that a lot of Nash's behavior was in response to Carson's bullying. Still, Nash's response was often very aggressive. The guard was always careful around him and had even wondered sometimes, at the wisdom of allowing him to work in the infirmary. But Palin liked him, and it seemed to help the inmate find some stability. So, time would tell.

Admittedly, after this last episode, Kenny was ready to accept that he had made a mistake in recommending Nash as Palin's new assistant; that the inmate really was too volatile and could not be trusted. Then he met Jack Kiefer and was given a whole new insight into what exactly was going on. Then, there was the pastor, Dr. Soames, who knew both these men and seemed to think they were worthy of her time and friendship. More food for thought.

He went back to watching Nash. He was an enigma, and Kenny wasn't quite sure what he was going to do about him. The thought did occur to him that it probably wasn't going to be his decision to make, anyway. Nash's privileges had been revoked for a month, when normally, the behavior he had exhibited on the work floor would have warranted a far harsher punishment, with privileges revoked indefinitely. If, after the month was up and Leon was back working in the laundry room and the infirmary, then Kenny would know that what Jack Kiefer had told him was probably true; that Warden Mitchell believed Nash was working for him.

If, on the other hand, Nash's privileges were not reinstated after the allotted time, then Kenny might be safe in assuming that Jack had lied to him to protect his friend from further punishment. Their loyalty apparently transcended prison walls, and one would willingly sacrifice anything, to ensure the safety of the other.

Kenny sighed. Like he thought before, Nash was an enigma. Only time would tell what was really going on here, and to be honest, Kenny wasn't sure which way he hoped it would go.

CHAPTER SIX
SETTLING IN

Laramie, Wyoming, 1886

The month of punishment went by slowly for Leon.

His left forearm did not cause much of an inconvenience, as the break was clean. The infection and fever that had developed in the dark cell cleared up quickly, once it got hit with quinine. The arm did need to stay in a cast for six weeks but not in a sling, so Leon was able to perform many of the duties required of him on the work floor.

But he missed his visitors and his books, as well as the variety of duties that helped keep the mundane from ruling his life. When he was finally able to return to the infirmary as an assistant, he found he appreciated the privilege even more than he had when he first started it.

The other person who appreciated Leon's return to his regular duties, was Dr. Palin. When Leon had first been thrown into the dark cell, yet again, as punishment for fighting, ole' Doc Palin had raised quite a stink. Not only was he losing the aid of the best assistant he'd ever had, but the risk of infection and fever to all three of the inmates was high. And even more so for Nash, who was denied medical care for the two days of his punishment. Leaving him for that long went against his medical judgment.

In fact, it rankled the doc so much that the next time he saw Kenny, which happened to be the morning the guard smuggled Jack Kiefer into the infirmary, Doc Palin quietly but firmly stated his case.

"What the hell did ya think you were doin'?" Palin complained. "All three of 'em had injuries that should have been tended to right away. Harris wasn't too bad and fortunately didn't have any problems develop, but Nash had quite a fever when he was finally brought in here. And you're lucky Boeman didn't choke to death on his own blood."

"Don't go chewin' me out, Doc," Kenny said in his own defense. "Carson ordered it, and he's the boss."

"Yeah, but you coulda said something."

"Yes, I coulda," Kenny agreed, "but to be quite honest, I was so mad at all three of them, I didn't feel much like getting into an argument with Carson right at that moment. Nash damn near gave me a concussion when he head-butted me, not to mention this black eye from Boeman. So, I wasn't feeling too compassionate about the fact they'd been injured turning the work floor into a battlefield. Not to mention inciting a riot."

"What do ya mean, 'damn near gave ya a concussion'? I told ya it was a mild concussion, and you should take a couple of days off, but did you listen to me? Nooo! Everybody knows better than the doctor. Damn well serves ya right."

Kenny stopped arguing, realizing he was getting pissed off all over again. He took a deep breath and brought his anger level down a few notches. He found himself drawn to the inmate, now interacting with his partner, but he wasn't really seeing what he was looking at.

"Yeah, yeah, okay. I know you're right, Doc," the guard conceded, "but it was still Carson's call, and those three idiots have been dancing around each other for months now. Maybe after this, they'll think twice about pushing for a fight. I hope so—enough of this bullshit."

"From what I hear, Carson's been pushin' for it too. Maybe he's the one who needs to back off," Palin pointed out. "Nash isn't the only one being punished here; now I have to go for a month without my assistant, and that's just downright depressin'."

Kenny nodded. "I know, Doc. I don't think even Carson expected things to get as far out of control as they did. Maybe he will leave them alone now and let them work out their own truce. As for your other complaint, you're the one who pushed to get Nash over here. You could have requested any number of inmates to be your new assistant, ones who aren't so likely to be getting into trouble. I warned you what Nash was like."

"I know, I know," Palin grumbled. "But he's still the best

assistant I've ever had, so I guess he's worth the problems he causes."

Both men stopped their conversation and looked over at the inmate in question. He was happy, almost playful, in his conversation with his two friends, now that Dr. Mariam had joined them. Both men silently noted to themselves that they were witnessing yet another facet of the convict's character that neither of them had seen before.

"Well, I got paperwork to do," Palin grumbled. "You gonna be much longer?"

"No," Kenny answered. "I'll give them some time to visit, then we'll be gone."

"Fine," he continued to grumble as he headed to his office. "Just don't send me any more patients; I'm gonna be shorthanded for a fuckin' month."

Kenny smiled and nodded agreement, then returned to his observations and quiet musings concerning those two most notorious outlaws; Jack "Kansas Kid" Kiefer and Napoleon Nash.

***

Much to everyone's relief, things did settle down at the prison after the big blowout. Everyone eventually got back to their regular duties and Kenny had pretty much accepted the information that Nash playing at being a double agent, was indeed the truth. It wasn't so much that Nash's behavior had changed, but more because it hadn't. Not to mention, his privileges were returned to him right on schedule, and Warden Mitchell suddenly was taking more of an interest in how that particular inmate was coming along.

Nash himself was pleased that, as he had hoped, both Boeman and Harris decided to back off him. They made a point of avoiding Nash whenever they had the choice, and if they were forced into one another's personal space, well, body language and the lack of eye contact did a lot to convey the message; you leave us alone, we'll leave you alone. Since that was all Leon wanted in the first place, this new arrangement suited him just fine.

So, time went on. Spring gave way to summer and Leon discovered that the prison could be just as hot during that season as it could be cold during the winter. Opportunity to join a work gang and to get outdoors for a few days, was jumped at by just about everyone.

But even this break from the mundane carried a price.

The first time Leon stood in line for a work detail, he wondered if he had made the right choice. A ball and chain would have been preferable to the concrete and iron shoe the guard strapped onto Leon's right foot. Even though he'd heard the Oregon Boot being mentioned as a form of punishment, this was the first time he became personally acquainted with it.

Made of heavy iron, a four-inch-wide band was strapped around Leon's ankle along with an iron support strap bolted to the heel of the shoe. It weighed close to 30 lbs. and was extremely effective in minimizing the inmate's mobility.

When the boot was first designed, it was intended as a deterrent to keep high-risk inmates from escaping. Then, a warden in Oregon had the brilliant idea that if he strapped the boot onto all the inmates in his charge, then he wouldn't need as many guards.

This strategy proved to be successful to the point where all prisons adopted the practice.

But the damage this contraption did to the ankle with long-term, continual wear, was extensive. It caused such painful injury to skin and bone, that even after release, an ex-con would be left crippled for life.

Public outcry put a stop to the barbaric use of the boot as a permanent deterrent and now could only be used as punishment, or, as in this case, for work details leaving the prison grounds. It was certainly no longer allowed for prolonged periods of time.

Once Leon got used to the boot, and how to drag it around with the least amount of effort, it became an acceptable hindrance of spending the day away from the prison grounds. The warehouse became a stifling oven in the heat of a summer's day, and even though the Wyoming breeze was hot and dry, it was better than being cooped up.

As an added incentive, some of the locals, whose fences needed repairing, or new barns erected, often came out with water, or even lemonade, to help quench the thirst of the convicts. There was even one little old widow-lady who brought out iced tea, chicken and apples, not to mention sweet and endearing conversation for the lonely and tired work gang.

A couple of the guards tried to shoo her away, but she just shooed them back, threatening to give their backsides a paddling if they didn't learn some manners. No harm came from her visits, and the convicts, to a man, were considerate and polite to her, so eventually she was allowed to carry on with her visiting unhindered.

Despite the sweltering heat, life was better during the summer than it was during the winter, and Leon settled in and thrived during the warmer months.

***

Arvada, Colorado.

Jack was frustrated. Penny worked consistently, sending out fliers and letters asking for support to get their friend pardoned from prison.

Unfortunately, as with most things that carry on over time, people who were very accommodating at first, lost interest and got on with their own lives. Penny's requests were more and more of a nuisance in people's busy schedules, and most of them were ignored.

Jack's own attempts at getting in to see Governor Warren got about as much notice as Penny's fliers, and Steven suggested he back off the harassment for a time just in case the governor decided to obtain a court order against him.

Jack and Penny both had hit a brick wall. What else could they do? Whatever information Gabriella might have obtained to use as leverage was now obsolete, since Governor Warren's questionable business practices were becoming public knowledge anyway. General opinion was, he wasn't long for the office.

"Just wait," Steven had strongly suggested. "Wait and see what happens."

"But now would be the time to hit him the hardest!" Jack insisted. "If he's about to be thrown out of office anyway, what more damage could be done by pardoning Leon?"

"He's fighting for his political life," Steven countered. "When your boat is sinking, the last thing you're going to do is add more water to it."

Eventually, Jack had to concede. Even Taggard wasn't getting in to see the governor these days, and any requests for an audience from Kiefer were being blatantly ignored.

It was proving to be a difficult summer in other ways, as well. Water was always scarce this time of year, but this summer was dryer than usual. Word was Montana got the worst of the drought, but all the plains states felt the pinch of it.

Cameron was fortunate with his property. After the disaster of his previous ranch in Wyoming, he learned how to judge the land and the water rights to it. He knew how to look beyond the green grass and lush vegetation and see what the normal situation was for any specific parcel of land. He made sure this property was sound before plunging into ranch ownership again.

Even at that, the Rocking M felt the strain of a dry spring and an even dryer and hotter summer. Everyone looked forward to the autumn months and the promise that the cooler temperatures and damper weather would put things to right again.

One pleasant respite from the heat and the frustrations was the much-anticipated marriage of Sam Jefferies to Maribelle Willis.

The wedding day in mid-summer had been hot but promising for the young couple, and since just about everyone in town had been invited, it really turned into quite a shindig, and an enjoyable time was had by all.

Only two minor details marred the festivities for a couple of the guests. One being that Caroline, not ready yet to forgive Sam for his transgressions, had decided to be extremely busy that weekend and therefore, much to her mother's disappointment, would not be attending.

The second minor incident was that Penny caught the bouquet, much to Jack's consternation.

But, those two things aside, everyone had a good time and the dancing and consuming of punch went well into the early hours.

Everyone slept late the next morning. Even Jean, who was usually up with the dawn, allowed herself a couple of extra hours to recuperate from the festivities of the previous day. Fortunately, the youngest member of the Marsham family was content to allow her to do this and didn't start complaining for breakfast until he heard his mother start to stir.

Jean quietly rolled herself out of bed so as not to disturb her snoring husband, then, donning her housecoat and slippers, she glided to the crib to tend to the baby. She quickly and quietly changed his diaper and, hoisting him onto her shoulder, carried him downstairs amidst happy coos and gurglings. He really was getting heavy.

Once downstairs, she put him on the floor so he could crawl

or attempt to walk anywhere he chose while she lit the stove and started the coffee. Oatmeal was next on the agenda. She was busy with all these preparations when she heard the door to the downstairs bedroom open and she turned to see a rather disheveled Jack Kiefer stumble into the kitchen.

"Good morning, Mathew."

"Hmm."

"Coffee?"

"Oh, yes."

There came some delighted gurgling from Eli as he maneuvered his way to his favorite "uncle". Little hands grabbed onto a pant leg and he pulled himself up to his very unsteady feet, making it quite clear that he wanted some attention.

"Oh, hey there, little man," Jack greeted him, sleepily. "What do you want?"

"Ahhg.'

"What's that?"

"Ahhg—"

"Up?"

"Ahhg!" A little fist punched a manly knee.

"Oh, you want up." Jack teased him. "Well, why didn't you say so?"

Jack reached down and swung the willing tyke up and over his shoulder like a sack of flour that reverberated with wild shrieks and excited laughter.

"If that doesn't get the rest of the household up, nothing will," Jean commented. "I guess we all had quite a late night."

"Uh huh," Jack agreed. "But the horses will still be wantin' their breakfast, and since I am supposed ta be fillin' in for Sam here, I guess I better get to it."

"Well here," said Jean as she handed him a cup of coffee. "I'll trade you."

Jack smiled as he took the cup from her, then leaned down a little to help shuffle Eli over into his mother's arms. The little guy protested at first, but once he realized that mama was about to feed him breakfast, all thoughts of play went out of his mind.

Jack headed outdoors just as Penny and her father were making their way downstairs.

It was still early morning, but the air was already heavy with heat, and Jack yawned and stretched as he headed for the barns. At least the coffee still tasted good; once the real heat of the day set in, water would be the only thing worth drinking, and that they had to use it sparingly.

Then the onslaught began. The three dogs were the first to realize the humans were finally on the move, and they came running over with their tails wagging, indicating a desire to be fed. Rufus greeted Jack with one loud woof then turned, and with an important air about him, led the way toward the barn where the food was stored.

Peanut and Pebbles danced and yapped joyously about Jack's feet as they helped to escort him in the right direction.

By the time he entered the barn, the horses had been well informed that food was on its way. He was greeted by loud snorts and nickerings, and a stamping of impatient feet. He went into the feed room and began dishing out the various different portions and quickly got the dogs out from under foot. Then he put a large bag of feed into a wheelbarrow, and making his way down the aisle, he scooped a serving of oats into five of the six occupied stalls. Soon the barn was filled with the contented banging and munching of most of the horses.

Karma was not pleased. Why was she not getting her grain at the same time as the others? Her ears went back, and tossing her head in agitation, she began pawing at her stall door. Then, as soon as Jack appeared out of the feed room, carrying a special bucket of feed, her ears shot up straight and she nodded at him in anticipation.

Opening her stall door, he had to push her searching nose away so he could dump the supplemented feed into her manger. At this point, she eagerly tucked in and began to devour it. Jack smiled and gave her a rub on the neck.

"There ya go, young lady," he softly murmured to her. "Eatin' for two now, ain't ya?"

He was answered with a contented snort.

Next on the agenda, Jack climbed up the ladder to the hay loft and, dragging a bale over to the opening, he pushed it through and let it tumble down to the aisle floor. He climbed back down after it and dragged it into the feed room, thinking how much easier it was these days to feed the livestock.

As far as Jack was concerned, the invention of the hay press was the best thing to happen in ages. He broke the bale apart, and putting six flakes into the same wheelbarrow, he headed down the aisle again and tossed a flake into each of the six stalls. That done, he gave his gelding a pat on the neck, then pushed the barrow back to the feed room and headed to the house for his own breakfast.

Once he was done with his morning meal, then the horses would also be done with theirs, and Jack would turn them out to pasture for the day and then set about cleaning the barns.

All in a day's work. It was Sunday, so Jean and Penny would be hitching up their little pacer, Monty, and going into town for services. Cameron often used that quiet time to catch up on the ranch's paperwork. Jack expected to be putting in a quiet, laid-back afternoon. At least, that was what Jack thought, as he headed into the house for breakfast.

Later, after the ladies had returned, and a very casual lunch of sandwiches and tea had been dispensed with, Jack was out by the pasture fence, making sure the horses had water for the rest of the hot day. Satisfied that the animals had what they needed, he turned around and nearly walked into Penny. She looked fresh and pretty, wearing a light summer frock, with her blonde hair pulled back into a pony tail. She smiled openly at him, her brown eyes sparkling.

"Ahh, hi Penny," he began tentatively.

"Hello Mathew. Are you going for a ride this afternoon?'

"Hadn't planned on it." Jack took off his hat and ran a sleeve across his sweaty brow. "It's pretty hot and Midnight's still kinda tired from the ride inta town and back yesterday."

"He's tired just from that?" she asked with knitted brow.

"Well, He ain't a spring chicken no more," Jack explained. "And the heat we're gettin' these days is hard on 'im. It's gettin' even warmer as we speak."

"Yes, I suppose it is," Penny agreed with a shy smile. "Wasn't that a lovely wedding yesterday? Maribelle looked so pretty and happy too."

"I hope she'll be happy," Jack commented. "She's gonna be spendin' the rest of her life with Sam, so if she ain't happy about it, there's somethin' wrong."

"I suppose," Penny said. "I guess when you've met the right man, you just know, don't you?"

"Well, sometimes."

Penny brightened. "I caught the bouquet. Did you know?"

"Yup," Jack nodded. "Uh huh." He felt a knot of dread hit him in the pit of his stomach.

"You know what that means, don't you?"

"Yup," Jack admitted. "I wouldn't put too much stock in that though: it's just an old wives' tale."

"Oh." Penny's gaze dropped.

Jack smiled and put a hand on his friend's shoulder. "C'mon, Penny. You've got lots a' time before ya gotta start thinkin' about that stuff. Live a little first. Get out there and enjoy life, give yourself a chance ta find out what you really want."

"But I know what I want," she insisted with a bit of a sulk.

"At seventeen?" Jack asked, with an incredulous tone to his voice.

"I'm almost eighteen," she insisted, indignantly. "I think I'm old enough to know my own mind."

"Aww Penny," Jack was sympathetic. "Believe me, you don't know yet. The last thing you wanna do is rush inta a marriage before you've had a chance ta explore your options. I've seen it happen too many times. Marryin' too young and then livin' ta regret it. And once you're married, you're kinda stuck, and then you'll be miserable for the rest 'a your life."

"But I wouldn't be miserable," Penny insisted. "And I'm not too young to know."

Jack sighed and leaned back against the fence. He looked off into the distance for a moment, then down at his own hands, trying to put into words the thoughts that swirled around him. How to explain this without hurting her feelings, without treating her like a child?

He gently squeezed her arm and she looked up at him, into those brilliant blue eyes, and her heart did a little somersault. But the look that he sent back to her was one of compassion and concern, not love, and it scared her.

"I remember when I was seventeen, almost eighteen," he said, quietly. "I remember thinkin' that I knew what really mattered and what was important. Penny, you were at my trial, you heard me admit ta doin' certain things. I'd already killed when I was younger than you are right now. I'd made the worst mistakes 'a my life, all before I was twenty years of age. And all the while, thinkin' I was right, I was justified, that that's what I wanted. By the time I was twenty-five, the choices I had made had already set my life onto a path that was dangerous and self-destructive. All the while, I was thinkin' we were in the right, that we were the smart ones—that we had life by the horns, and we were gonna live it to the fullest.

"It took a long time ta realize the selfishness of those choices, the conceit. And now Leon is payin' for both of us. Payin' the price for our bad decisions and our arrogance in thinkin' we was better than everybody else. That because of what we had been through, we had the right ta do what we did.

"I'm just gettin' to a point in my life now, where I only know what I don't want. I'm not gonna be able ta think about what I do want, or even who I really am, until all the consequences of them bad choices have been dealt with and cleared away. And I have no idea how long that is gonna take. You can't possibly know what you want yet, Penny. Ya need ta take the time ta get to know yourself first."

"But, a lot of those choices you made were because of the things that happened to you when you were a child." Penny felt like she was fighting for her life. "I never had to go through any of that. I had a happy childhood, so it would only make sense that I would know myself better now. I'm not a child, Mathew."

"I know, Penny," Jack agreed. "I can see that. But you're still—"

"Caroline's only a year and a half older than I am, and she's being courted by Steven. Two of her friends got married last year and one of them already has a baby. My friend Jane, who is three months younger than me, got married this past spring, and my other friend, Ruth, is betrothed . . ."

"It ain't a race, Penny," Jack pointed out. "And there is one big difference between them and us."

"What?"

"I'm fifteen years older than you," Jack said, blatantly. "All your friends married young men who are around their same age. They've all known each other for years; they grew up together. That makes a big difference."

"Caroline didn't grow up knowing Steven," Penny pointed out. "She's only known him for a year."

"I know that," Jack admitted. "But they are still a lot closer in age than we are, and they share a lot of things in common. And believe it or not, Penny, at your age, a year and a half encompass a whole lot 'a livin'."

"But Mama is a lot younger than Papa—almost fifteen years. And they have a wonderful marriage."

Jack sighed. This was not going well.

"I know that," he admitted. "But your papa had a lot more ta offer as a husband and a father than I do. I've got nothin' ta offer ya, Penny. I got no money, very little education and even fewer prospects—you could do so much better."

Penny almost stamped her foot in frustration.

"I don't want 'better'. I want you. Why don't you want me? Don't you like me?"

"Of course I like ya," Jack answered her, gently. "I like ya a lot."

"But you still go into town to see those upstairs girls," Penny pointed out. "If you like me so much, why do you go to see them?"

Jack stood dumbfounded for a moment, his mouth hanging open. He had no idea how to answer that. How do you explain to a maiden the difference between having sex and making love? He looked at her, and her big brown eyes stared back at him, awaiting an answer.

"Aww, Penny. Ahh . . ." he sighed, a hand on her shoulder. "Penny, you don't . . . that ain't real . . ." Oh brother, what now? "You don't want me comin' ta you for that. That's just for fun—it don't mean nothin'. You want a man ta respect you, ta come courtin'."

"Hmm," Penny commented, thoughtfully. "That's what Mama said."

"Well, she's right," Jack backed it up, though he felt a little exposed, knowing that Penny had already spoken to her mother on this topic. Couldn't a man have any privacy around here?

"So, if you like me, then why . . .?"

"Penny, please," Jack begged her. "I'm still tryin' to work out who I am now, and what I need ta do ta help my partner. I'm just not able ta even think about marriage, or even courtin' anyone 'til I get them other things in my life sorted out. Can you understand that?"

"But that could take years," Penny complained. "All of my friends are either married or getting married soon. At this rate, I'm going to end up an old maid. I'm not getting any younger you know."

Jack couldn't help it, and he laughed out loud.

"Ho, ho! Penny, darlin'. You're so young it scares me." Then, instantly, he realized he had said the worst possible thing.

Penny drew herself up with indignation, coupled with a horrified look that soon became awash with tears. She pivoted and made a wild dash toward the house, taking a hurting heart with her.

Jack slumped against the fence, having been hit with his own level of regret and frustration. And yes, hurt too.

"Aww, no. Jeez." He stood up and shouted after her. "Penny. Penny, don't. Please, Penny!"

But she had disappeared into the house and wasn't listening to him. He started to run toward the house himself, then stopped halfway and realized the futility of that. He sighed again, and with sagging shoulders, turned and walked toward the barn.

Dammit! I sure put my foot in it this time. Why does everything have ta get so complicated? He tried so hard not to hurt her feelings and then ended up saying the worst thing ever. *What the hell is the matter with me, anyway?* He kicked an empty bucket and hit the wall with a fist.

Rufus startled awake and noting that the human's mood was edgy, he decided it was time to go outside and sleep in the sunshine. His old bones rather liked the heat.

Jack continued to pace around inside the barn, mumbling to himself and shaking his head with the frustration of not knowing how to deal with this very sensitive situation. Finally, he stopped and sighed, then thought about what he usually did to help clear his mind and settle his nerves. That was easy; target practice. *Oh, but damn. My holster and gun are in my bedroom, and I sure don't wanna go in there just yet*. He sighed again. *Damn.*

A small sound caught his attention and he looked up to see Cameron standing in the doorway of the barn. *Oh, damn again! It's bad enough, causin' a scene with a young lady who's sweet on ya, but when the father of that young lady is well within earshot, it can be downright inconvenient.*

"Problem?" Cameron asked him with a casual cock of a brow.

"Aw, Cameron. I donno," Jack fussed, running fingers through curls. "I didn't mean ta upset her. I like Penny—a lot." Then added as an aside; "Maybe too much." Both Cameron's brows went up. "But I just can't give her what she wants right now."

Cameron smiled and walked deeper into the barn.

"The problem with being young, especially a young lady, is that everything hurts so much. Penny thinks she knows what she wants—and I don't know, maybe she does. But because she is so certain of her feelings, she can't understand how you could not be, so she takes it personally."

"No, she shouldn't take it that way," Jack insisted.

"I know that," Cameron assured him, "but she doesn't. Unfortunately, it might take a heartbreak or two for her to realize it."

"But I do care about Penny," Jack repeated, then sighed again, feeling even more frustrated. "I don't wanna be the one who hurts her like that."

Cameron shrugged. "Sometimes we're not the ones who get to decide that. All you can do is handle with care."

Jack snorted.

"No, I've been watching you," Cameron admitted. "You've always treated Penny with respect and consideration—and kindness. A father can't ask for more than that. You've never led her on or played with her affections, and she's just going to have to learn the difference between friendship and romance. And that can be one of life's more difficult lessons."

"Oh brother." Jack did not sound convinced. "I donno, Cameron. Maybe I should just leave after all. I don't want to. You folks, well, you ain't 'like' family no more, you are family. And David is a good friend. I guess I've gotten kinda used ta havin' that now. And without Leon, well, bein' on the trail seems kinda lonely. But, this ain't fair on Penny. I should just get outta her life for a while, give her a chance ta get over it and meet someone else more akin to her."

"That's up to you," Cameron said. "We'd all be sorry to see you go—not just Penny. Don't make any rash decisions, Jack. Why don't you saddle up ole Spike and go for a ride? Clear your head. You can bet your bottom dollar that Jean is in the house, right now, having a talk with Penny. By the time you get back, well, there could be a whole new slant on things."

Jack thought about that, then nodded.

"Yeah, okay. That's probably a good idea."

"Fine."

***

Jean finished cleaning up the kitchen after the midday meal when she heard Jack shouting her daughter's name. This got her attention, and she turned away from her cleaning just in time to see her youngest daughter come running through the front door. Obviously, something earth-shattering to a teenage heart had just transpired, as Penny hurried to her room with a hand over her mouth, fighting the anguished sobs of operatic tragedy.

With a resigned sigh, the mother of three scooped up her son, and amidst squirms and complaints from that young man, headed up the stairs to try and calm the flow of tears. When she got to the door of Penny's room, she was surprised when all she heard was silence from inside. She knocked and waited for her daughter's permission to enter. A strained little "come in" followed, and Jean opened the door to find Penny sitting quietly on her bed, looking tear-stained, but sheepish.

"What happened?" Jean asked, as she put Eli down to explore his sister's floor. "Are you all right?"

"Yes," came the sloppy answer, as she gulped and sniffed away her tears. "I have been such a complete idiot."

"I think that is a bit of an exaggeration," Jean countered, as she sat down on the bed beside her daughter. "Do you want to talk about it?"

Penny sighed. "It just dawned on me that I have been doing exactly what you told me not to do."

Jean smiled. "It's always nice to have your children acknowledge your wisdom," she said. "And what was that exactly?"

"You told me not to chase after him; to wait until he was ready to come to me," Penny explained. "But now, I realize I have been doing just that. I didn't think I was, I only wanted him to like me. But you were right; all I've done is push him further away."

"Oh, I see."

"Now, I'm sure he hates me." Penny's anger at herself took over from the tears.

"I highly doubt that," Jean countered. "From what I have seen, Mathew very much enjoys your company."

"Really?"

"Of course, he does," Jean insisted. "You just need to give him some room."

Penny nodded, emitting another large sigh. Then, she caught her breath when an alarming thought occurred to her, and she turned large, frightened eyes to her mother.

"You don't suppose he's going to leave, do you?"

Jean only got as far as opening her mouth to respond, when Penny jumped up from the bed and ran toward the door.

"Oh no!" Penny wailed. "He can't leave . . ."

She stampeded down the stairs and out the door in a way that only a teenage girl can do.

Jean sighed and glanced at her son.

"Thank goodness you are a long way off from putting us through this."

Eli smiled and gurgled at his mother while he stuffed one of Penny's socks into his mouth.

***

In the first barn, Jack was in the process of throwing a saddle onto the back of a very nice skewbald gelding when Penny made a self-conscious entrance through the open double doors. She quickly, though a little belatedly, began to straighten out her hair and her frock, making sure the last of her silly tears were gone from her face. Then she took the plunge.

"Mathew?"

Jack turned, surprised to see her there. Then he looked awkward, himself.

"Oh, Penny . . . ahhmm."

"No, Mathew," she assured him as she quickly stepped forward and put a hand on his arm. "I'm sorry. I've been pushing, and I shouldn't have done that."

"Oh, well . . ."

"I know you've been through a lot this past year," Penny acknowledged, "and for a lot longer than just a year. You're having to re-discover who you are, all over again." She smiled mischievously. "In a way, you could say that I'm older than you."

Jack snorted, then laughed. "Yeah. I suppose you have a point there."

She turned serious again. "I also know you are very worried about Peter."

"Yup," Jack nodded. "He's havin' a hard time, Penny. I don't know how much longer he's gonna be able ta hang on there, and ta be quite honest, I'm at a loss as ta what else I can do about it. Taggard and Steven are doin' everything they can, but a lotta doors are gettin' slammed in their faces. And the governor sure ain't any more accommodatin' toward me."

"I know," Penny agreed. "It's the same with my letters. Nobody seems interested anymore. It's like they'd rather just forget all about Napoleon Nash."

"Yeah, well I don't intend ta forget about 'im," Jack insisted with a bit of heat. "I just gotta figure out another way of comin' at 'em."

"Caroline is working as Steven's assistant now," Penny pointed out, then smiled and put both hands on Jack's arm. "Will you let me be yours? Let me help you."

"You have been helpin'. I know it was all the work you and Caroline did that saved my neck. And you've carried on doin' the same for Leon. You have been helpin'."

"But we must do more, because the letters are no longer working," she said. "Won't you let me come with you when you go see the governor, and when you go see Peter?"

"Oh now, Penny," Jack backed off. "I told ya that Leon don't want ya comin' ta see him there. On top a that, I really don't think your papa would approve of you travelin' around the countryside with me and no chaperone."

Penny sighed in frustration. "Oh, that is so silly. But I suppose you're right. Still, I want to do more to help you with this. Will you let me?"

"Yeah, a course," Jack agreed. "I could use all the help I can get."

"Good." She smiled and presented her right hand for him to shake.

Jack laughed, but still took her hand, and they shook on it.

"Friends?" she asked him.

"Friends."

"Good."

"Now, would you like to join me for a ride before supper?" Jack suggested.

"I'd love to. Papa said that it was still all right to ride Karma, just so long as I don't gallop her."

"Good," Jack agreed. "She could do with a stretch. I'll get the horses tacked up while you go get changed. How's that?"

"Sounds like a plan."

CHAPTER SEVEN
MEETING NAPOLEON NASH

Laramie, Wyoming,
Summer 1886

Leon sat in the processing room, waiting for his company to arrive. Not surprisingly, Jack had been his first visitor right after the punishment period had ended, and now Leon anticipated a session with his lawyer.

The cast had been removed from his arm, and the bone healed straight and clean. Leon was not oblivious to the favor Kenny had done him. He had no doubt in his mind that Carson had meant it when he warned Leon that he had crippled inmates before and wouldn't mind doing it again. Leon knew he had been lucky that Kenny was the one who had landed that blow, since Reece's intent, always, was to subdue, not to cripple.

Leon sighed and sat back while he awaited his legal counsel. His thoughts returned to Kenny Reece and the unusual relationship that had developed between them. There seemed to be mutual respect there, but at the same time, neither one ever took the other for granted. Kenny was an old hand and knew his business, so he sure wasn't going to take any nonsense from a youngster like Leon. But at the same time, the guard was aware of the inmate's reputation and acknowledged him as a step above the average convict. Still, there was an order to things that had to be maintained, and as long as both accepted that, they'd get by.

Leon was brought out of his inner musings when the door opened, and Steven stepped into the room. Leon smiled a greeting, but then when he saw the two women enter upon the heels of the lawyer, his expression changed from acceptance to surprise and, lastly, to anger. He was on his feet so abruptly that he knocked his chair over and Officer Pearson, still edgy from the riot, thought Leon was going to attack his visitors.

The guard jumped forward and, grabbing Leon by the belt, yanked him back and into the wall. Leon lost his balance and went down, the business end of the guard's rifle staring him in the face.

"No! No, don't treat him like that!" came the feminine protest, and the young lady ran around the table to protect her friend.

Pearson was instantly between them. "No! Miss! Stop," he ordered her. "This inmate is dangerous. Get back to the other side of the table. Now."

"He's not dangerous. . ."

"Caroline," Leon yelled at her. "Do what he says. Now!"

"Caroline, come on," said Steven. "You promised me you would not approach him . . . no matter what. Remember?"

"Come on, sweetie," came Josephine's soothing tone. "Come on back here, so we can all sit down and be reasonable." This last bit was aimed directly at Pearson.

Caroline reluctantly submitted to the logic of her friends and retreated to the other side of the table, but she continued to glare daggers at the guard.

Once Pearson was satisfied everyone was where they should be, he grabbed Leon under the arm and hauled him to his feet. He pressed a hand against his chest and pushed him into the wall.

"Just wait there, Nash," he ordered. "Don't move."

The inner door opened and Officer Murray stuck his head in. "Everything all right in here?"

"Watch Nash for a minute, will ya?" Pearson asked him. "Let me get this sorted out."

Murray stepped inside the room, his rifle ready, while Pearson righted the knocked over chair, then looked to the lawyer.

"I don't think this is a good idea. I know you're his lawyer, and you have the right to a private session with him, but he is unpredictable, and with these ladies here—"

"No, it's all right, Officer," Steven assured him. "Both these ladies are friends of his, he won't hurt them."

Pearson did not look convinced.

Steven smiled at him. "I'll take full responsibility. He'll be fine. I'll call you if we need any assistance."

"Fine," Pearson conceded. He motioned to the inmate. "All right, Nash, sit down. You better behave yourself, or you'll be back in the dark cell for sure. I'm beginning to think you like it in there."

Leon rolled his eyes, shuffled his way back to the table and sat down.

The two guards left and shut the door behind them.

Leon sat silently; he was not pleased. When he'd said he didn't want Penny or Caroline visiting him in this place, he'd meant it. No one seemed to care what he thought anymore.

"Peter . . ."

Leon snapped his eyes onto Caroline; they were in a slow burn.

Caroline felt a slight twinge of fear. She had never seen her friend angry before; she had heard him angry, in the jail cell back in Cheyenne, but never had she seen it, and certainly not aimed at her.

The Peter she knew had always been so kind and amiable, but now she was getting a glimpse of the threatening and intimidating gang leader that the law had always insisted he was. She wondered, briefly, if this side of him had always been there and he had simply hidden it away from them, or if being in this terrible place was the cause of it. Most likely, it was a bit of both.

Caroline took a deep breath and summoned her courage, reminding herself that he was still the same man she loved and had come to think of as a brother. She looked him straight in the eyes and met his anger.

"I'm sorry I overreacted," she told him, "but before you get all accusing on me, I should let you know, I have every right to be here."

Leon opened his mouth to argue that point, but Steven cut him off.

"She's right, Mr. Nash. Caroline is my assistant. She has come with me on numerous occasions to the prison in Colorado and has always conducted herself in a professional manner. Until today." He raised his eyebrows at her.

Caroline rightfully looked contrite.

"I already apologized for that," she defended herself. "But you are right, that was not professional." She looked to her friend again. "But is that normal? Is that standard procedure for the guards to treat you like that?"

Again, Leon opened his mouth to answer, and again, Steven cut him off.

"It is a prison, darling—"

Leon's eyebrows went up at the use of the endearment.

"—not a church social. Many of the prisoners here are very violent people. And that reminds me . . ." Steven turned his attention to his client. ". . . the warden stated that you caused a riot. What was that all about?"

Leon started to answer but was again cut off before he could get a word in edgewise.

"Oh Leon," Josey tutted. "Can't you be anywhere without needing to be in control? What was it this time? Did one of the other inmates try to tell you the proper way to crack a safe or something?"

Leon clenched his jaw and would have crossed his arms if he had been able to. He sighed in frustration and went into a pout. The other three people at the table sat silently, waiting for him to respond.

"Oh," he sniped. "I'm expected to speak now, am I?"

"Peter . . ." Caroline mumbled.

Josephine sent an accusing look to him. "Well, I can certainly see that prison hasn't done anything to sweeten your temperament. Still growling like an old bear."

"Steven's my lawyer, Caroline is his assistant. What's your excuse?"

"Well, for one thing, I wanted to see you, although now that I'm here, and you're being so sulky, I'm wondering what the point was." Josey took on an air of self-importance. "Besides, I'm also Caroline's chaperone. Whenever Steven and Caroline need to go on a business trip, I go along to make sure no hanky-panky takes place."

Leon snorted.

"Hey!" Josey was indignant.

"She is correct, Mr. Nash," Steven confirmed. "That was a condition that Mr. Marsham insisted on when Caroline came to work for me. She was to have a chaperone. It's mainly so she could have a friend with her, this being her first time away from home, but it is also the proper thing to do."

"Apparently, Cameron doesn't know Josey very well."

"Hey!" Josey frowned at the insult. "My, but you are in a snarky mood today."

"Ahh, perhaps we should get on with the business at hand," Steven suggested. "It's not like we have all afternoon."

"Fine," Josey agreed, though still feeling defensive.

"Fine," Leon grumbled.

"I was able to get in to speak with a Supreme Court Justice concerning the possibility of an appeal to that Court," Steven explained. "He wasn't terribly optimistic, considering Judge Lacey is currently Chief Justice and it is his ruling we will be attempting to overrule. However, if you were willing to make a formal statement apologizing for your behavior during your trial, and answer those questions concerning the other people involved with the con, then you might get a reduction of your sentence through the Supreme Court appeal."

Leon looked at Josey, almost feeling like it would serve her right if he did. She and Caroline should not have come to this place.

"What does Miss Jansen say about that?" he asked, with just a hint of sarcasm.

"Leon, you know I already said I would come forward with the information," Josey reminded him. "I told both Steven and Jack that I would do it, but nobody would let me."

"And the Court Justice doesn't want it from her," Steven clarified. "He wants to hear it from you."

"Ahh." Leon nodded and smirked. "Wants me to admit that prison broke me, is that it? Wants me to come crawling back to them to apologize for showing contempt of his court? That I've learned my lesson—that I'll tell him anything he wants to know."

Steven sighed, knowing this wasn't going well. "Something like that, yes."

"But Peter," Caroline was almost pleading, "don't you want out of here? Josey has agreed to it, and Steven doesn't believe he would send her to prison, especially when she explains the circumstances."

"It's not just Josey, sweetheart," Leon told her, his anger beginning to abate. "The other person involved probably would be sent to prison, and I can't do that to him."

"But we miss you so much," Caroline pushed. "We all want you to come home."

Leon could almost feel his heart break in two. He swallowed and cleared his throat.

"I want to come home, too." Even to himself, his voice sounded choked. He cleared his throat again, then not being able to look into Caroline's misting brown eyes, he turned his attention to Steven. "Is there really any point to making an appeal to the Supreme Court while Lacey is still Chief Justice there?"

"Since this is a case Judge Lacey presided over, he would have to excuse himself from the proceedings. If we could get five of the eight remaining Court Justices to vote in our favor, then Judge Lacey would not be able to argue against it."

Leon huffed. He wasn't impressed with that situation. "And on the very slim chance that we can get those five votes, you think we might get a reduction of my sentence, perhaps even a pardon?"

Steven nodded.

"By how much?"

Steven shrugged. "It's hard to tell. The court might consider ten years."

Leon closed his eyes and groaned. He looked at Granger again, shaking his head. "The law wants me to turn in my friends, just to shave ten years off my sentence?"

"It would still be cut in half, Mr. Nash," Steven tried to be positive about it. "I know that looking at it from this end, it doesn't seem worth it, but I'm sure that in nine years' time, you'd be happy for the reduction."

"Mr. Granger," Leon explained, "one way or another, in ten years' time, I don't intend to still be in this prison."

The statement was met with three sets of shocked eyes, staring at him.

"Oh Leon. Don't talk like that."

"But Peter . . ."

"What do you mean by that comment, Mr. Nash?"

Leon was silent for a moment, looking down at his shackled hands.

"Just that, Mr. Granger. I'm sorry, but I won't betray my friends just to reduce my own sentence." He shook his head and reiterated. "I simply won't do it."

***

"What did he mean by that comment?" Caroline asked, as the threesome made their way out of the prison and over to the waiting surrey. "Surely, he meant that he was confident we would have him out of here by then, right?"

Steven and Josey exchanged a quick glance.

"Oh, I'm sure that's what he meant," Josephine insisted. "Leon has always been so melodramatic. Don't you worry about him; he's a survivor."

"I don't know." Caroline pondered the different possible intentions of her friend's words. "It didn't really sound like he was feeling very positive."

The group stepped into their buggy, with Steven giving a gentlemanly hand to the ladies. Once aboard himself, he picked up the lines and clucked to the pacer to move them along. Everyone was quiet, busy with their own thoughts and concerns.

Finally, Caroline sighed and looked up from her musings.

"Well, either way, we're going to have to tell Mathew about this. Maybe he'll have a better idea of what Peter's intent was."

"Ahh, we can't really do that, Caroline," Steven reminded her.

"Why not? Mathew is his partner; he has the right to know what is going on."

"Caroline, you know anything said in a private consultation is privileged communication and considered confidential. You cannot tell anyone what was discussed in there." In the back seat, Josey opened her mouth to speak. "And that goes for you too, Josephine."

Both ladies pouted. Josey pursed her lips, wondering how he had even known she was about to protest.

"Surely Peter wouldn't mind if I told Mathew what he said," Caroline continued with her case. "They are best friends, not to mention family—"

"And if Mr. Nash wants his nephew to know what we discussed, then Mr. Nash can tell him, himself," Steven insisted. "We cannot."

"But Steven—"

"Caroline, you knew this beforehand," Steven reminded her. "Confidentiality is one of the most important tenets of our profession. You better decide early on what matters to you. If you can't keep a secret, then working in a law office may not be for you."

Caroline was stunned into silence. An icy dread encircled her heart as she feared she may have disappointed her suitor. Being away from home and working in a law office brought with it a whole lot more responsibility than she had ever imagined. But she loved her job and she loved her man and didn't want to lose either one of them.

"You're right, Steven. I'm sorry," she finally stated, feeling disappointed in herself. "And that's the second time today I've had to apologize for being unprofessional."

"That's all right," Steven assured her. "You're still learning the ropes, and I know it was a shock for you to see your friend like that."

"I didn't think it would be," Caroline admitted. "I saw those inmates at the Colorado prison, so I thought I had prepared myself for what to expect. But I suppose, seeing someone you know and care about in that situation—and being treated like that can be a shock, even if you think you're prepared for it. There was no reason at all for the guard to be so rough with Peter; he wasn't going to do anything."

"I know," Steven agreed. "He's your friend, and you care about him. You know he would never do anything to hurt you."

"That's right."

"But I also know that Mr. Nash has proven to be a difficult and unpredictable inmate," Steven continued. "And as far as those guards are concerned, he has been violent in the past and is considered dangerous. That guard was well within his rights, and he was only doing it to protect you."

"Well, perhaps the guard did feel that he was doing his job," Caroline argued, "but to say that Peter is dangerous, that's just nonsense."

"But he is," came Josey's voice from the back seat. "At least, he can be."

Caroline swung around on her friend with an indignant and accusatory tone.

"How can you say that? You've known him longer than either of us."

"Exactly," Josey pointed out. "I've known Leon and Jack for most of our lives. They're loyal, loving, considerate, compassionate, not to mention just plain, well—passionate." A knowing, devilish smile flitted across her features that might have caused Caroline some concern, if she had seen it. "But they are also lazy, self-centered, arrogant, manipulative—especially Leon, and if the need arises, dangerous. Taking into consideration the situation Leon is finding himself in now, I can see why the guards might consider him to be unpredictable and requiring extra caution. He never did give in to authority easily."

Josey sighed, sadly watching the scenery roll by as they made their way into the town of Laramie.

"Poor Leon," she murmured, more to herself than the two people up front. "He never could stand being cooped up, either. This must be killing him."

The rest of the ride to the hotel was conducted in silence.

***

Later that same afternoon, Leon found himself being escorted to the warden's office for their monthly discussion. It was becoming increasingly difficult to come up with tidbits of information that would keep the warden happy and himself safe from inmate retribution. As it turned out, Leon needn't have worried about that end of their agreement this time, because Warden Mitchell conveniently provided him with something else to worry about instead.

"You do realize that Dr. Palin is an alcoholic, don't you?"

"He is?" Leon asked, his eyes widening with innocence. "No sir, Warden. I wasn't aware of that."

"Oh, come now," Mitchell chided him. "You're over there, working with him every week. Do you mean to say, you have never noticed anything unprofessional in his habits?"

"No sir, Warden," Leon lied. "He's a fine doctor."

"I'm not disputing that," Mitchell conceded, "when he's sober. But that's not the point. If he is drinking while on duty, then he's a danger to his patients, and we can't have that. Have you ever noticed him taking a drink while on duty?"

"No sir, Warden." Again, Leon lied without missing a beat.

"Well, that surprises me, yes it does," Mitchell continued. "Still, he's probably just hiding it from you. I want you to look around his office and the infirmary, just to see if you can find any evidence of him drinking."

"Like what, sir?"

Mitchell was beginning to wonder if Nash was as intelligent as his reputation suggested.

"A bottle of alcohol would be a good start," the warden pointed out. "Empty shot glasses would be another indication. Alcohol on his breath. How about that? Do think you could manage to take note of anything like that?"

Leon shifted, uncomfortably. "I donno, Warden," he mumbled. "I would think that stuff like a bottle and glasses would be kept locked up. Especially if he knows he's not supposed to be drinking."

Mitchell sighed with exasperation. "I am aware of your talents, Mr. Nash. Do you really think I permitted you the privilege of working there because you are such a model prisoner? I'm sure you would have no difficulty getting past any locks he might have on his cabinets."

"Well, I'd need special tools—"

"It's an infirmary!" Mitchell lost his temper. "It's filled with special tools!"

"Oh! Yes sir. Hadn't thought of that."

"Tell me, Mr. Nash, how is it that you were able to avoid capture for so many years?"

Leon sent him a vacant look. "Luck?"

Mitchell rolled his eyes. "That'll be all, Mr. Nash. Just let me know if you find anything."

"Yes sir, Warden."

Murray escorted the inmate out of the office.

Mitchell sat back, shaking his head. That was disappointing. Nash seemed to be very intelligent upon his arrival at the prison, but now apparently, that façade was beginning to crack. But then the warden became reflective as another possibility occurred to him.

He recalled the inmates sudden switch in behavior when the warden first offered Nash this opportunity. The man was a master at verisimilitude and could switch from one persona to another with barely a wrinkle.

Obviously, something here is a façade, but which is it? Is Napoleon Nash a fool, just putting on airs of intelligence, or a smart man pretending to be dumb? Yeah, dumb like a fox. Only a real fool wouldn't know the answer to that one.

The warden smiled to himself. *If Nash wants to play games, I can go along with that. For now. Give it some time and then we'll see who's the cat and who's the mouse.*

***

Leon had been deep in thought during his escorted walk back into the prison proper. This new situation was not good. He was not only being asked to spy on one of the few friends he had in this place, but the warden was also telling him to "break and enter". That was something Mitchell had initially assured him he would not be expected to do. Just keep your eyes open. *"It's not like I'm asking you to sneak into their cells and rummage through their belongings."*

Hmm. It seems the rules have been changed. What a surprise.

***

The next time Leon found himself in the infirmary, he already knew what he was going to do. There was never any question of it; he wasn't about to turn Doc in.

"Hey, Doc," Leon got his attention once they had some time to themselves, "you still got that bottle of whiskey stashed away somewhere?"

"Sure," he admitted. "Why? Ya want a drink?"

"No!" Leon cringed, then lowered his voice. "No, Doc. That's not it."

"What's the problem then?"

"It's the warden," Leon explained. "He knows you've been drinking on the job, and he's just itching to catch you at it, so he can fire you. I don't know why he'd want to do that though. It can't be easy finding a decent doctor who'd be willing to work in this place."

Doc shrugged that off. "Ahhg! Me and Mitchell never did get on. Fuckin', pompous little ass . . ." Then he frowned and flashed a suspicious look at his assistant. "How did you know about this?"

"Because Mitchell asked me to spy on you, Doc," Leon admitted. "To look around and see if I could find any evidence. Even to break into your cabinets if I needed to."

Now Palin was ticked.

"That fuckin' son of a whore," he swore. "Who the fuck does he think he is? It's bad enough havin' to work in this fuckin' shit-hole of a place without that little prick pokin' his fuckin' nose into my business! I oughta take that whiskey bottle and shove it up his ass!"

Leon couldn't help but smile at the torrent of profanities that flowed from the good doctor's mouth. He waited quietly until Palin stopped to come up for air.

"He knows who he is, Doc," Leon pointed out, "and he is out

to get you. If he gets evidence that you're drinking on the job, you will be out of a job."

"Shit!" Palin grumbled. "As much as I bitch about working here, I'd be in real trouble if I lost this job."

"Well yeah, that's what I figured. And that's why I'm telling you; you have to get rid of that stuff. Get it out of here."

"Why?" he asked. "You're not planning on snitchin' on me, are ya?"

"No! Of course not!" Leon was indignant. "But if Mitchell asked me to spy on you, what's to stop him from asking somebody else to do the same? Somebody who doesn't care about what happens to you."

"Hmm," came the familiar response. "Ya got a point."

"Yeah. So, like I said, you have to get that stuff out of here—tonight, if possible. Okay?"

"Shit!" Palin let out one last obscenity, then sighed with acceptance. "Yeah, you're right. I will." He gave Leon a pat on the shoulder. "You're a good man, Nash, a good friend. I won't forget this."

Leon's dimples made a rare appearance. "Gee, thanks, Doc."

***

Arvada, Colorado

The fourth of July found Steven, Caroline and Josephine coming out to the Rocking M Ranch for the holiday weekend to enjoy the festivities with family and friends. When Sunday morning rolled around, everyone pitched in to get the necessary chores done, and then a number of horses were either saddled up, or hitched to buggies, and the whole gang headed to Arvada for the 11:00 am services.

The town was alive with celebrations, and the population seemed to have doubled in size, with everyone from miles around coming to join in. By 12:45 our group of celebrants casually walked along the boardwalk, taking in the sights and sounds of the town done up for a party.

There was the inevitable town band, making its noisy way along the main street. Banners and flags were flying. Paper pinwheels spun and brightly colored ribbons attached to sticks snaked through the air, mimicking the gyrations of the children who wielded them. Everyone was in a holiday spirit, and the idea of a picnic lunch was in the forefront.

Taking the lead, Jean and Cameron kept the pace slow since they had little Eli with them, and he insisted on doing his share of the walking, along with everyone else. He still wasn't quite able to manage this feat on his own and clung to a hand belonging to each parent, while doing his best to put one foot in front of the other. This was a slow process, but no one seemed to mind, and Jack, especially, got a kick out of watching the little fella having the time of his life.

Jack was second in line, with a lovely lady on each arm. Josey, on his left, chattered away as usual, prattling on about everything from the extremely revealing line on the dress that so-and-so was wearing, to what an interesting aroma wafted from the sweets shop.

Penny, on Jack's right arm, was quiet, but smiling with the enjoyment of the day and watching the antics of her younger brother. Sometimes, competing with Josephine, when she got on a roll, just wasn't worth it.

Behind them came Steven, with Caroline on his arm. They were content to keep the pace slow, as it gave them all the more time to be together without having to interact with anyone else. They laughed and flirted and chatted about everything and anything that caught their attention. They were lost in a world of their own that only two young people in love can create.

Eventually, this group made it to the town square where tables were set up for families to sit and sample the culinary delights of the different venders in the area. Cameron scooped Eli up in his arms and walked on ahead to find a table that would accommodate the lot of them.

It didn't take long before they found one that would do, and both father and son started waving at the others to get their attention.

They had all settled down with various lunches, when they were joined by one more acquaintance.

"David!" Cameron greeted him. "Come on and join us."

"Yes, that was my intention," David admitted with a smile of greeting for everyone present.

Room was made at the table, and David slid in to sit between Jean and Penny.

"Where is Tricia?" Jean asked him. "Will she be joining us?"

"No, I don't think so," David answered. "She's not feeling well and just wanted to stay home and drink tea."

"Oh," Jean commiserated. "Nothing serious, I hope?"

"No, no," David assured her. "Just a summer cold, I think. But she wanted me to leave her alone and kicked me out of the house. She says I'm a pest—can you believe that?"

Both Jack and Cameron snorted.

David smiled but did his best to ignore their opinion.

"How is everyone on this fine fourth of July?" he asked around the table. "Any great plans for the rest of the day?"

"No, I don't think so," Cameron answered him. "I think after lunch the ladies want to take in the flower show and the baking competition. As for we gentlemen, well, I do believe Ned has brought in samples of his fine beers, and there is also a shooting competition. You might be interested in that, Jack."

Jack shrugged. "Yeah, maybe. The problem with shootin' competitions is I always gotta hold back. Used ta be dangerous for me ta enter them things, 'cause it would bring unwanted attention. Now though, I might just end up embarrassin' myself."

"I don't know about that," Penny commented. "I've been watching you practice, and you've improved a lot over the last few months.

Jack smiled. "Why, thank you, Penny. But I'm still a long way from top form."

"How is your shoulder coming along?" David asked through a mouthful of potato salad. "Have you been keeping up with the stretching?"

"Yes David," Jack assured him with a long-suffering sigh.

David laughed. "Yes, okay. Onward! Let's have some fun."

***

As the afternoon progressed, the group naturally split up and went their own way. The four gentlemen went off to the saloon, while Jean, with Eli in tow, joined some of her friends to follow their interests. And, of course, to gossip. The three younger ladies went off to window shop and indulge in their own chit-chatting.

The three friends eventually ended up at the soda parlor. With some sweet treats in hand, they found themselves a lovely private little table outside, where they could sit and visit without too much concern about eavesdroppers.

"How was he?" Penny asked, full of concern. "Is it really as bad as Mathew insists?"

"Yes," Caroline answered. "It was worse. It was heartbreaking. I thought I was prepared to see him like that, but it was such a shock. And then that guard being so mean."

"Mean?" Penny repeated in a quiet voice. "But Peter has always been such a kind man. Why would they treat him badly?"

Josephine rolled her eyes. "You girls really do need to grow up."

Both young ladies sent defensive looks to their older friend.

"What's that supposed to mean?" Penny demanded.

"There you go again," Caroline accused Josie. "Condoning the treatment that Peter was receiving! How can you say that it's all right? That he deserves it?"

"I'm not saying that," Josephine defended herself. "I'm just saying you have to harden your hearts if you want to be of any use to Leon. You have to get over this naivety about prison life and about how 'it's not right', and 'how dare they treat him like that', etcetera, etcetera. One thing you girls really need to understand is that Napoleon Nash is not Peter Black. Leon was the most successful ever, leader of the Elk Mountain Gang, and you don't get to that station by being the nice guy."

Both sisters looked at her now, their eyes bright and shining. Neither of them wanted to hear what Josey was saying, and yet they were hopelessly fascinated by it, as well.

"Leon was an outlaw. He was a gambler, a flim-flammer and a crook," Josey continued. "Those guards know exactly what Leon was—and is, better than you do. They are not going to take anything for granted when it comes to dealing with him. Leon can be a handful, and that is for sure." Then Josey, seeing the frightened yet totally enthralled faces looking at her, softened her stance and smiled warmly in memory. "And yet, he is one of the most generous and kindest men I have ever known—Jack too." Big sigh. "They really are ones to set a young lady's heart 'afluttering."

Caroline and Penelope both smiled appreciatively.

"So," Josey continued in a more businesslike air, "if we are going to help Leon, then you two have got to toughen up. You have to stop crying over 'what is' so we can start deciding what exactly to do about it. Goodness knows, we've left it in the hands of the men for long enough."

The sisters nodded agreement; their expressions changed to ones of hardened determination.

"I have to get in to see him," Penny insisted. "I need to see for myself what we are going to be up against."

"Well, yes, of course," Josey agreed. "But how to get you in there. I don't think your parents would approve."

"No!" Penny agreed.

"That's for sure," Caroline seconded. "And Peter won't be pleased about it either. He was quite angry with me for going to see him."

"Why?" Penny asked. "I thought he would be pleased to see you."

"Stubborn male pride," Josey chimed in. Then seeing the confused expressions coming back at her, she tried to explain the male ego. "He knows he's at a disadvantage. He also knows that you two look up to him, maybe even admire him." Two enthusiastic heads nodded vigorously. "So, put yourself in his shoes. He's been subjugated; knocked down to the lowest level of humanity, his pride and his confidence beaten out of him. He's ashamed and embarrassed. Do you really think he would want you to see him like that?"

The sisters sat quietly for a moment, digesting what Josey had said, then nodded in acquiescence. Of course, Peter would find that difficult. Actually, now that Josey had explained it to them, they reprimanded themselves for not having realized it sooner.

"I guess that's why Mathew refused to take me to see him," Penny commented, reflectively. Then she gave a determined sigh. "But, I still want to go. I need to see for myself how he is and what conditions he's living in."

"Neither of us is arguing that point," Josey assured her. "But, we still have to find a way to get you there—without your folks or Jack knowing what you're doing."

Penny thought about it for a moment. "Mathew mentioned a woman preacher who has access to the prison. Apparently, she knows both Peter and Mathew from before and has helped to care for Peter when he's been sick or injured."

The other two ladies sat and looked at her, waiting for her to explain how this might be helpful.

"Well, perhaps if I can get in touch with this lady and explain what we want to do, maybe she would take me in," Penny continued.

"Umm, that's debatable," Josey commented. "And besides, you would still have to find a way to get there."

"You could always tell Mama and Papa that you're coming to stay with us for a week or so, just for a visit," Caroline suggested. "Steven and I are already planning to come here for Christmas, so if you were to come visit us for Thanksgiving, that wouldn't be suspicious."

"Yeah," Penny commented, "but then, what happens when Mama and Papa ask Steven about my visit?"

"You can actually come for a visit. There's plenty of room at Miss Hardcastle's boarding house. It'll be fun." Caroline explained. "Where you go after that is your business."

Josey was skeptical. "Do you have any idea how much trouble I would be in if Steven and your folks found out I was helping you with this? I'm supposed to be your chaperone. I'm supposed to make sure you stay out of trouble."

Both girls looked at her with their big brown eyes imploring her solicitousness.

"Oh, for goodness sakes!" Josey declared. "I don't know how I get roped into these things. I swear."

Then all three ladies nearly jumped out of their chairs when someone, probably a member of the local male child population, set off a string of fire crackers that split the air.

Instantly the street was increasingly more active than intended, with horses rearing and trying to head for the hills, and people running in circles attempting to control the horses and catch the culprits. The fireworks were for later that evening, not in the middle of a family-filled festive afternoon.

***

Jean, with Eli in tow, sat down at an outside table with her own group of friends. The four ladies had tea and pastries to attend to, and, with Eli settling in for an afternoon nap on the blanket Jean laid out for him, they all looked forward to some time to chat.

"That was certainly a lovely wedding, wasn't it?" Mable commented, sipping her tea. "Maribelle looked so pleased, and Sam was very handsome."

"Yes," Jean agreed. "They seem well suited. And Sam is

certainly a hard-working young man. He should do well for himself."

"Yes. But what a shame about he and Caroline," Suzie piped in, always the one to look for the cloud behind the silver lining. "You must have been quite disappointed when that all fell apart."

"Oh, good gracious, no," Jean contradicted her, and Suzie frowned. She had hoped to stir things up. "Not that Sam isn't a fine young man, but I knew Caroline wasn't too serious about him. She was just flirting, you know. The way young ladies do."

"Ohhh yes." Her three friends all nodded, knowingly.

"She was very hurt at first by his betrayal of her friends," Jean admitted, "but I think it was more wounded pride. We were all surprised by Sam's behavior, but her most of all."

"And my, but she's found herself quite a beau now," Millicent exclaimed. "Being courted by that handsome lawyer. A young lady couldn't ask for anyone better."

"Yes," Jean was happy to agree. "Mr. Granger is indeed a fine young man."

"And what of Penelope?" asked Suzie, again digging for a sore spot. "She's done with school now and is of an age to be thinking about marriage. As you know my Lucille is already betrothed to young Mr. Thomas, and they plan to be wed over the holidays."

"Yes, we know, Suzie, dear," chimed in Millicent, "and we're all sure Lucy and Theodore will be quite happy together. They've known each other since they could crawl, for goodness sakes." Then Millie looked to Jean again. "But what of Penny? She's such a pretty little thing—have you no one in mind for her? Don't want to wait forever you know, or all the good ones will be snatched up."

"I think Penny is making up her own mind about that," Jean answered. "I believe she has decided to hold out until the right one comes along."

"Oh, such childish nonsense," quipped Millicent. "The right one. She should set her sights on an eligible young man and go for it—otherwise she'll be left an old maid. Surely, there must be some young men in the county whom you would consider acceptable. What about Michael out at the Twin Star ranch, or Philip, right here in town?"

"I do believe Philip is already taken, Millie dear," Suzie

informed her. "He and Sharon Wilson are probably going to be wed very soon."

"That was quick," Millicent responded with wide eyes. "Why they just barely started to notice one another."

"Apparently, they did a lot of noticing when no one else was noticing," Suzie continued, with a knowing air. "It seems they have to get married—if you catch my drift. And soon, too."

"Ohhh!" Millicent cocked a knowing brow.

Jean smiled. "Well, these things do happen, don't they?"

A chorus of "Ummmm hmmmm," made its way around the table.

All the ladies smiled and took more tea.

"Might I mention my own boy, Charlie?" Mable took up the topic again. "He's a fine young man and is still quite available."

"Yes, yes, ladies! I know," Jean smiled. "But Cameron and I believe in allowing our girls to make their own decisions when it comes to choosing a husband. Unless, of course, we had a very strong aversion to the young man in question. But, we can hardly complain about Mr. Granger, and I'm sure Penny will make just as wise a choice."

"Oh, I don't know about that," Suzie commented dubiously, "the way Penny hovers over that Mr. Kiefer. Tch, tch!" She smiled with a dreamy look to her own eyes. "Still, I can certainly understand the attraction; he is a handsome man. I can see how a young, inexperienced maiden could be smitten with him. Considering who he was and all." Then she became serious and shook her head, knowingly. "But, hardly a wise choice, given his—background."

"But who's to say?" Jean responded. "We are all quite fond of Mathew. He's gone through a difficult time, but he seems to be coming out the other end of it now. And he is proving himself to be quite worthy. If he and Penny decide that is what they want, we would not have a problem with it."

This declaration was met by three buxom gasps from around the table.

"Surely, you don't mean that?"

"He's an outlaw and a gunslinger!"

"He has no prospects. What could he offer her?"

"Well now, he was an outlaw," Jean corrected them. "He has turned his back on that lifestyle, of that I have no doubt. As for him having no prospects, I don't believe that's true. Mathew has a lot to offer a young lady. He is a very intelligent and resourceful man. I'm sure once he finds his footing, he'll find his niche."

"From what I hear," said Mable, "all Mr. Kiefer cares about now is getting that partner of his out of prison. Just where do his loyalties lie? If he has turned his back on that life, as you say, then shouldn't he be thinking more about his own future rather than wasting his time on some convict? Since only Mr. Kiefer was given a pardon, then it would appear obvious that Mr. Nash was the true scoundrel and was sent to prison for a reason. I think Mr. Kiefer would be wise to sever all ties with that swindler and get on with his own life."

This statement was met with some vigorous head nodding and murmurs of approval from two of the other women present.

"Oh ladies. Please!" Jean was adamant. "What happened to poor Peter was the biggest travesty of true justice I have ever seen. It's all politics. Governor Warren crucified one, in order to justify giving to the other what had been promised to both. My opinion of Mathew would be poor indeed if he were to turn his back on his friend now, simply to get on with his own life. It would be poor indeed."

"Well, if that's what actually happened then, I suppose . . ." Mable quickly backstepped.

"Still, that could take years," Millicent said. "Just how long would Penny be willing to wait?"

"And is it worth it?" Suzie added her opinion. "How do you know Mr. Kiefer is even interested in—?"

All four ladies nearly jumped out of their seats as the festivities were loudly interrupted by the explosion of firecrackers renting the air.

Eli was startled out of his comforting nap and began to cry.

CHAPTER EIGHT
MEETING JACK KIEFER

Jack, David, Steven and Cameron were gradually making their way to the saloon where they knew some fine home-brewed beers were waiting to be tasted and then voted on.

Jack could hear the fast draw contest in full swing down one of the nearby side alleys, but had discreetly decided not to join in. He was with friends now, and he would enjoy the day as part of a family group.

They were all stepping onto the boardwalk in front of the Arvada Saloon when, quite unexpectedly, Jack walked very much accidentally into one of the local young ladies who just happened to be passing by on her way to the soda shop. Jack stepped back and smiled down at the pretty brunette and tipped his hat in apology.

"Oh, excuse me, ma'am, ah, Miss Baird, isn't it?" he asked.

"Why yes, Mr. Kiefer," she smiled sweetly up at him, "how kind of you to remember my name."

"It's easy to remember the name of such a pretty young lady," he commented casually.

Miss Baird smiled even more sweetly. "Why, thank you, Mr. Kiefer. Will we be seeing you at the fireworks later this evening?"

"I do expect to be there, yes ma'am."

"Lovely! I'll look forward to seeing you then," she flirted back at him, then she moved on, with a very sweet and smoldering brown-eyed look back at him.

Jack settled his hat back on his head and watched the enticing young thing walk away from him to join her friends at the cafe. Then he looked around toward the saloon to find his three friends smiling at him.

"Oh, don't even start," he warned them. "That was just a—"

"An encounter?" finished David.

"Yeah. No!" Jack floundered. "That was nothin'."

"Yes, of course it was nothing," David teased him.

"Better not tell Penny," Steven commented.

"There's nothin' ta tell!" Jack was getting flustered.

Finally, Cameron took pity on the young man, and getting in between him and the other two, he draped a conciliatory arm across his shoulders and headed him into the saloon.

"C'mon, Jack," he assured him, "don't listen to them; they're just jealous because some pretty little lady isn't fluttering her eyelashes at them."

"There was no fluttering of eye lashes!"

"Uh huh."

The four men settled themselves at the bar and began in earnest to sample some of the fine beers that were being made available. They looked around, hoping to find an empty table that would accommodate all of them, but no such luck. It seemed the saloon was a popular place for the numerous husbands of the county, and every table was occupied. The friends turned back to the bar and continued their conversation while leaning there and enjoying their drinks.

"How's business going, Steven?" Cameron asked his future son-in-law. "You keeping busy?"

"I'll say!" Steven admitted. "Since I still have my office in Cheyenne running, and now, the one in Denver, I'm kept very busy."

"Why are you keeping two offices running?" David asked him.

"I still have ongoing cases in Cheyenne, including Mr. Nash's," Steven explained. "It didn't feel right, simply walking away from them."

"Napoleon's case is still open?" Cameron asked.

"Oh yes," Steven confirmed. "I'm doing what I can to get a reduced sentence, but unfortunately, neither party is willing to compromise."

"How do you mean?" asked David.

"Well, Governor Warren won't even speak with me," Steven explained. "If we want to push for an appeal, it would help if Mr. Nash will concede and give up the information he refused to release during his trial, which he is still refusing to do. The Supreme Court may not even be willing to listen to our argument without some acknowledgment on his part."

This was met by a chorus of frustrated sighs, then everyone looked at Jack.

"What?" Jack asked them.

"He's your partner," Steven pointed out. "Can't you talk to him?"

"And tell him what?" Jack asked. "That he should knife two of our friends in the back so he can get out of prison?"

"Actually, it wasn't in exchange for a total pardon," Steven reluctantly revealed. "The judge I spoke to said an appeal may help to reduce Mr. Nash's sentence to ten years instead of twenty to life if we can offer proof of mistreatment, and he surrenders the required information."

Jack snorted in disgust. "That'll never happen."

"No," Steven admitted. "So Mr. Nash has already informed me."

This announcement was met with another chorus of sighs.

"Well," began Jack, "what's the next step? What else can we do?"

There was a moment of silence as everyone considered this question.

"I will say that the best step is to wait and see what happens with Governor Warren," Steven commented. "I doubt he is going to be in office much longer. Once we get a new governor in there, well, maybe he will consider honoring the pardon."

"Yeah, right," Jack mumbled. "We've been through this before. A new governor is gonna be too concerned about keepin' the big-budget business men happy to be willin' to pardon Napoleon Nash. I don't see it happenin'."

"I know," Steven acknowledged. "And there's not much point in appealing to the Supreme Court as long as Judge Lacey is Chief Justice there. He would, of course, have to excuse himself for the hearing, since it is his sentencing that we are challenging. But politics being what they are, I doubt his fellow Supreme Court judges would undermine him. Perhaps once he steps down, if he does . . ." The lawyer paused and shook his head, indicating his own lack of confidence in this happening any time soon. "Caroline is still writing to various newspapers about the promises made and broken. There's just not much else we can do right now."

"Penny is busy, doing much the same thing," Jack concurred. "Keepin' in touch with the individuals who helped out before. Askin' 'em for more letters to the Governor's office and all that. I donno. It just seems like everyone is ignorin' us now. Nobody wants ta think about it anymore."

"What about your Texas rancher friend, Mr. Coburn?" Cameron asked. "Is he still involved?"

"Yeah," Jack answered. "I know he's still puttin' pressure on Governor Warren, but again, he's gettin' shut out. Max has money and influence, but mostly in Texas. Wyoming don't really care. But he's still tryin'."

"What about the other judge," Cameron asked Jack. "The one you boys knew from before?"

"Who? You mean Judge MacEnroe?"

"Yes," Cameron agreed. "He seemed to be quite supportive of you. Is he still in the picture?"

"I guess," Jack answered. "He ain't well these days, and I suppose Warren figures that givin' me the pardon sort of makes 'em even. I don't know if Judge MacEnroe is really up to continuin' the fight. Maybe Penny could get hold a him again and see if he can still help out."

The bat wing doors of the entrance slammed open, interrupting their discussion. Six young bucks exploded into the saloon, laughing and hooting and slapping one particular fella on the back.

"Hey! Harry here just up and won the fast draw competition. Beers all around for us."

"Woo Hoo! That was some mighty fine shootin' you fellas missed. Ya all should 'a been there."

"Yeah. I ain't never seen nobody faster."

Jack casually glanced at the group as they collected their beers, and he met the eyes of the excited Harry, who was all puffed up with his victory. Their gazes locked only for an instant, then it was broken by the celebratory group heading away from the bar and taking possession of a table that had recently opened up.

Jack sighed, almost regretfully, then turned his attention back to the conversation.

"Yeah," Steven was commenting. "Keeping pressure on the powers that be can't hurt. I still think our best bet is to wait for a new governor to be appointed and go from there."

A dejected Jack stared down into his half empty glass of beer. It's all well and good for them to just wait and see, but what about Leon? He was the one who really had to hang on and wait. Just how long would he be able to do that? All the doors seemed to be getting shut in their faces and nobody was coming up with a feasible next step.

He sighed and took another swallow of beer. Then the blood went cold in his veins.

"Kansas Kid!" came a yell from behind him. "I'm callin' you out!"

Jack's three friends all turned as one to look at the young man doing the yelling. It was Harry, the winner of the fast draw competition. He apparently was feeling his oats and with the support of his friends, got to thinking that he was invincible.

Meanwhile, once the instant chill had left Jack's body, his well-honed instincts took over. His heart rate and breathing slowed, and a calmness settled over him as his right hand dropped inconspicuously to rest quietly by the handle of his gun.

"What's he look like?" Jack asked Cameron, who was standing the closest to him. "Is he wearing his gun tied down?"

"Yeah," Cameron whispered. "Much like how you wear yours."

"Damn it," Jack cursed. "Get away from me," he told his friends in a whisper, "and for god's sake, don't stand behind me."

"No, Jack, you can't be serious," Cameron argued.

"I ain't the one callin' him out, Cameron," Jack responded in a whispered hiss, "and he sounds serious. Move away from me—now!"

"You hear me, Kiefer?" Harry called to him again. "Or have you gotten soft since you become all legal?"

Everyone in the silenced saloon quietly shuffled away from the two gunmen. The atmosphere inside the establishment had gone from carefree and festive to one of oppressed anticipation, as the seriousness of the challenge became apparent. Even Bill, the bartender, had snatched up some of the more expensive bottles and taken cover behind the bar.

Jack took a deep breath in preparation, then straightened and turned around to face his adversary.

"Listen," he said, trying to defuse the situation, "this has been a nice, quiet—"

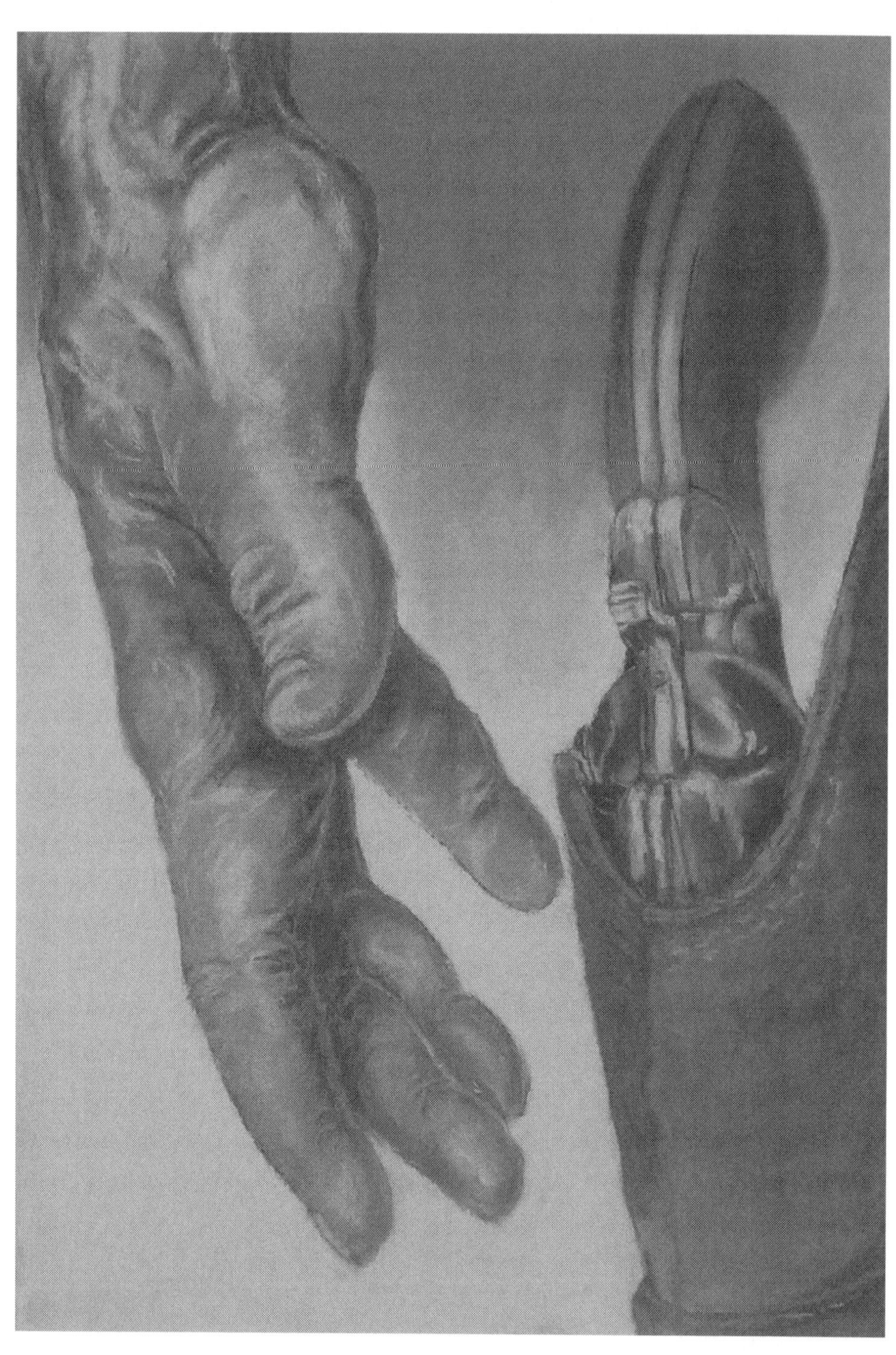

His right hand dropped inconspicuously to rest quietly by the handle of his gun.

Harry made his move.

Jack didn't even have time to think about it. His body reacted on pure instinct. The muscles in his right shoulder contracted, and like an electric shock running down through his arm and into his hand, the nerves and tendons responded instantly. His Colt exploded with the report, then the wisp of smoke and the smell of gun powder filled the air.

Harry lay writhing on the floor, clutching his right thigh, his own gun still nestled safely in its holster. There was stunned silence for a heartbeat, then everyone was brought out of their stupor by the sound of firecrackers taking over the scene. This was followed by frightened horses stampeding down Main Street, and people shouting in an effort to get things under control.

Then, everyone in the saloon was talking at once, with the occasional "Whoop!"

"Did you see that? I ain't never seen anything so fast."

David was on the run to tend to the stricken man, and someone else dashed out in search of Sheriff Jacobs. Steven stood with his mouth open, not so sure he had seen what he'd just seen.

Jack returned his Colt Peacemaker to its holster and leaned back against the bar, looking disappointed.

Cameron put a hand on his shoulder.

"Jeez, Jack," he said quietly, "is that how it happens? So fast, with no real warning?"

"Yup," Jack nodded sadly, "usually it does."

"Well," Cameron sighed, "at least you know you're still fast."

Jack shook his head. "No," he said. "I'm way off. If that had been Quincy Bartlett, I'd be dead right now. And I was aimin' for his holster, not his leg. I didn't wanna actually hit 'im."

Cameron and Steven exchanged looks at this admission; it had seemed plenty fast to them.

David looked up from his ministrations and beckoned to the lawyer.

"Steven, could you run over to my place and get my medical bag?" he asked. "I need to get this bleeding stopped, then we can move him to my surgery and I'll patch him up over there."

"Oh, sure," Steven agreed. "I'll be right back."

Cameron gave Jack another pat on the back.

"C'mon, Jack," he said, "let me buy ya a shot of whiskey. You're shaking."

The two men turned back to face the bar just as Bill came up with a bottle of the good stuff and three glasses.

"No fellas, it's on me," he offered as he started to pour, "and I'll join ya. That has got to be the dangest thing I ever seen. Talk about a Fourth of July! Whooee!"

The three men downed their whiskey just as Sheriff Jacobs entered the building. He did one quick look around, then headed over to speak with David first and get the prognosis for the young man bleeding on the floor.

"No, it's not bad, Carl," David assured him. "I'll get some padding onto it and then move him over to my surgery. He'll be limping, but he'll be walking tomorrow."

"Good," Jacobs nodded. "Did you see what happened?"

"Yes, I did."

"Good," Jacobs said again. "When you're done with him, come to my office and give me your version."

David nodded, then went back to soothe the whimpering contest winner.

Jacobs turned his attention to the bar, sighed and shook his head. Always something on the Fourth of July. He started over toward the bar, practically having to push eager witnesses out of his way. Suddenly, everybody wanted to offer up their version of what happened.

"I saw everything, Sheriff. It was absolutely amazing."

"You're not gonna believe it, Sheriff. What a gunfight. I ain't never gonna forget this."

"Hey, Sheriff, I'll be happy to tell ya what happened. I had a real clear view from behind that table over there."

Jacobs nodded politely to all the townsfolk who were so eager to be of assistance, but he still steadily made his way to the bar and to the man he really wanted to have a conversation with.

"Mr. Kiefer," he greeted the gunman.

"Sheriff."

"Howdy, Cameron."

"Hey, Carl."

With the pleasantries dispensed with, the sheriff turned his attention to Jack.

"You want to tell me what happened here?"

Jack sighed, this was never going to get any easier.

"We were just havin' a drink at the bar when that young fella called me out," Jack explained. "I tried ta calm him down, ta talk him out of it, but he went for his gun, and I just reacted. I'm sorry. I tried not ta hit 'im, but I guess I still ain't as accurate as I used ta be."

"Uh huh," Jacobs sounded skeptical. "No reason for it? He just decided outta the blue to call you out?"

"That's right, Sheriff,' Jack said. "I guess he was feelin' punchy, havin' just won that fast draw contest, and I suppose he'd already had a few beers before comin' here. He saw me at the bar and figured he'd make a show of it. I guess he found out the hard way that shootin' at a spinnin' plate ain't quite the same as shootin' at someone who could shoot back."

"Uh huh," Jacobs nodded. "Is that pretty much how you saw it, Cameron?"

"Yes," Cameron agreed. "That young fella started it. Jack did try to talk him down, but it wasn't going to happen."

Jacobs let go of a big sigh, and all three men looked to where David was helping Harry up onto his feet. A couple of Harry's friends were each getting under an arm to help escort him over to the doctor's office. David sent a quick smile to the three men at the bar, then a look of concern flashed across his face when he noticed Jack supporting his right arm with a thumb hooked into his belt. Then he was gone, tending to the more immediate need, but making a mental note all the same.

Steven came over to rejoin his friends. He gladly accepted a welcoming shot of whiskey.

"How about you, Mr. Granger?" Jacobs asked him. "You agree; that young man started the whole thing?"

"Oh, yes, Sheriff," Steven backed up the story. "No doubt about it." Then he smiled. "And if you have any intentions of arresting Mr. Kiefer here, well, I'll be quite happy to defend him—free of charge."

Jack sent him a look. *Why did you have to bring that up?*

But Jacobs laughed and shook his head.

"Oh, I don't think that will be necessary," he assured the group. "On the contrary, I believe I will ask the doctor how much he's going to charge for the medical services and then, whatever's left over from that fella's winnings will conveniently be the amount of his fine for disturbing the peace and inciting a gunfight." He tipped his hat to the group. "Good afternoon, gentlemen. Enjoy the festivities. But, please try and stay out of trouble."

"Yes sir, Sheriff," Jack answered with a relieved smile.

"See you later, Carl," Cameron added.

Jack slumped in relief, then poured himself another shot from the bottle.

"I am never gonna get used to talkin' to a badge," he mumbled into the glass.

Cameron smiled and gave him a pat on the back. "C'mon," he said, "let's go find the ladies. I'm sure rumors of what happened will be all around the town by now, and they'll be worried."

***

A couple of hours later found the group re-connected and seated around an outside table, enjoying supper.

David had tended to his patient, given him a dose of laudanum, then sent him to sleep away the rest of the afternoon in his hotel room. The doctor then rejoined the festivities, though he was disappointed that his wife was still not feeling up to snuff and had again decided to stay home and rest.

"What an exciting afternoon," Jean commented while she helped her son get food into his mouth rather than all over his face and hands. "Thank goodness it wasn't that serious."

"Yes," David agreed. "It turned out to just be a graze. Painful, but hardly life-threatening. Hopefully he's learned his lesson."

"Yeah," Jack grumbled. "Unfortunately, for everyone who learns the lesson, five more still need teachin'."

"Don't you think the majority of them will leave you alone, now that you've been pardoned?" Cameron asked him.

"I donno," Jack shrugged. "I hope so. But like I said at my trial, there's always one who wants the reputation. And knowin' my shoulder ain't what it used to be might just make it all the more invitin'."

"That's silly," Penny said. "Where's the honor in out-shooting a man who's been injured?"

Everyone at the table smiled.

"A woman's logic," Jean commented.

"Let's hope you're right, Penny," Jack told her. "But, in the meantime, I'm gonna keep on practicin' just in case you ain't."

"That reminds me," David piped up, "how's your shoulder feeling after that? I noticed you supporting it. Is it still bothering you?"

"No David, it's all right," Jack assured him. "It's just a little stiff. It'll be fine."

"Okay. But if it's still sore tomorrow, come in and I'll work on it for you."

Jack groaned. "David, it'll be fine."

"Oh, don't be such a baby," David threw at him. "You know it feels better after I've worked on it. I swear, I've never known a grown man to whimper as much as you do."

Jack glared over the table at him, but David met it with an innocent smile; obviously teasing his friend.

The young ladies giggled.

Soon, all the supper plates were cleared away and everyone was enjoying dessert and one final cup of coffee before evening plans were brought up for discussion.

"I'm sure you young people want to stay for the festivities tonight," Cameron assumed. "There's going to be dancing and of course fireworks once it gets dark."

"Yup," Jack agreed. "I believe that's a fair assumption."

The three young ladies smiled, sparkles dancing in their eyes with anticipation of a fun night in town.

"Well, that's fine," Cameron continued. "Though I do believe Jean and I will be heading home shortly." Jean nodded a tired but enthusiastic agreement to this statement. "Our young man here needs to get to bed—not to mention the old man! I just ask that when you people do get home tonight, that you try to be quiet. Please."

"Of course."

"Certainly."

"And you young men," Cameron took on a stern manner, indicating Jack and Steven. "You'll be escorting my girls, so I expect you to behave like gentlemen. You understand me?"

"Of course."

"Certainly."

"Good." Cameron and Jean exchanged a look. If Cameron had any concerns about honorable behavior—or lack thereof—his daughters would not be staying in town for the evening. "On that note," he continued. "I believe we will call it a night."

***

Everyone who stayed in town for the party ended up having a wonderful time. The tables in the town center were cleared away to make room for dancing, and the local band got set up to play, and the fun soon began.

Even though the Marsham party tended to stick together when it came time to eat or drink, or just sit one out, when it came to dancing, no one was sticking with just one partner. This wasn't too surprising, since most of those in attendance were of the same age group and had basically grown up together. But even the newcomers were familiar enough faces around town to feel like they belonged, and it was one big happy family, having fun.

Jack got a scare added on to his day when he left the group to tend to necessity and he spotted two of Harry's friends heading toward him. He felt a twinge of resentment that they might be coming over looking for revenge, but that supposition was soon laid to rest when both young men smiled at him and offered hands for shaking.

"We sure do want to apologize for Harry, actin' like such an idiot there this afternoon, Mr. Kiefer," one of them started in. "He's not a bad fella, but he can be a bit frisky sometimes, especially when he's had a few ta drink!"

"Oh. Well, that's okay, fellas," Jack responded, relief washing over him. "No hard feelings."

"Good! Good," stated the other. "I must say though, it sure was an honor to see ya in action. We ain't never gonna forget that."

"Yeah, for sure," agreed the first. "It was almost worth Harry gettin' shot to be able to see that, yes sir!"

"Uh huh."

"And ah . . ." started the other, a little more somber this time, "we really want ta thank ya for not killin' 'im. Like we say, he's not a bad fella."

"Yeah, sure," Jack mumbled. "No problem."

Then, with a few more handshakes and a slap on the back, the men parted company. Jack carried on with his mission, hoping he was never going to set eyes on those fellas again.

On his way back to his group of friends, one small incident did transpire that was taken quite seriously by some, and shrugged off as irrelevant by others, depending, of course, upon your gender.

Jack was returning to his friends when he found himself once again bumping into Miss Baird. He quickly back-stepped and apologized. She smiled and batted her lashes.

"Miss Baird," he said. "I do apologize. I seem ta be bumpin' inta you a lot today."

"That's quite all right, Mr. Kiefer." She smiled back. "And please, this is an informal gathering; feel free to call me Isabelle."

"Well thank you, Isabelle." Jack was smiling by this time. "My name is Jack."

"Yes, I know."

Jack then offered her his arm and they strolled back to the dancing together.

"I heard about that incident this afternoon," Isabelle commented. "How very frightening for you. And how relieved I was to learn that you had not been injured."

"I've gotten pretty good at takin' care a myself, Isabelle," Jack assured her. "It was hardly worthy a your concern."

"Yes, I'm sure you are quite able to take care of yourself," she flirted back at him. "You strike me as a very capable man, in more ways than one."

"Ohh, hoo, Isabelle," Jack teased her. "I do believe you are changin' the subject."

"It would seem that you are very astute as well."

Any further conversation was cut short by the appearance of Josey and Caroline, who were quick to intervene. Before Isabelle had any notion of the combined intervention being directed at her, those two worthy friends had nipped in between the couple and were ushering Jack off to a neutral corner.

By the time Isabelle was aware that her quarry had been absconded with and got her breath back to protest, she was instantly silenced by two sets of dark, smoking brown eyes just daring her to try that again.

Jack himself was surprised to find the very attractive Isabelle suddenly replaced by his two friends, one on each arm, hustling him off toward their table. As far as he was concerned, he was just being neighborly.

"Whoa!" he protested. "What's goin' on?"

"You don't want to be seen with her," Caroline explained. "She has a reputation."

"What? We were just talkin'."

"Besides," Josey added, "Penny wants this next dance with you."

"She does?" Jack asked. "Why didn't she just say so?"

"Well, she's shy," Josey explained. "Go on, get over there and ask her for the next dance."

Josey and Caroline, each with a hand pressed against the small of Jack's back, gave him a push toward the main focus of their discussion. Jack very nearly tripped over one of the chairs that were scattered about, but caught himself just in time, and came up face to face with a smiling Penny.

"Penny," Jack addressed her, politely, "would you honor me with this dance?"

Penny beamed up at him, smiling broadly. "Of course, Mathew. I'd love to."

Jack offered his arm to Penny, and they headed toward the dance area.

Caroline and Josephine rolled their eyes and shook their heads in astonishment.

"Men!" Josey declared. "Sometimes they can be so obtuse."

Then she smiled pleasantly as Steven and David offered their arms to the two ladies and everyone joined in to dance the evening away.

***

The next morning, no one was quick to rise and shine, but eventually, the household started to stir, and coffee was prepared and passed around. Fortunately, even Eli wasn't too interested in getting out of bed, so it became a very relaxing morning, mostly spent sitting on the front porch and drinking tea or lemonade.

Jack groaned as they all spotted David's surrey making its way down the lane toward the open yard. As usual, Midnight and Karma came dancing over to the fence to greet the visitors, and David's little gelding tossed his head and sent them a nicker.

Jean stood up and waved at him as he turned Rudy to the hitching rail and disembarked.

"David," she greeted him. "How good to see you. How is

Tricia today?"

"Feeling better, I think," he answered with a smile. "Just a twenty-four-hour thing."

"Good! Would you like some tea or lemonade?"

"Some lemonade would go down very nicely right now, thank you."

"Fine," Jean answered. "Come on up and have a seat. I'll get you a glass."

"Morning, David," Cameron greeted him. "What brings you out this way?"

"Yes, David," Jack cocked a suspicious brow. "What does bring you out this way?"

David came onto the porch, stepping over the three stretched out dogs as he headed for the empty chair. So much for being on the alert. He sat down between the two men and smiled at Jack.

"I think you already know what brings me out," he answered. "I decided I wasn't going to wait for you to do the right thing, so I included you in on my rounds for this morning. You can thank me later."

"David, I'm fine," Jack scowled, not wanting to mention he had hardly slept the previous night, due to the aching in his shoulder.

"Umm hum. Oh, Jean, thank you." David accepted his drink while Jean pulled up another chair and joined them. "I take it everyone got home all right last night. Quite an event, wasn't it?"

"I'll say," Cameron agreed. "I don't think anyone is going to be forgetting this Fourth of July for some time to come."

The conversation carried on in this vein for half an hour or so, then David put down his empty glass and stood up.

"Well Jack, c'mon, let's get to this," he said. "Best if we go inside, get you sitting in a straight back chair."

"How about we just don't bother doin' it at all?" Jack grumbled.

"Nope." David headed inside, secure in the expectation that Jack would follow him.

Jack sighed, but didn't move.

"You'd best get it over with, Jack," Cameron suggested. "You know he won't let up until you do."

Jack grumbled, but started to push himself to his feet. "My shoulder's fine," he mumbled as he headed indoors. "Why does he have to be such a pest?"

***

"Ouch."

"Sorry."

"Ouch!!"

"Sorry."

"Shut up!"

David stepped back, a little surprised at the level of hostility.

"What's the matter?" he asked his friend. "Why are you in such a snarky mood today?"

Jack sighed and slumped his shoulders. "I donno—just am."

David moved back in and continued to massage the shoulder.

"Here you go again," the doctor accused him. "You do know why. You just don't feel comfortable talking about it."

"Yeah, fine," Jack agreed, then grimaced in pain. "David, that hurts."

"Yes, I know. So, what is it you don't feel comfortable talking about?"

Jack sighed again. Poke prod, poke prod. Jack couldn't understand why he liked this man so much.

"All right," he finally snarked. "I'm frustrated—okay?"

"What about?"

"Leon!" he shouted. "What else? Here we are, doin' everything we can do that's legal, and nothin's happenin'. And people wonder why we went outside the law to get what we wanted. Ya turn old and gray, tryin' ta do it the right way. All summer long, he's been workin' outside the prison walls. All I gotta do is get some of the boys together from Elk Mountain and go cut him loose. Head down to Mexico or somethin'. But here I sit, waitin' for the next new governor, just on the outside chance he might be agreeable. Well damn 'agreeable'. I should just go get him. To hell with the pardon."

"Hmm," was David's comment as he moved behind Jack and began massaging both his shoulders; the man was getting tense. "Have you mentioned this to Napoleon?"

"No."

"Are you going to?"

"No," Jack admitted, calming down. The massage was helping. "He'd just get mad at me. He's already told me not to blow my own chances now. Even said he'd understand if I decided to just forget about him and get on with my own life. Can you believe that? That he would say somethin' like that to me? Damn."

"I guess he's just trying to let you know that you have choices," David commented. "I can certainly understand him not wanting you to do anything illegal now that you have your pardon. Maybe he sees it as after all that hard work, at least one of you has benefited. If you go and blow it now, well, what was it all for?"

"Yeah," Jack conceded. "I suppose."

Then a stampede of giggles and skirts came charging into the front room, being followed by a more sedate Jean.

Jack quickly put his shirt back on.

"David," Jean said, "would you like to stay for lunch?"

David smiled.

***

Later in the evening, the family was relaxed in various positions between the dining room table, living room armchairs and the front porch.

Jean was comfortably settled in an armchair where she was busy with her knitting for the upcoming cooler months. She was quiet in her mood, as she knew Caroline, along with Josephine and Steven, would be heading back to Denver in the morning. She had known they would not be staying for long, but she was still sad to see her daughter going away again.

Those same three people were on the front porch, laughing and talking together like the old friends they were quickly becoming. Caroline, as is usual for a young lady leaving the nest, was eagerly anticipating getting back to her new life in Denver and had no clue how difficult this whole transition had been on her mother.

Jean certainly wasn't going to let her know.

Cameron, Jack, and Penny were all sitting at the table, quietly involved in their own endeavors.

Cameron was doing the never-ending paperwork involved in running a business.

Jack was busy cleaning his gun, again. This was something he did every evening, but much to Jean's relief, always after Eli had been put down for the night. Penny was sitting quietly and watching with fascination while her friend dismantled his gun, cleaned every single little piece of it, and then put it all back together again without missing a beat. She'd watch him do it night after night, and still couldn't keep up.

The quiet comradery was then broken by a gentle enquiry.

"Have you asked Peter what he would like for Christmas, Mathew?" Jean suddenly asked from her corner.

"Ah, no I haven't," Jack admitted. "But I do recall him sayin' that a woolen hat would be appreciated."

"A woolen hat?"

"Yeah. They shaved off his hair, remember?" Jack reminded her. "His head gets kinda cold. They have cloth hats for summer, but nothin' more for winter."

"Oh, my goodness," Jean admonished herself. "I had completely forgotten about that. I suppose it's because I haven't seen him. Whenever I think of him, I still see him as he was here, with that lovely thick head of hair. I guess he looks quite different now, doesn't he?"

Jack sent a sad look to her. "Yeah, he does," then he smiled, trying to lighten the mood. "So, a woolen hat and some mittens, maybe a scarf if'n ya have the time."

Jean smiled. "Of course, I have the time. Peter takes priority these days. Do you know what you're going to get him?"

"No. I ain't really thought about it. I suppose I should; Christmas will be here before we know it." He stopped and looked down at the small cleaning tool he held in his hand, and he turned reflective. "Leon gave me this cleanin' kit for my birthday, I guess, about five years ago. I already had one, but some of the tools were missin' and I was just kinda makin' do. I hadn't said nothin' to him about needin' a new kit, 'cause I knew we didn't really have the money for one. But I guess he saw that I needed it, and he found the money somewhere."

Jean sent him a gentle look. "That was very considerate of him."

"Yeah."

"Do they do anything at the prison for Christmas?" Penny suddenly piped up.

"Oh yeah," Jack answered her, pulling himself out of his reminiscence. "There is a woman doctor there who gives services and lectures on Sundays for the inmates, and I believe she holds special services for Christmas and Easter."

All three heads looked up from what they were doing.

"Really?" asked Penny, feigning innocence. "A woman preaching at the prison?"

"Yeah, that's what I said, too," Jack agreed. "We know her from before, and she impressed us with her manner. I never thought she'd be accepted as a preacher though."

"Well," Jean commented, "who would have thought? I hope Peter is getting some enjoyment out of the services and lectures. Someone else with an intellect, perhaps to keep him interested?"

"Yeah. I donno," Jack admitted. "I think lately, Leon has been backin' off that stuff. Keepin' more to himself, you know."

Jean frowned. "That doesn't sound good," she commented. "Peter has a very active mind. If there is someone there who is willing to give lectures and spiritual instruction, he should take advantage of it."

"Leon never was very spiritual," Jack pointed out.

"Yes, I know," Jean conceded, "but there's something to be said about the spiritual side of things, especially during hard times. It might make his life now a little easier for him."

Jack sighed. "Well, she seems to have taken Leon on as her new project. Maybe she'll have some influence without him even knowin' it."

Jean smiled.

Penny saw her opportunity. "Oh, I remember now. You have mentioned her before. Didn't she and the Sisters from the orphanage bring gifts for the inmates last year?"

"Ya, that's right," Jack confirmed. "That's how she found out Leon was there."

"Oh. So the orphanage is right in Laramie?"

Jack became reflective. "Well, I guess. I ain't never been there. It must be close though, for her ta be at the prison as often as she is."

"Oh." Penny kept her tone neutral. "So she's there a lot?"

Jack shrugged as he started putting his gun back together. "From what I can tell. Usually when the doctor there needs help, she'll come ta act as nurse. I know when Leon was sick last winter, she did a lot ta get 'im through it."

"Yes. That was frightening," Jean remembered the episode. "I certainly hope he doesn't get that sick again."

"He's eatin' better this year, so hopefully not," Jack assured her. "And a nice, woolen hat and mittens will certainly help him to stay warmer."

"We'll just have to make sure he gets them, then," Jean declared, then pushed herself up from her armchair. "I'm in the mood for an evening cup of tea. Anyone else?"

"That would be nice," Cameron responded.

"Sure," came Jack's answer.

"Not me, Mama," said Penny as she got up from the table. "I'm still really tired from our late night, yesterday. I think I'm going to go up to my room and read a little, while there's still light."

"Oh." Jean was surprised. "All right, Penny. I suppose you all did have a rather boisterous evening."

"Yes. Goodnight."

"Goodnight, Penny."

"Goodnight, sweetheart."

***

Penny made her way up the stairs and into her room which she was now sharing with Caroline and Josephine while there was such a full house. She quietly closed the door and went over to her little writing desk, and sitting down, took out a piece of clean paper along with her ink jar and pen. She sat for a moment, reflective, wondering just how exactly to word this very sensitive letter. She must have sat for at least ten minutes, just staring into space, when finally, she dipped pen into ink and began to write.

To Doctor Mariam Soames
Orphanage, Laramie, Wyoming.

Then she stopped and thought about it some more. It wasn't much of an address, but it was all she had. She could only hope her letter would find its way to the proper recipient. Pen went to paper again.

Dear Doctor Mariam . . .

CHAPTER NINE
A YEAR IN THE LIFE

**Laramie, Wyoming,
Fall 1886**

Leon and Jack sat across from each other in their usual manner. Each, in their own way, was trying to ignore the fact that Pearson was standing behind the inmate with a loaded rifle, probably eavesdropping on everything they said. Jack was at a loss; he'd run out of conversation. Leon wasn't helping; he was in a mood. Stoic, depressed—silent.

"Weather's kinda strange these days," Jack finally commented, falling back on the typical topic that people tend to fall back on when there's nothing else to say. "Startin' ta feel a chill in the air, but we're still not getting any rain. The livestock around the barn are doin' okay, but Cameron's getting worried about the range stock."

"Hmm."

"Karma's lookin' good," Jack continued, then forced a smile. "She's startin' ta look a little plump, if ya know what I mean."

"Yeah."

Jack sighed, frustrated. "C'mon, Leon, give me somethin', will ya? The snows are gonna be flyin' soon. I don't know how many more times I'm gonna be able to get here before winter sets in."

"Yeah, I know."

Silence. Even Officer Pearson looked bored.

"Oh!" Jack brightened up as he remembered a piece of good news. "Seems like David and Tricia are expectin'—finally. David's walkin' around with his head in the clouds. He's just tickled pink—if you can say that about a man."

"Hmm. Well, he is a doctor. He oughta know how it's done."

The smile dropped from Jack's face. "C'mon, Leon. What kinda talk is that? David's one of the good guys—remember?"

It was Leon's turn to sigh, but then he had the good grace to look contrite.

"Yeah, I know. I'm sorry Jack, it's just . . ."

"What, Leon? What's been eatin' at ya?"

"It's just . . ." Leon couldn't look his nephew in the eye, "it's been a year."

Jack's attempts at pleasantries dropped, and once again, a strained silence fell between them.

Leon looked like he was going to cry, almost. But he didn't, and with a subtle cough and a shifting in his chair, he simply stared off into space, focusing on something beyond Jack's left shoulder.

"Yeah, I know," Jack commiserated. "I was hopin', maybe ya wouldn't realize it. Stupid really, thinkin' ya wouldn't realize it. But, I was hopin', that's all."

"Yeah." Leon shifted again, and this time brought his eyes down to meet his partner's. "I donno, I guess I just kept thinking something was going to happen, you know? Like it always does. We always seemed to be able to talk or fight or just plain scam our way out of these things, so I figured something was going to happen. Some miracle. I mean, surely this wasn't it. This wasn't going to be my life from now on. This was just a bad dream, and I would get out and we'd look back on it and laugh about what a close call it had been, and how we showed them. You know, the usual."

"Yeah, I know."

"But, it's been a year and suddenly it does feel like this is my life from now on," Leon continued, "that this is it. There is no exit out the back. My life outside of these walls doesn't exist anymore."

"Leon, it does exist," Jack assured him. "C'mon, don't give up on that. I know it's takin' longer than we thought, and doors keep on getting slammed in our faces, but we're not givin' up on ya. You gotta know that."

Leon sent his nephew a soft smile. "Yeah, I know that, Jack," he said and then sighed deeply. "I guess I have to just dig in and hang on. Right?"

Jack didn't answer him. The sarcasm in his tone was subtle but obvious to one who knew him so well.

"Are ya goin' ta' services at all, Leon? Or readin' them medical journals? You seemed to be getting quite a lot outta them things before."

"Yeah, I know," Leon agreed. "I just haven't been really interested in that stuff lately." He smiled again, a hint of sadness coming through his warm eyes. "I think I should just leave the doctoring to David. I don't really have the knack for it."

"Yeah? Well . . . have ya been talkin' to Mariam, lately?" Jack was grasping at straws. "She's a friend."

Leon shrugged. "Yeah. One of the other inmates was sick for a while, so she was here to help with him. But since then, she hasn't been around much. I guess she's been busy with orphans and such, what with Christmas only a couple of months away."

"Well, maybe you could write her a letter, or write David a letter, or write somebody a letter. What about Taggard?"

"What about him?"

"Well—write 'im a letter."

"I don't have anything to say."

Jack slumped. "Is Kenny workin' today?"

"Why? You want me to write him a letter?"

"No," Jack retorted, sending him a frown. "It's just that Jean sent some things for ya. They're actually Christmas presents, but since we didn't want to take the chance of everybody getting snowed in, she asked me ta bring them to ya early. You'll probably be needin' 'em soon, anyway."

"Oh," Leon mumbled. "Yeah, I think he's here today. Just ask for him. You know the drill."

"Yeah, I do."

Leon remembered something akin to manners. "I guess you should thank Jean for me. It's good of her to put the effort in."

"She's happy ta do it," Jack assured him. "She's always askin' after ya. She's worried you're gonna get sick again."

Leon smiled. "Tell her I'll try not to."

"Yeah, I will. I'd appreciate ya not getting sick again too."

"Hmm." Leon sat silent, then changed the subject. "How are the girls?"

"They're fine." Jack brightened, hoping this topic would be more positive. "I think Penny is gonna be spendin' Thanksgivin' in Denver, weather permittin'. Then they're all gonna be comin' out to the ranch for Christmas."

"Hmm," was Leon's only comment.

He stared off into empty space, a sadness enveloping him; a sadness that was deeper than any Jack had ever seen before, and it scared him. It was as though Leon had lost yet one more piece of himself, like he was giving up.

Then Pearson shifted his weight ever so slightly, but Jack had come to recognize that little bit of body language as time to wrap it up, and he was angry with himself for feeling relieved. This had been a difficult and awkward visit, and part of him was glad it was over. Yet, on the other hand, Jack felt anxious about leaving Leon when he was in this kind of mood. He was no longer sure about what Leon was, or was not, capable of doing.

"I guess our time is up," Jack told him. "I gotta go."

"Yeah, okay."

"Don't do anything stupid, all right?"

"No, I won't."

Jack smiled. It had been a very simple exchange, but it was enough of a reassurance that Jack was able to relax a little and feel confident he would see Leon again.

"I'll try to get in to see ya one more time before winter really hits," Jack promised him as he got to his feet.

"Yeah, okay Jack. Oh, and Jack?"

"Yeah?" He looked at his uncle to see a sparkle in those dark brown eyes, and a dimpled grin upon his face.

"Try not to worry so much, okay?"

Jack gave a quiet laugh. "Yeah, okay. See ya later."

***

Once out of the visitor's room, Jack hung around waiting for his belongings to show up. Within a few moments, Officer Murray arrived with said belongings in hand.

Jack accepted the items then enquired about seeing Officer

Reece.

"He's busy," the guard told him. "What do you need to see him for?"

"I need to give him this parcel," Jack explained. "It'll only take a moment."

"Like I said, he's busy," Murray reiterated. "You can leave it with me; I'll make sure he gets it."

Jack smiled. Not his friendly smile, but his I'm talkin' to an idiot smile.

"Sorry, can't do that," Jack informed him. "I have to give it directly to Officer Reece."

"He could be a while."

"That's fine. I'll just sit over there and wait."

"Suit yourself. But like I said, he's busy."

Jack went over to the bench and sat down, settling in for the long term. Since the guard was making no move to let Kenny know he had a visitor, Jack was preparing himself for a lengthy wait. Then, twenty minutes later, much to his surprise, Mr. Reece appeared.

Jack stood up and the two men shook hands.

"Afternoon, Jack," Kenny greeted him. "How are you?'

"Yeah, good," Jack told him. "How did you know I was here?"

"Pearson let me know you wanted to see me," Kenny informed him. "I also wanted to have a word with you before you left. I asked Officer Murray to let me know when you were here, but apparently, he forgot."

"Oh," Jack answered, sending a quick glance to where that guard had been standing. "Yeah, he forgot all right." Then Jack shrugged it off and focused his attention back on Kenny. "Well, first off, I wanted ta give you this, so you could make sure Leon got it. It's just a woolen hat and some mittens, but they're a gift from a friend."

"Yes, okay. I'll be sure he gets them," Kenny said as he took the parcel. Then he sent Jack a quick searching glance. "I guess you noticed his mood."

"Oh yeah," Jack raised his brows and nodded. "What brought that on? Is it just the 'one year' thing?"

"Partly." Kenny gestured him back into the now empty processing room, where they could sit and talk in some privacy. Then he continued. "The one-year anniversary is hard on many of the inmates, especially the lifers. It seems to be when they start to recognize the reality of their situation. Don't worry about that part of it too much, Jack. He'll get over it, and when he does, he'll be more accepting, and things will get a whole lot easier for him."

"Yeah, okay," Jack felt some relief at that. Obviously, Kenny recognized the pattern. "But you said partly. Has somethin' else happened?"

"Yeah," Kenny admitted. "One of the other inmates, a young fella who was due to get out in six months, well, he died last week."

"Oh. What happened?"

"Pneumonia," Kenny stated. "The thing is, by rights, he shouldn't have died. He was young and healthy; never been sick the whole two years he was in here. He should have been able to fight it off. Nash was looking after him in the infirmary, was with him when he died. He took it hard."

"Aww jeez," Jack groaned, looking toward the door which led into the back hallway. "Why didn't he tell me? Dammit. He mighta felt better if he'd talked about it."

Kenny shrugged. "Who knows? Maybe by not talking about it, he could pretend it didn't happen."

"Yeah," Jack reflected. "I suppose I can remember thinkin' along those same lines myself not too long ago. It don't work."

"No, it doesn't," Kenny agreed. "He cares about people. I've seen so many convicts come through here and most of them don't give a damn about anybody but themselves—especially the lifers. That's why they're lifers; most of them are criminally insane and they can't function out there. But not Nash. I mean, he comes across as being dispassionate, doesn't he? But it's just an act; he really does care about people."

"Yup," Jack agreed. "Losin' that young fella would have been hard on him." Then Jack became contemplative for a moment. "He's also used to bein' in control a things. I guess in here, that control has been taken away from him. Maybe workin' in the infirmary and just havin' a better understandin' of how things are, made him feel like he had some say again, in things that happen around him. Losin' a fella like that; a fella who was young and strong, and, as you say, shouldn't a died in the first place—yup, that would have been real hard on Leon. Always was, losin' a man he feels responsibility for. He takes it personal."

"Yes. I mean, it's obvious, isn't it? He is not insane or antisocial. It kind of makes me wonder why he was given such a harsh sentence," Kenny commented.

Jack smiled. "Yeah, it do, don't it?"

The two men locked eyes for a moment and it seemed to Jack that a whole conversation passed between them. For this to happen between him and Leon was normal, but considering Jack had not known Kenny for very long, it was an unexpected occurrence.

Kenny nodded, then continued with the verbal aspect of their communication.

"I was hoping—again, that since you do know him so well, you might have some insights on how to get him to engage like he did when he was first introduced to the infirmary. He was doing well for a while, and I hoped we'd had it beat, but now he is withdrawing more and more into himself. He's also becoming more violent, just like he was when he first came here. He stopped going to services a while back and now, after what happened to the other inmate, well, he doesn't seem to be getting much satisfaction out of the infirmary anymore either. Bad timing really—that incident happening right on his first anniversary here."

Jack sat quietly for a moment, becoming reflective and thinking back on the Napoleon Nash he knew way back when.

"The problem with havin' a mind like Leon's, is that it needs ta be constantly doin' somethin'," Jack explained. "It needs to have new and challenging problems to deal with or it starts to create its own problems and then gets itself inta trouble."

"Yes, I'd noticed," Kenny emphasized. "I never know what to expect from him. He can be volatile, unpredictable, explosive even, and then at other times, he's thoughtful, inventive and creative. Then, suddenly, he'll turn around and be sullen and moody or, like now, downright depressed. I'm at a loss."

"You can hardly blame 'im, being stuck here," Jack pointed out. "Leon has always been a doer, always somethin' on the go. He can't stand bein' cooped up, and you're surprised he's unpredictable? Even winterin' at Elk Mountain, he kept himself busy plannin' the jobs for the comin' year, otherwise, he'd a gone stir crazy. I know you're tryin' ta help him. Far more than I would have expected anyone here to be willin' ta do. Hopefully, once he's passed this one-year hurdle, he will be more acceptin' a things, like you say. But he is still gonna need things ta challenge 'im, or he's gonna end up retreatin' deeper and deeper into his own mind, just ta escape the boredom."

"I agree. That was mainly why Doc Palin and I worked so hard to get him in at the infirmary. Keep him interested and challenged, and then, hopefully, he would stay out of trouble." Kenny smiled, ruefully. "It partly worked. I had hoped he would find some interest in the lectures that our minister delivers here after services. She's very knowledgeable on many subjects and puts every effort into getting the inmates to engage. But again, he seemed interested at first, then gradually became bored with it all, and eventually stopped attending all together. Dr. Soames herself is feeling frustrated with him."

Jack nodded with understanding. "Maybe a word with Dr. Soames would help. We know her from before, but I don't think she understands how quickly Leon can get bored. She's likely focusing her lectures more for the average inmate.

"Ya gotta understand that Leon really is a genius. I'd always tease him about it," Jack smiled in recollection, "he could be so arrogant sometimes, he needed ta get knocked down a peg or two, or his head would explode. But he had ta understand numbers an' stuff, to pull off a lot of the jobs we did. That is what put us above the average outlaw—if'n ya get my meanin'."

"Uh huh," Kenny nodded. "I remember reading about that robbery in Denver, when Nash blew that state-of-the-art safe without so much as singeing the contents. And to do it, right under the noses of two of the major detective agencies in the country." He smiled in admiration. "That was nothing short of brilliant."

Jack beamed. It always pleased him to hear others recognize his partner's abilities.

Then Kenny's smile dropped as he realized he was condoning an illegal act.

"Umm, hmm," he coughed to cover his indiscretion. "Anyway, Dr. Soames and I have been discussing this situation. Perhaps if I suggest she make the lectures more challenging for him, give him something to latch on to. At least until this mood passes and he finds his footing again."

"Yeah." Jack became reflective, trying to think of alternatives. "Or maybe she could try somethin' completely different. Like I said, Leon is already real familiar with numbers and science and stuff. Maybe he needs somethin' completely new. After all, that's what drew him to the infirmary; medicine was new to 'im, that's what made it challengin'."

Kenny nodded. "All right. Thank you, Jack. I'll discuss this with her and maybe she'll come up with something. She's nothing if not inventive, and tenacious, and determined, and tireless . . ."

Jack smiled. "Sounds like someone else we know."

Kenny laughed. "You're right. We need to get everyone on the same track." He nodded again and stood up. Jack followed. "Thank you again. And now, I'd better get back to work. I'll see that Nash gets his parcel."

"Thanks."

The two men shook hands and parted company.

***

Once Leon was let loose into the prison proper, he decided to head outdoors for a while in the hopes of clearing his head and lifting his spirits. Even before he arrived in the yard, he felt guilty over the way he had treated his partner. Jack made the trip from Colorado every month just to spend one hour talking with him, and then Leon sat there all sullen and moody, and was even downright rude. Dammit! He'd tried to lighten it up at the end, "but too little too late" as they say.

Unfortunately, going outdoors didn't help him feel any better. At least Jack got to leave this place, got to go home, back to a life that meant something. When Jack started talking about events at the ranch, even minor ones, it reminded Leon even more of how he was stuck in here. So now there's David and his wife expecting their first born. Normally, this would be happy news, but here it was just another time piece, ticking away the months, and now, the years.

There was nothing like children to make the passage of time so apparent.

Geez, last time I saw Elijah, the boy was still an infant in arms. Now he's sampling solid foods, making attempts to walk and talk. Jack's like an older brother to him, or an uncle; a member of the family. As far as Eli's concerned, I'm a stranger; a nobody. Just a name that gets mentioned from time to time but had no real substance.

Now David and Tricia are expecting. Well, isn't that nice. I suppose I should be happy for them. But all that is to me is another little time piece coming into the world.

Caroline and Steven are courting and by the way things are going, they'll be betrothed soon. Then married. Then more children will arrive. And time ticks on, and I'll still be here, walking around the perimeter of the territorial prison. Where time stands still.

His shoulders slumped and a deeper sadness entered his eyes. *Why did Billings have to die? God dammit. He shouldn't have died! He was so young; barely twenty, and he was going to be out of here in six months. He had a life waiting for him*—Leon kicked a pebble and watched it bounce across the yard, before it banged into a wooden bench. Deep sigh. He felt responsible.

Mariam had been there as usual, tending to the sick man, helping him through the fever and the coughing and the nightmares. She was so diligent and never left his side.

Then Leon went into the infirmary for his day on the job. He had taken over for her, so she could have some well-earned rest and a meal. He sat by the young man's bedside, holding his hand and keeping the cold compresses caressing his forehead and neck, trying to keep the fever at bay.

Billings seemed to calm down during the late morning. Palin had given him something to ease the coughing and to help him sleep. He really did seem like he had turned the corner and was getting better.

Then, for no apparent reason, the fever spiked again. He became distressed. It seemed to Leon that no matter what he did, the patient would not quiet down and the fever only worsened. Leon thought he knew what to do to break a fever. He'd read all about it in the medical journals. He'd even helped other inmates go through it and come out the other end, just as healthy as before their illness. He'd had all the confidence in the world that he would see Billings through this just as he had the others.

But Billings wasn't improving, and Leon had started to get worried. But when he had just been about to call for Palin, Billings finally calmed down and seemed to be settling. Leon breathed a sigh of relief.

Then, he heard the death rattle and the young man died right there, with Leon holding his hand and staring in disbelief at the silent face upon the pillow. He found himself willing the form to move, to breathe, to do something! He silently pleaded with the man to give any kind of sign at all that life still lingered so Leon would not have to admit he had failed.

This was how Palin found them when he returned to the ward ten minutes later. Leon was sitting beside the bed, staring blankly into space and still holding onto the dead man's hand. Doc came over to them and did a quick check on the patient's vitals, even though one look told him it was already too late. He sighed and put a consoling hand on Leon's shoulder.

"Don't take it too hard, Nash," he tried to comfort his assistant, "sometimes that's just the way it goes."

"But why?" Leon asked in a quiet, shocked voice. "He was young and strong; he should have been able to fight it off. It's like he just gave up."

"There's no rhyme or reason to it," Palin rationalized, "why one person pulls through and another doesn't. I could never figure it out." He started to walk away, mumbling as he went. "Why do ya think I drink so damn much? Could use a fuckin' drink right now, I tell ya. . ."

Leon hung his head, still holding the lifeless hand. Even though Palin hadn't meant it as an accusation, his comment made Leon feel guilty, as he was the one who told Palin to get rid of his stash in the first place. Now, more than ever, he could understand why Palin always had a bottle on hand, because now, more than ever, Leon felt like he could do with a drink, too.

***

Leon stood in the prison yard, staring at the walls and thinking absently about how impossible it would be to scale them. It had nothing to do with the barbed wire that was strung along the tops of them, or with the ever-watchful guards up in the corner towers, with their ever-ready rifles always on hand. No, it was the walls themselves that defied any attempt to scale them. It was like they knew it too, standing there all rigid and stark, towering over the inmates, closing in on them, suffocating them. Laughing at them.

"What ya thinkin' about, convict?"

Leon just about jumped out of his skin. *Dammit. Here I am again, daydreaming and not watching my back. I really do need my partner in here with me. Why am I so bloody stupid all the time?*

He was startled into eye contact, then quickly looked away and down. It was one of the new hires, a younger guard named Thompson. He was a bully in the making and it riled Leon that he had to submit to him, knowing, that in his own element, Leon would have chewed this youngster up and spit him out before breakfast.

"Nothing, sir," Leon answered to the guard's shoes. "Wasn't thinking about anything, sir."

"It sure as hell looked to me like you was thinkin' about somethin'."

"No sir. Just daydreaming."

The end of the billy club caught Leon in the middrift and caused him to catch his breath and stagger, but he didn't go down.

"I don't recall askin' you a direct question. Was that a direct question, convict?"

Leon tried to unclench his jaw and start breathing again when the club came in for another blow because Leon wasn't fast enough to answer the question about it being a direct question. Leon's lips pulled back in rising anger, both at himself and at the guard. Of course, that hadn't been a direct question. The guard had thrown the bait out there and Leon had walked right into the set-up like some green newbie. What an idiot. Surprisingly enough, he kept his anger in check, which was quite a feat considering the foul mood he had already been in.

He answered the "direct question" as meekly as he could.

"No sir, it wasn't."

"Good," Thompson gave mock praise. "I was beginnin' to think you were so stupid you didn't know the difference. A little word of advice; you wanna be out in the yard, that's fine. But don't be standin' around, starin' at the fence like you're makin' plans. You understand me, convict?"

"Yes sir."

"Good. Nice to see ya learnin'."

Thompson sauntered away, swinging the billy club like he was out for a Sunday stroll.

Leon stood where he was, clutching his gut and reprimanding himself for his own stupidity. He really was beginning to lose his mind.

Although, in some ways, having to cow down to that boy did bring some understanding as to how it must have been for Gus Shaffer. All those years ago, in another place and another life, Leon had jumped the queue and taken over command of Elk Mountain. How that must have rankled the older man, who had been in the gang longer and ranked higher while Joaquin Cortez had been the boss. Then that little up-start-know-it-all, with his gun-slinging partner, had decided they were going to run things. The fact that the gang had then prospered better than ever before had only made it a more bitter pill to swallow.

Yup, Leon got a little more insight into how that must have rankled the older man, and now Gus just might be thinking that Leon was getting his just desserts. Or maybe, Leon was just feeling so down on himself that it would stand to reason that everyone else must be feeling the same way about him.

Leon took a deep breath and slowly made his way to the entrance to the cell block, making sure he didn't send a fleeting glance back toward the fences again. Thompson was probably waiting for him to do just that and would love a reason to justify inflicting another beating on the inmate. Leon made sure he didn't give him one.

***

Leon made a quick trip to the kitchen for a coffee, then spent the rest of the afternoon in his cell with the hopes of lifting his spirits with a good book. At least that was the plan.

When he returned to his cell, he noticed a parcel waiting for him. He smiled, remembering now that Jack said he'd brought one. After Kenny had performed the required search and re-wrapping, he had been prompt in delivering it to Leon's cell so it would be ready and waiting for him.

He set his coffee down on his side table, settled into his pillow, and opened the parcel.

Sure enough, it was a hat and mittens, but more socks and a scarf as well. There was also a tin container with some of Jean's wonderful Christmas baking inside. Leon's grin widened; some of those cookies would go perfectly with his coffee.

I'll have to keep these hidden, though I might take some over for the Doc and brighten his mood a bit. These days, we could both use some Christmas Cheer, even if it is a little early.

There was also a thick letter from Jean, which was a nice surprise, as Leon hadn't heard from her for some time. He settled even more into his pillow and got himself as comfortable as his bruised ribs would allow.

I swear, if I ever get out of here, I'll be sporting a permanent array of bruises made by those damn clubs. I don't know why it is, but every new hire or latest transfer just has to prove himself to the boss, and, apparently, their brain capacity can only conceive of one way to do it. He shifted again to ease the aching. *Somehow beating up an inmate goes with the territory. Why can't they hire more guards like Kenny? Although, I suppose, Pearson's not bad . . .*

Once settled, Leon laid the letter out on his drawn-up knees, and with coffee cup in one hand and a tasty Christmas cookie in the other, he began to read.

September 1886

Dearest Peter:

I have been meaning for some time to sit down and write a letter to you, as I'm sure things must get very dreary there. So, finally, this afternoon I have taken some time to do just that. I'm sure I'm only repeating what Mathew has already assured you of, but the truth does not suffer from repetition. Just know that we all miss you very, very much and look forward with anticipation to the day when you can come home and sit around our dinner table again and enjoy this family that is yours.

I'm not sure if Mathew will have told you (since this is hardly news that young men would find of interest) but David and Tricia are expecting their first child, which is due in early spring. Both young people are very excited and insist they can hardly wait for the big day. I can't help but smile to myself at their joy, and think, playfully, that I should loan them Eli for a week just to give them a taste of what they are heading into. But common sense prevails, and I continue to keep young Eli at home. Don't want to scare the new parents-to-be out of their joyous anticipation.

As for Elijah, he is growing in leaps and bounds. I'm sure you would not recognize him, all brown eyes and blonde hair. And mischief. Now that he is crawling, and even attempting to walk, everywhere, nowhere is safe. I am still amazed at how different he is from the girls; so much more of a handful. But thank goodness Penny enjoys him so much, as she does take a lot of the strain off me. And believe it or not, so does Mathew. He has quite a fondness for the boy and will often play with him and even take him for rides around the yard on his ever-patient gelding. In return, Eli loves him to pieces and pesters him, no end.

The ranch is doing all right, and better than most, considering this drought that won't let up, despite the change of seasons. Cameron quit his teaching job some time ago and is focused completely on running this business. He is thinking now that perhaps he was too precipitate in this decision, as the drought has been hard on the range stock and we may not get the price at market that we are accustomed to.

Our hay fields also suffered, and we only got two cuttings off them, rather than the usual three. We'll have enough for our own livestock, but not much left over to sell. Fortunately, our lumber sales have helped. But even at that, Cameron and Penny often spend the evenings with their heads together, going over the finances, just to be sure we'll be all right.

Karma is also doing well and seems to be blossoming with her pregnancy. She is loving all the extra attention that Penny doles out to her and, of course, is happy with the extra feed she is receiving. She is such a lovely mare, Peter, and I can certainly understand why you are so fond of her. Rest assured, she is well looked after here and seems to be quite content with her lot.

Penny will be spending Thanksgiving in Denver with Caroline and your friend Josephine, and is very much looking forward to it. I do hope that Miss Jansen doesn't mind being invaded by our two daughters! She seems to be a very energetic and agreeable young woman, and I'm sure has a life of her own, so having two young maidens suddenly dropped onto her must have been quite a shock.

Still, they do seem to enjoy one another's company, and I have heard no complaints, so hopefully she is all right with the current arrangement. Of course, Penny will stay at the boarding house with Caroline, but I suspect that they will not be spending much time there.

I have invited Miss Jansen to join us out here for Christmas as a way to thank her, and I am hoping she will attend. Another full house!

Dear Peter. I know you must be feeling very frustrated by now that no progress has been made toward your pardon, but please let me assure you that no one here has given up. We are at a bit of a stalemate now, but I'm sure this is just temporary. Goodness knows, whenever Steven is out here, the after-dinner conversation always focuses on you and what the next step should be. Even David gets involved whenever he can.

I must admit though, there are times when I fear for Mathew. He gets frustrated just sitting back and waiting for the legal system to start working. I suppose he is so accustomed to taking whatever measures are necessary to achieve his goal, whether they are legal or not, that having to do things by the book is very infuriating for him.

Cameron, David and Steven (not to mention your friend Sheriff Murphy) have done a lot of talking to him over the months to keep him from giving up his own pardon in a bid to break you out and then head for Mexico! So far, we have been able to keep him focused on our joint goal, but we can all tell that the enforced inactivity is wearing on him.

All I can ask of you, Peter, is that you keep the faith and know that we all love you and that we are still doing all we can to bring about your pardon. And please stay safe. The little that Mathew has told me of your life in that horrid place is enough to send shivers down my spine! Every night, I pray for your continued safety and well-being—and please, keep your strength up. Your illness last winter was a trial for all of us.

Keep safe.
With all my love and warm thoughts,
Jean

Leon sat back with a sigh. He took a nibble of his cookie and a sip of coffee while contemplating Jean's letter. He wasn't sure if it made him feel any better or not. Again, hearing about all the things going on at home was frustrating for him, as it was more reminders of how life was carrying on without him.

But that comment referring to Jack breaking him out, and the two of them disappearing south of the border—that wasn't acceptable.

I'll have a word with him about that, next time we get together. There is no way Jack is going to throw away his life now, in order to save me—that is not going to happen! Leon smirked and shook his head. *Trust him though, to be thinking along those lines. I don't know anyone who is as bullheaded and stubborn as Jack, but he's going to have to learn self-control and patience, and start getting used to doing things the legal way.*

Then Leon groaned as he again regretted his sullen mood during Jack's visit. *It's one thing for me to be feeling this way, but I really need to hide it from Jack. All this stuff is already hard enough on him without me making him feel guilty. This isn't Jack's fault, I know that, but it would be just like him to feel it as such, and that could make him throw all our hard work to the wind, just to get me out.*

His frustration came out in muttered curses.

Why do all these things have to come at me at once? The one-year anniversary was bad enough, but then Billings dying on me. His heart ached with his failure. *I'm no good as a doctor. Ole Doc Palin can get himself another assistant. Yeah. Someone who isn't going to just sit there and let a man die.*

He looked at the letter still in his hand and his jaw tightened.

Now, here's Jean, stating that Jack is contemplating an illegal act to get me out of prison.

He leaned his head back to rest against the propped-up pillow, and he closed his eyes and tried to think.

It's going to be another month before I'll be able to speak to Jack again, and there's nothing I can do about it. Hopefully, other, calmer heads in the group will continue to talk sense to that nephew of mine and prevent him from undertaking such a desperate maneuver. Maybe it's a good thing that the colder weather is approaching. There's nothing like ten feet of snow to put the damper on any escape attempts.

Leon sighed again, finished his cookie, then his coffee, and stretched out, thinking about his next move. He knew he should write to David. Not so much because of his pending state of fatherhood, although Leon would of course offer his congratulations along those lines, but more so, because Leon needed to discuss with his friend what had happened in the infirmary.

Palin, of course, had assured him that it wasn't his fault. Mariam had offered comforting words and solace, but they had all sounded empty to Leon, like they were simply patting him on the head and placating him, as though he were a child who couldn't have helped it simply because he didn't know any better.

Leon was certain that if Dr. Palin had been in the infirmary at the time, then Billings wouldn't have died. Palin, of course, denied this, but Leon still felt it was his own inexperience that had allowed it to happen. For a man who was usually so confident in his abilities, this was a crippling blow to his ego.

So, he would write to David, knowing in his heart that it was simply because he needed reassurance; needed someone whom he respected and admired to tell him that these things happened and that he shouldn't blame himself. Indeed, all the things that Palin and Mariam had already reiterated to him but just didn't seem to mean anything until David said it too.

Then, since Leon was only allowed to write one letter a week, he would include comments to Jean and a lecture to Jack all in the same transcript and instruct David to pass them along.

There! Leon stared up at the ceiling he could see, *kill three birds with one stone, and that'll be everyone taken care of.*

"Convict."

Leon jumped. He tensed, then looking to the door of his cell, he instantly scrambled to his feet. Kenny stood there, awaiting his convenience.

"It's time we had a chat. Follow me."

Kenny turned and walked away, assuming, and rightly so, that the prisoner would do as ordered.

Leon pushed away his confusion and followed the senior guard down to the main level and then into the processing room. It was unusual for Kenny to escort him down into this area for any reason and the fact that they hadn't stopped for the usual shackles caused him uneasiness.

Then he saw his visitor and a smile tugged at his lips, but then concern took over again. "Doctor Mariam . . ." He glanced around at Kenny and instantly felt like he had walked into a trap. Why would Kenny escort him down here to speak with the doctor?

What are they up to?

"Napoleon, please don't be concerned," Mariam assured him, "and I do apologize for disturbing you during your leisure time."

"That's all right," Leon stammered, "it's no disturbance at all. I just wasn't expecting . . ."

Mariam smiled. "I hope you will not be offended when I tell you that Officer Reece and I have been discussing you."

"Discussing me?"

Kenny moved around to stand beside the doctor. Leon glanced at him and then back at Mariam. He fought the impulse to high-tail it back to his cell.

"Yes. We have both been concerned about you," the doctor admitted. "You have stopped coming to services, even though you seemed to greatly enjoy it when you were coming. Especially the singing. You do have a very fine singing voice on those rare occasions when you allow it to come forth."

Leon's awkwardness increased, and he continued to stare at the floor with his hands behind his back, not quite sure what he was supposed to say.

"Ah, thank you," he finally stammered out.

She smiled. "Why have you stopped coming to services, Napoleon?"

"Ahh." Leon stood there with his mouth open, but his silver tongue had gone into hiding. He glanced again at Kenny, but there was no help coming from that quarter. "Ahhmm. I just . . . I, ah, had been given some books that I wanted to read, so was staying here to read them." Even to himself, this sounded lame.

"Really Napoleon, do you think that we haven't noticed your change of mood?" Mariam tutted, shaking her head. "Mr. Reece has suggested we offer you something new and challenging to assist you through this difficult time."

"I don't think that would be necessary—"

"On the contrary, I feel it's a good idea."

Leon sighed with resignation. He was being ganged up on; he could tell. He couldn't help but send a subtle but accusatory glance to the guard.

Kenny chose to ignore him.

Mariam hinted a smile. "Why don't you come and join us at our next service? I can't help but feel that you will be pleasantly surprised."

Leon sent another glance toward Kenny, and a quick, silent conversation took place between them.

Kenny broke eye contact with a slightly raised eyebrow. It was an unheard-of occurrence for a guard to look away from an inmate, but it was Kenny's way of telling Leon that the decision to attend chapel was completely up to him. But the raised brow added, in no uncertain terms, that he better make the right decision.

The left corner of Leon's lip twitched in a slight smile that he tried to hide.

"Yes, ma'am," he agreed. "I will certainly attend the next service. I'll look forward to it."

"Good. I'll look for you there."

With the conversation at an end, Kenny escorted him back to his cell.

The smile dropped from Leon's face as resentment and irritation took over.

Crap. Why can't these people just leave me alone?

CHAPTER TEN
FRIENDS AND ENEMIES

Arvada, Colorado

As soon as Jack stepped off the train in Arvada, he knew something was wrong. When you finally get the chance to put down roots in a place, you slowly begin to get to know it just as you would get to know a new friend. In time, you begin to recognize its moods. It was a subtle shift in the feel of the town when something tragic has happened. A drifter, passing through, might not pick up on it. But Jack was no longer that drifter, and he knew something had transpired while he was away.

He stood on the platform of the train depot and tried to get an inkling of what was wrong. He watched the people moving up and down the boardwalk, going about their daily business, and there was nothing apparent in their moods or expressions to suggest anything amiss, and yet . . .

He furrowed his brow and thought on it for a moment. Where was the best place to go to get information? The sheriff's office was always a good start—well, hadn't been "always" until recently, but now—yeah. Then there was the telegraph office or the mercantile, they generally knew what was going on in town.

Hmm. He walked on. *The telegraph office is the closest, so might as well start there.*

"Hey, Clayt," Jack greeted the man behind the counter. "How's everything goin'?"

"Fine, fine," came Clayt's non-committal answer. "Nothin' for you today though. Ya wanna send somethin'?"

"Nope. Just checkin'," Jack commented. "Anything new in town?"

"Nope," Clayt answered, with a bit of uncomfortable shuffling, "everything's quiet."

"Uh huh," came the suspicious response. "Ya sure?"

"Yup."

"Okay, see ya later," and Jack turned and left the office, much to the relief of the other occupant. Those kinda things, well, men just don't talk about them. That's what women folk are for, dagnabbit!

Accepting that the telegraph office was a lost cause, Jack headed to the sheriff's office. Surely Sheriff Jacobs would know what was up and wouldn't be all squeamish about discussing it.

"Howdy, Sheriff."

"Oh—Kiefer," Jacobs acknowledged him. "You're back, huh?"

"Yeah." Jack looked at him, suspiciously. "What's goin' on? Everything all right out at the Marsham's place?"

"Oh yes, everything's fine out there," Jacobs assured him.

"What then?" Jack was getting frustrated. "I know somethin' has happened, but no one will tell me what."

"It's just not something people want to talk about, is all," Jacobs tried to explain. "You're friends with the doc, ain't ya?"

"Yeah," Jack concurred.

"Maybe you should just go talk to him," Jacobs suggested. "Actually, that might be a real good idea. I'm pretty sure you'll find him in the saloon."

"In the saloon?" Jack questioned. That was odd. David wasn't generally a drinking man. It got Jack a little worried if that's where the doctor was to be found.

"Yup," Jacobs reiterated. "At least, that's where he's been most of this morning, so I expect he's still there. Might not be sober though."

"Right." Jack nodded, and feeling very much on edge now, he left the sheriff's office and headed to the drinking establishment.

It was early afternoon, so the place was still quiet, but one quick glance around at the tables did not produce the desired result. Jack made his way to the bar and waved Bill over

"I was told the doc might be in here, but I don't see 'im,"

Jack explained. "Is he around somewhere?"

"Oh yeah," Bill answered with a nod," he's sittin' at that table over in the corner there. You know, the one that ya can't see from the door."

"The one under the staircase?"

"That's it."

"Okay, thanks."

"Ya want a beer to take with ya?" Bill suggested. "You could be a while. He's got a whiskey bottle with him, but I watered it down before givin' it to 'im. The last thing I need is the doc drinkin' himself ta death in my saloon."

"Oh." Jack frowned. This whole situation was odd. "Yeah, okay."

Jack collected his beer, then headed for the table. Sure enough, there was David, sitting quietly by himself, staring into space with a distant expression on his face. There was a half empty whiskey bottle on the table by his arm, and an empty shot glass still being held in his hand. The whole scene dripped with oppression.

"David?" Jack quietly spoke to his friend as he approached the table. "What's wrong? What's happened? Is Tricia all right?"

David looked up at his friend as though suddenly realizing he was there. He then looked at the whiskey bottle and decided to pour himself another drink.

"Yeah, Trish is all right," he answered, blandly.

"The baby?"

"Baby's fine."

"Well, what then?" Jack asked as he sat down and put his beer on the table without taking a drink. "What's the matter?"

David looked at him with a sad and dazed expression in his eyes. Jack had never seen his friend looking so distraught. It scared him a little. Jeez, first Leon and now David—was it a full moon or something? David always seemed to be so much in control.

"I don't . . . I don't really want to talk about it," David said, then looked away.

"Oh, no ya don't," Jack countered him. "You never let me get away with that and now I'm gonna return the favor. What the hell happened, David?"

David looked at him again, then tears spilled from his eyes and rolled down his cheeks. He gasped in his breath and quickly wiped the tears away.

"Aww, David," Jack whispered. "C'mon, tell me what happened."

David sighed deeply, then relented. "You remember the Robertsons? They were expecting a baby, due right around Thanksgiving."

"Yeah, I know who ya mean," Jack acknowledged. "They have that small spread 'bout five miles south a here."

David nodded. "Two days ago, Wendy started having contractions."

"Eww, that's early." Even Jack knew this wasn't good.

"Yeah," David agreed. He downed his whiskey, then poured another. "I knew as soon as I got there something was wrong—not just that it was early, but something was really wrong. Wendy was in agony; the contractions were strong, and she was bleeding, but nothing else was happening. The other two children were scared and crying, and poor Floyd was beside himself, trying to keep it all together." Down went the next shot of whiskey, and another was poured. David released a deep, shuttering sigh. "Turns out the baby was breech. I've delivered breech babies before, but this one was bad and in distress."

"Breech?" Jack asked quietly, his own beer forgotten. "What's that?"

"Feet first," David explained. "The baby hadn't turned around the way it should for delivery, and it was hung up and not moving. Of course, Wendy was pushing, the contractions were strong, just like they should be, but nothing was happening. I knew we were running out of time; the baby was going to suffocate if I didn't get it out quickly, but the birth canal wasn't wide enough, and I couldn't get in there to maneuver the baby into position. I was preparing to do a caesarian—"

"What's that?"

"It's when the birthing canal is blocked. You make an incision in the woman's abdomen and get the baby out that way. It's an extremely risky procedure for both mother and baby, but—" David shrugged.

"Oh." Jack went a little pale.

The next shot of whiskey went south, and David poured another.

"So," he continued. "I was getting prepared to do this when Wendy screamed and suddenly the baby was born. But it wasn't right. It was small—well, that's not surprising really, considering how early it was, but it had a bluish tinge, so I knew it hadn't gotten enough oxygen. I got hold of him and cleared his mouth and tried to massage his lungs to get him breathing, and he did! You know, he coughed a little and started to squirm and he took a couple of breaths, but then . . ."

"What David? What happened?" But Jack had a dreadful feeling he already knew.

David shook his head and the tears rolled down again.

"He died," David whispered. "One minute I was holding this small, precious little life in my hands, and the next, it was just gone."

"Jeez, David, I'm sorry."

"Then I had to simply set him aside and tend to his mother," David continued. "Wendy was bleeding something awful. She was torn up inside and by this time, she was very weak. Poor Floyd was in shock—he was holding her hand and trying to comfort her, but she had passed out by then. The two other children were screaming. I was doing everything I knew how to do to stop her from bleeding out, but nothing worked." Another shot of whiskey disappeared. "I kept hearing Napoleon yelling at me: 'You're a doctor. You're supposed to save people. Save him!' And I was trying to. I was doing everything I knew how to do to save her." He turned imploring eyes to Jack. "Please tell Napoleon, I really was trying."

"Aw, David," Jack tried to comfort his friend. "Leon didn't mean any judgment on you when he said that. You told me yourself that he was terrified—he was graspin' at straws; at anything. He didn't mean ta imply that you weren't tryin'."

"Yeah. And I was trying."

"And you saved my life, David."

"Yeah," David acknowledged this, then sobbed. "But I didn't save hers!"

Jack felt his heart break. He didn't know the Robertsons very well, but they seemed like a decent enough family. He put a hand on his friend's shoulder and tried to offer what solace he could, but he knew it was far from being enough.

"I lost both of them, Jack," David stated through his tears. "With her husband and her children right there, waiting for me to save the day and to make everything all right. I lost both of them."

Jack sighed. His beer forgotten, he got up and walked to the bar. He returned a moment later with another bottle of watered-down whiskey and a second shot glass. This was going to be a long afternoon.

The two men sat quietly together while David worked his way through his misery. Jack poured himself a drink and re-filled David's glass from the bottle that was already open. Might as well finish that one before starting on the second. At least David lived within walking distance of the saloon, so both men could sit here and get drunk and not have far to sleep it off.

Half an hour later, Sheriff Jacobs entered the establishment. He did a quick scan of the premises, figured they were sitting in the corner and sauntered over to check up on them.

"I see ya found him all right," Jacobs stated the obvious.

"Yeah," Jack answered. "I think we'll just be sittin' here for a while."

"Well, okay," Jacobs answered. "Not going to be any trouble is there?"

"No, Sheriff. No trouble," Jack assured him. "I'll make sure I don't get quite as drunk as he does."

Jacobs chuckled. "Yeah, okay. At least ya know where he lives."

"Yup," Jack concurred. "Does his wife know he's here?"

"She did this morning, but I'll head on over there and let her know he's still here," Jacobs offered. "I'll also let her know you're with him, and she should expect both of you to stagger in together at some point during the evening."

The sheriff tipped his hat, then headed off to accomplish his errand.

Jack sat back and poured them both another drink.

"What if I lose her, Jack?" David suddenly asked, out of the blue.

"What? Lose who?"

"Tricia," he stated. "What would I do if I were to lose her like that? She's my life. I'd be lost without her."

"David, ya can't be thinkin' on it like that," Jack tried to be reasonable. "Look at all the babies you have delivered, and they're doin' fine. Things happen. Like you said, the baby was early and a breech, and there was probably a lot more things wrong with it that you don't even know about. It died so quick after bein' born; it must have had other things wrong with it. Trish is young and healthy; you're gonna have a beautiful baby, just you wait and see."

"I'd rather not have a baby at all, if it's going to mean losing her," David mumbled as he stared off into space. "We were so happy. Finally, a family—Finally. But now . . ." He shook his head. "I'm scared to death I'm going to lose her."

"Yup. I suppose I can understand why you'd be feelin' that way right now. But, ya can't let that hold ya back. Bad things happen and life just ain't fair sometimes, but ya gotta keep on tryin'."

Jack sat quietly for a few moments, wondering if he was giving that pep talk to David or to himself. Goodness knows, he'd been feeling hard done by, lately, thinking that life hadn't handed Leon a fair shake at all, and Jack had been feeling angry about that. But sometimes, ya just gotta keep on pushing.

Jack sighed and shook his head. What happened to the Robertson family did kind of put things into perspective. Not that what was happening with Leon wasn't bad enough, but Jack couldn't even imagine what it must be like to lose your wife and your child like that. Devastating doesn't even begin to describe it.

He remembered back to that first conversation he'd had with Rick Layton while they were in the barn at the Marsham's place. Rick had commented, almost nonchalantly that he had lost his wife and child the same way. Jack recalled stating, even then, that it must have been a tough thing to go through, and Rick had agreed, then promptly changed the subject. Something like that—well, it's just not something you can walk away from.

"C'mon, David," Jack suggested while he poured more whiskey, "what do ya say we have a few more drinks and put all this misery behind us?"

"Yeah, okay."

***

Fortunately, David had a head start on getting drunk, and considering he wasn't normally a drinking man, it didn't take long for him to achieve full intoxication.

Eventually, Jack helped his friend to his feet and they headed for the exit of the saloon. A few of the regular patrons had ambled in by that time, hoping for a couple of beers and some social time before heading for home. Many of them glanced up when the odd couple made their move, but to a man, they all quickly averted their eyes once they saw who it was.

Nobody wanted to acknowledge the tragedy that had taken place; it made for awkward conversation, and though they all felt bad for Floyd, losing his wife and child like that, it really was up to the women folk to do the consoling.

But nobody really knew how to console the doc. On the most part, all the sympathy and kind words went out to the bereaved family, and the doctor who had attended was a non-entity. But now, seeing that doctor—who was well thought of by most of the citizenry—drunk, and being assisted home by his friend, well, it just kind of made everyone a bit uncomfortable.

It was a chilly evening when David and Jack exited the saloon, and though David didn't feel the cold, Jack certainly did. He hurried them along toward the Gibson residence just to get into the warmth again. The stove was going, and lights had been lit, when Jack hauled David up the porch steps, through the front door and into the kitchen.

Tricia was on her feet instantly and came over to help get her husband settled in.

"Thank goodness you're home," she told Jack. "I wasn't getting worried quite yet, but not far from it."

Jack smiled. "He'll be all right. Just needs ta sleep it off."

"Hi babe!" David slurred. "Juss havin' a drink wi' ma' friend 'ere."

"I know, David," she answered. "Do you want anything to eat?"

"Eat?"

"Yes."

"Naw. How 'bout 'nother drink?"

"I think you've had enough to drink, dear," Trish informed him. "Why don't you go lie down?"

"Sure! You join me."

"Not right now. I'll come join you later."

"Oh, okay."

Jack helped Tricia shuffle her husband down to their bedroom, then he left them alone and made his own way back to the kitchen. He poured himself a cup of coffee from the ever-present pot on the stove, then sat down at the kitchen table to await instructions.

Fifteen minutes later, Tricia returned and poured herself a cup of coffee as well.

"He settled in okay?" Jack asked as she sat down at the table with him.

"Yes," she sighed. "I think he was asleep before I got his shoes off."

"Good," Jack answered. "Kinda rough couple a days, huh?"

"Yes," Tricia answered again. "Thank you for watching out for him. I was worried about him until Sheriff Jacobs came by and said you were with him. I knew he would be all right then. Thank you."

Jack smiled. It was nice to be trusted with precious cargo.

"That's okay," he said. "Glad I could be of help. Funny thing is; Leon is goin' through somethin' similar himself, right now."

"Oh? How do you mean?"

"Ya know he's been workin' at the infirmary in the prison."

"Yes," Tricia confirmed. "Hard not to know it. The letters that have been flying back and forth between Napoleon and David on that very topic have been keeping the postal service in business."

"I think it's about to get swamped again," Jack announced with a laugh. Then he became serious at Tricia's questioning glance. "Leon had a young fella up and die on him a while back. He's takin' it kinda hard. I'm hopin' he'll write to David about it, maybe give him some perspective."

"Oh," Tricia responded. "I'm sorry to hear that. It is difficult to deal with. Some doctors get hardened to it and simply don't feel it anymore, but I don't think David is ever going to be one of those. He takes it so personally."

"Yeah. Leon too," Jack agreed. "Maybe it'll do 'em both good ta talk it out between 'em."

"I hope so." Tricia was emphatic. "David has lost patients before, and children are always the hardest. But to lose a newborn and then the mother as well . . . it's going to be a while before he'll be able to look Floyd Robertson in the face again."

"Yeah, I suppose."

She thoughtfully ran a hand across her belly, which was only just beginning to show signs of her own pregnancy—if you looked real hard.

"Bad timing, too," she commented. "He was so excited before, but now, I know he's worried. He tried not to show it, but I can tell. He's scared the same thing is going to happen with us."

"Yeah. He did mention that."

Tricia looked up and met his eyes. "It won't though," she

insisted. "We're going to have a healthy, happy baby, and everything will be fine."

Jack just nodded. It wasn't exactly a topic he was comfortable discussing, but he was doing his best.

Tricia pushed herself away from the table. "I've got some stew I can heat up for supper, and then, of course, you'll spend the night. Your old room is all set up for you."

"Oh, well . . ."

"Jack, now don't be silly," Tricia insisted. "It's dark now, and it's not safe being on the roads alone at night. You know that. Besides, I'm sure David would like your company tomorrow when he wakes up."

Jack smiled. He hadn't been looking forward to the ride out to the ranch by then. Not only was it dark, as Tricia had said, but he'd had a few to drink as well, so the invite to stay in town was tempting. On top of that, to be able to settle into a familiar bed rather than amble over to the hotel, made it even more appealing.

"Yeah, okay."

***

Jack ended up staying with the Gibsons for most of that week, simply because David appreciated his company, and Tricia appreciated his support. Jack also knew that when he headed out on his monthly trip to Wyoming, the Marshams never expected to see him until he showed up. Often, he would stop by to visit Taggard or even go and try to harass the governor, so his arrival back home again was unpredictable.

There was a somber funeral service held for Wendy Robertson and her tiny son, Caleb Floyd, who had only known barely a minute of life. Just about everyone in town who could attend, did. The Gibsons joined up with the Marshams, but David felt uncomfortable, as though he was imposing on the family's time of grief, and he and Tricia did not stay long.

Jack stayed a little longer to visit with the Marsham family, and to talk to Cameron about what was happening with Leon. But nobody lingered. Aside from close friends, who stayed to help the Robertsons deal with life as they knew it now, most families departed early, showing their support by sending out baked goods and prepared meals. Jack returned to the Gibsons' home for a few more days, until David began to find his footing again, and then he too headed for the Rocking M, and everyone began to look ahead to Thanksgiving.

***

A few days after Jack had gone home, a letter from Leon arrived for David, but the good doctor wasn't sure if he was ready to read it yet. He suspected what was going to be in it, and he was afraid that reading about Napoleon's difficulties would cause his own wounds to open again, and he didn't feel up to dealing with all that yet.

Finally, though, his natural compassion for a friend in need won him over, and he settled in to his comfortable armchair, and, with a cup of evening tea by his side, he opened the letter.

David:

I have been sitting here for over half an hour now, staring at this blank sheet of paper, trying to think of what to say and how to say it. How do I even begin? First off, I must ask you to please apologize to Jack for me, as I was in a foul mood when he was here and I very much regret it now. He is good enough to come all the way here to spend time with me and I want him to know I really do appreciate it. Although, knowing Jack, he probably already does know this.

Jean also mentioned in her letter that Jack has been making noises about breaking me out of this hell hole, and both of us then heading for Mexico! She also assured me that everyone else was doing everything they could to convince him otherwise. I just want to include my support to your endeavors. Goodness knows, I would give just about anything to get out of here, but my nephew's pardon is not one of those things. So, if you have to tie him down and gag him to prevent him from acting irrationally, you have my permission to do it. You may also feel free to inform him that I said so!

Also, I would appreciate you sending my thanks to Jean for the wonderful Christmas gifts she sent, they will be put to good use, for sure. The cookies were certainly a delightful change from prison food, and are already gone.

I also want to offer congratulations, as I hear that you and your wife are expecting a new addition to your household. I'm sure you are both very excited at the prospect of becoming parents, and I have no doubt you'll be a natural at it.

At this point, I am almost tempted to close the letter off and leave it at that, but then I will berate myself for being a coward and have to wait another week before being able to write to you again. So . . . here goes.

I'm hoping Jack told you what happened here, as I really don't feel up to going into details about the incident, and knowing Kenny Reece (one of the guards), he filled Jack in on it all anyway. Let it suffice for me to say that a young man who was in my care passed away from pneumonia a couple of weeks back, and I suppose I'm having a hard time accepting it.

I certainly don't presume to be any kind of a doctor, and certainly not one of your caliber, but I thought I had learned enough to be able to help someone get through a fever. Goodness knows, I've spent many a sleepless night helping Jack get through his bouts of illnesses over the years, and this was before doing any studying up on the subject.

How is it that I could have lost someone so easily? He was a young man, David! Young and strong, and before the fever hit him, healthy. What did I do wrong? Palin insists that it wasn't my fault; that there often is no apparent reason why one person will survive and another not, but I still can't help but feel I should have been able to do something.

At this point, I'm feeling like I should just stay out of the infirmary, that Dr. Palin should find himself another assistant. I don't think I'm any good at this. I'm used to things working the way they're supposed to work. With dynamite or nitroglycerin, you know what you're dealing with; you do things a certain way and certain things happen. When you follow a mathematical calculation, the end result will always be the same, and if it's not then you did something wrong. So, what did I do wrong?

Anyway, I'm running out of paper, so I guess I should wrap this up. I feel kind of silly burdening you with this nonsense. I am sure you are shaking your head at my incompetence and thanking the fates that I'm not a licensed practitioner, going around and letting people die from the most common of illnesses. I just don't understand what I did wrong.

N.N.

David sighed and stared off into space for a few minutes, thinking about what he had just read. Napoleon's feelings of inadequacy really brought home to him how he himself had been feeling about his own recent failure. Far from opening up those wounds and bringing forth the pain again, seeing those feelings written out in black and white, actually helped to clarify things in his own mind and to deal with them more realistically.

Obviously, Napoleon was feeling lost, and his self-confidence had taken a beating. The fact he had repeated numerous times, his insistence that he had done something wrong, indicated how deeply he was feeling remorse over it. In fact, Leon's feelings so perfectly mirrored his own, David knew that responding to his letter would be a healing process for himself, as well.

Having realized this, David also realized it was not something to be taken lightly, so he decided to leave the letter for now and allow himself to sleep on it. In the evening of the following day, he would settle himself at the table and do some soul searching for himself, and thereby, hopefully, help to heal them both.

***

Napoleon:

My dear friend, your letter could not have come at a more appropriate time for me. I am glad you plucked up the courage to write it, not only for your own sake, but for mine as well. I recently lost a young woman and her infant during childbirth, and I found myself in a depression, filled with the same self-doubts you have expressed in your own narrative. So, please understand and appreciate that what I say to you now comes from my heart and is what I know to be true but still need to reiterate to myself at times like this.

Though pneumonia is a common enough ailment these days, especially for those who are already weakened by their circumstances, it is never a sure thing that the person suffering from it will survive. I know Jack has had bouts with this infection in the past, and has always come through it, largely due to your insistence that he do so, but there are many young and strong individuals who do not.

Your patient could have had any number of health problems before developing this infection, that you knew nothing about. He could already have had weak lungs, or a heart condition that would easily have gone undetected until such a time as this. I know you blame yourself, but please try not to—easier said than done, I know, but you must keep in mind that a human being is not a stick of dynamite, nor a mathematical equation. There are way too many variables to accurately predict how a patient is going to respond to treatment. Your friend, Dr. Palin, is correct; there is no way to tell who is going to survive an illness and who isn't.

Why did my patient bleed to death? She'd had two previous children with no problems; she was healthy and strong. There was no logical reason for it, but nonetheless, we buried her and her infant son last week, and I have to live with the fact that her husband is now without his wife, and his two surviving children are without their mother. Believe me, I felt like packing my bags and heading for Alaska where I wouldn't have to look that family in the eye again!

But, of course, this was impractical. I am a doctor, it is what I love to do and I will keep on doing it. Besides, I don't think Tricia would let me go anyway.

You seem to have shown an aptitude for helping people in the infirmary, and I'm sure Dr. Palin would greatly miss your assistance if you insist on leaving that position. I hope that you do not. You cannot allow this one failure, which indeed, was not a failure at all, to push you away from something you obviously take pleasure in doing. And if it helps you to stay sane in that insane place, then all the more reason to stay with it.

It was not your fault, Napoleon; you did not do

anything wrong! Please believe me when I say this, and keep in mind that I am saying it to myself just as much as I am to you. Somehow, if you don't believe it, then I won't either, and we both need to believe it! Okay? I am asking you for my own benefit as well as yours that you accept what I am saying, and that you pick yourself up and get back to it.

As for your other requests, I will indeed let Jack know you regret your mood when he was last there. I also agree that, knowing Jack, he already knows you meant nothing by it, and far from having to forgive you, never took any insult from it in the first place. Still, even if unnecessary, an apology is never wasted.

"I'm not sure if I'm willing to make an attempt to tie him down, though. Even with a stiff shoulder, he is still the fastest gunman I have ever seen. But rest assured, those of us here will continue to impress upon him the importance of patience, and that he must not take the law into his own hands. Indeed, from what conversation I have had with him on this topic, he has indicated that he is well aware of the foolishness of such an attempt and that you would not go for it anyway. I don't believe you need to concern yourself about it, nor to expect a rescue from that quarter.

I agree, Jean's Christmas cookies are the best I have ever tasted (don't tell Tricia)! I am sure that once I tell her your supply is already gone, she will get busy and bake you some more—which also means more for the rest of us. I am also glad that she knitted you some more clothing, as I am sure the winters get terribly cold in that place.

Be sure to eat a lot, even if you don't feel hungry, eat as much as you can. And stay as warm as you can, and by all means, stay as dry as you can! As I'm sure you are aware, especially now, pneumonia cannot be taken lightly; so stay healthy.

Parenthood! Yes! What a terrifying, but glorious event. I have delivered many babies and have always been thrilled by the arrival of new life, but I never once considered the overwhelming changes that come into one's life once that new little bundle arrives. I must admit to being scared to death, especially now, after what happened, for the well-being, not only of my wife, but also of our child. And now Jean tells me that those feelings of absolute terror only increase once the little creature is out and walking about. How will I ever survive this?

Still, I am thrilled and am pushing my fears away so as not to let them ruin this amazing experience. Tricia really is glowing, and despite some queasiness during the mornings, is wonderful and happy, and we are both so looking forward to being parents.

Though I have noticed that Jean tends to laugh whenever we comment on this. I don't quite understand why.

I will close off now, Napoleon. I hope this letter helps you to find your footing again, and that you continue to do whatever you need to, to stay sane and safe and healthy. It seems inappropriate somehow, to wish you a Happy Thanksgiving and a Merry Christmas, but I do so anyway, in the hope you will keep them in your heart as we all do you—on those days, as on all days.

Take care.

David

David folded the letter and got it prepared to send off with the next mail run in the morning. He hoped it would help his friend get back to his usual level of self-assurance, and that it didn't come across as too preachy. He knew he could be a pest sometimes; everyone told him so. But that was the problem with caring about people so much; it was difficult to back off and let them find their own way. Especially when they can be as stubborn and bull-headed as . . . well . . . stubborn.

Trish had retired to bed some time ago, so with the night closing in and cooling off, David shut down the stove, took the light and made his way to bed.

Tomorrow was another day.

***

Laramie, Wyoming,

Fall 1886

Leon grumbled. His mood had not improved and though he put in his time at the infirmary, he felt like he was imposing, like he really had no business being there.

Palin was supportive and kept him busy doing menial tasks until his self-confidence had a chance to re-assert itself. He knew it would; Leon was far too egocentric and vivacious for it not to. It would take time, but Leon had a lot of that on his hands.

Still, when Sunday rolled around, all Leon wanted to do was sit in his cell and read. He did not want to go to services. He did not believe in the doctrine, and the pleasure he once found listening to Mariam's lectures had been replaced by irritation. He found the lectures boring and elementary, though he had to admit he did enjoy the singing. Still, he was in no mood for song and would probably just sit in the back row and send out dark vibes to anyone within range. So, why bother?

He decided he was going to skip the sermon, even though he had promised to go. He was fed up with being told what to do by everyone around him, and it was time he made a stand. He was going to do exactly what he felt like doing; sit in his cell and read.

Then a guard appeared at his open door, and Leon looked up to meet Kenny's eyes. Briefly

Dammit! Doesn't that man ever take a day off?

"Convict. Follow me."

Leon felt his jaw tighten, but he knew better than to snap at the hand that fed him. He reluctantly got to his feet and did as instructed. He had no choice now; he had to go. So off to the common room he went.

Kenny stayed with him long enough to make sure he got seated and settled in, then sent him a look that told him he better stay put. Once satisfied, the guard turned on his heel and walked away to carry on with his other duties.

Yeah, fine for him. He can just leave. But I have to sit here and listen to this rhetoric whether I want to or not.

He crossed his legs and his arms, and scowled at no one. He was determined to be miserable.

Mariam soon arrived at the makeshift pulpit and began her sermon. She had such a manner about her when speaking to the assembly that each convict was sure she was speaking to him alone.

She made her sermons rousing and sometimes rambunctious, filled with tidbits of humor and references to everyday occurrences. She often quoted from well-known authors of the day and used examples from their adventurous stories to make her point more plausible. Indeed, if Leon hadn't already decided to stay in his foul mood, he might have enjoyed himself.

Then Mariam did something new, and Leon couldn't help but have his interest sparked. She brought out a victrola and set it up on a desk so the sound would carry throughout the room. Everyone who wished to stay after services and listen to it were welcome to do so.

Leon enjoyed music when he could get it, but there hadn't been too much opportunity to indulge in that pastime in the lifestyle that he'd led. So, seeing the victrola being set up and the discs prepared to send forth their melodious tones, he found himself sitting up straighter and leaning forward in anticipation.

Then it happened. Mariam Soames made an introduction that Leon would never forget simply because of the whole new world it opened for him in such an unexpected manner.

"I am now going to play for you a violin concerto in D major, by Pyotr Tchaikovsky."

The music began. Music that was grainy and tinny at best, but still glorious and impossible, washed over Leon. It enveloped him, stimulating his senses in a way he could not have imagined. He had never heard a violin played in such a manner before, would never have thought it possible The notes were so strident. So harsh and grating on the nerves, and yet wonderful and overwhelmingly chaotic.

How is it that an instrument could be pushed to such ear-shattering heights and yet be so soothing to the soul? His heart raced when the tempo plunged ahead and soared with the floating lace of the bow, then the crazy notes would jump in again and spiral you down to the depths. Then catch you and bring you back up to the height of ecstasy, to leave you floating in the clouds; your senses aware only of the music in your mind.

Leon sat and listened to that concerto being played on that old victrola and pictured himself hearing it the way it should be heard. Being played the way it should be played. Inside his vivid imagination, he could easily see himself buying tickets for himself and his friends: Jack, David, and probably Steven too. Of course, Steven and David were each accompanied by a woman, which made sense. But then his own thoughts surprised him; he and Jack also had a lady on each of their arms. Though Jack's companion looked surprisingly like Penny, his own lady was shrouded in mystery. Perhaps it was Gabriella, but no, it didn't feel like her. Maybe she was just a ghost, a hint of what might have been, but he was happy to take her for now.

They would go and listen to Tchaikovsky. To listen to his music the way it was meant to be listened to—being played by the Vienna Symphony Orchestra using instruments of the finest quality in the large, acoustically designed auditorium in Denver.

That would be heaven, sitting back in his cushioned seat, with eyes closed, fingers laced, and a small smile playing about his lips. That was where he was meant to be; that's when he would truly be at home. He was surrounded by his friends and family, by those who had helped him to find his way back from the abyss, and he would be happy again. Happy and content. And he would remember back.

Remember back to that day in the common room of the Wyoming prison when Dr. Mariam Soames introduced him to the most wondrous sounds he'd ever heard; sounds and notes and melodies that would stay in his mind and keep him sane. In those times when the loneliness, the fear, and the pain of his existence would become almost too much to bear, he could let his mind disappear into that music, sending him to someplace else where he was free.

Leon went back to Sunday services just about every week after that. Dr. Soames brought in other recordings of the classical masters: Beethoven, Mozart, Bach, and Chopin. But Tchaikovsky remained his favorite, and given the chance, he would sit for hours and listen to the violin and piano take his reality away for just a little while.

To give Leon even more incentive to keep on coming back, Mariam decided to give him something a little more challenging for his intellect than her normal lectures could offer.

One Sunday, after the service was completed, she once again had Kenny escort Leon to the processing room, and, once again, that inmate was instantly suspicious of a conspiracy. He couldn't help feeling awkward with Mariam being so intent on singling him out and not allowing him the option of sinking into despair.

"Napoleon," she greeted him with a warm smile. "I trust you

got something out of the sermon today."

"Oh, yes, ma'am," Leon answered her.

She cocked a brow at him. "You're back to calling me ma'am."

"Oh. Sorry. It seems more appropriate, considering."

"Considering that we're friends?"

Leon looked at the floor. "But you're also the preacher-lady. Whether I agree with what you say or not, there is still a certain etiquette to be observed."

A sadness floated down over Mariam's features. She ignored protocol and set a reassuring hand on his arm. "But we are still friends. Please don't lose sight of that."

Leon met her eyes and a smile twitched his lips. "Yes, ma'am."

Mariam sighed, but accepted what she could get. "So, what did you take away with you from the lecture this time? And don't hold back; say what you think."

"Oh. Ummm." Leon had to think about it for a minute. "Well," he began, with an air of sincerity, "that apparently even Christians enjoy sex, ma'am."

Kenny rolled his eyes. Well, she had asked for it.

The doctor's smile broadened.

"Yes. You're right," she laughed. "That is certainly one way of looking at it."

"Oh. Yes, ma'am." And Leon smiled back.

"I thought I might offer you another opportunity to exercise that rather brilliant mind of yours," she informed him, and Leon tried to look serious again. "Dr. Palin tells me you like to play with words, and that you easily retain most of the complex medical information you read in the journals he loans you. Obviously, you have quite the thirsty intellect."

"Ahh, yes, ma'am." Leon creased his brow, not sure where this was going.

"She reached into her pocket and brought out a single, folded sheet of paper.

"I thought I might help you to quench that thirst and perhaps have a bit of fun at the same time," she explained. "If you would like, I can give you a new word every week, and then the following week, you can return the word to me with the definition and a sentence with that word being used. Does that sound like something you might find interesting?"

"I don't know," Leon admitted, having been caught flat-footed. "If I don't know the meaning of the word, how am I supposed to use it in a sentence?"

Mariam smiled. "There-in lies the challenge, Napoleon. You must use your resources to discover the definition."

"Oh, I see," Leon smiled.

Mariam offered him the folded sheet of paper and, accepting it, Leon opened it up to look at the word written on the top of the page: *'Impecunious'*.

"Im-pec-u-ni-ous," Leon sounded the word out. Both he and Kenny looked confused. "What does that mean?" Leon asked, then laughed. "Oh. Ha, ha. Right."

"Next week, after service, I expect you to be able to tell me what it means. Have fun with it, Napoleon."

"Yes, umm hmm," Leon nodded. Looking down at the word and rolling it around in his mouth a few times, he didn't even notice that Mariam had left until Kenny touched him on the arm to escort him back to his cell.

***

That evening after supper, Leon lay back on his cot with an arm behind his head and looked up at the ceiling without really seeing it. David's letter lay open on his side table and Leon contemplated the words of comfort and support his friend had sent him. He had to admit they did make sense, and if David himself, who was about the best doctor Leon had ever come across, could lose a patient for no apparent reason, then who was Leon to think he should be able to do better?

He also appreciated the ingenious way David had turned things around to put the responsibility onto Leon to help both of them recover from their similar experiences. It kind of made them equals; each helping the other, rather than David coming across as superior and the one who was in control. Leon always knew David was a smart man.

David was right, of course; Leon did enjoy working in the infirmary. There was the constant learning curve which Leon found exciting, and it was also satisfying to some degree, to see how medical techniques were applied, and how they generally worked.

Now he had even more incentive to carry on in the infirmary; Dr. Palin and his stash of books were about the only resource he could think of to help define new words.

David could probably help him, but a week wasn't long enough to send a letter to him and get the response, so he would have to rely on resources that were at the prison. Leon smiled; he was feeling better already. This was going to be fun.

Then Leon sighed when he again allowed the dark cloud to over-shadow the silver lining.

A year in the life.

He still found it difficult to wrap his mind around the fact that he had been in this place for a year. Part of it seemed as though it was just yesterday when he had first arrived and received his instruction on what the rules were. Then, another part of him felt as though he'd already been here for an eternity; that his previous life was just a dream.

It didn't seem logical that these walls could contain him. It felt as though he should be able to simply walk out the front gate and leave here whenever he wanted to, just like Jack did. *So why can't I do it? Why can't I just leave?* Then he gave a soft huff. *Maybe it has something to do with the locked doors and all the guns pointed in my direction.*

Yet, it didn't seem real to him. It felt like a nightmare; a dream-scape. But it was one that he was trapped in, and all the conning and silver-tongued bantering wouldn't give him the golden key that would unlock the nightmare and ultimately allow him to escape.

He sighed and shifted a little to get more comfortable. It was starting to get chilly at nights again, and he contemplated getting up and pulling on his sweater, then decided against it for the moment.

He reflected on this past year, on all the things that had come and gone that made the days turn into weeks, the weeks into months, and now, that big leap of the months dragging into years.

He thought about the friends he'd made here—something he never had anticipated before his arrival. Who would think that one could actually make friends in prison? But he had.

Hmm, let's see. I suppose Kenny is the oddest example. A guard? Leon snorted. *That doesn't seem likely. But are we friends? No, not really. Allies? Hmm, again; no, but—well, maybe. A comrade in arms, perhaps; standing on opposite sides of the line, but living under a truce? Maybe, again. But I do trust him, and in here, that means a lot.*

Doc Palin? Yes. He has become a friend, and a mentor. He certainly isn't someone I would normally be drawn to on the outside, but in here, yes. We're two opposites being drawn to each other in order to join forces. Yeah, there's a bond between us now, all right; a bond built on trust and mutual respect. Palin doesn't treat me like a prisoner; he treats me like an equal, and I suppose, I do the same back.

Doctor Mariam is, most definitely, a friend. But then, we know each other from before. Still, she hadn't turned away when she learned my identity. In fact, she seems to be working harder at keeping me interested. He frowned, his eyes narrowing to slits. *Maybe she's working too hard at it.* He rubbed his eyes, and, with a definitive grumble, he shook away those thoughts. *She is a friend, and a good one, too. Stop being such a cynic! Besides, if Doc Palin is to be believed, it was she who had pulled me through that illness.*

So yes, most definitely, a friend!

My enemies are a lot easier to identify. He chewed his lip as he contemplated that sorry lot. *Carson is the biggest thorn in my side. There is no telling what that man is going to do. I always get the shivers when he gets too close to me. The man enjoys being a bully. Outside of this place, I could deal with him. I've put more than one bully in his place, and they know not to mess with me. But in here? Ha. In here, Carson holds all the cards, and he knows it. That makes him more dangerous than anybody else. Myself included, if I must be honest.*

Murray, Davis, and Pearson, well, hmm, they're more like non-entities. They're too junior to have any real power. It's who's giving the orders that dictate what actions those three would take. They're not bad fellas; they're just working for a living, like the other junior guards. I remember one of them, hmm, can't remember which one now, had given me and Jack extra time during one of our visits, because Jack had obviously been feeling the need to talk. Although Murray does tend to be a bit of a toad-licker. Oh well.

Thompson! Leon grimaced. *Now there's a young man worth watching out for. Another one who obviously hired on as a guard so he'd be able to exercise his need to beat on people, without ending up behind bars himself. I dread to think what life could become if he and Carson decided to buddy up. Jeez—no self-respecting inmate would be safe.*

And, of course, Boeman and Harris cannot be counted out. Just because they've backed off for now doesn't make them harmless. Boeman isn't going to accept the fact that I trampled him into the dirt. Sooner or later, that bastard will be after his own form of retaliation. I'll have to keep my eyes on those two.

As for Harris, that man isn't right. He's got a look in his eyes, like Lobo, but worse. Lobo only gets that crazy glint when he smells blood, but Harris has it all the time. I don't know what he's in for, but I do know he's over in North Cell Block, the one reserved for the real bad cases. Hmm. I wonder why I'm not over there. Ha! Probably because Mitchell wants me to think I'm special. Ha! That ass.

And, speaking of the warden. Leon rolled his eyes. *Well, if ya gotta have enemies, ya may as well start at the top.*

Leon still threw tidbits at the man, but he could tell the warden was losing patience. He probably knew Leon was just playing him, and Leon wondered what would happen the first time he got wind of something really important but kept the information to himself.

Yeah, but then, what would happen if I got wind of something important, and I snitched?

Another sigh. This time, he did get up to pull his sweater on.

I wish I had more cookies.

It was getting dark inside the prison now, though the lights in the aisle were still lit, and it would be a while yet before the nighttime lockdown. The prison was quiet, just the occasional cough floating up from somewhere, and the ever-present footsteps of a guard making the rounds.

Leon considered lighting his own candle but decided to save it for when he felt like reading or writing a letter. He settled onto his cot again and allowed his mind to wander. Much safer to do that in here than out in the yard.

I don't have to watch my back when it's lying on the cot.

Yes, he had made enemies in here, but he knew who they were. And he knew who his friends were as well, and that was equally as important. He had learned the rules, and he had learned how to circumvent them. He had also learned how to manipulate the punishments as a means to an end. How to use them to send out the message loud and clear that he was a force to be reckoned with, that he was someone to be feared. He'd learned how to weigh the pros and cons; knowing that if he broke any of the rules, then he could expect certain punishments, then to decide if accepting the punishment was worth breaking the rule.

It was a game of strategy and Leon played the game well. He still knew how to exact his own form of retribution on other inmates if they got on the wrong side of him, but the longer he was here, the fewer times he had to do it.

The other inmates got the message and left him alone.

The year had been quite a learning curve for the ex-outlaw leader, but he had learned the rules and the subtle strategies, and he had learned them well. And even though, through his own bull-headedness and his strong sense of loyalty he would suffer the indignities of other punishments, it would be some time before Napoleon Nash found himself in the dark cell again.

But when that time came, it would not be for breaking any of the rules. It would not be for fighting, or for talking back to a guard. The next time Napoleon Nash found himself in the dark cell, it would be for revenge.

CHAPTER ELEVEN
GROWING PAINS

School for Waywards and Orphans, Laramie
November 1886

Mariam sat at her small desk in her sparse room at the orphanage, contemplating a very odd letter. She wasn't sure what to make of it, and she had a feeling there was more to it than what was written on the sheet of paper.

> *Dear Doctor Soames:*
>
> *My name is Penelope Marsham, and I am a friend of both Jack and Napoleon, as I believe you are.*
>
> *I am interested in writing an exposé on prison life, but of course, going through official channels would be self-defeating. I'm sure the warden would only show me what he wanted me to see, if he allowed me into the prison at all.*
>
> ~~*Mathew*~~ *Jack has spoken of you often and with a great deal of respect, so it occurred to me that you might be willing to escort me into the prison in the guise of a novice. In this way, I would be safe from harm, but I would also be able to get a more realistic view of what life is like for the prisoners. From what I have heard from Mathew about conditions in that horrid place, I think it is time for the system to be challenged and hopefully some reforms put into place.*
>
> *I am much older than I look, so it would not appear out of place for me to be a novice under your guardianship, and I am quite willing to accept responsibility if by chance I am found out. I feel that this*

is very important and that someone must step up and do something about what goes on behind locked doors!

I would also appreciate you not mentioning this to either ~~Peter~~ Leon or Jack. For one thing, I don't want Peter to feel uncomfortable, knowing that I was there and watching him, since I would hardly be getting a true experience of prison life if that were the case. He would try to sugar coat it to protect me, and that is not the idea at all!

Jack would try to prevent me from going in the first place, and again, though it would be out of a desire to protect me, it can be quite infuriating sometimes!

They first came to know me as a young girl, and I think that neither one of them can get used to the idea that I am now an adult and quite capable of making decisions for myself. So please, if you are agreeable to helping me with this undertaking, I again ask that you not discuss this with either of my friends, as I know they would both try to hinder me.

I will be in Denver, Colorado for Thanksgiving, so if you would be so kind as to send me your response in care my friend, Miss Josephine Jansen, who resides in Denver, then I will be sure to receive it. If you are agreeable to my request, I would like to meet with you shortly after that holiday, as I really feel it is important to start my investigation as quickly as possible.

Yours sincerely,
Penelope Marsham

Mariam sat for some time contemplating this letter. As mentioned before, she honestly did not know what to make of it. Obviously, the young woman was a friend of both Jack and Napoleon and cared about what Napoleon was going through.

Meriam smiled at the young woman's attempt to use her friends' proper names. It seems there were still those who thought of them as anything but outlaws.

Still, her request that the Doctor not inform either of them of her intentions set off some quiet alarm bells.

The only thing that stopped her from disregarding the letter altogether was the fact that she found conditions at the prison difficult to ignore, and it often pained her to see the suffering that was inflicted upon the inmates. She had thought of raising a protest on some of the injustices she had witnessed there, but she feared if she did so, she would not be permitted to return, and that was not acceptable. She truly felt, and rightly so, that her work in the prison infirmary was important and she was needed there. So, she carried on and played by the rules and tried not to see the things she saw.

Now, this letter had arrived. Part of her wanted to play it safe and refuse to assist this young woman in her quest. But another part was getting tired of playing it safe and that here, possibly, was someone who, with just a little help from her, could make a difference.

Mariam decided she would think on it awhile—but not too long, as the Thanksgiving holiday was fast approaching, and Miss Marsham would need her answer soon. But the morning would still be soon enough, and Mariam set the letter aside and prepared to settle in for the night.

***

"Hey, Doc, what does *impecunious* mean?"

"Impecunious?"

"Yeah."

"How the hell should I know?"

"Well, you're an educated man."

"Who the fuck told you that?"

"You're a doctor."

"And I got my training from the school of hard knocks. I might have been drunk, but I do know I told you that much. I had a hard enough time, learnin' medical terms, why the fuck would I go outta my way to learn what impec . . . whatever, means?"

"Oh." Leon was disappointed. "Any idea how I could find out?"

"Hell. I donno." Then Palin sighed and forced himself to think about it for a minute. "Why don't ya try the dictionary? They got lots of words in there that don't mean anything."

"Yeah," Leon agreed. "You got one?"

"Nope."

"Any ideas where I could find one?" Leon was getting

frustrated.

"How about the library?" Palin answered with a touch of sarcasm. He didn't know why Leon's request for information irritated him, but it did. Maybe it was because the inmate was always asking for information, always wanting to learn more, and it tended to make the Doc feel a little intimidated. But, of course, he wasn't going to admit that.

"Yeah," Leon agreed again. "It's just that the library here doesn't have much in it, and I don't recall seeing a dictionary there."

Palin sighed again. Obviously, this wasn't going to go away. "Okay, what about that lady chaplain or doctor or whatever she is? She's all high-educated; there's a pretty good chance she'd know what it means."

Leon's shoulders slumped. "Yeah, I think it's a pretty good bet she does."

"Well then, there ya go." And Palin moved off to tend to other duties, thereby ending the conversation.

***

That evening, after supper, Leon ambled over to the far wall of the common room where the small library was housed. He did a quick survey of the books on the shelf, and, to his surprise, did come across a dictionary. Then, to his disappointment, it was quite elementary and didn't help to further his education any more than Doc had.

He sauntered back to his cell and settled in for the evening. He sat down on his cot and, with knees drawn up and chin resting upon a hand, he contemplated his options. He could think of numerous ways to discover the meaning of the word, but they would all take time, and his time was running out.

Kenny was the best educated man amongst the guards, and he didn't know what it meant. Leon sure wasn't about to ask Carson, even if he did get an opportunity to talk to the man without ending up covered in bruises.

Hmm, what to do? Leon had to admit, he was stumped on this one, at least for the time being. He focused on setting his mind onto other matters.

Unfortunately, by the time lights out and lockdown came about, Leon was still stuck on his word and couldn't get his brain to leave it alone. He was angry with himself. Not because he didn't know the meaning, but because here he was, once again, with his mind running amok and not listening to him when he told it to please shut down for the night.

Later, after lights out, Leon lay in bed and for the first time that season, he began to shiver under his blanket. It was definitely getting colder, and he realized if he was going to get any sleep at all, then he better make the effort now to layer his clothing. The temperatures during the night were only going to get chillier and his friends' requests that he stay warm and well fed during the winter months was starting to have an impact on him.

He pulled on his sweater, his socks and his new knitted toque and settled back into bed.

Now I'm too warm. Humph.

Off came the toque and down went the blanket.

There, that's better. He'd probably be pulling the blanket up again in a few hours and he kept the toque close by, but for now, he'd found a happy medium.

He closed his eyes as his thoughts wandered back to his nephew and his regret over his mood during their last visit. He hoped Jack would be able to get back to see him at least one more time before the weather really closed in. He'd be sure to make the next visit more enjoyable, because he didn't want Jack worrying about him all winter long.

Leon thought back to the previous winter and how miserable he had been when he thought his nephew had turned his back on him. How relieved he was when Jack finally made the trip out to come and see him. Since then Leon realized he had, at times, taken Jack for granted, and he had to remind himself to keep on reminding himself that Jack made quite a long, and surely by now, boring trip to come and visit him.

I need to let him know how important that is. Maybe I'll ask him for a dictionary for Christmas. Hmm . . . there's a thought.

***

After breakfast the following morning, Murray came and got Leon for his annual trip to "the other side of the tracks" so he could report any discoveries to the warden. All the way through the proceedings of being searched and shackled and then escorted down the hallway, Leon was busy racking his brain for anything of use, but not of any real importance, to tell the warden. Nothing came to mind.

Once he found himself in the warden's office, he was still trying to dredge up something, and the skeptical expression on Mitchell's face wasn't helping.

"Are you quite sure you have nothing to report—again?" the warden asked.

"Yes sir, Warden. All's quiet," Leon insisted, then shrugged with the unimportance of it and began scanning the bookcase along the side wall. "Well, except for the usual—you know."

"No, Convict. I don't know," Mitchell snapped. "That's why you're here. To keep me informed of what's going on. Remember?"

"Oh, yeah," Leon mumbled, moving his eyes away from the books. He hadn't spotted a dictionary yet. He sighed. "Well . . . let's see . . . Carson beat up on Johnston the other day, 'cause Johnston tripped over a broom that MacIntosh had just finished trimming, and the handle broke. So then Mac got mad and took a swing at Johnston, but missed and ended up hitting Thompson, and Thompson fell over backwards and knocked into a work table, spilling tobacco all over the floor, and then Harris, whom I believe is allergic to tobacco, started sneezing and his eyes were watering, so he couldn't see what he was doing and ended up tripping over that same, now broken, broom handle and bumping into Carson, who then got pushed over into—"

"Yes! Yes! All right!" Mitchell stopped the avalanche of descriptive narrative. "Anything of importance? Were you ever able to get into Dr. Palin's medical cabinets? Have you found anything suspicious over there?"

"Oh. No sir, Warden," Leon lied. "I checked all those cabinets, like you said, but I never found nothin'."

"I find that most odd," Mitchell commented, irritably. "I know the man is drinking on the job, I just don't understand why you haven't found any evidence. Unless, of course, you're covering up for him."

"Honest to goodness, Warden, since you told me to keep an eye out for Doc drinkin', I haven't seen him put liquor to lips even once."

"I find that most odd indeed," Mitchell repeated. He creased his brow in irritation as he noticed Leon's attention drifting. "Am I boring you, Convict?"

Leon snapped his eyes away from the book shelf.

"Oh! No Warden. I was just . . . ah . . . I was—"

"Never mind." Mitchell was beyond frustrated. "Why would that man stop drinking? I know darn well he was, but now you say that there's no alcohol in the infirmary at all."

"Well, no, there's alcohol there," Leon corrected him, and Mitchell perked up. "You know, for disinfectin' and such."

Mitchell slumped again. Something wasn't right here, and he had a good idea what it was. He knew darn well that Nash was playing games with him, and Mitchell was getting tired of it. It was time to put Mr. Nash to the test and then he would see just exactly what he was going to do to this particular inmate.

Meanwhile, Leon had a mild epiphany and decided, what the hell; he had nothing to lose by trying.

"Perhaps Dr. Palin is impecunious."

Mitchell looked at the inmate, his brow creasing again. How was it that an uneducated outlaw would know that word? But then, the warden smiled inwardly and reminded himself that this was no ordinary outlaw. Nash was highly intelligent and all the reports coming back to him from the officers on the floor substantiated this. Mr. Nash was again, trying to play him for a fool, and something was going to be done about that.

"I hardly think this is the case," Mitchell answered him, casually. "If it were, then it would probably be because he was spending all his money on liquor, and you would be seeing some evidence of it. Don't you agree?"

"Ahh, yes, I suppose so." Leon hesitated. He wasn't sure if that answer helped him out or not.

"That'll be all," Mitchell dismissed him. "Officer Murray!"

***

For the rest of the afternoon, Leon was on the work floor rolling cigars and stuffing them into boxes. Fortunately, it was mindless work, because his mind was far away and working on something else.

Does impecunious have to do with money? He mused. *Or liquor? Or lack thereof? Or both, or neither? Hmm. I could guess, and submit a sentence using the word as referring to money, or liquor, or lack thereof . . . but what if I'm wrong? I can't submit something that might be wrong. That would be embarrassing. Damn. Where can I get my hands on a dictionary? Well, Kenny might have one. But then again, how am I supposed to ask him about it when I'm not allowed to talk? Hmm. I need to get him over to the infirmary, that way I can—*

WHAM! A billy club whacked the edge of Leon's table, and he was startled out of his meanderings.

"Convict! Wake up!" It was Thompson. "You sure spend a hell of a lot of time daydreamin'. It's a marvel to me that you get anything done at all."

Leon kept his eyes down and didn't say a word, but he did notice that he had been stuffing six cigars into a four-cigar box, and making quite a mess of things while doing it. Apparently, even a brainless job needed some level of focus to accomplish it correctly.

Leon snatched back the boxes that were overly stuffed and began to rearrange the cigars to set things right.

Thompson smirked and moved on.

The other guards seemed to think that Nash was something special, but Thompson hadn't noticed anything so far. The fella seemed a bit dim-witted to him.

Leon heard Johnston snicker beside him, but a quick look from the outlaw leader wiped the grin off Johnston's face and sent his attention back to his own duties.

Finally, the long day was over, and the inmates headed toward the common room for supper.

Leon sat down to a plateful of corn beef hash and limp vegetables. He stared down at them, wondering what combination of vegetables this mush consisted of, and very nearly turned away from it in disgust. Then, he heard Jean's voice telling him to stay healthy and how worried they all were when he got sick last winter. Then David practically repeating the same message. Eat as much as you can, even if you're not hungry.

Another heavy sigh. *Maybe if they saw the food that was being offered, they would understand why I don't want to eat.*

He looked down at the gray mess on his plate and wondered if he would ever see a nice red T-bone steak again. At least during the summer, they had all those fresh vegetables from the prison garden, but now, winter was beginning to look even more bleak. This muck was disgusting.

Oh well. He resigned himself to the fact that he should eat something. He didn't want to get pneumonia again, especially after what happened to Billings. One more bout with that infection, and he might not make it back either.

But then, would that be such a bad thing?

No. Leon shook his head and worked up the courage to eat. Don't think like that. What was it Cameron said? "At least in prison you have life and when you have life, you have hope." Something like that, anyway.

Leon sighed as he looked at the slop before him.

I don't know, Cameron. Hope seems to be dwindling away these days. Oh crap! There I go again, slipping into melancholy. Things must be really bad, if all it takes is a plate of disgusting food to bring me down like this. Let's face it, there were times in Elk Mountain when we'd be happy to get this. Smarten up and eat something!

So, he did.

Forcing down as much of that fare as he could, he pushed himself away from the table, fully aware of Boeman's eyes upon him. Leon knew as soon as he left, the alpha inmate would slide Leon's plate over to himself and finish up whatever Leon left behind. It was a win/win situation; Leon wouldn't get into trouble for not cleaning his plate, and Boeman could feel all smug about getting something for nothing.

Leon followed his normal routine and, grabbing himself a cup of coffee, he headed back up to his cell to spend the evening reading. He'd found *The Complete Works of Shakespeare,* which wasn't complete anymore, but close enough. He got a lot of enjoyment out of reading the oddly-worded English text and would often sit on his cot right up until lights out and allow himself to get lost in the old world filled with intrigue and murderous plotting. And, of course, love.

When he arrived at his cell, however, he found that someone had left another book on his cot. Leon assumed it had been Kenny, since no one else would care to leave him anything. Leon tried to pick the book up with one hand, since his other hand held the coffee, but found the text was far too heavy for that attempt. He quickly gave up the effort and simply flipped open the front cover to see what treat he had in store.

It was a dictionary. It wasn't new, but it was intact and that's all that mattered.

Then, he discovered it was more than just a dictionary, it was a dictionary and a thesaurus all in one. Leon had never seen such a marvelous thing. He'd never even had a thesaurus before.

Ohh, this is going to be fun.

He pushed Shakespeare out of the way, settled into his cot with his pillow against the wall and, hoisting the heavy book up onto his knees, he opened it and started to search.

"Impecunious: Having no money. Poor. Penniless."

Leon snorted. *I can relate to that!*

Now all he had to do was come up with a sentence before Sunday. This shouldn't be too difficult, so he would let the word play around in his head for a few days until it got comfortable there. He was sure by Sunday morning he would be able to present Dr. Mariam with his finished assignment.

For the rest of that evening, he continued to flip through the heavy book and read word after word along with their definitions, right up until the buzzer sounded to indicate evening lockdown. He put the book aside, stood up from his cot and went to stand by his open cell door for the head count. This had become such a mundane routine, Leon hardly noticed himself doing it anymore, and he stood quietly while the guards walked by, doing their count, ticking off names, and closing each cell door in the process.

Leon's mind wandered again, thinking about all the words he had come across just in that short evening of browsing. He was amazed at how complex the English language was, and how many words there were that he didn't even know about. This little challenge Dr. Mariam had started with him was going to be an interesting learning curve. Now that he had his first word deciphered, he looked forward to Sunday, so he could get going on his next one.

Thompson walked by Leon's cell and noticing, yet again, the vacant look on the inmate's face, shook his head in disgust. He had been looking forward to meeting Napoleon Nash when he was hired at the prison. He'd grown up reading all those dime novels about the infamous outlaw, about how brilliant he was—and how dangerous. How he could turn a grown man into jelly just by looking at him, and open a locked door simply by tapping it with his finger.

Damn. How disappointing. The man was obviously an imbecile and couldn't even count high enough to package up a small box of cigars. He could understand why he was given laundry duty, as it kept him out of everybody's way. Just how many brain cells do you need to fold a sheet? But how in the world he got working in the infirmary was totally beyond Thompson. He must have polished somebody's brass the right way was all that guard could reason.

Leon stepped back into his cell and stood there for a moment. He watched as Thompson pushed his cell door shut and heard the heavy clang as the mechanical lock was set in place. It was one thing Leon never really did get used to, being locked into his cell at night. He was comfortable and felt safe there, so long as the door was open, but the sound of the lever sliding the bar across the tops of the doors always sent a shiver of claustrophobia down his spine. Though over time, he adjusted to it, he never really did forget that he was locked in.

Leon sighed and turned back to his cot. He could still light a candle and carry on reading if he wished to, but he preferred to save his candles for when he was writing his letters. So, he cleared his cot of the books strewn about and settled in to relax and put his mind to rest for a while.

Darkness slowly invaded the cells as night closed in once again. He thought briefly of Gabi, but knowing this would only get him worked up again, he brought his focus inward to one of his favorite sonatas and listened to music in his mind until he quietly drifted off to sleep.

***

Throughout the next few days, Leon tried to catch Kenny's eye and find a way to ask him about the dictionary, but the guard was not cooperating. Then, when Sunday rolled around, and Leon thought he might sneak in a quick question at chapel, it turned out to be one of Kenny's days off, and the guard was a no-show.

This was frustrating. Leon never could figure out the schedule of the guards who worked the floor. Eventually, he decided it must be on a rotating system, so no guard ended up always working Sunday, or at night, or on holidays. Another purpose for this was what Leon had already found out for himself; keeping the schedules erratic would prevent the inmates from learning the pattern and thereby knowing who was going to be on when. That made an assault or escape that much more difficult to plan if you didn't know who you'd be dealing with.

So, Leon went to the sermon and sat through the lecture. As usual, when he allowed himself permission to do so, he did get some enjoyment out of it.

Then the victrola came out again and those inmates who wished to stay longer to listen to the selection for the week, settled in for another hour of a musical interlude.

Leon sat back and, closing his eyes, he imagined what the passages would sound like when played live in a concert hall. He hoped one day he would be able to find out, but in the meantime, he could soak up the notes as they were presented to him here. So, for a short time anyway, he was able to disappear into another world and drift away.

Not surprisingly, he possessed the kind of mind that could hear the arrangements one time through and he would know it; he could remember them all, so he could pull them up and listen to them again, whenever opportunity or need presented itself. This ability proved to be a sanity-saver on more than one occasion, and often helped him fall asleep at night when nothing else could.

Too quickly the hour was over. Those inmates who had left before the music, now began to saunter back in again in anticipation of something resembling lunch.

Leon stayed where he was. He frowned as he considered the likelihood of having to force down another meal in this place. At least soup and sandwiches were too basic to really mess up.

He took a deep cleansing breath and glanced up to see Mariam Soames being escorted in his direction, with Murray in attendance this time. The inmate smiled and stood up to greet the doctor.

"Dr. Mariam."

She smiled. "Well, at least that's better than ma'am. Were you able to complete your mission?"

"Yes, ma'am," he announced, with just a hint of pride in his demeanor. He produced the sheet of paper and presented it to her.

Mariam accepted it and read what he had written down.

Impecunious: penniless, without money.

The Kid and I never had to worry about being impecunious until we decided to go straight.'

She smiled.

Murray, who had read the sentence over the doctor's

shoulder, sent Leon a reproving look.

Leon grinned.

"Very good," she congratulated him. "You certainly have an understanding of this word, though I suspect you had some help."

"You said, 'whatever resources become available'."

Her smile broadened as she noticed Leon becoming more comfortable around her again. She handed him another folded piece of paper.

"Let's see what you can do with this one," she challenged him. "See you next week."

"Oh, yes." Leon dropped his head in thanks as he took the proffered paper.

She smiled a farewell and carried on with her day.

Leon unfolded the paper and looked at his new word.

"Mettlesome." Leon frowned. This was a simple word, and because of that, he instantly suspected a trap. Was there some little thing about it that gave it a different meaning other than the obvious? He decided he would double-check before he did anything with it. It would be most embarrassing to be wrong on the assumption that it was too easy to bother with.

***

When Kenny finally showed up on Monday morning to escort him to the infirmary for his day of work with the doctor, Leon got the chance to ask him about the dictionary. The walk there was made in silence, since Leon knew the rules well enough to know not to open his mouth while in the aisleways. Even Kenny would let him have it for that.

However, once they'd crossed the threshold into the infirmary, Leon sent the guard a quick glance and brought forth the question.

"So, you know anything about a dictionary that was left in my cell last week?" he asked.

"Dictionary?" Kenny cocked a brow. "What dictionary?" But then he smiled and, turning on his heel, he left Leon to his daily duties.

Leon grinned, and he nodded to himself. Yes, Kenny had left it.

"What are you grinnin' about?" Palin demanded. "Get over

here, I need your help."

"Oh. Sorry, Doc."

Leon hurried over to the examining table to find one of the new inmates sitting there with the palm of his hand sliced open. Apparently, the knife used to trim the broom bristles had slipped and caused an injury. Leon smiled to himself but was careful not to show it. It seemed this type of injury was quite common among the newbies.

Officer Davis stood quietly off to the side, waiting to take his charge back to work once he was stitched up. Leon hadn't even noticed him there until now; the man was that good at blending into the background.

Palin brought his assistant's attention back to the matter at hand.

"So, what do ya think? Does it need stitches?"

Leon looked at the cut that had already been cleaned and disinfected, but still looked nasty.

"Ah, yup." was Leon's diagnosis. "Looks that way to me."

"Good. You're right," Palin agreed. "Go get the needle and suturing thread."

Leon nodded. He sent a quick look into the dark blue eyes of the patient and saw fear there. This was a young man, younger than Billings had been. He was obviously scared right down to his core at having been dropped into this new and hostile environment.

Leon smiled quietly in reassurance.

"It's all right," he said. "It's not going to hurt."

The newbie barely responded. He was obviously still in some shock and not sure yet whom he could trust and whom he couldn't. Leon felt for him but there really wasn't much more he could do, other than stay close to him on the work floor. He would give moral, albeit, silent support, whenever he could.

Leon went to the counter and opened the drawer containing the supplies that Palin had asked for, then he stopped dead in his tracks. Right there in the drawer, laying innocently on its side next to the suturing thread, was an unopened bottle of whiskey. Leon swallowed nervously and sent a quick glance at the doctor. That man was busy sprinkling powder over the wound and wasn't paying any attention to his assistant.

Leon gathered the supplies, grabbed a role of gauze, gently closed the cabinet door and returned to assist Palin with the injury.

He sent a furtive glance to Davis, hoping the guard hadn't seen anything, and by the guard's bored expression and casual stance, it would appear to be a safe bet.

Leon held the patient's hand steady while Palin stitched the lips of the cut together, then wrapped it in gauze and some bandages.

"There ya go, Ames," Palin stated. "You're fine to go back to work." He then looked at Davis. "Maybe just get him packaging cigars, or something else light, for the rest of the week, all right?"

"Yeah, sure, Doc," Davis agreed without too much conviction. "I'll see what we can do."

Ames smiled weakly in thanks, then got to his unsteady feet. More nerves than injury, Leon surmised as he gave the man a smile and a pat on the back. Then Davis had the new inmate by the arm and headed him back toward the exit.

Leon and Palin watched them leave.

"Seems like a nice enough kid," Leon observed. "What's he in for?"

"Apparently, he likes to set fire to things," Palin informed him. "Burned their school house to the ground. Fortunately, the only one inside at the time was the schoolmarm, but she only made it out because some of the older students saw the flames and ran in to get her. It seems she had been knocked unconscious."

"Oh," Leon's lip twitched. "No candles for him, then."

The two men exchanged glances, and both looked toward the door where Davis and the inmate had exited the infirmary.

"Yeah, well, back to work," Palin mumbled. "Not too much for ya to do today, Nash, barring the unexpected. You can tidy up in here and make sure all the supplies are topped up, you know."

"Yeah," Leon replied. He hesitated a little, then forced himself to continue. "Ahh, you been replenishing the liquor supply, Doc?"

Palin sent him a confused and slightly irritated look. "What do ya mean by that?" he demanded.

"Well . . ." Leon almost shuffled his feet. "When I was getting those supplies for you, I came across a whiskey bottle in the drawer."

"What the hell are you talkin' about?"

"Are you saying you didn't put it there?" Leon asked, hopefully.

But Palin was already on the move, heading to the cabinets.

By the time Leon caught up with him, he had the drawer open and was staring at the bottle laying there.

“Fuck,” Palin swore. “How the hell did that get in there?”

“So, it’s not yours?”

“Hell, no,” Palin retorted. “Ya think I wanna lose my job?” He rubbed his chin and looked contemplative. “Still, since it’s here, do ya wanna—”

“No!” Leon had to be strong for both of them, because he had to admit, he was pretty tempted as well. It’d been a long time since he’d had a decent shot of whiskey. But, “No Doc, we can’t. Obviously, someone has planted it here to set you up. You start actually drinking it, then you’ll just be walking right into the trap.”

“Hmm,” Palin sounded disappointed. “I suppose you’re right. But who the hell would do that? I get along fine with everyone here. Well, pretty much. Who’d want to see me get fired?”

“I don’t know,” Leon admitted. “It doesn’t make sense.” Then he stopped and frowned as another reason occurred to him. “Unless it’s not you they’re trying to set up.”

“Well who else?”

“Me,” Leon stated. “The warden can’t understand why I’m not finding any evidence of your drinking because he knows you are, or were. He came right out and suggested that I was covering up for you.

“Of course, I denied it, but I don’t think he believed me. Now, I’m pretty sure he didn’t believe me.”

“Shit,” Palin swore again. “Now what?”

“I don’t know. If I don’t tell him about this, then he’ll know for sure that I’ve been covering for you, but if I do tell him, then you’ll lose your job.” Leon sighed. “Let me think on it for a bit, Doc. I’ll figure something out. I always do.”

CHAPTER TWELVE
TURNING THE TABLES

The following morning, Leon caught Murray's attention and silently let him know he wanted to see the warden. Murray smiled slightly, sent him a subtle nod and went off to see if it would be convenient for his boss at this time.

Leon's eyes narrowed at the guard's apparent satisfaction at the request. He decided it was time he began to pay a little more attention to what that guard did when not on the work floor.

Two hours later, Leon found himself standing in front of the warden's desk, trying to look servile.

Mitchell oozed superiority. He sent the convict a knowing smile.

"Have you something to report?" he asked the inmate.

"Ah, yes, sir, Warden," Leon admitted, "but ya gotta agree ya won't punish me."

"Punish you," Mitchell repeated. "Why would I do that, Convict, unless you are guilty of some misconduct?"

"Yes . . . well . . ." Leon looked as though he was going to shuffle his feet again, and he kept his eyes averted, putting on the air of a guilty conscience. "Ya gotta agree ya won't punish me."

"You are hardly in a position to make demands, Convict," Mitchell pointed out. "Tell me what you know and then I will decide if the information is worth ignoring any misconduct you have committed."

Leon gave a resigned sigh, apparently giving in to the warden's authority.

"Well, ahh . . ." Leon began, "a couple of evenings ago—I can't remember which one—I kinda snuck over to the infirmary. I know I shouldn't have done it—but I had a splitting headache, and I know Doc keeps some real good painkillers over there, so . . ."

"How did you get through the locked doors?" Mitchell asked, and Leon raised his eyebrows as though that answer should be obvious, and obviously it was, because Mitchell quickly shook his head and waved the question away. "Yes, yes—never mind. So, what happened?"

"Well, Doc had gone by then, so I was just rummaging around for some of those painkillers when I heard the door unlocking. I quickly hid until I could see who it was."

Mitchell was suddenly uncomfortable.

"So, who was it?" he asked.

"I couldn't tell 'cause it was gettin' dark in there, but I could see what he was doin'."

"Yes?"

"He went over to the counters and I heard him open the drawer there, the one that isn't kept locked, and then he took a bottle of somethin' out of a small bag he had with him. I couldn't see what kind of bottle, but I knew it was a bottle. And then he put it in the drawer, closed everything up and left the same way he'd come in."

Mitchell nodded. "And you don't know who it was?"

"No. It was dark, and I couldn't see his face."

"That's very interesting, Convict," Mitchell stated. "What did you do next?"

"I made sure the guard—"

"How do you know it was a guard? You said you couldn't see him."

"No, no, I couldn't see his face," Leon explained, "but he was wearing a guard's uniform. I could tell that much just from his silhouette."

"Right," Mitchell conceded with a tinge of disappointment. "Continue."

"As I was sayin', I made sure the guard was well away and not comin' back, and then I went over to that drawer and opened it. Wouldn't ya know, there was a bottle of whiskey in there."

"Indeed?" Mitchell commented. "And how do you know that the bottle of whiskey hadn't already been there for some time? As I have already told you, Dr. Palin does tend to drink while on the job." The warden smiled. "You may have just given me the evidence I need to fire the man."

"No, I don't think so," Leon disagreed, though he looked

nervous, contradicting the authority figure. "I mean, I saw the guard put a bottle in that cabinet and that was the only bottle in there. If it had already been there, then I would have found two bottles of something. Right?"

Mitchell sighed. "Yes, I suppose you're right about that."

"Yeah!" Leon nodded, showing enthusiasm. "Seems to me, somebody's tryin' to set the doc up or somethin'. Don't know why anyone would want to do that though. Now even if I were to find more bottles lying around, I'd be real suspicious of them being legitimate—if ya get my meanin'."

Mitchell's jaw tightened irritably. "Yes, I suppose you have a point."

Leon smiled broadly, puffing himself up with a job well done.

"So," he surmised, "we can just forget about me bein' there after hours an' all? 'Cause if we can pretend I wasn't there, then we can pretend nothin' else happened either . . . right?"

Mitchell sent Leon a suspicious look. "Are you threatening me, Convict?"

"Threatening you, Warden?" Leon asked, then smiled. "Why would I be threatening you?"

"Right," Mitchell agreed, but he did not look pleased. "I will keep this information confidential for now. You may return to your duties."

"Yes, sir, Warden."

***

"Hi'ya, Kid!" Leon's broad smile greeted his friend. "How are ya?"

"Good, ole man," Jack answered as he sat down in his usual spot. "You're sure in better spirits than ya were last time I saw ya."

"Yeah." Leon was contrite. "I'm sorry about that. I know I was down. David passed along my apology, didn't he?"

"Oh, yeah," Jack assured him, "and I understand why, considerin' what had happened and all. Ya coulda talked to me about it, though."

"Yeah, I know. I just wasn't ready to talk about it yet, that's all." He sighed. "I guess sometimes it's easier writing stuff like that in a letter rather than talking face to face."

"Uh huh," Jack agreed. "I have to admit, it was good for David to get that letter from ya. He was kinda goin' through a hard time himself right around then. I get the feelin' the two of ya talked it out?"

"Yeah, we did," Leon admitted. "It was good."

"Good." Jack smiled. "I got some good news for ya, Leon."

"Oh yeah?" Leon asked. "Did Judge Lacey finally see the light and is going to rescind my sentence and let me live my life as a free man?"

Jack looked disappointed. "Well, no . . . not that good."

Leon smiled. "I was just ribbin' ya, Jack. I knew it couldn't be that good. So, what is the good news?"

"Well, now that you've taken the oomph out of it, it don't seem all that important no more."

"Oh no, Jack. Come on," Leon insisted. "I was just teasing you. Don't leave me in suspense. What is it?"

Jack smiled again. "We were right, Leon," he informed his uncle. "President Cleveland finally got fed up with Warren and some of the business dealings he was involved in, and booted 'im outta office."

"Oh," Leon responded, suddenly quite serious. "So, Warren's not the governor of Wyoming anymore? That is good news."

"Yeah. A fella by the name of George Baxter is in office now," Jack explained. "Taggard and Steven and me already have an appointment to go speak with 'im, early in the New Year. And I tell ya, there's gonna have ta be an avalanche coverin' the train tracks to prevent me from bein' there."

Leon looked disappointed. "The New Year? You couldn't get in sooner than that?"

"No. Steven tried. I guess Warren left quite a mess behind, and this new fella is already swamped with complaints and people wanting to see him. We got the earliest appointment we could."

Leon smiled, realizing his friends were doing everything possible to help him out.

"Yeah, that's good, Jack. Let's hope he's more agreeable to our situation than Warren was."

"Couldn't be worse."

Leon raised his brows and nodded agreement. "How are the girls?" he asked.

"They're fine. Penny is all excited about spendin'

Thanksgivin' with Josey and Caroline." He smiled mischievously. "She's fun ta watch. I just hope she don't get herself inta trouble, this being her first time kinda out on her own. Josey ain't what you might call a strict chaperone."

Leon laughed. "Uh huh. And those two girls can get quite rambunctious when they're together. And knowing Josephine, any trouble they get into, she'll be right up to her neck in there with them."

Jack smiled. "Yup. Still, Steven will be there to make sure they behave themselves. And the matron of the boarding house where Caroline stays is apparently quite strict, much ta Caroline's annoyance. Ha, ha! She'll be keepin' an eye on 'em."

"Hmm," Leon nodded. "Probably a good thing. So, how are you doing, Jack?" he asked, changing the subject. "You're working? keeping busy?"

"Oh yeah. The problem with ranch work is that there is always somethin' that needs doin'. One thing ya gotta promise me, Leon, is that when you get outta here, we're not gonna buy ourselves a ranch."

Leon smiled. "I promise. It's good that Cameron keeps you working though, and paying you as well. I'd hate to think you were impecunious now, after all we've been through. Although, I know how mettlesome you get once gloaming sets in. Are you behaving yourself and staying away from the meretricious side of town these days?"

Jack sat still as stone and stared at Leon, not quite sure what he had just heard and no idea how he should respond to it. Finally, he looked away, and he and Officer Pearson locked eyes for an instant. Pearson shrugged; he had no idea either. Jack looked back to Leon's inquiring gaze.

"So—what's your answer?" Leon asked, innocently.

"What's my answer?" demanded Jack. "What the hell was the question?"

"I simply stated that I would hate to think you were broke, but I also know how restless you get once evening settles in, and I hope that you're staying away from the brothel, or at least, that part of town."

"Leon, there weren't nothin' simple about that question," Jack pointed out. "What the hell are you doin' anyways? Readin' a dictionary from cover to cover, or somethin'?"

Leon grinned like the Cheshire cat. "Yeah, something like that."

Jack waited for further explanations. Leon relented, though teasing his nephew had been enjoyable.

"Apparently, Dr. Mariam felt I needed some mental stimulation, so she gives me a new word every week to define and put into a sentence," he paused, excitement lighting his eyes. "It's kind of been fun; you should try it."

"Uh huh." Jack didn't look enthusiastic. "Ya mean she has actually found words that you don't know the meanin' of?"

"I know! Amazing, isn't it?"

Jack rolled his eyes; Leon's head was starting to swell again.

"So, how do ya figure out what they mean?" he asked. "Ya got a dictionary or somethin' in there?"

"I didn't at first," Leon admitted, "and it was proving to be quite a dilemma. I was even thinking of asking you for one for Christmas. But then somebody else beat ya to it."

"Oh yeah?" Jack asked, feeling a little resentful. "Who?"

"I'm pretty sure it was Kenny, but he won't admit to it. I went back to my cell one evening after supper and a dictionary, with a thesaurus, was sitting on my cot."

"What the hell is a thesaurus?" Jack asked. "Sounds like it oughta be extinct."

"Oh," Leon answered, taking on an important air, "well, a thesaurus is a book that gives you samples of different words that mean the same thing."

"Oh." Jack rolled his eyes. "Great. Now you're gonna be givin' me even more words that don't make no sense. Why don't ya just use the same words the rest of the world uses? You'd be a hell of a lot easier to put up with."

"Don't you want to learn new words, Jack?" Leon asked him, feeling disappointed.

"Why?" Jack shot back at him. "I can communicate good enough with what I got. Dang. No wonder your head is so swollen all the time—all them big words floatin' around in there."

"Oh," Leon mumbled, looking down at his shackled hands.

Jack instantly felt contrite. Here he had been telling Kenny that Leon needed something new to get him out of his depression, and now that he had, Jack was complaining about it.

"Yeah. I'm sorry, Leon," he apologized, "you're right."

Leon perked up, a small smile tugging at his lips.

Jack noted the rekindled spark and decided to encourage it. “Maybe this is somethin’ we can do together. Mariam gives ya words to define, then you can pass ‘em on ta me, and I’ll take ‘em home and figure ‘em out too.”

Leon’s smile grew into a big dimpled grin. “Yeah! There ya go, Jack. It’ll be fun.”

Jack smiled and nodded, though “fun” wasn’t exactly the word he had in mind.

“Yeah. Although, I hate to say it, Leon,” Jack reminded him, “but with the way the temperature has been droppin’, we could get hit with some heavy weather soon. I may not be able to get out here next month.”

“I know,” Leon admitted. “I’m trying not to think about it. Still, when that happens, I’ll send them along in a letter. The mail slows down in the winter, but it does usually get through eventually.”

“Yeah, that’s true.”

Shortly after this, the two friends finished up their visit and went their separate ways. It had been harder this time, saying goodbye, since they didn’t know when they would be able to see one another again. But they had to do it, and eventually they accepted the inevitable and parted company.

Leon returned to his cell to read, since it was too cold outside for a walk around the perimeter. He dreaded another winter here, as he had no problem remembering how cold it had been the previous year. However, he did acknowledge the fact that he was better prepared for it this year, with more knitted clothing and, well, maybe not so much a layer of fat, as just not so much ribcage showing. Plus, he had a better idea of his place in the scheme of things; he wasn’t the new fish out of water anymore. He’d be all right.

***

“Really, Officer Murray, I’m very disappointed in you,” Warden Mitchell lectured the young man. “I give you a simple job to do and you totally botched it.”

Murray frowned. “I don’t understand, Warden. I did what you asked, and there were no problems. I’ve been wondering why nothing has come of it yet.”

"Yes, you did what I asked," Mitchell growled, "but you didn't watch your back and you were observed!"

"No sir, Warden," Murray insisted. "I was real careful. Nobody saw me go into the infirmary."

"Maybe nobody saw you go in, but someone else was already in there and he saw what you did."

"What?" Murray didn't believe it. "No sir. Nobody was in there. I did a full check of the ward before I placed the bottle. Who says they saw me?"

"Nash! That's who." Mitchell's fist banged on his desk. "The very man I was trying to test. The absolute last person that should have seen you, saw you."

"Nash?" Murray repeated with indignant amazement. "Nash was nowhere near the infirmary that morning. All the inmates were still locked in their cells."

"Morning?" Mitchell asked in a slightly quieter tone. "Don't you mean night?"

"No sir. I went in there early in the morning, before the Doc showed up for work," Murray explained, "and I swear—there was nobody else in there."

Silence ensued within the warden's office. Murray stood nervously. He was confused and not quite sure why he was getting chewed out like this. He'd done his job.

Mitchell was into a slow burn, his upper lip pulled back in anger. It was a good thing the coffee cup he held was made of stout ceramic or there would have been a minor explosion and a large coffee puddle all over his paperwork.

"That bastard," Mitchell cursed in an angry whisper. "He's still playin' me."

Murray made no comment. This was all going right over his head, but he did pick up on one fact, the warden's anger was no longer directed at him, and for that blessing, he was relieved.

"That's all, Officer Murray," Mitchell finally dismissed him. "Return to your duties."

"Yes sir."

***

Thanksgiving came and went without so much as a ripple. The prisoners had turkey and fixings for supper, and the Sunday sermon was a little different in its message. But all in all, it was just another day. In the week that followed the holiday, Leon found himself in the warehouse as usual. Back to making brooms again.

Ho hum. Nothing changes.

Then, one quiet morning, pandemonium broke out. Since there was no talking allowed, when a dispute developed between the inmates, it was usually a silent one, and nobody other than the two adversaries were even aware of a disagreement until the fists started flying. And that's exactly what happened this time.

Leon didn't know what it was about, nor even who was involved, and he didn't want to know. He had enough to deal with without getting involved in another man's dispute. Unfortunately, it did not take long for the other inmates on the floor to get caught up in the action. Pretty soon, they had made a circle around the two combatants and were making it very difficult for the guards to get in there and break it up.

Before Leon could get himself out of the way, he got caught up in the throng and the harder he tried to get out of it, the deeper into it he was pushed. Within seconds, he found himself with a front row seat to the fist fight and it took everything he had to stay on his own feet.

The fight was getting brutal and nobody could tell the identity of the two combatants. For one thing, both of them had bloody noses by this time, and they were so at each other, it was hard to distinguish who was who.

The fight took a sudden turn toward viciousness when the man on top grabbed one of the dull work knives from a table, and before anyone could stop him, he plunged it into the right side of his adversary. He then scrambled to his feet and disappeared into the circle of men standing and jostling around him.

Leon could see the stricken man writhing on the floor and made a run for him to assist where he could. The guards were swinging their clubs to break up the crowd and disperse them, but Leon still managed to get around them. He got into the clear just in time to see Thompson bend over the injured man, grab the knife handle and prepare to pull it out.

"No!" Leon shouted and made a run for him.

Thompson looked up just as Leon collided with him, and the two men ended up sprawled on the floor, with Leon on top.

Leon scrambled away from the guard and hurried over to the

injured man. He grabbed a rag from one of the work tables and began to wrap it around the wound at the base of the knife handle, being oh so careful not to dislodge the weapon. One thing he did know: if the knife were to be pulled out now, chances were good the man would bleed to death before they got him to the infirmary.

Leon's hands trembled, his confidence at a low ebb. All he could see was the blood seeping through his pressure point and the terror of losing another patient threatened to overwhelmed him. He focused enough to recognize the wounded man as the new inmate, Ames, and that he was in desperate need of Leon's help.

Ames gasped for breath and looked even more scared than Leon was. He grabbed hold of Leon's tunic, his eyes pleading for the older man to save him.

Leon was still shaking, his own breath coming in anxious gasps. A scream was building up at the back of his throat and all he could see was his best friend bleeding out in his arms, the blood seeping from the bullet wound and soaking into the ground around his knees.

Then a jolt came from behind. Thompson yelled at him and had grabbed the back of his tunic, trying to pull him away. To Leon, it was a re-enactment of Morrison grabbing him and preventing him from helping his partner. He yelled his anger and, shooting up, he sent his elbow into the guard's gut, sending the man staggering back to crash into a work table.

Thompson regained his balance, and filled with self-righteous indignation, came at Leon, swinging his club and swearing.

Leon felt the blows hit his back and shoulders, but he ignored them and continued to apply pressure to the injured man's wound, hoping and praying he was doing the right thing.

"Thompson!" came Kenny's angry voice. "Back off!"

Then Kenny was there, between the guard and the inmate.

"Back off, Officer Thompson," Kenny repeated. "Nash is just doing his job."

"What do ya mean, his job?" Thompson sneered. "That convict attacked me, and he's gonna get punished for it."

"All Nash did was stop you from killing that man," Kenny shot back. "If you had pulled the knife out, Ames would have bled to death right here and now. So back off!"

Kenny was still between the three men, his hand against

Thompson's chest, their eyes locked.

Thompson fumed but he knew his place. He succumbed to Kenny's authority, and dropping his gaze, he backed away from the senior guard.

Kenny gave a sigh of relief and took a quick look around.

The other inmates had been dispersed and were back at their own duties, even though a few of them were still sending furtive glances their way. As for the assailant, nobody was saying who he was or where he went. A quick wiping of blood off his face and back to his workstation, and none of the guards would know which one it was, and none of the inmates were going to let on.

"How is he, Nash?" Kenny asked, as he knelt beside the two men.

"I don't know," Leon admitted, still shaking from the assault. "I think I have the bleeding slowed for now, but the sooner we get him to the infirmary, the better."

"I sent Davis for the doctor. He should be here any minute," Kenny assured him. "So, just hang on."

"Yeah."

Though it seemed like an hour, Palin arrived on the scene in less than a minute. He knelt beside Ames, across from Leon, and did a quick assessment of the patient's condition. That done, he let out his breath and nodded.

"Good job, Nash. Ya slowed the bleeding, and he's still with us. Now, we just have to get him back to the infirmary without causing him too much distress." Palin glanced up to someone standing behind him. "Ma'am, could you take over for Nash and keep applying pressure to the wound while we move him?"

"Of course, Doctor," Mariam responded.

Leon looked up and smiled with relief as Mariam came around and knelt beside him. He also noticed another woman standing there, wearing the black dress and long white head covering that indicated a novice. She stood back from the group, with her eyes down, obviously not wanting to get in the way. Perhaps she was also feeling a little intimidated by all these men, some quite menacing in their appearance, standing around her. Leon dismissed her, as his focus returned to the job at hand.

Mariam placed her hands over top of Leon's, then he carefully slid his hands out from under hers, and she continued to apply the pressure needed to keep the blood from flowing.

Leon breathed another sigh of relief now that these two, more experienced, people had taken over. He stumbled to his feet and awaited further instructions.

"Okay, Nash," Palin said, "if you could grab hold of his legs, I'll get his shoulders and we can move him to the infirmary."

"Sure, Doc."

The small procession made its way out of the warehouse, across the open yard and back into the main building.

The young novice followed along behind, keeping her head down and not looking to either side, as she stayed focused on the group in front of her.

Kenny brought up the rear, just to make sure they got the wounded man into the infirmary without any further mishaps.

Thompson watched the group leave, his jaw set tight in indignant anger.

Carson watched Thompson, a subtle smile growing on his face.

Boeman watched all of them.

***

In the infirmary, Palin led the way to an examination table, and they laid the patient out on it.

"Okay," he said. "Ma'am, you keep applying that pressure. Don't let up. Nash, go get the suturing thread and a needle."

Both assistants nodded and carried out their tasks while Palin prepared a dose of morphine for the patient. The novice stayed out of the way.

Kenny approached Doc. "Shall I take Nash back to the work floor?" he asked. "It doesn't really look like you need him here."

"No, leave him be," Palin answered quietly so the others wouldn't hear. "Nash's self-confidence took a beating after Billings died. I think it'll be good for him to stay here for now and help out. Come back and get him in a few hours."

Kenny glanced at Nash getting supplies out of the cabinet. Once collected, the inmate hurried them over to the patient, then laid a comforting hand on the man's forehead and shoulder.

Kenny nodded. "Yeah, okay. Good luck. I'll see you after lunch."

The senior guard discreetly left the infirmary while Palin

returned to his patient and administered the morphine.

Within moments, Ames was completely sedated, and the three adults concentrated on withdrawing the knife and keeping the flow of blood to a minimum. The procedure itself did not take long. Once the knife was out, Palin used the forceps to locate and remove the piece of material that had been pushed into the wound by the dull knife, and he was then satisfied that they were done. He sprinkled the whole area with morphine powder and stitched the wound together.

Once this was completed, everyone stood back with a sigh of relief.

Leon wiped his bloody hands on his tunic and stepped back. He was still shaking from the stress and the memories all of this brought back to him. Was he never going to be able to see blood again without it triggering this response? He went and sat down by the counter before his knees gave out under him. With another deep sigh, he ran his hands over his eyes, then over his scalp; he still couldn't get used to the fact that there was no hair there.

Palin sent Nash a scrutinizing glance, and noting that Mariam and her novice were busy bandaging the wound, he walked over to his assistant and placed a reassuring hand on his shoulder.

"Ya did good, Nash," he complimented him. "Your actions probably saved his life."

Leon looked up and met Palin's eyes, then smiled. For the first time in a long time, the convict felt some pride in himself.

CHAPTER THIRTEEN
PENELOPE'S DECEPTION

Earlier that day

"Come child, snuggle up so we can keep each other warm."

Mariam opened her thick blanket as a welcoming gesture for her young companion to tuck in beside her, so they could use both their blankets and combined body heat to make the coach ride to the prison a little more comfortable.

Penny smiled. Though she had her own blanket and was wearing long woolen underwear beneath her heavy black novice habit, she was still cold. The invitation to snuggle was instantly accepted and Penny moved in quickly. Soon both ladies were feeling more civilized.

During the colder months, when Mariam could get to the prison at all, she usually stayed for a least a couple of days—longer if the need arose. There was a string of cells alongside the infirmary, set aside for women prisoners, but since it was rare for all of these cells to be occupied, one of them had been converted into a comfortable room for her. It consisted of a wood stove, a writing desk with a chair, a chamber pot and two hammocks, stretched out, one above the other.

It was not unusual for Mariam to bring a companion along with her, since helping in the prison infirmary was a good eye opener for any new novice who was contemplating a life in service to her God. After this initiation, there were many who decided to simply pack it in and go home.

Mariam's current companion, though obviously not a true novice, seemed determined to accompany her to the prison and had overcome a great many obstacles to attain that goal. Mariam admired her for that much, but still had some doubts about the legitimacy of her claim.

The young lady insisted she was an emancipated woman, and a reporter in her own right, wishing to do an exposé on the prison system, but it didn't set right. She came across like a brown-eyed doe caught in the sights of a hunter's rifle, rather than the sophisticated woman of the world she claimed to be.

Still, Mariam admired her spunk and determination—and her courage as well. This was not going to be a walk around the park during a Sunday social. The Territorial Prison was a daunting institution, even for the hardened criminals who had been sentenced to do time there. For a young woman, barely out of her teens, if indeed, she was out of her teens, it could prove to be quite terrifying.

"How long have you known Jack and Napoleon?" Mariam asked her companion.

"About five years now, I think," Penny answered, omitting the fact that there had been a long stretch of separation during that time. "We had a ranch here in Wyoming and they showed up on our doorstep one Christmas Eve, during one of the worst blizzards we'd had in ages. They were nearly frozen to death. Of course, we took them in. They stayed on and worked the ranch for quite some time after that."

"Very admirable for your folks to have done that, but also very risky. Two drifters coming from out of nowhere; that was awfully trusting. Did you never wonder what they were doing out and wandering about in such weather?"

Penny shrugged. "It was not unusual for drifters to show up at the ranch, looking for work or even just directions. And we couldn't very well turn them away; they and their horses were in desperate shape. And it's not like they stayed in the house. Once they had recovered, they slept in the bunkhouse." She paused and thought back on that time. "But, we knew we were safe with them. There was something about them, something that made us trust them. Even after we discovered who they were, we still trusted them. I never once felt threatened by either one." She smiled. "I suppose you think that was awfully naïve."

"No," Mariam denied. "I know exactly what you mean. The first time I laid eyes on those two drifters, I knew they were decent men. Oh, a little rough around the edges, I suppose, and not at all comfortable with me lecturing them about how they had neglected the spiritual side of their lives."

Penny giggled.

But Mariam became serious again. "Oddly enough, considering their background, Jack opened up to me right away. He told me they had been raised in an orphanage but had run away while still quite young. They'd had to make their own way in a hard world. Now Leon, he was far more cautious. He was not happy at all with his friend discussing their past with me and was quick to shut it down. I suppose he was afraid that dear Jack was going to get carried away and give up all their secrets, right then and there, amongst the tumble weeds."

Penny giggled again. "Mathew is sweet, isn't he?"

"Yes," Mariam agreed, then she sighed, reflectively. "I must admit to being very shocked when I discovered their identities. It didn't seem possible. They were both such kind men." She shrugged her shoulders. "Yet, Leon has been in the prison for a year now, with no denial that he is who they say he is—it doesn't seem right, somehow."

"Yes," Penny agreed. "They were arrested at our ranch in Colorado. Did you know?"

"No."

Penny nodded. "It was the worst day of my life. Mathew was so badly injured I thought for sure he was going to die. I was so scared. I love him so much."

"Oh?"

"Both of them," Penny quickly covered her tracks. "I love them both; they're like brothers to me. That's why I must see for myself what Peter is going through. He's a dear friend and doesn't deserve to be mistreated. I want to do everything I can to help him."

Mariam smiled and gave Penny a tighter hug. "Good. And I want to do everything I can to help you."

***

On a good day, it only took an hour or so to make the trip from the far side of town all the way to the outskirts at the other end, but this was not a good day. Snow had been falling for some time, and when the coach finally pulled up to the front door of the prison, both ladies were happy to disembark and get the blood flowing again.

Once the coach was halted, ole' Bart, the orphanage's handy man, stiffly clambered down off the box. He stamped his cold feet, then with a mittened hand, unlatched the coach door and assisted the two ladies to step out.

"Thank you, Bart," Mariam acknowledged him. "With the way the snow is coming down, I suggest you stay here for tonight. Get the horses settled and tell the trustee to escort you to the kitchen for a meal. I'll make sure you have a place to sleep."

"Yes, ma'am. Thank you," Bart answered. He smiled underneath his woolen scarf, remembering the impromptu poker game he got into the last time he'd had to spend a night at the prison. "You just send word when you're ready to head back."

With that, Bart climbed up onto the box and clucked the horses into motion again. Their gait instantly picked up when they found their noses turned toward the stabling area; such a welcome alternative to heading home to their own stalls in weather like this.

Mariam and Penny made their way into the front foyer. Mariam had been there many times, but for Penny, just walking through the entrance was like walking into a whole new world. Even though the hallway and the rooms situated on both sides of it, could have been from any office building in Laramie, there was still a feeling of oppression about it. The guard who awaited them, complete with billy club, side arm, and rifle, added immensely to this impression.

Officer Davis had been expecting them, and though his greeting was friendly enough, Penny still found herself holding back and keeping Mariam between herself and this imposing man. Davis ignored her or perhaps, had already written her off as a non-entity and hadn't noticed her discomfort. He did his job and escorted them to the infirmary, having already made sure that there were no inmates loitering around the area.

Just like Leon, and then Jack before her, as soon as Penny entered the cell block of that institution, she felt the oppressiveness of those walls closing in on her. She followed Mariam and their escort across the cold floor, feeling a little frightened, with her eyes looking everywhere around her. She was certain there were ghosts floating above and behind them, keeping just out of sight. She stayed close to the doctor.

Davis led them up the stairs to the second floor, and they followed him into the section which housed the women inmates. He stopped at the first cell and opened the door for them.

"Here you are ladies."

"Thank you," Mariam said. "Do we have company?"

"No ma'am, not at this time. Our last female inmate was released five days ago."

"Oh yes, I recall her telling me that. Thankfully she has family to stay with."

"Yes, ma'am." Though he didn't appear interested in the fate of the released woman.

He motioned the women into their sanctuary.

The wood stove had been lit in anticipation of Mariam's arrival and the small room was warm and inviting. Penny knew it would be difficult to leave this cozy sanctuary when it was time to venture into the real world again, but she was resolved to do so. This room was a lovely reprieve, but she wasn't about to chicken out now.

"There's hot soup in the kitchen, ma'am, if you and your assistant would care for some," Davis offered. "The inmates are all busy with their duties, so you can head over there, unimpeded. There's nothing pressing in the infirmary right now, anyway."

"Thank you, Officer," Mariam answered. "I will let Dr. Palin know we are here and then I believe some hot soup would be very welcome."

Davis nodded and tipped his cap to both ladies. "Ma'am, Miss. I'll see you later, then."

Penny stepped into the cozy room and instantly felt the heat begin to invade her toes and fingers. She smiled, and putting her overnight bag down on the floor, she began striping off her outer layer of clothing and vigorously rubbed her hands over the stove.

Mariam soon did likewise, giving them both a chance to warm up before heading next door to the infirmary.

Once both ladies had taken the time to melt away the chill, they made themselves presentable after the discomfort of their journey. That done, Mariam led the way the short distance to the end of the corridor and tapped lightly on the door. Within a few moments, they heard a key from the inside turning in the lock, and it opened to present to them an older, balding man who looked a little grizzled and worse for wear, but still managed a smile in greeting.

"Ma'am," Palin greeted them. "I've been expectin' you. Didn't realize you were bringing a novice with you this time though."

"Yes, I know," Mariam answered. "It came up suddenly. I hope you don't mind."

"No, of course not," Palin responded, waving them into the larger room. "The more the merrier."

The two ladies entered, and Palin couldn't help but watch the novice glide gracefully in behind her mentor.

What a pretty little thing, he thought to himself. *And what a shame she's gonna hide away her beauty inside a nun's habit.* Then he felt guilty; not because he was having thoughts like that about a servant of the church, but because he didn't feel guilty about having thoughts like that. He shrugged. He was an amoral man, and he'd learned to live with it.

"Not much goin' on right now, ladies," Palin informed them as he closed and re-locked the door. "Might be a good time to show your student around the infirmary. You never know when things could get busy here."

"Yes, of course," Mariam agreed. "I will take some time to do that now, then I believe we will head down to the kitchen for some hot soup. It was a rather chilly ride over here from the school."

"Fine," Palin agreed, "whatever you want."

Palin left them to it and returned to his ever-present paperwork.

Mariam took Penny around the facility and showed her all the little nooks and crannies, and where all the different supplies were kept, etc. They then left and went downstairs for some much-needed sustenance.

It just so happened that the two ladies were in the kitchen, sitting at a little side table beside the stove having their soup and bread, when Leon happened to walk in. He had an armful of towels and table coverings that had been laundered the previous day, and were now being returned to their proper station.

"Oh look," Mariam whispered, as she pointed him out, "there's Leon now."

"Oh no." Penny was mortified. "He can't see me here." She began to look around for a place to hide.

Mariam smiled at her discomfort then put a calming hand on her arm. "Don't worry," she said, "He'll only see what he expects to see: another of my novices coming for the day. Just relax."

Though still a little tense, Penny nodded. Once she realized the truth of the reassurance, she did relax and, seeing that he was distracted, she allowed herself a moment to scrutinize her friend.

Leon stood at his ease, talking to one of the other trustees over by the linen shelves. He noticed Mariam and her novice sitting in the corner, but he chose not to disturb them while at their lunch. Besides, he knew how intimidating the first visit to this prison could be for a young novice, and he didn't want to add to her discomfort. He sent Mariam a quiet nod in greeting then carried on with his duties.

So it was, Penny could watch her friend and remain unnoticed herself. Despite what she had already heard from Caroline and Jack concerning Leon's condition, she was still shocked and heart-sickened by what she saw.

He was so thin. That was her first observation. She wasn't even sure if she would have recognized him if she passed him in the corridor. It was only because Mariam pointed him out that she could see it was indeed her friend.

He finished his chat with the trustee and turned to leave. She saw him smiling, and her heart nearly broke; he had such a beautiful smile. But his cheeks appeared hollow and his complexion was pale and tired-looking. And his hair! His beautiful thick dark hair was all shaved off which made him look even more gaunt.

Her hand came up to her mouth as a silent sob escaped her, and she quickly looked away from him, hoping to block out the image. But of course, she couldn't, and she looked back again to watch him walk away and disappear around a corner to return to his duties in the laundry room.

"Are you all right, my dear?" Mariam asked her.

"Oh, my goodness." Penny allowed her sob to come forth. "Oh, my goodness. He has changed so much. I would not have known him. Mathew and my sister both warned me, but . . . to actually see him like that. Oh, my goodness."

Mariam put a hand on her arm. "Are you sure you want to continue with this?" she asked. "This is what life is here. If you don't think you can handle it—"

"No, no," Penny assured her, taking a deep breath and wiping away the tears. "This is ridiculous. I must harden myself if I expect to be of any use at all. I get frustrated with these tears; they come so unbidden. I hate it, this crying over every little thing. I must stop doing this or no one is ever going to take me seriously. The only power a crying woman has over men is one of pity and condescension, and I will not play that game. I have a job to do here; I have a mission, and I will not let these silly tears have control over me."

Mariam sat back in surprise. Right before her eyes, this quiet, unassuming young girl had changed into a determined woman who was not going to let anything, or anybody, stand in her way. Penny had already exhibited this perseverance simply by having made it this far, but now Mariam was seeing it manifest into a true defining spirit.

Sitting before her was a young woman who was not going to allow the powers that be control her life or her decisions. Even if it meant defying her own parents, which is something Mariam had by now come to realize she had done.

Mariam smiled and patted her arm again.

"Come, finish your soup," she said. "Then we will return to the infirmary and I'll show you more of our duties there."

***

The rest of the afternoon went by quietly. There were some minor cases to tend to, but mostly it was follow-up for returning patients.

Penny settled in, helping with the cleaning up and bringing supplies over to the doctor as he asked for them. By the end of the day, she felt relaxed and confident about what would be expected of her in this new environment.

The next day would prove to be another matter altogether.

***

The morning started out just as quietly as the previous afternoon had been, and Penny was beginning to wonder if Caroline and Jack had been overreacting with their testimonies of deplorable conditions. The inmates, whom Penny did see and assisted attending to, did not seem overly hard done by, and everyone was civil to one another.

Leon had certainly appeared underweight when Penny had seen him, but perhaps that was just her imagination; seeing what she expected to see. It may have been the prison garb and his shaved head which made him appear emaciated.

The status of the day changed when Davis burst in upon their morning, all huffing and puffing, and full of self-importance.

"Doc! We got a fight happenin' in the warehouse," he announced. "Don't really know what's goin' on or who's involved, but we might be needin' ya."

Palin grumbled in frustration as he looked up from the instruments he was sterilizing.

"All right, we'll be along," he answered. "Ma'am, will you grab my bag over there by the desk? God dammit, I don't know if these fellas are animals before they come here, or if bein' here brings it out in 'em. Either way, I always seem to be patchin' somebody up."

Palin and Mariam headed out the door, and since no one had given any specific instruction to the quiet little novice, she decided to tag along.

Walking across the yard toward the warehouse, Penny pulled her collar tight in a futile attempt to ward off the biting Wyoming wind. She shivered against the cold, but as they approached the open door of the workshop, her trembling was more from anxiety than the elements of winter.

She heard men yelling and something banging against wood and metal. Then, as they came into the building itself, she could also smell them. Uncouth men who are only permitted to shower once a week, and in cold water to boot, cannot help but put out an aroma that would assault a young girl's nostrils and cause her eyes to water.

Penny put a hand to her nose and mouth to mask some of the odor, but she wasn't having much luck. Then, as they entered the work area itself, she almost lost her courage altogether and wanted to run screaming back to the safety of the infirmary. But she took herself in hand and muttered a reprimand.

Self, came the silent words*, this is why you are here. Don't you dare turn coward now and run into hiding.* And she didn't.

But the scene that met her eyes was daunting. Harsh men, dressed in the traditional prison garb, were being ushered back to their workstations, but they were not going willingly. They were silent in their protest, but they protested nonetheless, with eyes filled with resentful anger and mouths twisted in sneers of hatred at the guards enforcing the rules.

The yelling and banging came from the guards themselves,

using whatever means they had at their disposal to dominate and control the throng of prisoners who had been caught up in the aggressive adrenaline of the fight.

It seemed to Penny that the guards were just as harsh and brutal as the prisoners. The only real way to distinguish them, was by their clothing and the billy clubs they were so effectively wielding.

Her teeth chattered with the most basic of animal fears as she noticed the looks being sent her way by some of the inmates. Though most of these cons would have been civil to a young maiden, there were others who were used to taking what they wanted and didn't mind showing it.

Once they noticed that a youthful female had entered their domain, it didn't matter to them that she wore the uniform of the church. Their nostrils flared at the sight of her, and the looks of masculine lust sent a shiver down her spine and encouraged her to keep her face hidden. She made sure to stay close to her mentor.

Then all she noticed was the blood. She was taken back to that terrible day, a year and a half ago, when her dear friend had lain stricken in the dirt, just barely holding onto a life that was rapidly seeping away from him.

And there was Leon, down by the wounded man, and again, there was blood all over him, soaking into his clothing and smeared across his face. His hands were covered in it.

Penny thought she was going to scream; it was happening all over again.

Fortunately, before she could lose her courage altogether, Leon and the doctor were standing up, lifting the wounded man with them, then walking toward the exit.

Mariam was right in there, her hands keeping pressure on the terrible wound.

Then her safety net was walking away and, willing herself to stay calm, Penny fell in line with them. She was dimly aware of one of the guards coming up behind her, protecting her from the advances of what she conceived to be the threatening multitude of pent up male lust. She denied her legs the impulse to run.

Relief washed over her when she found herself back in the relative safety of the infirmary. She quickly got out of the way, since she had no real idea how to tend to the injured man, whereas everyone else in the room was quite capable of doing just that.

She watched Leon and felt a sorrow rise in her as she realized that it had not just been her own imaginings; he was indeed a different man now than the one she had known. It was as though there was a sense of brutality about him now; a darkness that lingered. Or was that simply because of the blood that was on him?

She continued to watch him, secure in the knowledge that he was too focused on his job to pay her any mind. He wasn't brutal in his behavior while tending to the patient; in fact, he was just the opposite. He was exhibiting compassion, a true sense of caring whether the man lived or died. He was quick and efficient in carrying out the doctor's instructions, and Palin himself seemed to trust in his abilities to do what was needed.

Yet, there was something; just a hint of the wild animal in him that she had never noticed before. She remembered the doctor's comment earlier that morning concerning the behavior of the inmates. "*Were they animals to begin with, or did being in this environment make them into animals?*" Knowing what she knew of her friend, Penny was certain she knew the answer to that question.

She briefly noted the guard leaving the infirmary, then her attention was again drawn to the activity surrounding the patient. She couldn't see too clearly what was going on and she didn't want to move in closer in case Leon would then take more note of her. More than anything else, he could not know she was here. Indeed, it had not been her intention to be in such proximity to him at all. She had, of course, hoped to see him, but at a distance.

It did not take long for the impromptu surgery to be completed, and everyone, including Penny, relaxed their stance and the atmosphere in the infirmary calmed down. Leon moved away to sit by the counter, and Penny noted how pale and drained he appeared. Even the hand he rested upon the countertop trembled with the shock of recent events.

Her resolve to stay incognito came close to breaking as her compassion for her friend compelled her to approach and give comfort.

Fortunately, Dr. Palin saved the day by giving her and Mariam a job to do in completing the bandaging of the patient's injury. Penny was not only relieved to be distracted from Leon's situation, but also to be given a task that she felt confident doing. Turning away from Napoleon, she stepped close to Mariam and turned her attention to the undertaking at hand.

Despite being occupied, Penny was still vaguely aware of the doctor speaking with Napoleon, apparently assuring him of a job well done. They spoke for only a moment, then Palin disappeared into his office to write up the paperwork on this latest incident. It was at this point that Leon's attention moved back to the patient and his attendants.

This was the first time Leon had taken much notice of Mariam's companion. She was quiet and unassuming in her manner, and indeed, was quite masterful at keeping her head down and her face hidden. Leon could not even say what color her eyes were, and her hair was hidden beneath her head covering. Yet, there was something naggingly familiar about her. He couldn't put his finger on it and it bothered him. He had that feeling he should know her, but was unable to get enough information from her countenance for him to place her.

Then the atmosphere in the infirmary changed for the worst. Carson and Thompson materialized at the doorway, and neither one looked like they were there on a social call.

Penny saw them come in and instantly felt the strained oppression settle over the room and its occupants. What she witnessed next removed all doubt in her mind concerning the safety and well-being of her friend while incarcerated in this institution. It awakened in her an anger and a resolution, to not only save her friend from this horrid place, but to have a hand in changing the very structure of the prison system itself.

Leon tensed. *Dammit! What now?*

He stood up, trying to be discreet, but also wanting to get himself into a better position. Sitting down, he was vulnerable, but now he moved so that his back was against the counter and cabinets, hoping to prevent Thompson from moving in behind him. He turned halfway toward the two guards, but he was sure to keep his head down and his eyes averted from them, not wanting to provoke a worse beating than the one that was already headed his way.

Carson moved toward him, tapping the end of that damn billy club against the palm of his left hand. He was looking mean, but that didn't say much, because even when he smiled, he looked mean.

Thompson, on the other hand, was smiling. He was looking forward to this.

The two guards got into position around the convict; Carson in front of him and Thompson to the side. Leon may have protected his back, but now he was surely trapped.

He locked eyes with Mariam, his expression apologetic.

Why the hell did Carson have to do this here and now, with these two ladies watching?

But then it occurred to him that this was exactly what Carson had in mind. Adding embarrassment and degradation to the physical assault would make it all the sweeter for the two men who had already proven themselves to be sadistic bullies.

"That has got to be a record for you, Nash," Carson commented. "You broke three of the basic ground rules all in one go. How about you show these ladies just how smart you are and tell us what those rules are."

Leon's jaw tightened. *Dammit! Where is Palin?* He maintained his eye contact with Mariam, though he didn't really know why. Maybe he just needed to focus on something other than Carson's boots. He couldn't bring himself to look at the novice, though he was very much aware of her looking at him. *Dammit! Not here, not now. This isn't right.*

"C'mon Nash," Carson chided him, "you have permission to speak—let's hear it. What are the three rules you broke?"

Leon looked down at the floor. His heart pounded. His brain did not want to work. *Ahh . . . three rules . . . what were the three rules?*

"I spoke out of turn," Leon answered quietly, "and I assaulted a guard."

"Okay. That's two." Carson could count. "What was the third rule, Nash? C'mon. It's probably the most important rule of all and yet, it seems to be the one you keep on forgettin'."

Leon was silent. *Where the hell is Palin? Dammit, I can't think. Which other rule did I break?*

Thompson snickered. "Just like I thought," he sneered. "He's a stupid redskin. Everybody keeps goin' on about what a brilliant man Napoleon Nash is, but I swear, I have yet to see it. And what kinda name is that for an Indian? "Napoleon Nash". C'mon, your injun ma musta given you one a her heathen names. What is it, Nash?"

Leon's hackles rose, and it was all he could do to refrain from smashing the guard's nose in.

Yeah! She gave me a Shoshone name," his mind screamed out, *but it's sacred and not for the likes of you to know!*

"Officer, really, is this necessary?" Mariam asked. "Please consider my young novice . . ."

"Just doin' my job, ma'am," Carson interrupted her, though still boring his eyes into Leon. "We gotta keep on top of these convicts or they're gonna start thinkin' they run the place. Especially these mongrel types. Perhaps next time, you'll leave your novice back at the orphanage."

Penny opened her mouth to protest, but Mariam laid a hand upon her arm, instantly silencing her. Mariam had dealt with enough bullies in her day to realize that the more you protested their behavior, the worse it would become.

"So, c'mon, Nash," Carson continued, "you've had a moment to think on it. What's the third rule?"

"I don't remember, sir."

"You don't remember," Carson repeated. "Sounds to me like you need re-educatin'. Thompson, remind Nash what the third rule is."

Leon felt Thompson lean into him, could feel the man's breath against his neck.

"The . . . guards . . . are . . . always . . . right."

Leon closed his eyes. *Oh yeah.*

"The guards are always right," Carson reiterated. "You seem to have a hard time rememberin' that one, Injun Nash."

"What the fuck is going on in here?" Doctor Palin had returned to the ward.

"Hey there, Doc," Carson greeted him with a mean smile. "I'm just remindin' Nash of the ground rules. He's been kinda forgetful of 'em lately."

To emphasize his good intentions, he gave Leon a couple of friendly pats on the shoulder.

Leon cringed with each touch.

"You know damn well you don't pull that crap in here," Palin threw back at him. "This is my infirmary, and Nash is my assistant. When he's workin' as my assistant, those fuckin' 'ground rules' don't apply. And you bloody well know it."

"Maybe in here they don't apply, Doc, but on the work floor, they sure as hell do," Carson pointed out. "And when he broke the rules, he was workin' on the floor, just like any other low-life convict."

"You wanna take this up with the warden, then you go and

do that," Palin challenged him, "but in the meantime, get the hell outta my infirmary."

"Sure thing, Doc," Carson agreed and turned to go, his hand still on Leon's shoulder.

Quick as the proverbial whip, he came around, full force, and whacked that billy club right into Leon's ribcage.

Leon gasped and doubled over, but Thompson grabbed him around his chest, holding him up so Carson could get in two more rapid blows.

Then all hell broke loose.

"You fuckin' prick!" Palin yelled, then made a run at the guard.

Carson had no problem blocking the older man, and then, with a quick upper jab with his elbow, sent the doctor staggering back into an examination table. Palin tried to stay on his feet, but was unsuccessful, and he went down with a crash and a clatter, taking a tray of instruments with him.

Leon had fallen to the floor, clutching his ribcage and painfully gasping for air. He curled into a ball to protect himself from the onslaught he knew was coming.

Carson turned back to him, then both guards started kicking the fallen convict until, quite unexpectedly, they found themselves blocked by the devil in a novice habit.

"Stop it!" Penny yelled at them, all fury and clenched fists. "Stop kicking him!"

Both guards stopped out of surprise more than anything else. They stared at the unassuming young novice who was now standing over the fallen convict, her jaw tight and her brown eyes alight with indignant rage. This was not a frightened young girl, pleading with them for mercy, but a strong and angry woman demanding respect.

"You leave him be!"

Carson and Thompson smiled at each other. What a wildcat. This could be fun.

Mariam quickly got in between Penny and the two guards and pulled her out of the melee before anything more could happen. Palin was on his feet again, limping but coming at them.

"You get the hell outta here, Carson," he demanded. "And take your new little boot-licker with ya. And you better believe Mitchell is gonna hear about this."

Carson snickered. "Yeah, right." He knelt beside Leon and

grabbed hold of his tunic. Leon opened his eyes, but instantly looked away. "You look at me, Nash," Carson ordered him. When he didn't get the response he wanted, he gave the convict a shake.

Leon gasped.

Carson's eyes bore into him

"Here I am, givin' you permission to look me in the eye, and you ain't got the guts? Look at me!"

Leon sucked his teeth with the pain, but his lip curled in a snarl, as he deliberately turned and glared his hatred into the guard's eyes.

Carson smiled. "You ever assault one of my officers again, I'll hang ya. But I won't do it in a way that'll kill ya, Nash, I'll just make ya wish you were dead."

He gave the convict a shove, causing the back of his head to bang against the floor, then the guard stood up and addressed his audience.

"Doctor, ladies. Have a pleasant afternoon." He nodded at Thompson, and the two men turned and left the infirmary.

Everyone was on the move at once. Penny reached the fallen man first and cradled his head in her lap. She leaned over him, looking into his eyes, her blonde hair, which had escaped from her veil, was hanging loose about her face.

"Peter!" Her voice was a mixture of anger and anguish. She wasn't sure which emotion she felt the most.

"What the hell . . .?" Leon looked into her gaze, his face a picture of confusion. *I must be hallucinating; Penny couldn't be here. I must be seeing things. Surely Penny didn't run away from home to join the convent, did she? No, no, that doesn't make sense. Something's wrong here.* "Mariam?"

"Yes, Napoleon, I'm here," Mariam assured him. "It's all right."

"What . . .?"

"No, no. It's all right," she repeated. "I'll explain later."

"Oh. Okay."

"Nash." Palin managed to squeeze himself in between the two ladies. "Just relax, I wanna take a look at ya."

Leon nodded, and Palin pulled up his tunic, then frowned at the odd bump and discoloration on the right side of his torso. He gently applied pressure and Leon tensed.

"Yup," Palin confirmed, "it's that same damn rib again. Only this time, it is for true and surely busted. Three times lucky, eh Nash?"

Leon groaned. "It feels like there's a knife sticking in me."

"Yup, I'm not surprised," Palin commented. "It's a bad break. We move ya the wrong way and it's gonna pierce a lung. Damn that Carson. He's just a fuckin' sadistic bastard. I swear, he should be hung by his balls and left to swing until they rip off."

Leon cringed. "Jeez Doc, and you call him sadistic. Remind me never to get on your bad side."

"And really, Dr. Palin," Mariam admonished him. "I realize you enjoy your colorful idioms but I would appreciate you remembering there are young ears present."

Palin sent a quick glance to an embarrassed novice, then had the good grace to look embarrassed himself.

"Oh yeah," he mumbled. "Sorry miss. Don't pay me no mind; I'm just a vulgar old man."

Penny smiled, feeling self-conscious, then dropped her gaze to focus again on her friend.

"Well," said Palin as he stiffly hoisted himself to his feet, "let's see if we can get him onto a table. We're gonna have to be careful though; like I said, one wrong move and he'll be upchucking blood.

Penny paled, but also looked determined to do her bit. Both ladies stood up and prepared to assist in the maneuver.

Palin disappeared into his office again, but returned promptly with a stretcher. He set it down alongside Leon's prone body.

"Okay," he said, "now, miss, if you could just take my place here, beside the stretcher. Good. Ma'am, you kneel by his feet and I'll take his shoulders. We wanna roll 'im onto his side, so our young novice here can slide the stretcher underneath him. But we gotta be careful; keep his body straight. You understand? We can't let it twist at all."

"Yes, Doctor. We understand," Mariam informed him, while Penny nodded her agreement.

"Right then. Let's—"

"Wait a minute, Doc!" came the tense and nervous protest from the victim.

"What?"

"Ahh, how about a little morphine or something down here?" Leon asked. "I have a funny feeling this is going to hurt."

"Nope, can't do it," Palin informed him. "If we do start to hurt ya, I wanna hear ya hollerin'. Givin' ya morphine would kinda defeat that purpose, wouldn't it?"

"Well . . . yeah . . ." Leon had to agreed but his tone was apprehensive. He did not like this one little bit.

"Don't worry about it," Palin consoled him. "Believe me, I don't wanna have ta deal with a compound fracture or a punctured lung any more than you do. All that blood, and bones stickin' outta bodies—not to mention the hysterical screaming. And I don't think the ladies would appreciate it either."

Leon groaned. Palin picked a fine time to be funny.

"All right, ladies. Ready? One, two, three . . . roll."

Leon closed his eyes and tried to relax as he felt his body gently and smoothly rolled onto its left side. Penny pushed the stretcher underneath, and he settled down onto it. The broken rib was hurting like hell, but nothing stabbed at him. If he could have taken a breath without pain, he would have sighed with relief.

"Let's move him up to that exam table there, beside young Mr. Ames. Good thing that fella's still asleep. All I need is two damn crybabies in here."

Ten minutes later, Leon was lying on the table, trying to ignore the pain as he waited for the morphine to kick in. Palin had cut his bloodied tunic off, and Mariam was carefully washing away the blood from his chest and hands. Leon slowly started to drift away, but he could still feel the movements around him and hear the conversation.

"Oh, Doctor," Mariam was saying, as though from a distance. "I believe he has broken a couple of his fingers too."

"Oh crap. Yeah. That Carson—and now Thompson, too. What a pair of assholes. Mitchell's gonna be hearin' about this, that's for damn sure."

"Look at that," Leon heard Penny exclaim, her voice fading away. "I've never seen a bone broken like that before. Look at the way it's pushing up against his skin . . ."

What's Penny doing here? Shouldn't she be in school or something? Or maybe she doesn't go to school anymore. But she's only twelve years old, isn't she? Oh, Cameron and Jean are going to be furious. What is she doing here . . .? Then he was gone, drifting into dreams he would soon forget, completely oblivious to the procedures going on around him.

***

When Kenny returned to the infirmary to collect his charge, the scene that met his eyes when he walked into the ward was not at all what he had expected. He stopped, his mouth open, and with such a confused expression on his face, it couldn't help but bring smiles to the people sitting down to a cup of afternoon tea.

"What in the world?" Kenny finally stated. "What happened here?"

"It seems Carson decided Nash needed to be reminded of the rules he broke when he saved Ames's life," Palin explained. "He and that Thompson kid showed up shortly after you left and promptly taught him a lesson."

"Oh damn. Oh, I'm sorry ma'am, miss," Kenny caught himself, then he sighed with frustration. "Here we go again. I don't know how many times I've told Mitchell that Carson is too abusive with the inmates. This is getting out of hand."

"Yup," Palin agreed. "Well, c'mon Kenny, sit down for a cup of tea. I'd offer ya something stronger, but I don't have anything." Kenny hesitated a moment. "Oh, c'mon," Palin repeated. "If you've already had your break then have another one."

Kenny smiled and nodded, then sat down with the others.

Mariam poured him a cup.

"Officer Reece, I don't believe you have met the new novice. This is Penelope."

"Miss Penelope," Kenny greeted her with a slight nod. "I'm sorry about my harsh language there, but this convict isn't a bad sort. A bit hardheaded at times, but still, I'm getting tired of Mr. Carson singling him out for this kind of abuse. The warden doesn't seem prepared to do anything about it, either. Anyway," he added with a smile, and Penny couldn't help but notice what a handsome man he was, despite being old enough to be her father. "I shouldn't be bothering you with this stuff; it's none of your concern."

"Oh, but it is my concern, Officer Reece," Penny contradicted him. "Peter is a dear friend of mine, um, I mean Napoleon, and I intend to see that something does get done about this. And don't worry about your bad language. I think I'm getting used to it." She sent a sidelong glance at Dr. Palin.

Kenny smiled. "Yes, I'm sure you are, being in this

reprobate's company."

"That's the thanks I get for workin' in this insane asylum," Palin complained. "And nothin' in the cupboard to drown my sorrows with either."

"That's all you need, Doc, to get caught drinking on the job," Kenny said. "I thought you quit."

"Quit drinkin' here," Palin clarified. "Still put away a few good belts when I get off duty. How the hell else am I supposed to survive this fuckin' place?" He rolled his eyes as he realized he had cursed in front of the ladies again. Oh well.

"Oh." Then Kenny's expression turned serious as he looked across the ward to the two unconscious patients.

"So, you're a friend of his, are you?" he asked Penny.

"Yes. Him and Mathew both."

Kenny creased his brow. "Mathew?" He looked to Mariam.

"Mr. Kiefer," she informed him. "Miss Marsham first came to know them under their aliases, and she is having a hard time letting those names go."

"Ah."

"Oh dear." Penny bit her lower lip, looking sheepish. "I suppose I do still think of Mathew as the person I first came to know. It's difficult to think of them now in any other way. Especially outlaws."

Meriam smiled and patted her hand. "You and me both, my dear."

Penny brightened at this show of solidarity. She then returned her sparkling gaze to Kenny. "Mathew has told me all about you, Officer Reece. He says that you are doing a lot to help Peter, and that you watch out for him here. I want you to know that we all really appreciate that."

"Hmm," Kenny was contemplative. "So, you're a friend of both Nash and Kiefer, and here you are working in the infirmary as a novice. Isn't that interesting."

Penny and Mariam both appeared sheepish in light of this observation.

"Well, Officer Reece," Mariam commented, "as you know, many young ladies are sent to our orphanage as novices to experience that lifestyle. As you also know, most of them choose to move on to other things. A life in the service of the church is not for everyone."

Kenny nodded. “Am I to take this to mean that your current novice is not likely to be returning?”

“Not likely, no,” Mariam confirmed.

“At least, not as a novice,” Penny informed them.

Kenny’s eyebrows shot up. “Ohh?”

“As I said earlier, I intend to see that something gets done about this,” Penny further explained. “I plan to return here and have my own word with the warden.”

Kenny grinned. “Good. This stuffy old prison could do with a bit of shaking up.”

Penny mirrored his grin. She decided that she liked Officer Reece.

Kenny looked at the two patients again. “So, what’s your prognosis?” he asked Palin. “I know Ames is going to be here for a few days, but will Nash be able to return to work soon?”

“Not likely,” Palin answered. “Those two assholes busted his rib and broke two of his fingers. He’s gonna be laid up for a while. Still, it woulda been a lot worse except our novice here got in between them and stopped the lesson pretty quick.”

Kenny’s brow shot up a second time.

“Really?” His tone suggested admiration.

“They were hurting my friend,” Penny explained. “I couldn’t just stand there and do nothing.”

Kenny chuckled. “Well, it seems to me that Nash is lucky to have a friend like you watching out for him.”

Penny beamed her pleasure at the compliment.

Kenny sighed. “I swear, between illness, injury and working here, he spends more time in the infirmary than he does in his own cell. Anyway, I better be getting back to work.” He stood and nodded to the visitors. “Ladies. Doc. I’ll be back later to check up.”

***

Later that afternoon, while Mariam tended to other duties, Penny sat beside her friend, watching him sleep. She held his uninjured hand in hers and found herself becoming even more resolute in doing something about this deplorable situation.

Even in his sleep, Leon did not look restful. Just as she had noticed before, there was a change in his countenance that she could not quite put her finger on. But she knew it was something feral, something guarded. Even in a drug-induced sleep, he was watching his back.

She caressed his forehead, then cradled his face in her hand, again shocked at the angular feel of his cheekbone and jawline. And Jack said he had actually gained some weight since last winter. Oh my.

Leon moaned softly in his sleep and nestled into the feel of her hand on his face. Penny smiled; was it her imagination or had he relaxed a little, taking comfort from a friendly presence and a loving touch? She would try to be with him tomorrow when he woke up, since Dr. Palin seemed to think he would be out until at least midmorning. She hadn't wanted him to know she was here, but now that he did know, she would offer what support she could. Whether he liked it or not.

***

"Officer Carson. I have had no less than three complaints about your conduct in the infirmary the other day," Mitchell informed the head guard. "Would you care to elaborate?"

"Yes sir, Warden," Carson replied. "Nash, once again, forgot the rules right out there on the work floor, in front of everybody. I didn't think it was a good idea for the inmates to start thinkin' that it was all right to assault a guard for any reason, so Mr. Thompson and I made sure Nash got the message. The rest of the inmates now know he's spending some time in the infirmary, but as a patient this time, so they all got the message."

"Why did you take Thompson with you?" Mitchell asked him. "He's still new here, why not take one of the more experienced guards, like Pearson or Davis?"

"Because Thompson was the injured party," Carson reasoned. "I felt he deserved restitution."

"Hmm," Mitchell nodded. "I want you to understand that I have no concerns about the way you manage the prison, Mr. Carson. I have no trouble absorbing complaints from bleeding hearts like Reece and Palin suggesting that your methods are too brutal. Most of the inmates here are willing to comply with the rules once they've spent a day or two in the dark cell, or lose their privileges for a month."

Here Mitchell gave a resigned sigh and shook his head. "But there are always those few who refuse to accept the inevitable. Then we have to be tougher on them if we want to have any hope at all of breaking them in.

"If corporal punishment is all they understand then that's what we'll give them. Nash has been a particularly difficult egg to crack, and I certainly understand your need to get tough with him. I would even go so far as to say that you are doing a fine job of keeping everyone in line, and I wouldn't want you to feel you need to change your methods in any way."

Carson nodded, accepting the compliment, but wondering why he was here.

"The only thing I would suggest is that you use a little more tact next time," Mitchell explained. "I mean, really Mr. Carson . . . doling out punishment in front of Dr. Soames and her companion couldn't help but cause a stir. Indeed, Dr. Soames was very—uncharitable in her complaint." Mitchell groaned and rolled his eyes as another thought occurred to him. "And I'm probably going to be hearing an earful from that bloody lawyer, too. Goddammit."

Carson shifted uncomfortably, but remained silent.

Mitchell sighed. "That's all, Mr. Carson," he concluded. "Just, in future, when you need to discipline an inmate, please make sure you do it when no one from outside the prison facility is present to witness it. Outsiders don't understand."

"Yes sir, Warden," Carson agreed. "Next time, I'll be more 'tactful'."

"That's all I ask," Mitchell concurred. "How is Nash, by the way?"

Carson allowed a small smile to invade his lips. "He'll be a while recovering, Warden."

"Good!" Mitchell responded with some heat. "That'll be all Mr. Carson."

"Yes sir."

***

"You shouldn't be here, Penny."

"I had to see for myself how you were being treated," Penny insisted. "I was sick and tired of only getting sugar-coated answers from Mathew, and everybody treating me like I was too young to know."

Leon smiled weakly. He was lying in bed and propped up on some pillows, allowing his friend to encase his uninjured hand in both of hers. Her imploring eyes asked him to please not be angry, even while her voice demanded respect.

He gave a resigned sigh. "It seems nobody listens to me anymore. I make it very clear that I don't want either of you young ladies coming out here, and yet both of you completely disregard my wishes and find ways—devious ways, I might add—to make your way here anyway. Don't you people realize who I am? I'm the infamous Napoleon Nash. I was the most successful leader of the Elk Mountain Gang." Cough, flinch—heavy sigh. "I could crush an unruly outlaw with just a look from my cold dark eyes. Hardened criminals trembled in their boots with a reprimand from me. And yet, two young ladies, who are just barely adults, exhibit a total lack of respect for my impressive credentials and end up doing whatever they want to anyway."

Mariam, who was helping Ames with some soup, glanced over at the "great outlaw leader" and smiled.

Penny laughed out loud.

Leon sighed again and closed his eyes. "Nobody takes me seriously anymore."

Penny raised his hand to her lips and gave him a sweet kiss, then smiled at him.

"We love you too much to take you seriously."

Leon smiled, then bringing her hands up to his mouth, he returned the kiss she had given him.

"Your parents are going to be worried about you," he commented. "You need to get back home."

"We'll be leaving tomorrow, Napoleon," Mariam informed him. "It's been snowing steadily, but the road is still open. I'll make sure Penny gets on a train and heads for home before we're all snowed in for the winter."

"Good," Leon said, then closed his eyes because the lids were getting too heavy to keep open any longer. "I'll have to write to Jack all about this as soon as I'm able."

"Oh no." Penny was mortified. "Please don't tell him about this."

"Why shouldn't I?" Leon asked through closed eyes. "I expect he'll get quite a hoot out of it."

"Because he'll tell Papa, and then I'll really be in for it."

Leon chuckled. "Considering you're overdue getting home from Denver, I would not be surprised if your papa already knows about this, and you're already in for it."

"Oh." Penny was crestfallen. "I suppose you're right."

"Hmm."

"Well, I don't care," she stated, fervently. "I wanted to see you and I did, and I'll accept whatever punishment Papa gives me. We're going to get you out of here, Peter. I mean it. I won't rest until we can bring you home."

"Hmm."

"Come, Penny," Mariam stood up and settled Ames back into his pillow. "They're both tired and need to rest. We'll come back this evening."

"Oh, all right." Penny was disappointed, but looking at her friend, lying back in his pillows, she could see the truth of the statement. "I'll see you later, Peter."

Leon's nod was barely perceptible.

The two ladies glided away, and aside from Palin doing some work at the far table, the infirmary was left in silence.

"Hey, Mr. Nash," Ames called over from his bed.

Leon forced his eyes open and looked at him.

"You could do a hell of a lot worse than havin' a friend like that."

Leon smiled softly and nodded. He closed his eyes again and drifted off into sleep, thinking that Ames was right; he was a lucky man, having friends like that. A deep sigh and he was gone, dreaming about Karma, and galloping like the wind across a sea of grass with the warm sun shining down upon him, and the thrill of the ride causing him to laugh out loud.

CHAPTER FOURTEEN
NEW BEGINNINGS

Laramie, Wyoming,
Winter, 1886

Leon lay in the infirmary, eyes closed and resting. It was still night—early morning, actually, but dark and quiet. He was coming up from a morphine-induced sleep and still nestled in that feeling of comfort and well-being. He'd had strange dreams, but not terrifying ones, and now he contemplated their significance.

He knew what had induced them. Harsh comments from Thompson, demanding the revelation of his native name, had cut him deeply. Memories of his mother and her people had rushed to the surface of his mind, and the name she had given him, *Kwinaa*: Eagle, exploded into conscious thought.

Normally, Shoshone children weren't given a name until reaching the age of maturity, because only then was their true nature known. But his mother, *Huittsuu-a*, knew that his future was uncertain, so gave him a childhood name.

Not everyone was privileged to know that name. Huittsuu-a only used it in private, generally sticking with Netua: my son, among family members, and only using Napoleon when out in public. Even Jack had only been made privy to his secret name under threat of dire consequences if he dared repeat it. It was sacred; it was private. The name held power for its owner, but only if it was kept private. The more it was spread around, the less powerful it became, so to be permitted access to it was a great honor.

And there was Thompson, in his face, ridiculing him and his mother, demanding to be included in a ritual of which he knew nothing about.

***

Kansas, 1851 - 1861

The first ten years of Leon's life had been what every little boy dreamed of. His father had been strong and extremely intelligent. He could have done anything with his life, but the desire to be free of his wealthy, but stifling family, back East, along with his desire to be his own boss, outweighed any other interests. In his spare time, when he had spare time, he wrote poems and stories. On those dark and cold winter nights, when all the chores were done, he delighted his children by reading to them. Once they got to know the stories, they assumed roles and enacted plays, giving the tales new magic and life.

Leon excelled at it. He seemed able to change his voice, his mannerisms, and even his physical appearance to suit the character he portrayed.

His father often teased him that he was wasted being a farmer's son and should find his path upon the stage. It never occurred to anyone that the farmer's son would turn this talent to more nefarious activities.

Another thing Leon excelled at was his school work, even though his behavior in class would have suggested otherwise. He drove everybody to distraction, teacher and students alike, with his shenanigans and outright misbehaving. Their teacher was young but wise in the ways of education. She discovered early on that Leon's main problem was that his mind was too agile, too quick to stay focused on anything for long. As soon as the lesson had been explained once, he had grasped it, and boredom would set in.

As difficult as this behavior was to deal with, what was harder was seeing how Jack got pulled into mischief with his friend. Jack was a bright boy in his own right, but he learned differently than Leon. He needed more time to grasp new concepts, but Leon refused to give it to him. Jack would be right on the verge of understanding the lesson, when the older boy would pull his attention away and distract him with antics that were significantly more fun than learning his ABCs. Jack hero-worshipped his friend, and his education suffered for it.

Every summer, Leon and his mother made the journey to Wyoming to visit her people for a month. Before he gave permission for Huittsuu-a to marry this white man, her father insisted that she not lose her connection with her ancestors. Frederick Nash had agreed. Every year, *Huittsuu-a* would return to Yellowstone, where her family spent their summers hunting and fishing and preparing for the winter months that followed.

While living in Kansas, as the wife of a white man, *Huittsuu-a* adapted to that lifestyle. She wore the acceptable clothing, spoke English as though she were born to it, and agreed that her son should have a white man's education. She went to church on Sundays and participated in the socials on Saturdays. She was well liked in the community, and with her name anglicized to Hannah, many forgot about her Shoshone heritage.

But *Huittsuu-a* did not forget. While her husband made sure his children were well educated in the English literary classics and made aware of the most recent scientific and medical advancements, *Huittsuu-a* would take her son to the side, and in the language of her people, ensure his education became well-rounded in this area as well.

Whenever she could discreetly do so, she'd tell her son about his other people, his Shoshone people. Leon would go out of his way to help his mother prepare meals or with the cleaning up afterward just for the opportunity to hear stories of his ancestors, and of the Spirit Guides, of great warriors and strong women. He absorbed it all.

Leon loved it. He not only got to play at being an Indian, for one month out of every year, he was an Indian. He developed friendships with the other boys his age, learned how to play their games and function within their social system. He ran wild, his dark hair growing long and adorned with feathers. His skin tanned and his body firmed to the point that his friends back in Kansas would not have recognized him.

His uncle, *Mukua*, taught him how to track game and to ride a horse, Indian style, so that even as a young boy, he had developed these skills far beyond that of the average white man. Learning how to hunt with a bow and arrow, his eye/hand coordination was so acutely developed that he became an even better shot with a rifle than his father was.

He loved his grandfather and sat for hours in the evenings

His uncle, Mukua, taught him how to track game and to ride a horse Indian style

just listening to him talk. To young Leon, he appeared to be ancient in both years and wisdom. He was the medicine man, *Nat-soo-gant*, to this tribe, so he was respected by all members, and his council was always considered before any major decisions were made. Leon burst with pride to be the grandson of such an important man, and he so wanted to grow up to be just like him.

His homecoming to Kansas was always bitter sweet. He never wanted to leave Yellowstone, and if it had been up to him, he would have stayed there forever and become a full Shoshone warrior. But it was not up to him, and *Huittsuu-a* knew she had to return to her husband. She would miss her family and look forward to their next visit, but she loved the man she had married. Even without the disgrace that would befall her if she left her husband, she would never have considered such a thing. So, Leon would leave behind his feathers and bone breastplate, re-don his Anglican clothes, get a haircut, and board the coach back to Kansas with his mother.

Jack was always overjoyed at Leon's return. That one month without his friend's company seemed longer than all the other months of the year put together. He counted the days and often couldn't sleep the few nights leading up to his friend's homecoming.

Leon had to admit that, he too, would become restless and excited as the train took them closer to their homestead. Once they disembarked from the train, they still had to catch another coach that would take them closer to their town, then wait for his father to drive in with the buckboard to complete the journey home. By the time all this was accomplished, Leon had stopped missing his Shoshone family and was anxiously awaiting the reunion with his best friend.

All the rest of that summer, Leon would show Jack the new things he had learned while away. They went hunting and fishing, and rode the old plow horse when she wasn't working the field or too heavy with foal. She wasn't quite the same as the wiry mustang he'd gallop bareback across the open plains, but she was better than nothing.

Jack absorbed it all, and Leon was placed even higher on the pedestal that Jack had constructed for him. By the time Leon had reached his tenth year, he was already seeing himself as one separate and above his peers. It was an attitude that would stay with him well into his adult years, and would cause him more trouble and misery than even his wise grandfather could have foreseen.

Returning home from Yellowstone during the summer of his tenth year, he was not to know that it would be his last visit there as a child. Terror and devastation overran the family shortly after Huittsuu-a and her two children returned to their Kansas farm. Nothing was the same after that. Both Leon and Jack lost their families through horrifying events, then were thrown into an orphanage where life only brought them more misery.

Once they left the orphanage, Leon tried to get them back to his Shoshone family but was unable to do so. Life wasn't finished beating them up yet, and the need for food and shelter kept them close to the larger cities where it was easy to disappear into a crowd. Even then, by the time they were taken in to become flimflammers, they were a sorry, desperate pair of teenagers. All that mattered to them then was survival, and Leon forgot about his maternal heritage.

Then Jack left him.

Leon could not admit to being heartbroken. His grief came out in anger, spurred on by feelings of betrayal. His nephew, who was always following in his footsteps, always hanging off every word Leon said, always putting him up on that pedestal and gazing upon him with blind admiration, had walked out on him. Gone off to find his own way in life, a life that did not include his uncle.

Leon tried to find him, but anger and betrayal clouded his eyes and deafened his ears. Besides that, he had taught his nephew too well how to hide his tracks, and Jack had put those skills to good use. Leon gave it up.

Then Wyoming began pulling at him again. He traveled to the Shoshone reservation in Crowheart Butte, where his people, and the only family whom he recognized, now lived. The white man's world had given him nothing but misery and betrayal, so he went home to the last place where he could remember being truly happy. He threw away his Anglican heritage and returned to his true family, to his mother's people.

When he first arrived, he was welcomed with open arms. A feast was organized in his honor. There was dancing and music and many stories were told. A sadness fell over the gathering when Leon spoke of his mother's fate and of all the ordeals forced upon him since then. But his grandfather assured him that sad as this news was, it was not unexpected.

With so many years having gone by since *Huittsuu-a's* last visit, her family had smoked and entered the spirit world to ask of her fate. The Spirits showed them chaos, fire and blood, and much screaming. But nothing more, nothing concrete. Still, for those wise enough to know how to read the Spirits, it was obvious that Huittsuu-a was lost to them.

Since it is not polite to speak of the dead, nothing more was said about it, and Leon continued in his blessed ignorance of a lost sister whom he had forgotten ever existed.

He went through the rituals, going into seclusion to receive his vision and the image of his talisman that he must always have with him for luck and to keep him safe. He was also given his adult name during his contact with the spirit world, and just like the child's name his mother had given him, it was sacred and powerful. He would become full Shoshone and disappear from the white man's world.

But it was too late.

His vision told him that it was not to be. A coin was his talisman, but the Shoshone had no need for money; it was not their way. Money was the white man's burden.

The name his spirits gave him, *Napai'aishe*: Two At The Same Time, indicated that he would never be just one person and never settle in just one life. Always, there would be ambiguity, complexities and contradictions. He was a man apart, and his main path in this lifetime was to reconcile with all those different people whom he was and to ultimately find acceptance and contentment.

He stayed with the Shoshone through that summer and into the early fall, but try as he did, even Leon knew it wasn't going to work. He had been too long in his father's world and the simpler life of the Indians soon began to wear upon his brilliant mind.

As a young child, he had naturally adapted to the different culture, making friends quickly and holding no judgment. But, as a young adult, even those boys he had laughed and ridden and hunted with now looked upon him with adult suspicions. And his uncle was no longer with the tribe. Leon did not fit in, and he knew it. It was awkward, and he was unhappy.

When his grandfather called him to his teepee one evening, his heart sank because he knew what the discussion was going to be about. Accepting the truth himself was difficult, but hearing the same dictate coming from his grandfather was another heartbreak for the young man to endure.

It might have been different, his grandfather said, if they had still been living free and clear on their own land. But they were on reservation land now, and subject to certain conditions. Eventually the Indian Agent would know, and Leon would be forced to leave anyway. A white man would not be permitted to remain living with the tribe, and Leon was a white man now. He had been a white man's son and raised in the white man's world, so there he must return.

"There has also been other trouble that you do not know of," his grandfather stated. "Mukua, my son and your uncle, is no longer with us."

Leon's heart sank. "Mukua is dead? How?"

"No, he is not dead. He is simply not with us. The white man's agents came and tried to take Mukua's son from him. They have taken many of our children to go live at the Residential Schools to teach them White Man's ways. Mukua did not want this for his son. He killed the white man who had taken the boy.

"Many of us here thought it was a noble thing. He was protecting his family, so it was an honorable killing. But the Indian Agent did not see it that way. He came here, searching for Mukua, telling us that we must hand him over to face white man's justice. But we did not see it this way.

"Still, Mukua could not stay here. He left behind his family and has disappeared, so, to us, he is dead.

"Since it is impolite to speak of the dead, I tell you this for only one reason. It is not safe for you here. As I have said, once the white man knows you are here, he will take you away. Normally they leave us alone, and we could hide you, but not now. They watch us, and often drop by without being invited, which is very rude. But they are looking for Mukua, and they will surely find you.

"I don't understand the logic of the white man. Though you are a young man now and have completed the necessary rituals to move into adulthood, the white men may still see you as a child. They may try to put you in one of these schools, and they may try to convince you that your mother's people are worthless. That you should be all white man."

"They already tried that, Grandfather. It didn't work."

The old man nodded. "So, you know of what I speak. Even though you must leave here and live among the whites, I pray to the Spirits that you will not forget us. That you will honor your mother and your people."

Leon's eyes filled with tears. Not just because he had to leave, but because of the tragedy that had befallen his uncle and friend. And for his grandfather, who had suffered such losses. He nodded his acquiescence.

"I will, Grandfather. I will always honor you. I promise."

Leon's grandmother, Daa'za, made him a special gift. Traditionally, when a young man came of age, she would make him a breastplate of the finest quality, using only the best elk bone, buffalo leather, and silver acquired through trade with the more southern tribes. But since Napai'aishe would not be remaining with the Shoshone, she used the same materials to make for him a fine belt.

The belt was long enough that Leon also had a hat band made from it. He cherished these items for the gifts that they were, and he would wear them throughout most of his life.

It was with a heavy heart that he set out for lower ground before the winter snows began to blow. He felt lost and confused, and very much alone. He, literally, had no family left. His parents and siblings had all been massacred. His father's family had rejected him as an inferior before he was even born, and now his mother's family, though acknowledging kinship and affection, had also sent him on his way. His nephew had abandoned him, and as far as Leon was concerned, that was the end of it. He had no one left.

So, he decided, if neither world would accept him, then he'd have to make a whole new world for himself. He'd do it, too. Using his own intelligence, his finely tuned skills and the courage of his forefathers, he'd show them all. The West would come to know the name Napoleon Nash, and he would be respected; he would be somebody. And he didn't need anybody else to help him get there.

***

Laramie, Wyoming
Winter 1886

Now he lay on the cot in the infirmary at the Wyoming Territorial Prison, his body battered and beaten once again, and his life in a shamble.

What an arrogant young fool I was. Even when Jack and I got back together, I was still so full of myself. All we did was feed off each other's anger, and look where it got us. Well, me, anyway. But, I suppose, that's fitting. I always was the instigator, even when we were children.

I did forget about my mother's family. I promised my grandfather that I would not and yet I let it all slip away.

Am I ever going to smarten up?

Now, looking back at the time he'd spent with the Shoshone, his most powerful memory was of the gifts and the names he had received, first from his mother, and then from the Spirits. Thompson hadn't realized the sacred ground he had trodden upon when he showed disrespect toward those memories from the outlaw's troubled past.

***

Arvada, Colorado,
Winter 1886

Penny disembarked from the train with bags in hand. She felt trepidatious of the confrontation that was to come.

It was a cold and gray afternoon and Penny snuggled deeper into her warm coat as she paced up and down the platform. There was a light snow falling along with the temperatures, and the sharp scent in the air promised more snow to come. Penny suspected she had made it home just in time. But thoughts of the weather quickly dissipated when she turned and spotted her father.

They started toward one another, but neither was smiling. Indeed, Cameron's mouth was set in a hard line and Penny felt her stomach twist into an even bigger knot than it had already been in.

Father and daughter stood facing one another, and Penny put her bags down at her feet, then stood up straight and looked her father in the eye.

She loved him dearly, and it broke her heart to meet with his disapproval, but she was adamant that she would not back down on this.

Finally, after what seemed an eternity of standing and staring at one another, Cameron broke the silence.

"Penelope."

Oh, she knew she was in trouble now.

"Papa, I—"

But Cameron stepped forward and picked up her bags, then turned on his heel and walked back toward the waiting buggy. Penny hung her head, then silently followed.

The ride back to the Rocking M was anything but pleasant. Apparently, Cameron didn't have much to say to his daughter, and Penny felt she would have much preferred a chewing out over this stoic silence. All her resolve to not back down was being deflated by the simple fact that she was being given no obstacles to fight against. Kind of hard to self-righteously stand your ground when no one was challenging you.

Halfway home, all of Penny's resolve to be right had dissolved into anxious repentance, and she was overcome by the need to explain herself. She would try anything now to lessen some of this silent disapproval being heaped upon her, and she finally succumbed.

"I'm sorry, Papa, but I had to see him, and nobody was willing to take me. I asked Mathew and he refused. I asked Josephine, and she wouldn't go for it either. Everybody kept on insisting that I was too young and that Peter wouldn't want me to come anyway. But I had to. I had to see for myself. Please understand."

Silence ensued for a few more minutes as Monty paced on through the snow. Penny sighed, and with hanging head, snuggled deeper into her blanket. She knew her father would be angry with her, but he had never been so angry that he was not willing to talk.

Finally, Cameron relented, and though he still would not look at her and his voice was tight, he did open communication.

"Do you have any idea how worried we were? When I arrived at the train station last week and you were not there, all sorts of wild fears ran through my mind. And your mother—! You couldn't even bother to send us a telegram."

"I hadn't planned on being gone this long," Penny explained in a small voice, "and I didn't realize you would be meeting my train."

"How else did you expect to get home? Were you planning to walk out to the ranch from town?"

"No! I just . . . I didn't think."

"You're darn right you didn't think!" Cameron agreed. "Your mother was beside herself with worry. Thank goodness Dr. Soames had an address for Jack and she sent us a telegram to let us know where you were. Right now, I feel like locking you in your bedroom and throwing away the key until you're thirty-five. And I'm certainly going to have a thing or two to say to Caroline too—don't you dare deny she had anything to do with this, because I know darn well she did!

"You two were always good at instigating things together. I swear, Steven is going to have his hands full marrying into this family—especially when he realizes he's going to be inheriting the younger sister as well. Poor man—I feel like I should warn him now that he would be much better off packing his bags and returning to Wyoming, still single and worry-free." He released a big sigh as he shook his head. "Well, if this incident hasn't opened his eyes, I guess nothing will. Young and stupid. By the time he figures it out, it'll be too late."

Cameron finally quieted down and focused on keeping Monty on the road, since the snow was getting deeper and the track harder to distinguish.

Penny sat silently and sent a furtive glance to her father, hopeful that the worst of the onslaught was over.

Fortunately, anything more Cameron might have wanted to bestow upon his daughter would have to wait because they were soon pacing down the road toward the ranch and into the yard.

Monty needed no direction to find his way to the door of his barn.

Sam, who had been waiting for them, stepped out to take hold of the horse's bridle while the Marshams stepped down from the buggy.

"I'm sure glad you folks made it back," he stated as he patted Monty. "I was beginnin' to worry."

"Yes, it's falling heavily," Cameron observed. "As soon as you get Monty unharnessed and put away, why don't you head for home. I'm sure Maribelle is getting worried by now."

Sam smiled and nodded. "Yes sir, Mr. Marsham. Thank you."

Sam clucked to the little bay gelding and they moved into the carriage house.

Once inside, Sam quickly released the horse from the shafts and pushed the buggy back and out of the way. He unharnessed the animal and led him back over to the horse barn and tied him in the aisleway. He then gave him a quick rub-down to brush away the snow and to make sure he was as dry as he could be, before putting him into his stall with some hay.

Karma, Midnight, Berry, and Spike, along with Sam's own horse, Ginger, were all comfortably settled in their stalls by this time. They hardly gave the newcomer a second snort, while they contentedly munched on their own snack. Life was good.

Being inside a sturdy barn filled with horses on a cold and snowy day brings with it its own kind of peaceful pleasure. It can still be chilly, but the warmth from the horses' thickly coated bodies, along with the sounds of munching and snorting, and stamping of feet, made one feel cozy and welcome. Therefore, it was with some reluctance that Sam brought Ginger out into the aisle and commenced saddling her up so he could head for home, himself.

It was at times like these that he regretted home was no longer just across the yard in the bunkhouse. With that good wood stove quickly heating up the small room, as well as the coffee, the living quarters had soon become warm and comfortable.

Still, it was a trade-off. Once he did get home, he would be greeted by his wife, who could also make their small home warm and cozy. And he could be sure that the coffee would be on and ready for him as soon as he walked in the front door. All he had to do was get there.

His little sorrel mare wasn't all that pleased about being hauled out of her stall either, and stood stoically, with her ears back throughout most of her tacking up. She had been nice and comfortable right where she was, and now she had to go out in that? Life for a horse wasn't fair sometimes. But then, it occurred to her that Mrs. Human would have a nice warm mash waiting for her in her own stall at her other home, so perhaps a quick trot through the snow to receive that wasn't too much of a sacrifice for her to make.

Sam got her saddled, made sure everything in the barn was put away, then bundling himself up in his coat, hat and gloves, he led Ginger out into the whiteness. Sam noticed that the temperature didn't seem that cold; it was quite pleasant out. The snow falling, along with the thick white covering upon the ground, made everything seem quiet and peaceful—almost serene. He smiled, and giving his mare a pat on the neck, he mounted up and they headed out of the yard at a trot, toward his home and his wife.

***

Inside the ranch house, Penny was getting hit with a chill of another kind. She really must have messed up big time for her mother to be giving her the cold shoulder. Even Eli, who sat on the floor, coloring on some scrap paper, looked up at the three adults with a worried expression on his face. The atmosphere in the living room was oppressive even to him.

"Can I help you with dinner, Mama?" Penny asked.

"No," Jean answered, over her shoulder. "Why don't you go upstairs and put your things away. Perhaps I'll feel like talking to you after that."

"Yes, Mama," Penny mumbled and, with a quick sideways glance at her father, she took her bags upstairs to unpack.

As soon as she was out of sight, Jean turned to her husband and they exchanged knowing smiles.

"Do you think it's working?" Jean whispered.

Cameron nodded. "You should have seen her face while we were driving home. It was all I could do not to start laughing right then and there."

"Ohhh, thank goodness I wasn't with you," Jean said. "I don't think I could have handled it."

"Hmm. All I had to do was remind myself how worried we were about her, and that helped me keep a straight face. A little bit of the cold shoulder now should make her think twice about pulling something like that again."

The downstairs bedroom door opened, and Jack poked his head out.

"How did it go?"

Cameron gave him the thumbs up sign, then Jack came out to replenish his coffee cup. He was just heading back into his own room when Penny came downstairs. Seeing her friend, she sent him a warm smile.

"Hello, Mathew. I really need to talk to you about—"

"Not right now, Penny," Jack interrupted her, as he strode toward his door. "I ah . . . I have some words to decipher."

"But . . ."

He was gone, the bedroom door closing firmly behind him.

Penny looked confused. What did he mean, words to decipher? She looked at her mother, but Jean turned her back and continued with supper preparations. Penny frowned and turned to her father.

"I'm busy with the books right now, Penny," he commented as he settled in at the dining room table and began opening ledgers.

Then Penny smiled and turned to her little brother, who had been watching the unfolding drama with intense interest. As soon as he locked eyes with his sister however, he quickly turned away and was once again enthralled with his artful masterpiece on the floor.

Penny slumped, and with one last glance around at her family, she turned and sulked her way back up to her room. Dinner was going to be an uncomfortable affair.

***

As it turned out, the first fifteen minutes of sparse and cold dinner conversation was uncomfortable, but fortunately for Penny, the youngest member of the Marsham family decided the punishment of his older sister had gone on long enough. He finally broke under the pressure and started to cry. Penny, who was hurt more by his outburst than any of the other cold shoulders, was instantly on her feet and over to him.

"Oh, no, sweetie," she begged as she picked him up in her arms, "don't cry. Please don't cry. I'm sorry."

She gave her brother a hug, and Eli, still crying lustily, put his arms around his sister's neck and returned the hug. He didn't know why everyone was mad at his favorite sibling, but he'd had enough of it and decided it was time to put the matter to rest.

Everyone else at the table sat back and gave up the pretense of indifference, and the atmosphere improved. Penny continued to stand by the table, hugging her brother and whispering assurances to him until his sobs gradually settled down. He pushed himself off her shoulder, and staring into her eyes, he smiled through his tears. Penny smiled back at him and gave him a kiss. He giggled and leaned in for another hug and kissed her on her cheek.

No one could resist the child's antics and there were smiles all around as Penny returned her brother to his chair.

Once they were settled, silence returned to the table, and Penny realized it was time she faced the music.

"I'm sorry I worried you all so much," she confessed. "I was intent on how to get out there to see Peter, I didn't realize how selfishly I was behaving. But I can certainly see it now, and I truly am sorry. I'm not sorry that I saw him, but I'm sorry for what I put you all through."

Cameron and Jean exchanged looks and a quick, silent conversation took place. Jean smiled and nodded.

Cameron concurred.

"All right," he said. "Apology accepted. But don't you ever do anything like that again, or I will lock you up and throw away the key until you're thirty-five."

Penny smiled. "Yes, Papa."

By the time coffee and pie had made its way to the table, the conversation was in full swing. Penny was in her glory relating the events she had witnessed while at the prison.

"He got beat up again?" Jack queried, feeling his temper rise.

"Yes!" Penny was adamant. "And it was just for doing his job. He stopped one of the new guards from doing further damage to an injured man, but that senior guard—Carson?" Jack nodded. "He didn't think that was a good enough reason for Peter to break the rules, and he came into the infirmary later and, well . . . he really hurt Peter."

"Ah jeez," Jack groaned. "Now I'm stuck here and can't get out to see him. How bad was he hurt, do you know?"

"Oh yes." Penny then continued with a hint of pride. "I helped to patch him up. It was very interesting, watching the doctor set that broken rib. And then, with the fingers, he took each one and gave it a quick yank to get them looking like fingers again. You could hear the bones crackling as they got forced back into place."

"Oh dear," Jean commented. "I'm not sure this is quite the proper supper conversation. And it must have hurt poor Peter."

"Oh no," Penny assured her mother. "Dr. Palin wouldn't have done that to him while he was awake. He put Peter to sleep with morphine. I'm sure he didn't feel a thing."

Jack cringed at the mention of that drug, but only Cameron noticed.

"And it was interesting, Mama," Penny insisted. "Dr. Palin, he showed me how to splint the fingers and tape them to the other fingers, so they wouldn't be able to move, then we wrapped the whole hand in gauze. We also taped up the rib, so it wouldn't be able to move either, though I'm afraid Peter is going to be awfully stiff for a while." She creased her brow and reflected. "I wasn't sure about that Dr. Palin at first; he can be awfully crude, but he's actually a very nice man, once you get past his language."

Jack snorted. "Yeah, from what Leon has told me, I suppose that's one way of describin' Doc Palin. He is different, that's for sure."

"Palin?" Cameron asked. "Any relation to our deputy?"

"Oh yeah," Jack recalled. "Leon said Ben is the Doc's nephew. I don't know how much they keep in touch though."

"Hmm. Small world."

Jack nodded, then returned his attention to Penny. "What about Officer Reece? Wasn't he around through any of this?"

"Yes." Penny nodded emphatically. "He stopped the one guard from hitting Peter with that club thing, while Peter was trying to help the injured man, and he escorted us back to the infirmary. But then he left, and I suppose, now that I think about it, that's probably what Mr. Carson was waiting for, because he and the other guard showed up right after that.

"Dr. Palin tried to stop them from hitting Peter, but he got pushed out of the way, and Sister Mariam tried to reason with them, but . . ." Penny shrugged, indicating that no one was going to stop Carson once he got started. She wisely decided not to mention her part in stopping the onslaught, remembering the chewing out she had received the last time she had gotten in between one of her friends and potential danger. "When Mr. Reece came by later, he was really angry." She smiled. "Officer Reece seems like a very nice man."

"Yeah," Jack grumbled. "For a prison guard." He wisely decided not to mention the fact that it was Reece who had broken Leon's arm a while back. And worked him into the ground in the pouring rain, just for being drunk. Still, that all may have been justified, considering. So, he'd just leave it alone. "He does seem to be willin' ta help out, and he keeps me informed of what's goin' on there. I expect I'll be hearin' from him about this incident, soon enough."

"Oh," Penny commented, hoping that Officer Reece would not mention her standing up to the two guards with billy clubs. She looked to her father, building up the courage to breach a new, but related, topic. "Papa, I really feel that I have to do something about this. The conditions at that prison are terrible. Peter doesn't even look like himself anymore."

The two men at the table exchanged looks. Cameron had heard much the same concerns from Jack.

"Well," Cameron sighed. "I suppose it's a good thing winter is setting in, because I don't want you going back there."

"But Papa . . .!"

Cameron held up his hand to silence her. "Not yet, Penny," he compromised. "Perhaps in the spring you can join Steven and Caroline, if he's willing to take you."

"I could go with Mathew," Penny insisted.

"Ahh . . ." Jack started to protest.

"I don't think that's a good idea," Cameron confirmed.

"But why not?" Penny questioned. "Mathew would look after me."

"I have no doubt about that," her father commented, "but you are still a maiden, Penny, and it would not be proper."

"Arrgg!" Penny protested. "Mathew wouldn't do anything, Papa. You know that."

"I'm actually more concerned about what you might do," her father informed her. "You are a little bit too headstrong for your own good. Still, we'll wait until spring and then see. Besides, Napoleon may be out by then, anyway." He turned to Jack. "Don't you have an appointment to see the new governor in January?"

"Ah, yup," Jack confirmed. "Me, Steven and Taggard will be goin' ta talk to him about all a this."

"Well, here's hoping," Cameron commented. "In the meantime, Penny, you can always carry on with your letter writing. Let people know what you're trying to accomplish and perhaps describe some of the abuses you witnessed. You might get good results if you play on peoples' sympathy."

"That's true," Penny agreed. "And you're right. There really isn't much I can do through the winter anyway. I think I will start writing some more letters."

The other three adults exchanged looks. Penny had agreed to this decree a little bit too easily for their liking.

Then Eli started banging his cup and voicing his displeasure at still being trapped in his chair. Dinner was over with! Why was everyone still just sitting around?

CHAPTER FIFTEEN
FRIENDS, OLD AND NEW

Laramie, Wyoming

Kenny motioned to the newly-hired junior guard. "Officer Thompson, a word if you could."

"Oh, Mr. Reece. Umm, something wrong?"

"Just some words of caution," Kenny assured him. "Being new here, I realize you are still trying to find your footing. Also, seeing as how Mr. Carson is the senior guard, he would naturally be the best person for you to look to for instruction." Thompson nodded. "However, Mr. Carson does have a tendency to lean toward the aggressive side when dealing with certain inmates."

"Yeah," Thompson agreed, "but from what I've seen, some of 'em ask for it."

"Sometimes, yes," Kenny had to agree. "But these men are not ignorant savages; most of them know what fair punishment is and what it isn't."

"Yeah." Thompson was becoming suspicious.

"Now, again, I realize you are new, and you really haven't had the chance to learn your way around yet, or to know which of the inmates you can push and which ones you can't."

"I treat the inmates all the same, Mr. Reece," Thompson insisted, "and if one of 'em pushes me, I'll push 'em right back!"

"I certainly agree with the latter part of that statement," Kenny told him. "But if you insist on treating the all inmates the same, then you are going to get yourself into trouble."

"But the rules are the rules!" Thompson was trying to understand where this was going. "If an inmate breaks a rule, then he needs to be punished. They have to be kept in line."

"Agreed," Kenny confirmed. "But there are different ways of

doing that. Most of the inmates here are just young, down on their luck, fellas, who ran into some hard times. They want to serve their sentence and go home. They learn the rules and they obey them, and they don't generally give us much trouble.

"Then there are others, like Harris and Johnston, who aren't too bright, but tend to be mean. They learn the rules, but will go out of their way to break them every chance they get. Those fellas, yes; you have to come down hard on them or they will run you ragged.

"Then we have the others, like Boeman and Nash, who aren't stupid." Here, Thompson snorted. Kenny hesitated and sent him a hard look. "That's where you're making your first real mistake, and it's a mistake that could get you into trouble here."

"What's that?" Thompson asked, already feeling bored and slightly irritated with this conversation.

"Somewhere along the line, you've come to the conclusion that Nash is stupid."

"Yeah, well," Thompson shrugged. "Everyone says that Napoleon Nash is such a brilliant man, but I ain't seen any evidence of that. As far as I can tell, he's just some dim-witted half-breed."

"And that assumption is going to get you into trouble," Kenny reiterated. "Make no mistake about it, Napoleon Nash is a brilliant man—probably smarter than you and me put together." Another derisive snort from Thompson, which Kenny chose to ignore. "He knows the rules inside out, upside down, backwards and forwards, and he knows how to manipulate them. He knows how to use them to his advantage, and he knows how to circumvent them. Most importantly of all, he knows how to ignore them. If he feels justified in seeking retaliation, he will do so—rules be damned."

Thompson frowned.

"How can he ignore them?" he asked. "If he breaks the rules then he will be punished."

"Yes, and he knows that," Kenny continued, "but he also knows what's fair and what isn't. Often the loss of privileges or a stint in the dark cell is enough to dissuade the inmates from breaking the rules. Going after any of these men with the intent to do physical damage is usually a tactic that is not necessary to get the message across, and only serves to create resentment. If you continue to abuse your privilege here and dole out unwarranted punishments, Nash is the kind of man who will, eventually, retaliate. And he won't care about the punishment for doing so; he'll simply accept it as the price he has to pay."

"So, you're tellin' me not to punish him for breakin' the rules?"

"No, Mr. Thompson. I'm saying don't punish him unfairly. Respect the inmates and on the most part, they will respect you. Don't back down from them and don't ever assume anything. The best piece of advice I can give you for working in a prison, Mr. Thompson, is always watch your back, treat the inmates with respect, and always be fair when it comes to doling out punishment. If you can get through the day knowing you've done that, then you've had a good day."

"Yessir, Mr. Reece," Thompson responded. "I'll certainly keep that in mind."

"Good."

Thompson headed off to continue with his rounds.

Kenny felt some trepidation as he watched the junior guard leave. He had the feeling he hadn't gotten through to the man at all.

***

Leon shivered. He was back in his cell, though far from being healed enough to return to his regular work schedule. He was wearing every layer of clothing he could pull on, but he was still stiff and sore, making the cold temperatures bite all the harder. The two broken fingers on his right hand made it difficult for him to write any letters, so he contented himself with reading and deciphering new words.

The latest new word was *"Qualm"*. Leon had already known the meaning of that one, and in his present mood and condition, he had come up with a sentence very quickly.

Qualms? Yeah. I have some qualms. I have qualms about spending another freezing winter in this damn prison. I just wanna get out of here! Why can't I just go home? I'll be good, I promise . . .

***

Jack hadn't been able to make it out for his usual visit, and though it had been disappointing for Leon, it hadn't come as a surprise. Right after Penny departed for Colorado, the winter had taken hold with a vengeance, and the first of many blizzards soon closed roads and shut down the trains, so even the mail was having a hard time getting through.

It was a rough time of year for the inmates. Not only was Christmas now fast approaching, which tended to make lonely hearts even lonelier, but the dark days and darker nights made the cold more penetrating and the loneliness more acute.

Leon was better prepared for the cold weather this year, but he still felt the chill, and he wondered how he had even survived it the previous year, when he'd had very little apparel to stave off the freezing temperatures. Of course, come to think of it, he almost hadn't survived, so things were already better this year. He tried to remind himself of that while he lay on his cot, in his cell, in the dark, once again staring at a ceiling he couldn't see; things were better.

He grudgingly admitted that he was warmer. He was also eating, and he had friends. Jack Kiefer was still his partner and that was certainly better than where they were this same time last year. A new governor was in office, and though that wasn't a guarantee of anything happening, it was certainly better than the same old dictate.

Ohh, let's see, what else? Oh! The music. Yes, that has been a life-saver. He'd turn that on in his mind again, once he was ready to settle for the night. And Dr. Soames, with her lectures, and the new words every week. He had to admit that was fun.

Kenny was standing by him, and Dr. Palin, too. He wasn't quite sure where he stood with the warden though. Leon hadn't been taken up to see him since he was injured. That could go either way. If Warden Mitchell clued in to the fact that Leon had outright lied to him, there could be hell to pay. And Leon really wished Carson would go fall off a ledge somewhere. He could handle Thompson on his own, but him backing up Carson was not a winning proposition, at least, not for Leon.

He rolled onto his side and snuggled into his layers of warm clothing and blankets. The thought occurred to him that the worst thing about the colder nights was that he didn't have a nice, warm, soft body to snuggle into as well. He no longer thought about sex, and this was both a relief and a concern for him. It was frustrating becoming aroused when there wasn't anything he could do about it other than—what he could do about it.

Then, as a young and healthy male, the fact that he didn't fantasize much about sex, even though it was far more comfortable not to, the fact that he didn't caused him to worry. Was he going to forget how? What would happen the next time, if there was a next time, he found himself in the embrace of a warm and enticing feminine bed-mate? Would he still be able to, well—perform?

The things a man would worry about when he had nothing else to do but stare into the darkness. Leon sighed heavily and decided it was late and time to sleep. He closed his eyes for real and settled deeper into his warm cocoon.

Who to listen to tonight? Something gentle and relaxing. Something that would calm his mind and relax his body; something soothing . . . Chopin, yeah. Something by Chopin.

***

Warden Mitchell was busy at his desk, catching up with correspondence that had finally made its way to the prison. A series of nasty blizzards had slowed everything down from Dr. Soames's visits, to supplies, and to the mail service. But for now, the clouds had departed, the temperatures had dropped, and the cold sun shone down on the white world of a winter wonderland. The access roads were cleared, the snow packed down, and life started to move again.

The sunny morning found Warden Mitchell in a gloomy mood. The rush of backed-up mail had brought with it numerous letters that had brought irritating news. Who in the world were these people who seemed to keep coming out of the woodwork, thinking they knew more about running a prison than he did?

He was used to Mr. Kiefer, even though the man could be a major pain, and Dr. Soames, of course, had lodged her verbal complaint of unnecessary abuse. Then there was the lawyer, Mr. Granger, who refused to go away.

What was that about? Usually, once a case was settled and the convict incarcerated, the lawyer simply disappeared; he was no longer being paid, so why stick around? Indeed, Warden Mitchell had no contact with the inmates' lawyers. There was no point; the case was over, and the defendant was handed over to the prison system and forgotten.

But Mr. Granger had maintained contact. Not only with his client, but with Warden Mitchell himself, and seemed to be of the opinion that he had some say in the treatment of his client.

Somehow, word of Leon's most recent punishment had

gotten out, and the lawyer had been quick to send a letter of reprimand. Mitchell had dismissed it at first, after all, what was the lawyer going to do about it now that winter had set in? There was really nothing he could do; this was Mitchell's prison and he would run it his way.

Besides that, Nash's punishment had been legitimate; attacking a guard in the middle of the work floor, right in front of the assembly of inmates. Of course, he'd have to be punished for that.

But now, Mitchell was irritated as he worked his way through the pile of letters on his desk. Mrs. Gabriella Tanguay from San Francisco, California, who the hell was that? Someone else who seemed to think she knew better.

Her letter was professional and to the point, but there had been an underlying threat suggesting the warden was being watched, and that steps would be taken if the unwarranted abuses continued. Unwarranted abuses? Did Nash have his own telegraph office in his cell?

Now Mitchell found himself staring at yet another letter written by a woman—what was it with these women, anyway? Didn't they have enough to do, looking after their households and their children, without sticking their noses into mens' affairs? This latest letter was from a Miss Penelope Marsham.

Well, that explains it, Mitchell snarked. *She's not married, so has nothing better to do with her time.*

Her letter intimated that she, somehow, had first-hand knowledge of excessive punishment being doled out, and that this treatment of an inmate would not go unchallenged. Mr. Nash has friends. Obviously! And his friends were not going to stand by and allow this to continue. Something was going to be done . . . so on, and so on.

Mitchell sighed in frustration.

This was simply the ranting of a young and flighty female who needed a man in her life to take the young lady in hand and teach her her proper place. Something was going to be done, indeed.

Mitchell snorted.

Yet, a nagging doubt wiggled its way into his gut, and his jaw tightened as he sat and considered his options.

Perhaps it would be better, for the time being, to back off Mr. Nash. Let things settle down somewhat, and give his friends the opportunity to relax and direct their attentions elsewhere. Friends and family could be such a nuisance sometimes, but fortunately, most of the inmates didn't have much in the way of outside support. But apparently, Mr. Nash did. Mr. Mitchell decided that he was going to have to start dealing with this particular inmate in a different manner.

He would back off Nash for a while and let the inmate relax, let him get back into his regular routine. He could keep his privileges and his contacts, then they could both carry on pretending they were pulling the wool over the other one's eyes. But no low-life inmate and his friends—and lawyer—were going to tell him how to run his prison. Just let them try it, and they'd see then what Warden Michell was truly capable of!

***

So, life for Leon settled down again through the winter. The warden left him alone. Mitchell was no longer asking the inmate for much of anything, and Leon was relieved at not being put in a position where he was having to make things up.

Christmas came and went. He attended the special Christmas service in the common room, but decided not to stay for the handing out of gifts by the Sisters. He felt his relationship with Mariam was beyond that now. He had received so much more from her in the way of friendship and support, so let the others receive their gifts, and Leon discreetly departed.

However, Mariam had other intentions along those lines, and when she didn't find Leon in the assembly, she requested and received special permission for a guard escort her to Leon's cell, so she could deliver his gifts in person.

She was disappointed to find herself in the company of Officer Thompson, as she was having a difficult time forgiving him for his part in the assault upon her friend. In any case, she was civil and polite to him and kept her own personal dislike for the man under wraps.

"On your feet, Nash," Thompson ordered, "you have company."

Leon couldn't hide his irritation as he glanced up from *A Christmas Carol,* but then seeing who his visitor was, he quickly put his book aside and got to his feet.

"Dr. Mariam," he mumbled, feeling embarrassed now that he

had ducked out on her. But then he smiled. "Merry Christmas."

"And a Merry Christmas to you too, Napoleon," Mariam returned his smile. "I realize that perhaps you feel you are not deserving of any more gifts from the school—or from me, for that matter. But I must insist."

"Oh no. You really don't need to," Leon protested. "You've already given me so much."

"Nonsense! It's Christmas." Mariam was in her usual jovial good spirits. "The children at the orphanage made some cookies for you and they were very adamant that I be sure to give them to you—in person. So, here they are."

Leon accepted the small box that was apparently full of cookies, and then smiled abashedly. *The children made cookies especially for me?*

"Thank you," he murmured. "But why . . .?"

"They feel a connection to you," she explained. "They all know that you and Jack were orphaned at a young age, just as they've been. They read the dime novels about you, and the older ones have all the newspaper articles from your trial. Whenever I visit with them, they insist on hearing all about how you're doing and hoping that you are well. I can't count how many times I have retold the story of how we all met. They seem to like hearing that one over and over, and over again."

Now Leon really felt embarrassed. He saw Thompson roll his eyes, and was tempted to punch him in the face. But seeing as how it was Christmas and all, he refrained.

"They ask about me?"

"Oh yes."

"Oh." He looked at the box in his hands, not quite sure how to respond to this. "I hope I don't disappoint them," he finally commented.

"No, I don't think you do," she assured him and placed a gentle hand on his arm.

Thompson shifted uncomfortably. He really didn't like the lady parson getting that close to this inmate. He knew that, for some reason, he and the doctor were friends, but he didn't trust Nash, and Carson had warned him that the man could be unpredictable.

And yet, Dr. Soames seemed to know what she was doing, so Thompson let it go, but remained watchful all the same.

"They admire you," Mariam continued. "You give them

hope."

"Hope?" Leon was incredulous. "I've been an outlaw most of my adult life, only to end up in prison! How does that give them hope?"

"I don't know," she admitted. "All I do know is that they admire and respect you. I guess, they see in you someone who had a hard beginning, yet rose up to make something of yourself." Leon snorted. "I know. In the eyes of the law you are a criminal, but in the eyes of those children, you are a "gentleman bandit" who is dashing, romantic and even honorable, not to mention, very handsome—in the eyes of a child."

Leon laughed. "Yes well, as long as they don't go off to become thieves and bandits themselves. There's not much romantic or honorable about that!"

"I don't think they will," she assured him. "Most of them give every indication of growing up into fine citizens. But, in the meantime, a little innocent romanticism isn't going to do them any harm. I will tell them that you very much appreciated the cookies."

"Yes indeed," Leon agreed. "And wish them all a Happy Christmas from me."

"I will," Mariam promised. "And now, this second parcel is from the kind ladies in our parish who wished to contribute. I hope you will find it useful."

"Ah, yes, ma'am." Leon accepted the second parcel, having given up any thoughts of refusing the gifts. "Thank you."

"Goodbye for now, Napoleon."

"Goodbye."

***

Leon was left alone in his cell once again. He sat on his cot, holding his box of cookies and thinking what an odd circumstance this was. Eventually, he opened the box and took a look at the assortment of oddly shaped pieces of baked dough, each adorned with a different colorful design depicting little Christmas items. One was a tree, another looked like snowflakes, another was, well, Leon supposed it was a cross—and was that supposed to be a running horse? A sheriff's badge?

The convict smiled, and picking up the treat with the badge design on it, he took a sampling nibble. He had to admit, it wasn't too bad. Quite tasty, actually. Not quite as good as Jean's baking, but nobody's baking was as good as Jean's baking! He'd have to find a way to thank the children for this little pleasure. He didn't know how, but hopefully, something would come up somewhere down the line.

He finished the one cookie, then closed the box and slipped it onto the floor under his table. He then focused on ripping open the brown paper wrapping on his second gift. Woolen long johns! Yes, those will come in handy. And more socks. Good. He smiled and reprimanded himself for being too proud. He should be more willing to accept gifts when offered to him, especially at Christmas time, and simply be happy that people who didn't even know him were willing to give. He would be in dire straits again this winter, if not for unsolicited gifts.

He settled into his pillow and picked up his book, all prepared to read the afternoon away. Then he frowned and sent a speculative look toward the box of cookies. Oh well, it's Christmas, why not? He reached down and, grabbing the box of cookies, he brought them up to rest on his stomach and commenced to read the afternoon away while munching on sweet treats. Better him than the rats.

***

On the Saturday between Christmas and New Year's, Taggard came to visit. But as soon as Leon saw the look on his friend's face, he knew this wasn't just a social call. Something had happened.

"Hey, Taggard," Leon greeted him. "Nice to see you. Did you have a good Christmas?"

"Yeah, Leon, not bad." Taggard sat down opposite him at the table. "Had a nice supper there at the Widow Jenkins' place. You remember her, don't ya? Husband died last year from influenza."

"Ahh, no, can't say that I do. Sorry. Is she someone you've been seeing lately?"

"Well, yeah, a bit," Taggard admitted. "Nothing serious, you know. Just two people with nowhere else to be on the holidays."

"Uh huh."

Leon waited. He could feel something more coming.

"I'm sorry to have to tell ya this, Leon," Taggard finally

confessed, "but Governor Baxter has resigned his office."

"What? Already?" Leon hated to admit it, but he was disappointed with this news. He had been trying not to put too much hope into the possibility that a new governor might be more willing to review his case. Secretly, though, he had been looking forward to the meeting his friends had booked to speak with Governor Baxter. He had allowed hope to sneak into his conscious musings.

"Yeah," Taggard confirmed. "He put in his resignation about ten days ago, and all appointments have been canceled—for now."

"Well . . ." Leon was almost speechless in his disappointment. "What do we do, now? Can't we book an appointment with the next governor?"

"There isn't a governor for the territory right now," the sheriff explained. "President Cleveland has appointed the Secretary of the Territory, ahh, a Mr. Elliott Morgan, to fill in the office until a new governor can be sworn in."

"Oh," Leon murmured. "Can't we make an appointment to see Mr. Morgan? Considering he's temporary, he might be happy to give me a pardon." Leon was hopeful, but knew he was grasping at straws.

"No," Taggard told him. "The governor's office isn't taking any appointments right now. It seems that Mr. Morgan is in there just to tend to the necessary duties to keep the territory running. He's not legally able to make decisions like granting pardons or approving new laws or anything like that. Basically, he's just a figurehead until a new governor takes over the office."

Leon sighed and stared silently down at his shackled hands. This was hitting him hard, harder than he would have thought. He hadn't realized how much he was holding onto each and every little hope, until that hope got squashed. He felt like he was set right back to the beginning again.

"I'm sorry, Leon," Taggard said. "We didn't want to just tell ya this in a letter, and since Steven and the Kid are kinda snowed in, I offered to try and get to ya, since I'm the closest. I would have got here sooner, but well, the weather just wasn't cooperatin'."

Leon nodded, but didn't say anything.

Taggard sighed and quietly shook his head in frustration.

"I know we keep on sayin' this, and it's probably soundin' kinda hollow to ya by now, but ya gotta hang in there. We're gonna keep on tryin'."

Leon just sat, still looking down at his hands.

"How long?" he asked in a strained voice. "How long before a new governor will be in office?"

"I don't know. Hopefully, early in the new year. As soon as he can, Steven will book us a new appointment and we'll be in there to plead your case. So, like I said, just hang tight, okay?"

"Yeah. Okay." Then he smiled and tried to brighten up a little bit. After all, it wasn't often that Taggard came to visit. "It's good to see you, Taggard, and I do appreciate you coming all this way in the winter to tell me in person. That means a lot."

"I figured it was the least I could do," his friend responded. "I have to admit, I wanted to check up on ya, make sure you're eatin' again."

Leon rolled his eyes, but good-naturedly. "Yeah, I'm eating. There's nothing terribly appetizing here, but I sure don't want to get sick again."

"That's the smartest thing you've said in a while. And yeah, I guess you do look better than the last time I saw ya. Things been goin' okay, lately? You stayin' outta trouble? The Kid wrote me a letter sayin' you got punished again. What was that all about?"

Leon shrugged. "I overstepped the boundaries," he admitted. "But a man's life was on the line, so I still feel I was justified."

"Leon . . ."

"No, I know." Leon sighed with some resignation. "I'm learning my way around here, like who my friends are and who I need to watch out for. I'm still helping in the infirmary and I'm trying to stay away from the people who don't like me. I'm also working hard at keeping my mouth shut—" a snort from Pearson, standing by the door. ". . . and doing what I'm told." He smiled, ironically. "I think it's finally sinking in that if I just do what I'm told, and behave myself, then I won't get hit."

Taggard chuckled. "Yeah, well, you never were one for takin' orders, that's for sure. But sometimes, ya gotta bend a little, or you're gonna break."

Leon grinned until his dimples showed through. "Oh, you know me, Taggard. Go with the flow."

"Yeah, mmm hmmm," Taggard wasn't convinced. "Well, I'd better be headin' back, Leon. Just do me a favor and stay outta trouble, will ya?"

"Yeah, I'll try," Leon agreed. "And thanks again for coming.

It was good to see you."

***

Officer Pearson escorted Leon back to his cell after his visit with the sheriff, and even that guard could tell that the inmate's mood had once again dipped into melancholy. Of course, Pearson couldn't help but overhear the conversation between the convict and his friend, and it didn't take a genius to know the news had not been good.

Pearson didn't say anything to his charge all throughout the removal of the shackles, or during the walk back through the prison proper, but once they approached Leon's cell door, the guard put a hand on Leon's shoulder. Much to Leon's surprise, Pearson gave him an encouraging comment.

"Not all's bad, Nash," Pearson said. "The recent dump of mail has brought you some letters. Maybe those will cheer ya up a bit."

"Oh." Leon's surprise at the comment caused him to speak out of turn.

The guard ignored it. He turned and simply walked away, leaving Leon outside his cell to stand, looking at what was, indeed, an influx of letters scattered over his cot.

Leon frowned in concentration. He didn't think he had enough friends out there to account for that large a pile of letters. This was odd, indeed. Leon uprooted himself from the aisle and, going to his cot, gathered all the letters together. He settled into his usual position for reading and began to riffle through them to see who they were all from and which ones would have priority.

Well, there was one from Jack, that wasn't a surprise. But it was awfully thick, so it probably contained letters from Jean and Penelope as well. That one went to the top of the pile. There was also one from Caroline, separate from the others. It joined the first one. They were all probably going to be talking about the same things: Christmas and the fine supper, and how Karma was doing, and sending him warm thoughts, etcetera. He liked to read about those things, even if they did make him feel homesick. It would be far worse if they didn't bother to tell him about their holidays at all. That would be awful!

Then he started coming across letters that weren't in

envelopes. They were simply single sheets of paper, folded two times over, with a person's first name printed rather crudely on the outside. These had obviously not been mailed, but simply dropped off by someone who had access to the prison.

Leon's curiosity was roused, and he shuffled through them, mumbling the names out loud as he read them. He was hoping he might recognize some of them.

Melanie, William, Todd, Beth, Ben, Sally, Joshua, Gillian . . .

Leon felt even more confused; he didn't know any of these people. From the style of printing, these were obviously children, but why would a bunch of children be writing to him? Then a chill went through him that touched his heart. These must be from the orphans! The ones whom Mariam had mentioned.

He hesitated, suddenly feeling anxious.

He didn't know why receiving letters from those children would cause him distress, would make him feel vulnerable but it did. He wasn't sure if he wanted to read them. He didn't want to admit it, but he was afraid of what old emotions their words might stir up. Did he really want to go down that path?

What are these children to me, anyway? Don't I have enough heartache? Don't I have enough worries without including a bunch of orphans looking for a hero?

His brain kept telling him to cast the letters aside and move on to reading the ones from his friends, from the real people in his life. But for some reason, his body would not respond. He sat there, staring at the letter in his hand, reading the crudely written words that were scribbled upon it.

> *Mr. Nash. I hope you had a fun Christmas. We had chicken and even pie. Did you have a good dinner to? I hope you got lots of presents, I got a new sweater, it's to big for me, but Dr. Mariam says I will grow into it. I hope she's right, 'cause I really like it! Did the Kansas Kid come and have Christmas dinner with you...?*

Then, another one:

> *Mr. Nash; I'm sorry your in prison. That can't be much fun. Do you get to go outside? I really like reading about you in the stories. I hope I can be like you when I grow*

up. I'm sorry you lost your ma and your pa. I lost my ma and pa to, so I know what that feels like. Do you have any friends at the prison? I have friends here and they're important to have so I hope you have some there. Maybe Kansas Kid can come and live with you, that way he can be your friend there too, then you wouldn't be so lonely . . .

Once Leon got started reading the letters, he couldn't stop. He found himself going from laughing out loud at some innocent, but surprisingly accurate comment from one little girl, to fighting a tightening throat and having to swallow down emotion from another insightful comment from a youthful heart. By the time he had finished reading the ten or so letters from the children, he was emotionally exhausted. He leaned against his pillow, with his knees drawn up, and stared straight ahead at nothing for the longest time. He had absolutely no idea how to respond.

Finally, he sighed and began to gather the letters together into a pile. He tried to pull his mind back from the past and to focus again on the here and now. His first option, he supposed, was to talk with Mariam. Obviously, she was the one who had delivered these letters to his cell, or, at least, had someone deliver them. So, next time he ran into her at the infirmary, there would be some explaining to do.

Still, Leon had to admit to himself that it had been sweet, and he did, after all, appreciate it.

He stored the pile of loose letters in his box and slid that under his table. He then turned his attention to the letters that had arrived with the post.

There was the one from Jack, and the one from Caroline, and then… Ohh! A third one he hadn't noticed earlier. He picked it up, then froze. It was from Gabriella.

His cheek twitched. His gut knotted. Was that anger, resentment or excitement? He didn't know.

The letter had been posted some six weeks previously, but the bad weather across the country had delayed it. She hadn't written with Christmas in mind, just feeling the need to touch base.

Napoleon:

I do hope my last letter wasn't too upsetting for you. That wasn't my intention, but I felt compelled to write because of a telegram I got from Jack informing me that you had been neglecting your health and not eating enough. That has been preying on my mind as the winter has begun to close in again with a vengeance, and I do hope you have taken heed of Jack's advice and started being a little more careful.

For goodness sake! There are easier ways to kill yourself. Why are you putting your body through illness and privation? Are you dumb? I thought you were supposed to be smart, or is worrying the people who care for you, a matter of indifference for you?

Poor Jack is worried sick. If you can't look after your health for yourself, then at least do it for him and the others who care about you. Just think about the feelings of helplessness sweeping through your friends, and please, don't add to that.

Besides, you will get out of there eventually, and you surely don't want to be a broken man and unable to live a rich, full life when you are released, do you? Try focusing on the space between your ears and realize how much you are hurting people. If that doesn't work, think how pleased some people would be to see you destroyed and broken, and resolve to rob them of that!

Leon couldn't help but smile at this reprimand, as he could so easily hear her lecturing tone and see the finger being wagged under his nose.

Yes, mother.

He chewed his lip, as he realized how much he did miss Gabriella. She had been his once-in-a-lifetime, but now . . . he sighed and focused on the letter again.

Well, nagging over, but I can't promise it's completely over if I hear of anymore nonsense from you. I thought I'd update you on the efforts going on outside. Your friends are still working hard, lobbying, petitioning and making sure that every person of influence is fully aware that nobody is about to sit back and let you be forgotten. All the efforts continue and that should help you to realize that if they haven't given up, then you shouldn't either. You have a part to play in this too, you know.

For my own part, I have continued to apply my particular abilities to your issues. You may be aware of a few minor successes, but the change in faces has been frustrating, especially as I am working very much in isolation. I have to start again to find some new leverage. I have no doubt I will. It's the nature of the beast, and I have dealt with politicians for a large part of my life. But obstacles have been placed in my way, and doors, previously open to me, have been slammed in my face. Mind you, you know my philosophy; if people underestimate you, it only makes it easier to put one over on them.

These men see a woman and sell me short, not realizing that there's more than one way to skin a cat, and I have to fall back on more than just my persuasive arguments. As you are no doubt aware, I am not able to be as mobile as I previously was, so I am finding progress slow. Make no mistake though, it does continue.

I am sorry to tell you, but you have probably already realized, that so far, we have not been successful in doing anything other than ruffling a few feathers. We keep trying though. Remember that, and support us, as we continue in our battle to get you released. Water can cut through stone under the right circumstances, so we keep right on, drip, drip, dripping away at the resistance.

I admit, a part of me was afraid you would screw up my letter and throw it in the bin, without even reading it. I know how angry you were, but I don't know if that continues to burn in you. For my part, I set time aside and I have done as I promised. I will hold our best times in my heart again tonight. I do want to offer an olive branch and make some peace between us.

Gabriella

She wants peace now, does she? I don't know.

A flicker of his lost love hit his heart when he noted that, this time, she had included a return address. An open invitation for him to respond to her.

He sat for some time, just staring at the letter, waging a battle of wills between his heart and his brain.

I don't know if I can trust her, not after that . . .it would be nice though, wouldn't it?

He re-read the letter numerous times, until finally, he sighed and set it aside for now.

If I do write back to her, it's going to take some careful thought first.

He sat back, closing his eyes as he rested his head against the pillow. What an exhausting afternoon this has been. *What a bronco ride! I'm not sure I have the energy to read the remaining letters now. What if there are even more surprises? I'm not sure I can handle that.*

He chuckled to himself at how silly he was being. Of course, he wanted to hear how Christmas had been for his family; that was important! Maybe, if he tried real hard, maybe in reading about it, he could pretend he had been there too.

So, with eyes still closed, he reached to where he knew the letters were, and picked one up. Bringing it to his face, he opened his eyes and saw that it was the letter from Caroline. He opened the envelope and removing the sheets of paper, he discovered that there were two letters enclosed; one from Caroline and one from Josephine. Of course! How could he have forgotten about Josephine?

He picked up Caroline's letter first and began to read,

> *Dear Napoleon:*
>
> *What a marvelous Christmas this has been. We were all able to make it out to the ranch for the big day, and a good thing too, since Steven and I (well, actually, just Steven) had something very pressing to speak with Mama and Papa about! Of course, it was to ask Papa's permission for us to become betrothed and to start thinking about marriage!*
>
> *This was hardly a surprise for me, since Steven and I have been discussing the possibility for some time now, and I was certain that Papa would give his permission, as I know that both he and Mama are quite fond of Steven. Still, there are always those nagging doubts that things won't go the way we expect, and all through the journey from Denver to the ranch, my stomach was full of knots and butterflies!*

All my worries were for naught, however, since Papa did indeed willingly give his permission, and Mama was thrilled and couldn't stop smiling all day. Penny seemed a little put out, and I don't really know where that was coming from, but Josey just laughed it off and stated that that was her problem.

Fortunately, by the time we all settled in for Christmas supper, Penny had come around and seemed to be just as excited by the coming event as I was. Mathew didn't say too much of anything, which did disappoint me a little, but just a little. Nothing was going to dampen our day.

Of course, we were hoping to plan the wedding for some time this coming summer, as this would seem the logical course of action, and Mama declared that we must have the wedding here, at the ranch, that way, there would be lots of room for everybody. All of this is quite appropriate, but I must admit, there is one nagging issue that causes me to hesitate in setting a date.

That issue, my dearest friend, is you. In all the imaginings I've had of my wedding day you have always been there to share in the joy of it with me. It seems to me to be a betrayal to you and to our friendship if I were to go ahead and set the date of my wedding before knowing that you will be able to attend.

We are all trying so hard to attain your release from that horrid place, and it would bring me so much pleasure to have you with us on this special day, that I find it impossible to commit to a date until I know you are free.

At this point, Leon shook his head with some feeling of sadness, and mumbled to himself. "Oh no, sweetheart. Don't wait for me."

I love you so much, Peter. I miss you so much. All my hopes and prayers are that you will be home with us again soon! Please take care of yourself and don't you dare get sick again!

Caroline

Leon set the letter down and grabbed the tin box that had once held cookies, but now held his own stash of paper and a pencil. He knew he had to write down his answer to his friend before the thoughts and emotions of her loving words were washed away by the news from others.

He took one of his many books to use as support and began to write his response.

Dear Caroline;

First off, of course: congratulations on your betrothal! I must admit, I am not surprised at this news, as it was obvious that you and Steven were very serious about one another. I was also aware of the high regard your parents hold him in, so I would have been far more surprised if permission had been withheld.

I am also touched and greatly honored that you hold me in such esteem that you would be willing to postpone your wedding date to assure my attendance. But please, don't put off your special day on my account. I know everyone is working very hard to secure my release, and for this, I am very much indebted to you all, but even I am under no illusions as to how long this could still take.

Please have your wedding day and enjoy it to its fullest. I may not be able to attend in person, but I will be with you in my mind and in my heart, just as surely as I know that I will be there in yours.

I cannot help but think back to that gangly teenager I first met, not so many years ago. You and your sister both played at being such little ladies while Mathew and I were recovering from our ordeal, but soon your true natures burst forth! How many times did I see your poor mother dragging you out from the wood shed, doing her best to brush off the dirt and spider webs from your face and hair.

I knew in that instant that I liked you, and you have continued to amaze and inspire me as you've grown from that gun-toting tomboy into this intelligent and beautiful young woman.

Steven is a lucky man and has shown great wisdom in that he apparently realizes this himself. That once having met you, he would be willing to go to the ends of the earth (or at least to Denver) to ensure his continued attendance upon you. You are worth it. Be happy, Caroline. And you better write to me, in great detail, about every moment of your special day—so take notes.

All my love, Napoleon

Leon settled back and re-read his letter, hoping he had expressed himself eloquently, without coming across as too mushy. She was marrying Steven, after all—not him. He smiled, feeling like he was all done in.

What a day. And now I add aching fingers to the list of inconveniences. Why couldn't Carson have broken the fingers on my left hand. He harrumphed. *Not as effective, I suppose.*

Then, the buzzer sounded, announcing that it was supper time. If that swill could actually be called supper.

He sighed and, pushing the numerous letters off to the side, he swung his legs over to the floor and prepared to join the herd heading down to the common room. He knew he had to eat, so he may as well get it over with.

Perhaps once he had attended to that chore, he would feel rejuvenated. Even though all the inmates had to line up and head down together, once the meal was done, they were able to disperse as they wished. He could bring a coffee back up to his cell, then continue with his letter reading until the shadows of the evening, and the tiredness of his eyes and spirit, would settle him down for the night.

Leon did indeed continue to read letters for the rest of the evening, but he was tired by this time, and decided to focus on the lighter stuff. He set aside Jack's letter for the next day and settled back to read the note from Josey.

Dear Leon:

If you haven't already read the letter from Caroline, then I suggest you do so now, because I have no intentions of going over it again. She has been sooo gushy and excited about the whole business that I've about had it with weddings and rings and happily ever afters.

What is it about young ladies thinking that marriage is the be all and end all, and the only way to find happiness? Anyway, enough of that. I'm sure she will be very happy, and so on, and so on, and let's move on.

Christmas at the Marsham's place was enjoyable, even though I was surrounded by all the signs of domesticity. Not only were Caroline and Steven full of their happy plans for the summer, but the doctor, David Gibson and his wife, were there as well, and she's starting to show the bun in the oven, I can tell you.

I think Jack and I were both feeling a little out of place with all this family stuff going on, but I guess that's what Christmas is all about. So, we put on brave faces.

Penny was a little out of sorts with her older sister basically taking over the conversation for the day. All attention was on Caroline, and you know how sisters can get with that 'sibling competition' thing. Well, maybe you don't know—but it can get bad sometimes, believe me! Not that I'd know what a sister can be like, but I can imagine! Anyway, Penny settled down as the day wore on and seemed to be happy for her sister, after all.

Dinner was wonderful. You're right: Mrs. Marsham is a wonderful cook, and of course, everyone ate way too much! But it was Christmas, after all, so what better excuse to make a pig of yourself?

After supper was cleared away, we ladies adjourned to the sitting room and spent the evening talking about wedding plans and expected babies, and of course—you. Penny told us all about her adventures at the prison, and all the things she had seen there. She's busy writing letters again!

I certainly hope these things will all help in some way, Leon, although, by now, you must think it is all a waste of time. I know the men, who were all sitting around the dining room table with their brandies, were spending most of the evening discussing you and the plans they were making seemed rather intense. I was not made privy to those plans however, so I cannot relate them to you. Hopefully Jack will get around to that, and by 'that' I mean informing BOTH of us of their plans. I do so hate being left out.

I have spent the night here, at the ranch, and the

three of us will be heading back to Denver probably tomorrow, if the weather holds. So, I am writing this letter on the go, so to speak, as I hope to post it along with Caroline's in the hope that it will get to you quickly now that the weather does seem to have let up a bit. You'll probably be getting a whole stack of letters, all at once, but I guess that's okay.

I feel like I want to ask how your Christmas went, but considering where you are, I can't think it was all that merry. Still, I hope there was something of the holiday spirit to the day, and that you got a decent meal out of it, in any case. We all sent gifts to you in one big package, so if you don't have it yet, it should be arriving soon.

I hope you are healing up okay from your last encounter with the 'mean' guard, which is how Penny tends to refer to him. The 'mean' guard, and the 'nice' guard tend to come into her conversations a lot lately. I can't imagine there being a 'nice' guard at a prison like that, but I suppose it's all relative.

Anyway, bedtime now, so I must be off! Take care of yourself, Leon, and don't go getting sick again! We have enough to worry about with you, without adding that to it! Hopefully we will all be out to see you once the weather becomes more agreeable, and the next batch of news will be delivered in person.

Bye for now,
Josephine

Leon sat back with a sigh.

Jeez, even reading her letters is exhausting. Where in the world does that woman get all her energy?

Still, having read it, her comments about the others sitting around the dining room table and making plans concerning himself got his curiosity roused. So, even though his eyes burned with exhaustion, he looked at Jack's letter with the intention of reading it now, after all.

CHAPTER SIXTEEN
A NEW STRATIGY

He opened the thick envelope, and sure enough, there were letters from Jack, Jean and Penny, all folded into a neat package. He fingered through the pages and pulled out the ones from his partner, then settled in to read.

Hey Leon:

Well, if you've had a chance to read Caroline's letter, I suppose you can guess at what a commotion it made around here! If'n ya haven't read her letter yet, I suggest ya do so now, or I may end up ruinin' her surprise for ya—oh jeez, I hope you have it! Anyway, enough of that, I'll leave it to the ladies to fill ya in on all that stuff.

Penny did say that Carson—that bastard!—got you pretty good again, and this time just for doin' your job! I sure would like to send Gus Shaffer and the boys in there to teach him a lesson. He might have a different view of his situation if'n he had the entire Elk Mountain Gang to contend with.

Anyway, I hope you're feelin' better, and I'm sure that you've got the Doc and Kenny both watchin' out for ya.

We all got to discussin' things around the supper table after the dinner had been cleared away—funny how a lot of intense conversation happens at that time, kinda like us sittin' around the camp fire after a long day of ridin'. I can't remember how many serious talks we had, just sittin' there watchin' the fire, and drinkin' coffee. Jeez, in some ways, I kinda miss them days—well, not everything about them days, but parts of it. Oh well, back to what I was talkin' about. Steven has suggested another strategy that might have merit, but could take some time to work out (And Kenny, I know you read all of Leon's letters before he gets 'em, so, first off, I hope you and your family had a nice Christmas. Now second, listen up here, 'cause this just might involve you).

Like I was sayin', we were all sittin' around the table and, a course the conversation just naturally drifted over to talkin' about you (Leon that is, not Kenny) . . .

Rocking M Ranch

. . . "What's happening with your appointment now that Governor Baxter has resigned? Cameron asked the group. "Will you still be able to get in to present your case?"

Jack groaned, but Steven beat him to the answer.

"No," he regretfully admitted. "All the appointments got canceled and, apparently, Mr. Morgan isn't seeing anyone. I guess he has his hands full just getting the mess cleaned up that his two predecessors left behind."

"Oh brother," was Cameron's sardonic reply. "And no idea who the next governor is going to be?"

"Well, yes," Steven answered. "There are a couple of contenders, but unfortunately, the favorite, so far, is Thomas Moonlight."

Jack perked up. "Moonlight?" he asked. "That name sounds familiar—not that you'd ever forget that name, once ya heard it. But still, he did a lot durin' the war, didn't he?"

"Oh yes," Steven was emphatic. "He's originally from Kansas and rode with the Militia during the war. He had a great deal to do with bringing in Quantrill. He was also very active in the politics of Kansas after the war, until he moved out this way. He would be a strong governor for Wyoming, but not too sympathetic to outlaws, I'm afraid."

Jack sighed. "Yeah, I remember 'im now. Like ya say, he'd probably be good for Wyoming, but not so good for Leon."

"Still," Steven tried to perk things up. "I will solicit an appointment with him and see where it goes—the worst he can do is throw us out of his office."

The attitudes of the three other men seemed downtrodden, so Steven thought he would put forth an idea that had been simmering in the back in his brain for a couple of months.

"I do have a couple of other suggestions," he offered and was met with three expectant expressions. "I'm sure you have all noticed that our current course of action has not resulted in much success. What I might suggest next, well, it could take some time and might even be dangerous for those who are working in the prison. But, we might be able to set up a hearing with the Prison Commission to present our case. We would be expected to present evidence of 'wrong doing', or 'miscarriage of justice', that sort of thing. We would be presenting our case to board members, perhaps even to the governor himself.

"Also, I will begin the procedure to present Mr. Nash's personal case to The Supreme Court. The first step is for me to send in what is called a *writ of certiorari*, which is basically a request to have Mr. Nash's situation reviewed, and discuss the over-all conditions at the prison.

"If it is accepted, and I stress here that not many petitions are, I will submit what is called a brief, outlining our reasons for the review. This is where the rest of you come in. Others may also file a brief, called an *amicus curia*, to offer your views on this matter.

"After that, I will present our case in person to the Justices. If you wish to be present, you may be, but it's not necessary. Only myself and the opposing attorney, most likely the Solicitor General, can speak. Also, we won't know the outcome at this time. It could take weeks before we know the results."

Silence followed this announcement as the others tried to understand all of what the lawyer had said.

Once legal terminology came into a conversation, Steven may as well have been talking to himself.

Jack sighed and responded to what he did understand from Steven's information. "Yeah but, we talked about this before. You said there was no point since Judge Lacey was the Chief Justice and the other Justices weren't likely ta overturn his ruling."

"Yes, at that time, this was true," Steven said. "But Judge Lacey retired from the Supreme Court last month, so now this option has become available to us. Also, aside from an extremely harsh sentence, there was no evidence of wrongdoing. The length of sentence was at the judge's discretion and would not be enough, in itself, to warrant an official hearing. Also, up to this point, any punishments Leon has received have been justified."

Jack snorted in disgust.

"Yes, I know, Jack," Steven sympathized with him, "but, according to the law, as long as the warden stays within the boundaries laid out by the penal system, then any punishments he doles out are at his discretion."

"Then why would you think we could get a hearing now?" Cameron asked. "Nothing's changed."

"I disagree, Cameron," Steven said. "A lot has changed. I know you were angry at Penny for what she did, but I for one am glad she did it. The fact that she is not an employee of the penal system and did witness, first hand, an unwarranted assault upon Leon could be invaluable to us."

"You mean, all we have to do is take what Penny saw to a hearing and we could get Napoleon pardoned?" Cameron asked incredulously.

"Well, no. It's not quite that simple," Steven admitted. "Like I said, it could take some time, but it's a beginning. What I suggest now is that we all start keeping notes. Especially you, Jack, since you are in contact with Leon more than the rest of us. You need to write down everything Leon tells you of what is going on behind those locked doors. Take note of dates, and the names of the people involved. We need to build a foundation of wrong-doing, so we can walk into a hearing and present to the judges a solid example of ongoing abuses."

Steven paused, knowing his next suggestion might really cause some feathers to ruffle.

"I am also of a mind to challenge the validity of the penal system itself. Many of the standing rules, to my mind, over a period of time, could cause psychological damage to the inmates, and this open standard of corporal punishment leaves too much room for abuse. Things that are considered legitimate punishments, well, people behaving like that out here in the 'real world' would probably wind up in prison themselves for assault. I really feel it is time for this system to be challenged. I'm just not sure if we have the connections, and the evidence to succeed in forcing changes to be made. This would require setting up a hearing with the Prison Commission itself where those who are willing can step forward in person to state their case."

Steven stopped again and looked around at his audience.

Everyone was contemplating his words and trying to allow the enormity of his suggestion to sink in. Not wanting the conversation to end in a stalemate, Steven backtracked to his original plan and would give some time for the larger picture to be accepted.

"So, in the meantime," he continued, "just start keeping notes, and we'll see where this whole thing takes us."

"Can we include things that have already happened?" Jack asked.

"Yes, for sure," Steven agreed, "just put down the date, as close as you can; anything you can remember, just jot it down. And we need to get as many testimonies as possible, so the board members can compare notes, so to speak. Make sure everything correlates."

"You would need more than just Jack's statements then, wouldn't you?" David asked. He had been sitting quietly throughout this exchange, since he didn't feel he had any function in it. But he was still willing to contribute when a thought struck him.

"Yes," Steven again admitted, "we would need two or three corresponding statements of the same events before we could have any hope of this working. Even then, all it might accomplish is that the warden gets a slap on the wrist, and it may not help Leon in the long run.

"As I already said, the chances of the Supreme Court accepting Mr. Nash's case are slim, so appeal to the penal board may be our only option. If the Supreme Court agrees to hear us, then having already presented our case concerning abuses to the board may help."

"Still, gettin' the warden ta back off Leon is somethin'," Jack commented. "As long as he don't turn around and exact vengeance upon 'im, later on. Warden Mitchell has left no doubt in my mind that he would be capable a doin' just that."

"That is also a risk," Steven admitted.

Groans made their way around the table.

"I'm only suggesting this as an option," Steven reminded them. "It'll take time, it'll take coordination, and it'll take cooperation, and it may not even work. But gentlemen, I am at a loss to suggest anything else."

This time, silence made its way around the table.

It was Jack who broke the stalemate.

"I can keep notes about what goes on there, and I have no doubts about Penny bein' willin' ta write down her experience." He sighed, contemplating the other options. "I know Kenny and the Doc keep detailed records of everything that goes on in each of their departments, but I don't know if they would want ta present that information at a hearing. It could be dangerous for 'em."

"Yes," Steven concurred, "this is why I hesitated to suggest it. If we can develop a strong enough case, I could present them with a court order forcing them to make their records available, but I would rather they did it willingly."

Jack contemplated this new dilemma. Both Kenny and Palin were trying to be supportive of Leon within the prison system, but to ask them to go against their employer, and their fellow guards, might be asking too much.

"I don't know," Jack admitted. "They could get into real trouble, goin' against the system, and Officer Carson, in particular, can get real nasty, especially if he feels threatened. The only friends Leon has in that place could, at the very least, end up losin' their jobs, and at the worst, be found layin' dead in an alley somewhere."

Steven nodded, but silence reigned again around the table. They could hear the ladies in the other room laughing about something, and the jovial sound seemed out of place considering the current mood of the gentlemen's discussion.

"I don't know," Jack repeated. "I wanna help Leon—of course I do! But I hate ta put Kenny at risk like that. And I know darn well Leon wouldn't approve of it if it meant riskin' the lives of others. It's a lot ta ask."

"Yes, it is," Steven said, "but it's all we have."

"Jack, couldn't you just ask Officer Reece?" Cameron suggested. "No pressure, just present the option to him, then let him decide."

"Yeah, I suppose," Jack agreed, though he didn't sound very enthused. "I could mention this in my next letter to Leon. I know Kenny reads all of Leon's mail before passin' it on to him, so he'd get an idea that way of what we're thinkin' about. Then, I suppose the next time I get out there, he'll have had some time ta consider it. I guess, I could do that."

Everybody nodded; this sounded like a good plan.

"Well!" Cameron declared. "It's Christmas night. Steven is newly engaged, David is an expectant father, and it turns out to be my youngest daughter, rather than my oldest, who has become an undercover detective. Then, on top of that, it looks like we're all planning to tackle the very foundations of the entire Auburn penal system to boot. Sounds like we're in for a very interesting year."

"Here, here!" David agreed, and everyone raised their glasses . . .

***

Laramie, Wyoming

. . . so, that's where things stand now, Leon. I know it don't sound too encouragin', but we are workin' toward gettin' some things organized here. We are still plannin' on goin' in to see the next governor, whoever that ends up bein', but we are also gonna get started collectin' that information in case we end up havin' to take it to a hearin'.

Try ta stay outta trouble, okay? I know it's almost like a contradiction to say that, since incidences of uncalled for punishments are what we need ta challenge the powers that be, but I don't like ta see ya gettin' hurt. That Carson could end up killin' you if you're not careful—I'm sure he's done it before! Hopefully the information we already have, along with what Penny witnessed, will be enough, and all you need to do from now on is just lay low!

Do ya think Mariam would be willin' ta come forward? I'm sure she has witnessed a lot 'a things there that would make a sailor's toes curl. Anything at this point would be helpful.

Whatever you do, Leon, don't try to provoke a response from Carson, or the warden. Steven figures that any deliberate attempt to antagonize by you would become apparent under close inspection and would then be useless in a legal hearin', so, like I said, stay outta trouble!

I'll get out ta see ya as soon as the weather permits. In the meantime, take care of yourself, Uncle. I don't know what I would do if anything happened to you

in there.
Jack

Again, Leon sat back with a heavy sigh and tried to absorb all the information Jack had squeezed into this letter. Oddly enough, at this point, the main thing that stuck in Leon's mind was the way Jack seemed to be taking more control now, even to the point of lecturing him. It seemed to Leon that his nephew was moving away from their previous lives as outlaws and transients. He had a new life now, new friends and new beginnings. He was becoming his own man.

Leon felt a twinge of jealousy and resentment that his partner had been given the opportunity to let go of the past and move on, and part of him was afraid that Jack would simply leave him behind. Then, he admonished himself for being selfish.

Of course, Jack is going to move on, this was a good thing! He needs to rediscover who he is and learn how to function in a society as a legal, law-abiding citizen.

None of this means he's going to leave me behind. Leon smirked. *On the contrary, Jack made it clear, on more than one occasion, that he wasn't going anywhere until I was free to go with him.* Then Leon frowned, and his natural cynicism took over. *Still, I wonder how long it'll take before that resolve starts to crumble. Jack can be stubborn, but if the years begin to pile up and there was still no pardon in sight, how long could Jack remain true to the cause, and how long can I rightfully expect him to?*

By this time, the light inside his cell was beginning to wane, and though the oil lamps in the aisle were still lit, it wasn't bright enough for him to continue reading. He sat for a long time, just holding Jack's letter and staring into the dimness, thinking about the plans they were making. He felt guilty in a way, at the risks his friends had taken, and were apparently willing to take again, to secure his release. This new endeavor seemed to be even riskier than all the others.

People could get hurt—himself included. And personally, he was tired of getting hurt. The real lessons here were finally beginning to sink in; indeed, Leon was not the alpha wolf anymore, he was not the one in charge and it had taken a long time for him to finally accept this. He always had to look for a way around the rules; way to come out on top. He hadn't been able to let go of being the one in control, and all he'd gotten for his arrogance was battered and bruised—and broken.

Well, parts of him were broken, but not his spirit; they hadn't broken that yet, though Carson sure was trying. But no, he still had his heart and his soul intact—and his hope. They were limping often enough, but still intact. He was just getting more cautious. More willing to bend rather than break—like Taggard had said.

Yeah, Taggard's a pretty smart man. I would have done a lot better in life if I'd just listened to him more often. But I was a hard head in my youth, just had to do things my own way, and now look where it's got me.

Leon smiled and shook his head. *Now those people closest to me are willing to risk everything to get me out of a jam that my own arrogance has gotten me into.*

He frowned with these revelations. He was uncomfortable with that scenario, but just selfish enough, and homesick enough, to sit back, lie low, and hang tight—and let them try.

That night, he dreamt about Gabi. He woke up in the wee hours of the morning, out of breath and sweating, frustrated and relieved all at the same time. Thank goodness it was still a few hours before morning roll call, so he didn't have to worry about facing that particular dilemma again. He shifted and re-adjusted himself to get comfortable, then smiled.

At least this proves one thing; I'm still quite capable of 'performing', when the opportunity arises.

He closed his eyes and took a deep cleansing breath, then relaxed and listened to his pounding heart slowly drop back down to its normal rhythm. There was something comforting about the fact that it wasn't yet time to get up, and he settled himself back into a peaceful sleep.

***

The next day, Leon was back to work doing light duty in the laundry room. His broken rib and the two fingers were still taped up, but he was beginning to feel more mobile and not quite so sore, so he knew he would be able to start responding to the rest of his letters soon.

On the other hand, he was only allowed to post one letter per week, and this week, of course, it had been Caroline's. There was no rush to get started on the next one.

He looked forward to reading the remaining letters that were still waiting for him, even though he knew they would be reiterating what had already been said. Still, it's often fun to get differing points of view.

I wonder how long it's going to take for the parcel of gifts to get here. He smiled. *I hope there'll be some more of Jean's baking in there somewhere. Even if it's a bit stale, it'll still be a treat!*

Then his thoughts skipped to another topic. *And what's Kenny thinking? I know he read the letters; he had to, it's part of his job, making sure nothing covert is going on in the correspondence. He'll know what my friends have in mind. And if that's not covert, ha! Still, will he approve and stay quiet about it, or will he do his job and give his boss the heads up? Will he agree to help, or simply turn a blind eye?*

Kenny was there that day; Leon had seen him on the work floor, but the guard had given no indication that he wanted to talk. Indeed, it seemed to Leon that the man was trying to avoid him. Or was that just his imagination? Leon sighed as he folded the sheets; maybe he should just stay quiet and let Jack handle things from his end. That would probably be the best, but Leon still had trouble relinquishing control; he still felt the need to be in charge. Old habits die hard.

The day closed without Leon catching the guard's eye, and he returned to his cell after supper with his evening coffee, to settle into reading his remaining letters. He even had a new word to decipher: *verisimilitude*, and he had laughed out loud and almost spilled his coffee when he read the definition.

Jeez—Jack and I had been playing at that very thing for five years and didn't even know there was a special word for it! Jack will get a kick out of this one.

Leon settled into his usual position on his cot and got comfortable. He couldn't believe how much difference it made, having nice warm underclothing to wear. Though his fingers still got stiff and cold, he was, for the most part, more content with his lot this winter compared to last year. He smiled as he pulled out Penny's letter and began to read.

> *Dear Peter:*
> *I hope you are feeling better by this time and that*

you haven't gotten yourself into any more trouble!

As you predicted, I was certainly 'in for it' when I got home. Everybody was mad at me, but it was worth it as far as I was concerned, and now, even Steven thinks it was a good idea and that what I witnessed there could be to our advantage. So, there you go! I'm sorry if I made you uncomfortable with my presence, but in the long run, it may turn out to be worth it!

Now, Christmas Day—OH BROTHER! Or maybe I should say; Oh sister! Caroline took over the whole gathering with her 'wonderful' news! I felt like the last horse to get away from the start in a race! Oh, but then Mathew pointed out to me that I shouldn't think of life and marriage as a 'race', but still, I really do feel like I have been left behind.

Of course, Mama took me aside and gave me a bit of a talking to. Going on about how I should be happy for my sister and share in her joy, rather than be resentful of it, and of course, Mama is right! So, once again, I was being selfish and thoughtless, and I sort of knew it anyway, but having Mama point it out in her quiet way made it all the more apparent. So, I did change my attitude, and we ended up having a nice Christmas.

I suppose I do miss my sister quite a bit with her living in Denver now. We used to be such buddies, but she's moving on and is beginning a whole new life for herself, and I guess I'm a bit jealous. I think I'm also afraid that she's going to forget about me, that her new job and new husband are going to take my place, and she won't have any time for her little sister anymore. I guess we all must grow up some time, but I do miss her.

On to other things now; I'm pleased to say that Karma is doing very well! I am so looking forward to early spring, when her foal will finally arrive, and hopefully, all will go well with that. She is looking quite heavy, naturally, though I suspect some of this is her thick winter coat. All the horses look fat in the winter time.

I wish you could see her. She is such a pretty mare, and I know she misses you. I do my best to fill in for you, and I think she does like me, as she often nickers when she sees me, but you are still her 'special person' and she awaits your homecoming just as much as we all do.

The three dogs are doing fine, though Rufus is starting to show signs of aging. He is having a harder time getting up the steps and is looking stiff and sore when he walks across the yard. I'm hoping it's just the cold weather getting to him, but he does tend to spend most of his time sleeping in the hay inside the barn.

Pebbles and Peanut like to snuggle up to him for warmth now that Sam is no longer here to let them into the bunkhouse. But they're doing fine, and everyone is staying quite healthy this year.

I guess that is all for now and, hopefully, I will see you again once the weather improves. Please look after yourself. We all miss you and love you very much, and I just don't know what we'd do if anything were to happen to you in there!

Well, bye for now,
Penelope

Once again, Leon thought how odd it was that Penny was feeling much the same way about her sister moving on as he had about Jack moving on. He supposed then, that feelings of being left behind, or abandoned, must be universal with young and old alike.

I shouldn't be so hard on myself for having those feelings; everybody has the right to feel anxious once in a while. Even me.

The news about Karma was both bitter and sweet. As with so many things that were happening, he wanted to hear about them, but at the same time, it often made him feel as though life was passing him by. He missed Karma, too—a lot! He missed their wild gallops and her temper tantrums. He missed her nicker in the mornings, and her demand for food or attention. He missed their arguments and her angry stamp of a foot when she wasn't getting her way.

He smiled. Suddenly he was reminded of another red-headed lady in his life who had a very similar temperament. Funny, he'd never thought about how the personalities of both ladies were almost parallel, and how much he was drawn to a fiery female. He chuckled out loud when he thought of what Gabi would have to say about him comparing her to his horse!

That wouldn't be good; best to keep that observation to

myself.

He came back from his musings to realize he was still holding onto Penny's letter. He put that one down on the "already read" pile and turned to the last sheet of paper awaiting his attention. Just the very act of picking up Jean's letter, and unfolding it, was enough to make him feel safe and secure. She had such a very special place in his heart and "coming home" would not have the same emotional impact upon him, if she were not there. She was everything he missed about "family".

> *Dear Peter:*
>
> *I'm sure the ladies have already filled you in on the news of the day, so I will not bore you with repeating it. On the other hand, I must say, I got quite a chuckle out of Cameron giving poor Steven a very difficult time of it. Cameron can have such an evil sense of humor, and he was having way too much fun at Steven's expense . . .'*

***

Rocking M Ranch

"Oh good!" Steven stated, though his clenching of fists suggested that relief was the last thing he felt. "I was hoping to catch you both alone for a moment."

Cameron and Jean exchanged quick glances. They had a good idea of what was coming.

"That's kind of a contradiction," Cameron observed. "How can either of us be alone, if we're both here? Really Steven, as a lawyer, you need to be aware of inconsistencies in your speech."

"Oh, umm, yes. Sorry." Steven was already fumbling. "It's just that I have something rather important I need to speak with you about, Mr. Marsham. Oh! And Mrs. Marsham too, of course. Both of you."

Two sets of brows went up at the sudden change to their formal titles. "Cameron" and "Jean" had long ago become the norm.

"Really?" Cameron commented. "About Napoleon's case? That is a shame about Governor Baxter resigning his office so soon. Now your appointment with him has been postponed, or, more accurately, it has been canceled altogether. It is frustrating, all this political red tape, and I know it's driving Jack crazy. It seems to take forever to get anything done, and nobody wants to listen to what anybody has to say, so I can certainly understand why—"

"No, no, Mr. Marsham," Steven interrupted him, "that's not it."

"Oh?" Cameron feigned amazement. "What else could be so important on this Christmas Day?"

"Well, umm, sir, I would like—oh, and ma'am! You as well, yes. I would like to ask permission for your daughter's hand in marriage."

"Oh yes?" Cameron asked. "Which one?"

"Which one?"

"Well yes, Mr. Granger. I have two daughters. I would hate to misinterpret your intentions, or are you saying that either one would do?"

Jean tried hard to keep a straight face throughout this exchange. This was cruel but fun, all at the same time.

"No!" Steven wasn't saying that at all. "No, no. I mean, Penny is a very lovely young woman, and I'm sure she will make a fine wife for any young man who is fortunate enough to catch her eye. She really is very nice—"

"Now you're sounding confused, Mr. Granger," Cameron pointed out. "It would appear to me that Penny is the one you are interested—"

"No, no," Steven insisted. "No, it's Caroline . . ." He stopped and sighed, his shoulders slumping. A smile tugged at the corners of his mouth. "You're pulling my leg, aren't you?"

Cameron smiled.

Jean finally broke down and laughed, but she came forward and gave the beguiled young man a warm hug and a kiss on the cheek.

"You really must forgive Cameron," she said, then sent her husband a visual reprimand. "He really gets too much pleasure out of teasing the young men who gather around. I'm surprised he doesn't scare off all the suitors."

Steven visibly relaxed as Cameron came forward and extended his hand for shaking.

"I'm afraid my wife is right. But a man must take some fun where he can find it. Of course, you have our blessings and I have no doubt you will make a fine husband for Caroline."

Steven beamed with relieved pleasure, and Jean gave him another hug.

"I have no doubt about this myself," she agreed. "Welcome to the family, Steven, and what a wonderful Christmas present this has been!"

***

Laramie, Wyoming

. . . Then Steven went to inform what I'm sure, was a very anxious Caroline, that we had given our permission for their union. Within moments, her excited and very un-ladylike exclamations were vibrating throughout the household!

Penny felt a little put out about the whole affair, which I could understand from her youthful point of view, but still, it was unacceptable under the circumstances. Fortunately, it only took a few words from me to help her see what she already knew herself and she brightened up, and joined in on the celebrations.

We had a lovely Christmas with most of the family all around us. I could not help but think what an improvement it was over last year, when Mathew was going through such a difficult time. The girls had both been so disappointed when he didn't show up for the holiday, and then there was all that drama that came after it! Thank goodness things are so much improved this year.

The only thing I could wish for, for next year, is that you will also be able to join us around the dinner table. You were terribly missed, Peter, and I know Mathew felt your absence more than any of us. He did enjoy himself for the most part, but occasionally, when he thought no one was looking, his expression became melancholy, and it didn't take a genius to know that he was thinking about you.

I know he has written you a letter as well, and that he has told you of the plans Steven brought to the table. It all sounds so covert, that I can't help but feel a chill when I think of the risks you might incur with these plans. You are so very much at the mercy of the officials there, and some of them have already proven to be quite brutal.

My goodness! I thought Marshal Morrison was bad, but the stories I've heard from Mathew over the past year, and now from my own daughters as well, makes me ashamed to think that we have men like that holding positions of such authority.

Thankfully you seem to have a friend, as such, in this Officer Reece, and I hope Mathew and Penny have not overestimated his worth and support of you. Obviously, you need friends in there, and I pray every night that the ones you do have will help to keep you safe.

Goodbye for now, Peter. Know that you are always in my heart and in my thoughts. God be with you.

Jean

Well, that was it then, news and thoughts from all sides. He settled back with an arm behind his head and contemplated his letters and the responses he would send back. He realized then that he could include a letter to Josey with the one going to Caroline, so two of them could be taken care of in one shot. Then, Jean, Penny and Jack could all go in the same envelope as well. Yes, that's more like it. Then it wouldn't take so long to respond to everyone, as long as his healing fingers didn't lay in too much of a protest.

He would get started on those tomorrow; he was too tired now to do them justice.

The buzzer sounded and Leon sighed in irritation. For one thing, he was warm and comfortable, right where he was. Having to stand at the door to his cell, just for some stupid roll call, when they already knew he was here, was downright irritating.

Oh well.

Up he got to wait at the aisle.

Davis walked by, doing the count and checking off names. Everyone present and accounted for. Like, why wouldn't they be? A step back into his cell, and then slide, bang, as the door was closed upon him. This was followed by a loud, mechanical clang, as the locking bar slid into place, shutting him in for the night.

Another sigh and he moved back to his cot to get comfortable again. Maybe he would light a candle and read for a while. He was still so full of all the news from home, he really didn't think he would be able to settle into sleep any time soon. Yeah, he'd read for a while, then listen to some music in his mind, and hopefully, convince it to shut down and drift into the night.

***

Over the next couple of evenings, Leon managed to get letters written back to just about everyone who had sent him a note. It really wasn't too time consuming, since he didn't have very much to report; nothing changed at the prison. He mainly focused on assuring everyone that he was doing okay, and he was making himself eat more, even if he wasn't hungry. And that he was certainly keeping warm. He also included the new word for the week in Jack's letter. He smiled, almost wickedly, wishing he could see Jack's expression when he learned the definition.

That done, he took a fresh sheet of paper from his diminishing pile and contemplated his next reply. This was a letter he had not originally intended to write, but the more he thought about it, the more it seemed the proper thing to do. He just wasn't sure how to do it.

Well, just start writing and see where it goes.

To the children at the Sisters of Charity Orphanage:

Thank you very much for thinking of me at Christmas time. It was a very pleasant surprise to receive your cookies, and then all those kind letters as well. I greatly enjoyed all of it and it made this Christmas very special.

In answer to some of your questions: Yes, I do get to go outside, although these days it's a little too cold for outdoor activities, so I keep busy working indoors. I work in the laundry room and the infirmary, and I also work in the warehouse, making brooms and candles and cigars.

The Kansas Kid does come to visit me once a month, but I don't think he would want to come and live here, as it really is not that much fun. I also have other friends who come to visit when they can and send letters when they can't, so I'm not really alone. Friends are important, and I'm glad to hear that you value your friendships there at the orphanage.

Dr. Soames is also a very good friend of mine, and I'm pleased to hear that you value her kindness to you. You must also continue to study hard in school and realize how important it is to get an education. Whatever you do, don't follow in my footsteps!

Riding the outlaw trail may sound exciting and adventurous, but it's not. I can't count how many times me and the Kid had to sleep on the cold ground, and be wet and miserable because we didn't have money for a room, or we were on the run from some posse that just wouldn't quit! And now, I've ended up here, in prison, for goodness knows how long, and that's not fun either.

I realize we all share the same horrendous tragedy, and that was to lose our parents at a young age. I know that many of you must feel angry and resentful that life has handed you such a difficult path to tread.

We cannot choose many of the things that happen in our lives, but we can choose how we deal with them, and holding onto anger is not a good thing to do. It won't help you in your lives, and it certainly won't bring your parents back. Nor would your parents want you to be angry and resentful; they would want you to grow up to be happy and productive adults, and to have a good life.

When the Kid and I were orphaned, it was a different time than it is now. The Civil War was raging and the whole country was in turmoil. Nobody had time for orphans. The institution that took us in was a hard and cruel place for children to have to grow up in.

Both Jack Kiefer and I grew up angry, and that anger clouded our judgment and caused us to make choices that were dangerous and self-defeating. Not that I am justifying the decisions we made; the Kid and I were wrong in what we did, and we've both had to pay a heavy price for it.

I guess what I am trying to say here is that you have a safe and caring home with people who treat you with kindness and respect. They are giving you every opportunity to excel, and I want to emphasize how important it is that you all take advantage of that.

Well, enough lecturing. I certainly don't want to come across as just another boring adult! Thank you again for the gifts and the letters, and I hope you all had a very nice Christmas. Take care, respect one another, study hard, and above all else, have fun!

Napoleon Nash

Leon sat back and re-read the letter, then decided it was good to go. It was hardly a literary masterpiece, but writing to a group of children whom you don't know isn't exactly easy. Hopefully they would appreciate the note and maybe, he thought, it would be kind of nice if some of them decided to write to him again. So, he folded the letter and put it aside. He would give it to Mariam the next time he saw her, so she could then pass it along to the children.

Next, Leon picked out the letter from Gabi and re-read it.

He felt nervous about writing to her.

What to say? It's been so long since I've had any contact with her. It feels like writing to a stranger He frowned. *Well, just start writing, I guess.*

So, out came another sheet of paper.

Gabriella:

You are correct in your concern that I still feel some anger and resentment toward you. How could I not? As I pointed out to you at the time, you were doing to me the same thing that your in-laws had done to you. You knew how much you were hurting me, yet you did it anyway.

Having said that, I am trying to come to terms with it all. In my head, I know you were right. Trying to start a family while living the outlaw life is a bad idea. I have seen many men try it, and it has always ended badly. And I guess it did for us, too. The pain of that loss is with me always.

Maybe the anger I still feel isn't toward you at all, but at myself. So, I guess it's me I need to forgive, though I don't know that I will ever be able to. You did nothing wrong. It was all me, and I'm so sorry.

As to your enquiries, I am doing better this winter,

and yes, I am eating more now and staying healthy. It was not my intentions to kill myself through starvation. As you pointed out; there are far faster and easier ways of doing that, if that had been my design. Looking back on it now, I think it was all the stress of trying to find my footing here, in this place, and of course, facing the reality of really being here. Not only was I not prepared for how cold it gets in the winter, but Jack had shut me out and I didn't know why, so I must admit I was very depressed. I simply couldn't eat.

Later on, I became more aware of what Jack had been going through and why he hadn't been in touch, so I had a better understanding of it all. Now of course, he comes to see me every month when the weather allows him to do so. I know he is doing everything he can to convince the powers that be to grant me a pardon, but, as you know, he keeps running into blockades.

He is finding this just as frustrating as I do, but he and our other friends keep on trying, so, as you say, doing my best to keep hanging on here and to stay out of trouble.

Right now, visitors are few and far between, simply because of the snow piling up outside. So, I do get lonely. Oddly enough though, I have friends here, so I'm getting by.

Rest Assured, Gabi, even though it's hard to call what they serve here 'food', I am eating better, and even forcing myself to eat more than I want. I don't need to get sick again. Especially since one young man, whom I was looking after, got pneumonia and died, right there with me holding his hand. That was a shock. I'm the great Napoleon Nash! I was looking after him, so he wasn't supposed to die on me. Yeah right. Have I always been such an arrogant ass?

I know you are doing all you can at your end of things to try and help in procuring my release. I have no doubt you have been faithful in that endeavor, but I am also very much aware of your other commitments, and that those do, of course, hinder what you can do. Your other responsibilities come first and foremost. You hold our future in your hands, Gabi. There is nothing more important than that.

Though your letters bring a plethora of mixed emotions for me, I came close to throwing the first one away, but I did not do it. I guess that shows some progress.

Perhaps, as you say, if I ever do get out of this place, life will be better. I don't know if there is a future for you and me other than the connections we already share. But perhaps that connection is all that really matters.

I do appreciate your efforts and your letters, even if I'm not yet able to fully forgive. Keep writing if you wish to, and I promise I won't throw them away.

N. Nash

There, done. I'll let it settle, then go over it again and make some changes if I want before sending it out. Damn her anyway. Damn her for leaving, and damn her for coming back into my life. How can you love someone, and hate them at the same time?

He would send Caroline's letter first, since he felt it was important for her to hear his view on things. So, of course, Josey's letter would go along with that one. Gabi's would go next, because that one would take the longest to arrive at its destination. He would send the one to the ranch, last. He was hopeful the parcel of gifts would arrive before then, so he could also include a "thank you".

He settled back on his pillow and reached under the cot to retrieve his latest book. He had finished *A Christmas Carol*, and was now getting started on *Oliver Twist*, which was, of course, a story to which he could easily relate. He thought, fleetingly, that once he finished it he would suggest that Jack read it as well. Then he snorted softly.

Yeah, like that was ever going to happen.

***

Next day, in the infirmary, Leon did a quick scan of the ward and was disappointed at seeing only Dr. Palin sitting by his desk. There were absolutely no patients to tend to at all.

"Is Dr. Mariam going to be coming in any time soon?"

"Not unless we get a rush of sniffles and stubbed toes," Palin mumbled. "Why?"

"I wrote this letter for her to take back to the orphanage," Leon explained. "So, I guess I was kind of hoping she would be in today."

"Oh. Well, leave it with me and the next time she comes in I'll be sure she gets it." Then Doc looked up and sent a suspicious look over to his trustee. "What do ya mean you wrote a letter? What the hell have you been doin', Nash?"

Leon was taken aback. "What?"

"I told ya to give that hand a rest, to give those fingers a chance to heal," Doc reminded him. "It's bad enough that Carson has you back workin' again, but you gotta start writin' a letter in your spare time?"

Leon looked sheepish. "Well, they were important, Doc."

"They?" Palin's face turned red. "How many did you write?"

"Well, umm, let's see . . . there was one to Caroline, then one to Jack, and one to Jean, and—"

"Oh fuck! Get over here."

"What? Why?" Leon was unnerved. He took a step backward, thinking he was going to get punished for misbehaving. It did not occur to him for a moment that he could easily overpower the doctor, and he was nervous about the fact that he was in trouble.

Palin saw the anxiety level rise in the inmate and consciously calmed himself. Goodness knows, Leon had been brutalized enough at the hands of prison employees, and now, the inmate's automatic response to any show of disapproval caused him to become defensive.

"No, Nash, c'mon," Palin reassured him, "I just wanna look at those fingers and make sure they're still healing properly."

"Oh, all right." Leon relaxed and approached the doctor.

They both sat at the table, and Palin carefully untaped the broken fingers, then carefully began his own version of the poke and prod.

Leon flinched a few times but held his ground, and soon Palin finished with his exam. He re-taped the fingers.

"Yeah, okay," he said. "They're a bit more swollen than I would like to see at this point, but they're doin' okay. But still, if you ever wanna crack open a safe again, you better lay off the letter writin' for now. All right?"

Leon smiled. "Yeah, Doc. All right."

"Good! Now get to work."

"At what? You just said there's nothing going on."

Doc shrugged. "I donno. You're supposed ta be so smart, find something. But leave those fingers alone."

Leon sighed. It was going to be one of those days.

***

January 1887

When Saturday finally rolled around again, Leon found himself confronted with the long-awaited Christmas parcel sitting on his cot. It was two weeks late, but that didn't matter one bit. It was here, and Leon eagerly settled in to open the numerous rewrapped items.

One thing about Kenny, even though he had to unwrap any gifts that were sent, he always put some effort into restoring them to their original state, so that way, the inmate who would ultimately receive them could have the pleasure of opening the gifts himself. Little things like that made a big difference in a convict's life.

Leon sat down and opened the outer box. He gazed in at the items still wrapped in their brown paper and wondered whose to open first. He decided he wasn't going to decide, so he just grabbed one.

It was from Caroline.

He unwrapped the brown paper and discovered three sturdy candles and a handy tin candle holder. Candles he could use; this was good.

The next one was from Jean. Sure enough, it was more baked goods. They were a little broken up, but still quite edible. She had enclosed a brief note:

> *I know I already sent you your Christmas gifts with Mathew, but since everyone else was contributing to this box, I thought I would add in a little something again, myself. I hear through the grapevine that you appreciated the cookies before, so I've sent you some more. I hope they survive the journey intact!*
>
> *Jean*
>
> *P.S. Cameron sends his regards. You know how*

men can be about writing letters!

Leon smiled and took a nibble. They may not be intact, but they still tasted good.

The next one he pulled from the box was from David and Tricia. This surprised him, as he hadn't expected anything from them. He opened it to find another pair of warm socks and a scarf. And another quick note:

Napoleon;

Tricia seems to be suffering from the "Restless new mother fidgets" and she has been knitting up a storm since autumn! Thank you for giving her one more person upon whom she can lavish the end results. Stay warm and well fed, and keep in touch.

David

Okay, Leon agreed. If Trish's nesting syndrome resulted in him getting some of the finished results, well, he had no difficulty with that.

The next one was from Penny: Writing paper and two pencils. Again, something he could use, and to the point, as well; if they wanted him to keep writing to them, then he would need a stash of paper, more than what the prison supplied. This stash would do nicely.

Another reach into the box, and another parcel brought forth. This one was heavy, probably a book. It felt like a book, and indeed, it was. From Josephine. It was a copy of short stories and poems by Edgar Allen Poe, along with another note, short and to the point:

Leon: I don't knit. Josey.

Leon smiled again. This was all making him feel so good. It was a funny thing, considering where he was, but maybe, it was simply in comparison to last Christmas. Either way, he had to admit this was one of the nicest Christmases he'd had in a long time. His friends were all around him, perhaps not in person, but certainly in spirit, and he didn't feel quite so alone anymore.

He made one more reach into the box, and fittingly enough, the last gift he pulled out was from his nephew. It was a small box that fit comfortably into Leon's hand, and it was wrapped, like the other gifts, in plain brown paper. *From Jack* was printed, simply, across it.

Leon couldn't help the grin. The box felt so familiar to him, almost comforting to the point where he was afraid to open it, in case the actual item itself would destroy that feeling of camaraderie that had settled upon him. Finally, he did the inevitable and unwrapped the paper. His smile broadened. Trust Jack to know exactly what he needed.

It was a deck of cards.

A disturbing thought flashed across his mind, and he held the deck close to his chest and sent a furtive glance into the aisle. Maybe he wasn't allowed to have a deck of cards in here; maybe the guards would take them away from him. But then he relaxed. Kenny had already inspected the gifts. If Leon wasn't allowed to have any of these items, they would never have made it to his cell.

His dimples returned.

Despite his minor handicap, he opened the box and slid the deck into the palm of his right hand. His heart rate picked up, and he felt an excitement come into his chest.

He placed the deck onto his little table and spread the cards out with his left hand, then deftly brought them all back into a deck again. He picked up one card and weaved it in and out, through the fingers of his left hand, then slid it across the back of his hand and into his palm, then through his fingers again.

His dimples deepened.

The cards were stiff with their newness, but he shuffled them as best he could with his two fingers still taped up. They felt awkward, but he knew that working them would warm up both the deck of cards and his fingers. Wisely, he started with a simple mind teaser that would not put much strain on his hands.

He dealt out twenty-five cards then sighed and considered his options. Seeing the pattern already unfolding, he went about making the five pat hands that had gotten him into and out of so many scrapes throughout the years, that it felt like greeting an old friend.

Leon spent the rest of the afternoon playing with his new toy. The only time his smile left his face was when he was so focused in concentrating on the solitary game, that his brow would crease for a moment, and the smile would disappear. But only for an instant, then it would be back again, and he would shuffle the cards and deal them out, and start all over.

Yes, it had been a good Christmas. Now, they were into a new year. It was January 1887, and near the end of the following month, Leon would be thirty-six years old.

There had been new beginnings this Christmas, and some disappointments, but still, a lot of hope. Leon knew he was lucky, so very lucky, with the friends and family he had, and as Gabi had pointed out, they were all working toward that one goal, and Leon had a responsibility to them. He had to stay safe, stay healthy and stay alive. He had to surrender control of his life and trust to others to pick up the reins and steer the way.

Can I do it? Step down and stop trying to always be the man in charge? I suppose, if I want to stay alive in this place, I might have to. Let's face it, being stubborn hasn't worked. I can either comply with the rules or end up beaten and broken, maybe permanently. What would be the good of a release from this place then?

He sighed, his focus turning inward as he thought about all the obstacles he'd placed in front of himself.

Yeah. Time for a change in attitude.

It was a new year, and a new beginning, and Napoleon Nash had just made a gigantic leap of faith

CHAPTER SEVENTEEN
A CHANGE IN ROUTINE

Arvada, Colorado,
December 1886

"So, what do you think?" Cameron asked his wife.

Jean yawned and snuggled in deeper beside her husband.

"About what?" she asked.

"About Penny going back to the prison with Jack," Cameron reminded her. "I know she wants to go, but I'm not so sure Jack wants to take her." He hesitated, staring into the darkness, then he smiled. "I'm not so sure I want Jack to take her."

"Yes," Jean agreed. "It would be asking quite a bit of Mathew. Not just the responsibility of having a young lady with him, but the time he has with Peter is precious to him. He might resent having Penny along."

"Hmm," came the comment back to her. "I hadn't thought of that aspect. I suppose that is a point."

"What were you thinking?"

"The same thing all fathers think," Cameron confessed. "I know they're fond of each other, and I know how emotions and desires can take over, especially if they're off on their own like that. I've nothing against Jack; he's shown himself to be a fine young man, but still, he is a young man and things can happen."

"Yes, they can," Jean agreed. "I seem to recall another fine young man whisking a rather willing young lady off to the barn for some time alone. I sometimes wonder what would have happened if my father had walked in on us."

Cameron laughed. "Oh, my goodness. We probably wouldn't

have any children." He sobered and returned to his point. "That's exactly what I'm talking about. I'd hate to have to shoot Jack

"Yes, dear. I know," Jean teased him, then put the joking aside. "Penny can be quite flirtatious sometimes. It might be putting too much temptation into a young man's path. That really wouldn't be fair to Mathew." Jean became quiet again as she considered the options. "What about your other suggestion? That Penny goes along with Steven and Caroline? I'm sure Miss Jansen would be present as well, so Mathew and Penny wouldn't have much time to be alone together."

"Yes, I was thinking about that," Cameron admitted. "My main concern is that it would be quite a party converging on the prison all at once, and the warden may not appreciate it."

"Then, perhaps Miss Jansen would be willing to go along with them as Penny's chaperone, just for that one trip," Jean suggested. "Three people have been in before to visit with Peter, so that shouldn't be a problem."

"Yes, but Miss Jansen is supposed to be Caroline's chaperone," Cameron pointed out. "She can't very well be two places at once."

"I know. But Steven and Caroline are betrothed now, and really, I can't help but feel that their celibacy is no longer under our control. If they wanted to, they could find time alone together." She smiled and gave her husband's arm a squeeze. "We did."

"Is this conversation intended to make me feel better?" Cameron asked. "You keep on reminding me of 'us', and I am going to lock both our daughters up until they reach thirty-five!"

Jean laughed. "We turned out all right."

"Yes, we did," Cameron hugged his wife even closer. "It's just that having two headstrong daughters is trying on a man's nerves."

"Well, dear, let's sleep on it. We have agreed that Mathew and Penny cannot go to the prison without a chaperone, so we can sort the rest of the details out as the time comes close. Goodness knows, nobody is going anywhere in this weather. It's probably a good thing the appointment with the governor was postponed, because I doubt Mathew would have been able to get to it anyways."

"True."

***

Two bedrooms over, Penelope was also lying awake and worrying about life in general. First off, Peter was very much on her mind, and she couldn't help but be concerned about his safety in that awful place. She was thankful that he had friends there, and Dr. Mariam had assured her that she would let her young friend know if anything else happened. Not that Penny could do anything about it, other than keep notes, but just knowing she had contacts there at the prison, made her feel a little less useless.

The other thing occupying her thoughts was, of course, Mathew. They had been getting along very well since summer. Having once agreed to stay just friends for now, they had both relaxed and were simply enjoying one another's company.

She knew Mathew had been angry with her for sneaking off to the prison, but he seemed to get over that quickly enough. Especially when Steven pointed out that it might actually help their case. Anything that might help Peter's case was very quickly accepted by his partner.

They were all frustrated by the inactivity that winter had forced upon them, and she knew that as soon as the weather allowed it, Mathew would be on the train back to Wyoming. Penny hoped that she would be able to go with him, but she doubted her parents would allow it. Include the fact that Mathew apparently wasn't comfortable with her going with him either, well . . . it just didn't seem likely to happen.

This is all so silly. Mathew wouldn't do anything. He was always such a gentleman. Why don't Mama and Papa trust him? She sighed in frustration. *It seems the only way they might even consider my going back to the prison would be if I go with a whole group of other people. Really? Having Caroline and Steven along for the ride would be just so—crowded! Still, I suppose it would be better than not going at all.*

Then she thought back, with a mixture of pleasure and irritation, to the New Year's Eve party which was held in town the week before.

***

New Year's Eve

Steven and Caroline had not attended the get together, as they, along with Josephine, had returned to Denver right after Christmas. But at least David and Trish had joined in on the festivities, despite Trish's obvious disadvantage. It was agreed that Jack and Penny would spend the night at their place after the fireworks show, so they would not be trying to drive the buggy home in the dark, or have to pay for two rooms at the hotel.

The party had been held in the community hall, and it had been well lit and well attended by most of the young people who called Arvada their home.

Sheriff Jacobs had popped his head in a couple of times during the evening, but since everything seemed to be staying within reason, he was not too concerned about problems arising.

All in all, the young adults of the town were good citizens. There were also some older folks attending, with the intention of keeping an eye on things, and Deputy Ben Palin did his part to keep his peers in line. He was there to enjoy the festivities with his lady of interest, but he was also making sure nobody got too rowdy.

Sam and Maribelle were also in attendance and would spend the night at the hotel, making it a real holiday for them. It would probably be the last holiday for a while, since the announcement had been made that Maribelle was already in the family way. They would most likely be spending next New Year's Eve at home.

The hall was crowded with everyone in a festive spirit and wanting to dance until the fireworks show at midnight. With all that going on, it was not until Jack was returning to the table where Penny was awaiting their fruit punch that he became aware that Miss Isabelle Baird was also in attendance. He shouldn't have been surprised by her presence, since she was part of this group of young adults, but he still was taken aback when she inadvertently bumped into him and nearly caused him to spill the drinks.

"Oh, ah, Miss Baird—I mean, Isabelle," Jack smiled at her. "I always seem to be bumping into you. My apologies."

"Not at all, Jack," she assured him with a sweet smile. "How nice to see you here. We haven't had much chance to visit since last summer. You always seem to be off somewhere."

"Yes ma'am," Jack agreed. "I have been busy. But it is nice to see you here tonight. Perhaps you would honor me with a dance later."

Isabelle smiled coyly. "Why, of course, Jack. I'd be pleased to."

Jack smiled and, nodding a polite acceptance, started to move off.

Isabelle, however, had other plans, and she placed a hand on his arm, stopping him before he could even take a step.

He looked back at her, and her eyes traveled upward to the ceiling.

Jack followed her gaze and his heart came into his throat. They were standing under the mistletoe.

Oh dang!

It just so happened that David was walking by them, taking drinks over for himself and his wife.

"You walked right into that one, Jack," he whispered on his way by. "Or should I say, right under . . ."

"Ahh . . ." Jack looked down and met Isabelle's pleased and expectant gaze. He smiled nervously. *Dagnabbit. Penny's starin' at me. I can tell. Oh well.* "Yes ma'am, I mean Isabelle. Happy New Year."

Fortunately, he was holding a drink in both his hands, so he didn't have to worry about what to do with them. He leaned forward and gave Isabelle a friendly kiss on the cheek.

Isabelle however, had other ideas and at the last instant, she turned her cheek aside and Jack felt his lips settle onto hers in a rather warm and pleasing connection.

Much to his surprise, her lips parted a little, and he felt the tip of her tongue caress his mouth.

Jack pulled back from her and gazed down into the dark pools of her eyes; he was breathing just a little bit too fast for his comfort.

She smiled up at him. "Happy New Year, Jack," she purred, "until our dance."

Her claim staked; she then sashayed her way across the floor to her table where she was sitting with her group of friends.

They were all smiles and giggles at watching her set the trap and successfully ensnare her prey. She sat down with a smile of satisfaction, feeling confident that she had established her priority and had won the night.

Jack returned to his table where David, Tricia and Penny were awaiting him, each wondering how he was going to handle this situation. Jack sat down beside a dejected looking Penny, and putting the drinks onto the table, he draped an arm around his young friend's shoulders and hugged her to him.

"I ain't quite as obtuse as some people would have ya think," he whispered to her. "I know exactly what she's doin', and Penny darlin'—I ain't interested."

Penny smiled, and she returned his hug, giving him her own kiss on the cheek.

David laughed and raised his glass of punch.

"Well done, Jack. Happy New Year!"

***

Penny lay in her bed and smiled up at the ceiling. It had turned out to be a fun night after all. Though Isabelle did indeed get her one dance with Jack, he danced all the others with either Penny or Tricia. Even though dancing with Tricia, in her current state, did not really describe the awkward wallowing that her attempts on the floor amounted to. She did her best, but after one dance with Jack and two with her husband, she called it a night and was just as happy sitting at their table and watching others.

Naturally, this pleasant pastime was regularly punctuated by her numerous waddles to the necessity. David accompanied her on those jaunts, to make sure she didn't slip in the snow. And also, because he was a doting husband and father-to-be. Poor Tricia was quite ready for the baby to arrive. She was awfully tired of not being able to see her toes, and the extra weight she lugged around was exhausting.

The fireworks display had been loud and glorious, and Tricia did very well staying up for it, as by that time she was done in and ready for sleep. And yet, the walk back to the Gibson residence, with both David and Jack assisting the mother-to-be to keep her feet, had been filled with laughter and jokes, and a good time with good friends.

***

In the downstairs bedroom, Jack also lay awake, contemplating life as he knew it these days. As always, first and foremost, Leon was on his mind. No matter what else was going on in Jack's life or moods, there was always with him an underlying fear or dread. It didn't clutch at his heart or rise to choke him or cause him to lose his appetite, but it was still there nonetheless. Just a dullness in the pit of his stomach and in the back of his mind. It was always there.

What if somethin' happens ta Leon before we get him out?

What if he gets sick again and he doesn't pull through? What if Carson beats 'im ta death? I wouldn't put it past that bastard. What if Leon spirals into another depression and stops eating again . . . what if . . . what if . . .

Jack groaned and ran a hand over his eyes and through his hair. *Jeez, I thought Leon was supposed to be the worrier. He's the one who always had ta think everything ta death. He's the one who went over all the 'what if's'.* Jack would always go on instinct and say what he thought without worrying the idea into the ground.

Yeah Leon, that's a good plan. Or Ah no, Leon, you're just not thinkin'.

And he'd let his partner worry about the details.

But . . . what if . . .? Jack felt that familiar fear creep through him again; the one he always felt when he got too close to thinking about this. What if . . . and he was almost afraid to think it out loud. *What if Leon dies in there, before we can get him out? It would be unbearable, especially when I'm in a position ta break 'im out, without havin' ta put all that much planning into it. It'd be easy in the summer time, when the inmates are outside the prison doin' work for the townspeople. Just gather some of the boys from the gang and make a raid. It would be so easy.*

And yet, I ain't doin' a damn thing to organize it. Why? Cause I know Leon wouldn't approve. He wouldn't go for it. Leon wouldn't want me to be throwin' away my pardon just ta save him. So, here I sit, tryin' ta do things the right way—the legal way—and it's takin' forever!

Then the same question hit him again.

What if Leon dies in there before we can get him out? Jack silently groaned. *It sure would be hard to carry on without him by my side, figuratively or literally.* He rubbed eyes that burned with worry. *Jeez, I don't even wanna imagine that . . .*

Oh, this is gettin' too morbid!

Jack forced his mind away from that vicious circle and put it onto more pleasant thoughts.

New Year's had been fun. He'd come close to forgetting

about his worries while at that gathering. Everyone had a great time, the food had been good and plentiful, the fruit punch, though a bit "fruity" had been refreshing, and the company could not have been better.

Jack smiled at that thought. *Jeez, I must be gettin' old. He thought back to some of the raucous New Year's Eve parties he and Leon had been to over the years—especially the ones in Elk Mountain. Or even better, in the nearby town, that had no problem welcoming the outlaws and their money to celebrate the night away in their establishments.*

Wine, women and song! Or, more appropriate: whiskey, whores and tinny piano music. But they sure had fun!

Jack smirked. *Not too long ago I wouldn't 'a hesitated ta jump on a tasty invitation like the one Isabelle gave me. Jack shook his head in the darkness. Young Miss Isabelle has no idea; she thinks she's all worldly and seductive, but compared to the women I've spent time and money on durin' my outlawin' years, she's still innocent and pure. She has absolutely no idea.*

Penny's innocent too, but at least she don't pretend ta be otherwise. She's sweet and caring. She wants ta be with me 'cause she likes me, not because 'a who I used ta be. When we first met, I was just a down-on-his-luck saddle tramp who didn't even have enough money ta get outta the cold on Christmas Eve. And she didn't care; she just liked me.

Jack felt a calming warmth wash over him at the thought of Penny, and he smiled. Then the smile turned to a frown when Isabelle returned to his thoughts.

That one's only after the reputation. I know that; I ain't an idiot. She don't know me well enough ta like me. She just wants ta be the one who seduces the Kansas Kid. Well, that ain't gonna happen. Aw, she's sure pretty enough, and, like I said, there was a time, not long ago, when I would not have hesitated to partake of her treasures. But not no more.

He was approaching his thirty-fourth birthday and was finally beginning to grow up. He'd spent all New Year's Eve without having even one alcoholic drink, and also knew that he would be going to bed alone. But because he had spent the evening in the company of friends and family, he hadn't missed the boozing or even thought about hitting the whore house. And he'd had a really good time. His life had changed and so had his priorities.

Then his thoughts drifted back to Leon again—always back to Leon. But this time it was more about what they were planning on doing, not what they weren't planning on doing. Steven's prediction had been correct in that it was Thomas Moonlight who had been sworn in as the new Governor of the Territory of Wyoming. Just what that would mean for their concerns remained to be seen.

Moonlight had very little sympathy for outlaws and trying to use the Civil War as an excuse for their chosen lifestyle wasn't going to get them very far. But they did have a new appointment set for the middle of April. Steven was working on a presentation that might convince the new governor that Napoleon Nash had served enough time and was deserving of a pardon.

Just hang on, Leon. Just hang on and lay low, and stay outta trouble. That ain't askin' too much, is it?'

Oh, but what if . . .? No! Don't go there again. Get some sleep. Busy day comin' up.

Jack rolled over and snuggled deeper into his warm blankets. He closed his eyes for real and relaxed.

Upstairs in the third bedroom Elijah slept like a baby.

CHAPTER EIGHTEEN
THE BIG FREEZE

January 8th, 1887

They'd all been aware that a storm was brewing but whatever moisture it brought was coming too late to help the grasslands recover. The unusually hot and dry summer had sucked all the nutrients out of the ground, and the livestock was already suffering from the shortage of feed and water.

The approaching storm didn't bring any comfort with it.

Cameron stood in the middle of the yard watching as the sky darkened and the wind tickled his nostrils. A foreboding settled upon him and he chewed his lip with worry.

Jack left the barn and came to stand beside the rancher. He too looked up at the approaching storm.

"What?" he asked in response to Cameron's concerns. "It's just another storm comin' in. You said yourself that we could use more snow."

Cameron shook his head. "No, this is different."

Now it was Jack's turn to frown. "Different how?"

"Can't you feel it? The heaviness in the air." He sniffed. "And it smells different."

Jack also sniffed. "It smells like snow. But that ain't no surprise. It's January."

A gust of wind hit them, and both men snatched their hats to prevent them from blowing off their heads.

Jack shivered. "Brrr. It's gonna be a cold one, that's for sure."

"It's going to be more than that." Cameron spotted his hired hand exiting the coach house. "Sam! You know where we store the winter rope?

"Yes sir."

"Good. Gather it all up. We're going to need it."

Sam nodded and waved. "Yessir, Mr. Marsham."

"Rope?" Jack asked.

"Yes. We'll stretch two lengths of rope from the porch to the barn door, and another to the chicken coop and another to the outhouse. I suspect this blizzard is going to last for days and everything will be a white-out. I've known men to lose their sense of direction then get lost and freeze to death in the middle of their own barnyard." He glanced at the chicken coop. "We better fortify that coop or those birds are going be buried. We'll have to stuff the hen house with more straw as well, to help insulate it. Let's get to work. There's lots to do before suppertime."

Cameron walked toward the horse barn, his every stride powered by determination.

Jack stood for a moment, watching him go.

"Geesh." He glanced up at the darkening sky. "It don't look no different from any other storm ta me."

***

January 9th, 1887

By some accounts, the worst blizzard to ever hit the western states, hit them early in that new year. It swept down from Montana, and blew on through Wyoming, over Colorado, as well as east into the Dakotas and even sent its bite as far south as Texas.

Cattle died by the thousands. Large, powerful ranchers were brought to their knees. No one escaped the freezing blow, and cattle ranching, as it had always been known, was changed forever.

But when Jack awoke early that next morning, he was blissfully unaware of what was to come. All he was concerned with was the sound of the wind battering against the side of the sturdy house, and the fact that he was cold.

He shouldn't be cold. The blankets on his bed always kept him warm and cozy even through the coldest winter nights. But he woke up this morning curled in a ball and clasping the blankets snuggly around him.

He knew he should get up. The least he could do is get the stove going, and maybe even the fireplace, to take the chill out of the morning air.

He quickly dressed but as soon as he opened his bedroom door, he was hit with the aroma of coffee brewing, and lights were burning in the kitchen. Jean was already up and the stove lit so why was it still so cold?

"Oh, Mathew, let me pour you a cup of coffee."

"I'll get it, Jean. You're busy."

Jean smiled and nodded. "Yes. What a morning. Thank goodness Eli has gone back to sleep."

"He's already had his breakfast?"

"Yes. And Cameron is out feeding the livestock."

"But that's my job." Jack's tone belied his concern. He stopped pouring his coffee in mid-stream and set the pot back on the stove. "I better get out there ta help 'im."

"No, Jack, you can't."

Jack cocked a brow in surprise. In all the years he had known Jean, this was the first time she had used his given name.

"Why not, Jean? What's wrong?"

"In weather like this, only one man goes out at a time. If Cameron gets lost out there, we're going to need you to search for him. That will leave me and Penny in the house to tend to things here. Eli can't be left alone, not even for a moment."

Jack topped up his coffee cup as he considered Jean's words.

"How could Cameron get lost? We strung up the guide ropes. They'll keep him on track."

Jean replenished her own coffee as she shook her head with worry.

"In weather like this, we can't count on just one safety measure. You never step off that front porch without tying the third rope around your waist. The other end of that rope is tired to the railing. If the guide ropes break or get buried, you'll always have that third rope to get you back."

"Jeez. Just how bad is this storm?"

The expression in Jean's eyes was answer enough, but before she could voice it, the front door banged open and a buffalo hide coat covered in snow staggered into the alcove.

Both Jack and Jean set coffees down and dashed through to assist. The wind had forced the door out of Cameron's hands, causing it to crash all the way open and snow whipped into the house to scatter across the floor.

Jack grabbed the door and, putting all his weight into it, he pushed it closed and locked it tight.

Jean went to her husband and helped him unbutton the coat made even heavier by the layers of wet snow sticking to it.

"Cameron, are you all right?"

"I'm fine," came the muffled response from inside the layers. "I just need to get warmed up."

"Coffee and oatmeal are ready and waiting for you."

"Oh, good."

With Jack helping to pull the coat off Cameron from behind, it wasn't long before the rancher looked like himself again. Soon all the cold weather paraphernalia was set out in the sitting room in front of the blazing fireplace to sizzle and dry.

***

After the adults finished breakfast, Eli was awake and ready for attention. Penny took care of entertaining her brother, while Jean returned to the kitchen. There were going to be endless buckets of snow to melt into drinking water for people and animals both, so they were all in for a busy time.

Jack and Cameron sat at the dining table to discuss plans for the day.

"Did Jean tell you about the third rope?"

"Yes."

"Good. Don't ever step off that porch without tying it around your waist."

"Yeah, I know. She told me."

"And only one of us goes out to the barn at a time."

"Yeah, I know."

Cameron sighed and leaned back. "Sorry. But this is one of the worst blizzards I've ever seen. If it last more than a couple of days, we could lose the ranch."

"What? Lose the ranch? Why? The cattle on the Rocking M always winter fine."

"This is different, Jack. After the growing season we went through last year, the cattle have already been weakened by lack of forage and water."

Jack remembered back and nodded.

The previous spring and summer had been exceptionally hot and dry, with many cattle on the larger spreads not being able to find water, and ultimately dying of thirst. Those that survived were weakened by the heat and lack of moisture. Everyone had waited anxiously for the autumn coolness and rain storms.

But the storms didn't bring rain. Instead, they arrived as dry lightning and rather than bringing precious water cascading from the sky, all they sent was fire. Acres and acres of grasses, already scorched from the long, hot summer, burst into flames that ran wild across the prairie and then into the timber, destroying everything in their wake.

Many ranches across the western states were so vast that transporting feed and water to the dwindling herds was impossible. During a season when the range cattle would normally have been fat and healthy from the summer grass and the autumn rains, they were instead already starving. And winter hadn't even set in yet.

"And now this," Cameron continued. "You saw the snow that came in with me. It was wet and heavy. Cattle have thick, heavy coats that are ideal for keeping them insulated during the winter as long as the moisture doesn't penetrate to the skin. Normally, their coats are thick enough to keep them dry, but not with this kind of snow. Once those same heavy coats get weighed down by wet snow, and night comes, bringing the temperatures below freezing, many of those cattle will die. And it's going to get cold, Jack. It's going to get really cold."

"Aww, jeez."

"Then, on top of that, those that survive the freezing temperatures will likely die of thirst because they've never learned that snow holds moisture. Standing up to their bellies in white precipitation, they'll simply let themselves die.

"I'm afraid cattle are not the smartest beasts the Lord put upon the Earth."

Jack sat and stared at his cooling coffee. "I see what you mean; we could lose the whole herd."

"We might. It was a hard blow but I learned a valuable lesson from the failure of our first ranch in Wyoming. Don't buy a ranch at face value. Research it, study it. Find out what the water table was during the best and the worst seasons. Make sure there are valleys and hills for shelter during the winter months, and streams and rivers that will flow all year round. And, I try to keep my range stock at home. I don't allow them to spread out and mingle with my neighbor's herds. I did my homework before purchasing this second ranch, and I've never allowed it to become so vast that it was unmanageable.

"And, as you know, we harvest a lot of hay throughout the summer to ensure we have feed for the winter."

"Oh brother, do I know it." Jack groaned in memory of hay harvesting. "Some of the hands from those other spreads thought it was a great joke that we did that."

"I know," Cameron agreed. "It is hard, heavy work, and during the hottest time of the year. None of the larger ranches do it. They figure their spreads are vast enough and the range lush enough that they don't need extra feed. Up until now, they've been right." Worried darkened his eyes as he gazed at the front door. "I have a feeling this blizzard is going to change all that." He sighed then came back to the present. "Even for us, with this kind of weather, there's no way to get feed out to the range stock. They really are on their own until spring. I pray to God that this storm doesn't last too long."

"What about your horses, Cameron? You've got some real good stock out there."

"I'm not as worried about the horses as I am about the cattle. Horses know they can get moisture from snow. They also know how to dig down to get at grass." He gave a soft, ironic laugh. "Yeah, what little there is of it. But Belle is a good lead mare. She'll keep them safe."

Jack frowned. "A mare? I thought Gambler would look after the band."

"Nope. The stallion's job is to acquire as many mares as he can, protect them from predators and other stallions, and make baby horses. That's it.

"The lead mare is the one who decides when it's time to leave for the summer or winter grazing lands. She knows where the water always flows and where the sweetest grass grows. And she knows where the best shelters are to get out of this kind of a storm. Yup. I'm sure she has them all tucked up in some enclosed canyon or protected valley to wait it out. They'll be fine.

***

When it was Jack's turn to haul water to the barn and chicken coop, he suddenly understood what all the precautions were about. He stood on the porch, bundled up in the thick buffalo coat, scarf and hat, heavy gloves and insulated boots, and felt fear.

The rope was tied snuggly around his bulky waist, and he knew the two guide ropes were there even though he couldn't see them. Truth was he couldn't see anything but white and couldn't hear anything but the howling wind.

He carried buckets of water in both hands so he would have to count on the feel of the guide ropes against his arms to get him across the yard. And yet, he hesitated.

This was worse than the winter he and Leon had shown up at the Marshams' Wyoming ranch, injured and frozen to the core. He'd thought that was bad, but at least they could see a few feet ahead of them.

All Jack could see now was a wall of white; an impenetrable wall that swirled and stormed past him but kept him anchored to the porch. How was he supposed to walk through that?

He knew he couldn't let the ranch down now. With one big, deep breath, which he instantly regretted as the cold air stung his lungs, he stepped off the porch.

It seemed an eternity of feeling his way along the guide ropes as he inched forward. He had to drag his feet through the gathering snow along the pathway, but still stumbled a couple of times with the uncertain footing. An instant of panic hit him then, as he would lose touch with the guide ropes, and the snow whirling around him made him feel dizzy and disoriented.

Resting on his knees, he forced himself to relax and regain his bearings. Leaning on the buckets, he could push himself to his feet again and swing his arms until he made contact with the guide ropes. As long as he didn't spill any of the water and have to go back for more, he was making steady progress.

He pushed onward, dragging his feet through the heavy, wet snow until he came up, face first, against the barn door. Relief washed over him when he finally opened that door and was able to step inside the structure.

Horses whinnied their greetings, and the lone cow with her spring calf rustled in the straw bedding in anticipation of lunch. The dogs were nowhere to be seen and Jack assumed they were nestled inside their own nests with no intention of coming out to greet him.

Certain chores still needed to be done even though access to the manure pile out back was impossible. After feeding, then breaking through ice in buckets and topping up the water, he set about mucking the stalls. An indoor manure pile was established near the back and that's where the soiled straw had to go for now.

Twice as much bedding went back into the stalls to help insulate, plus the combined body heat of all the animals inside the barn helped to keep the freezing temperatures at bay. But it was still colder than Jack had ever experienced before. Not even wintering in Elk Mountain had been this bad.

He thought briefly of those fellas who were wintering in that drafty bunkhouse in the hideout. The leader's cabin was better, but still, those boys must be cold.

I sure hope Gus brought enough stores in ta get them fellas through this.

Then his mind was back to his own situation. Even though he worked hard and fast to get through the chores, he never felt the need to remove any of his layers. The only thing not covered were his eyes and still he was cold. And yet, this cold was nothing compared to what it must be like out on the range. His heart ached, knowing that those beasts were suffering and dying out there and there wasn't a thing anybody could do about it.

He noted, as he fought against the howling wind on his way to the chicken coop, that very little new snow had accumulated along their paths, even though it was still a solid mass of white falling from the skies. He thought it odd but with all the other concerns to deal with, that particular one did not linger.

As soon as he forced open the door of the coop, he was met with a chorus of relieved clucking accentuated by loud crowing from the rooster. Jack kept an eye on the rooster who tended to have an attitude about anyone getting close to his hens, but on this occasion, that bird seemed to know it was in his best interest to behave himself.

Jack broke through the ice in the water pans and replenished the grain, at which point, there was a rush of feathers amongst wild clacking as all the chickens made a rush for the feed pans.

Jack got out of their way. He did a quick fluffing up of the straw and checked the roosts for eggs just in case any of the hens were laying. They weren't.

Then he left and made his way back to the house, taking empty water buckets with him to be replenished for Cameron's next trip out to the barn in a couple of hours.

Coffee and a bowl of Jean's rich, beef stew was going to go down real good.

***

The hopes and prayers that the storm would only last a short time had all been in vain. For ten long, cold days, the wind howled and the skies dumped snow that got blown into impassable drifts. Firewood and coal were running scarce and the larder was starting to look bare by the time Mother Nature decided to move on.

Even then, getting off the ranch was impossible.

Jean worried about their neighbors, especially the older folks who refused to leave their small holdings and go live in town. She hoped they'd had enough to see them through and enough wood to stay warm. But she wouldn't know until the roads could be cleared and people started getting out again.

Jack thought he was in good shape from working the ranch, but ten days of hauling water caused his arms to ache. And yet, once the snows stopped, a different kind of work started and Jack's aching muscles would have to toughen up.

Looking out at the yard, the stretch between the house and the barn was unrecognizable. The reason for the lack of accumulation of snow on the flats became apparent. Every structure that stood in the face of those howling winds had huge drifts piled up against them. The well was buried, with only the battered bucket and the wooden cross bar still showing.

The outhouse resembled an igloo with only a small section cleared because the door was occasionally forced open. On the most part, everyone had used chamber pots and tended to their own dump duty.

The barn and chicken coop looked more like rolling hills under the huge drifts of snow with again, only the doors and the side away from the wind showing wood. The house itself was in no better shape.

Everything would need to be dug out and quickly too, before the weight of the wet snow collapsed any of the roofs. Both the barn and the chicken coop needed to be striped completely and new bedding put down. Though efforts had been made to keep the animals clean, it had been a losing battle and those structures reeked with the combination of urine and excrement. It was tough going, and all through it, Cameron worried over the fate of his cattle.

It was a week before the road into town was clear enough that a horse-drawn sleigh could make it through. Those who had sleighs made the trips into town, checking in on any homes along the way that they could access. They brought back supplies, checked in on stranded families and made sure that whatever was needed got done.

But no one was getting out onto the ranges until spring. Only then would the true devastation of those ten brutal days in January 1887 become clear.

CHAPTER NINETEEN
REJUVENATION

There was one bright spot that helped take some of the bite out of that cruel winter.

February rolled in and things didn't seem all that much different from January. It was still cold, it was still white, and nobody was going anywhere unless dire emergency required it.

David was getting anxious as Tricia's due date was fast approaching, and he didn't want them to get snowed in. Of course, their neighbor, Millie, was often over to help Tricia with the daily chores and to lend moral support. Tricia's mother tried to get in from their ranch as often as she could, but the road conditions kept her at home more than she'd like.

Fortunately, the Hamiltons were just a block away and on standby alert. John had done most of the doctoring in town before David had arrived, and his wife, Nancy, was an experienced midwife. Both would be in attendance for Tricia's delivery.

Jack wanted to write to Leon for his birthday, but he also wanted to hold off on the letter until the baby arrived. He wasn't sure if his uncle was really all that interested in the arrival of new infants, but David was a friend, so he would probably appreciate an announcement. Chances were, any letter written to Leon now would be late arriving anyway, so another week or two wasn't going to make much difference.

As it turned out, Tricia went into labor in the middle of the afternoon of a clear and bright sunny day. Millie had no problem making her way to the Hamiltons' home to let them know that the time was upon them. David was a nervous wreck, excited and scared all at the same time, and he was very much relieved when John and Nancy showed up and took control. Delivering other people's babies was one thing, but the prospect of having to deliver his own was proving to be more nerve racking than he ever would have imagined.

David spent the afternoon and evening sitting beside his wife and holding her hand. In between contractions, she spoke quiet reassurances to help keep him calm.

By the time late evening came upon them, both parents-to-be were worn out and wishing that this new little person would hurry up and put in an appearance.

By the time the wee hours of February 16th came, David was beyond nervous and was just plain tired. Tricia was holding her own and soon the contractions were coming close together, and everyone got busy.

"How arc you doing, David?" John asked his friend, who was looking pale.

"I'm okay," David answered as he wiped perspiration from his wife's brow.

"How are you doing, Trish?" John asked the wife.

Trisha simply nodded in between deep breaths and squeezed her husband's hand even harder.

David grimaced but held his ground.

Some hours earlier, word had gotten around the district that the new infant was on its way. Jack had been good enough to take on the role of cab driver for those who wished to attend the birth and he got the pacer, Monty, hitched up to the buggy in anticipation of a trip to town.

Jean got herself ready, organizing Penny to carry on with Eli and to take over the handling of the household for a while.

Penny was disappointed that she couldn't go too. Jean pointed out to her that there were going to be more than enough mother hens in attendance as it was, and Penny could come in later to give her congratulations.

Another consideration in the back of Jean's mind was that, even though there had been no indication of problems, this was Tricia's first pregnancy, and there was no telling how it would go. Jean did not want Penny there to witness things if it went badly.

Of course, Penny had been in the other room when Eli was born, but Jean had already had children, so chances were good that, even though Jean was older, this birth would also go smoothly.

Jack and Jean bundled themselves up in the sleigh, and they

headed out at a quick pace toward the Baxter ranch to pick up Tricia's mother, Mary. That done, and with the two ladies chatting excitedly in the back seat, Jack turned the horse's head toward town, and they made quick work of the hard-packed distance to the Gibson residence.

Jack dropped the ladies off and headed back to the Rocking M. He knew his attendance at this event was hardly necessary, and that they would likely be there all day and maybe into the night. The ladies would rent a horse and buggy to bring them home when they were ready.

Once inside, Millie and Jean settled in at the kitchen table, while Mary disappeared into the bedroom to add support to her daughter and son-in-law.

A couple of hours later, Mary returned to the kitchen to join the other ladies. Tricia had noted that her mother, who wasn't well at the best of times, looked fatigued and, assuring her that all was well, sent her off to relax with a cup of tea.

Jean and Millie made sure that tea and coffee were both kept available, along with the hot water needed for sterilizing and cold water for the numerous cloths that Nancy and David used to help Tricia deal with the pain and exertion of contractions. All three of those ladies had been through enough child birthings to know how things were going, and that there was no rushing it. Babies were born when they were good and ready to be born, especially first babies.

But when they heard Tricia yell out in pain, as a particularly strong contraction hit her, those wise ladies smiled across the table at one another and knew that birth was imminent.

Mary was tempted to return to her daughter's side but decided that holding her hand was what David was there for. After all, he was the one who had gotten her into this condition, so he should have to at least suffer through the labor pains as well.

Inside the bedroom, Nancy was in position to assist her husband, and David was doing his best to be supportive of his wife. He ignored the pain in his hand, as the contractions caused Tricia's grip to become vice-like in its intensity.

But David held true and caressed his wife and spoke encouragements to her, even though she felt like punching him in the face. Then another strong contraction, and John gave Tricia the okay to push. And push she did, with all her might as she allowed a gasp of pain to escape her.

"Here we go," John told her. "I can see the baby's head now, Tricia. Just a few more good pushes and you'll be done."

Tricia didn't answer but sent him a look indicating who else she'd like to be pushing right then. *Damn men! What do they know about this? If David thinks he's ever going to touch me again, he is sadly mistaken! Oh my God!* Another contraction and another push and—*Oh! When is this baby going to get out of me?*

"Just one more push, Tricia."

"C'mon, sweetheart," David coaxed her. "We're almost there."

We? When did this 'we' come into it?

Another contraction and Tricia gasped again, then suddenly—finally—the pain released, and everybody was on the move. Nancy came forward with the swaddling blanket, while her husband set about his business tying off the umbilical cord and getting the infant breathing.

David still held onto his wife's hand but stood up, trying to get a look at his new offspring.

John smiled at him. "It's a boy, David! A strong and healthy boy. Congratulations to both of you."

David's face split into a grin.

Tricia was just relieved, but as soon as the infant was wrapped in a blanket and placed in the new mother's waiting arms, her tired face lit up with pleasure.

David was already touching his new son's head and laughed excitedly when the baby wrapped a tiny fist around his finger.

Tricia instinctively put the baby to her breast, but he wasn't showing much interest in nursing just yet; still too much in shock over that violent passage from warm darkness into cool air. And life was just beginning.

Nancy returned to the kitchen to get more warm water and wash cloths, and to deliver the good news.

"It's a boy!" she announced.

Jean and Millie were pleased as punch.

"Finally, a grandson," Mary exclaimed. "All my children seemed determined to keep having girls!"

"Is Tricia okay?" Jean asked. "Did everything go all right?"

"Yes," Nancy assured them. "Baby and mother are doing fine. Father's a bit scattered though." She smiled. "Just give us a few minutes to get them cleaned up, and then you can come in to meet the new arrival."

Half an hour later, everyone was in the bedroom and gathered around the new family. Both parents smiled with pleasure through their exhaustion, while the object of all the attention suckled for a few moments, then promptly fell asleep.

"He's a beautiful baby," Jean complimented them. "Congratulations, both of you. You've waited a long time for this."

Both parents nodded emphatically.

"I have boxes of baby boy things, just waiting to come over and be of use again," Jean continued. "Eli outgrows everything so fast; it'll be nice to be able to pass them along."

"Well, everyone," John announced, as he and his wife finished with the cleaning up. "The sun is rising, and it looks like it's going to be another real nice day. How about we all head over to the cafe for breakfast and leave this new family to get acquainted on their own."

Everyone nodded assent to this and began shuffling toward the bedroom door.

"You're all going?" David was almost in a panic. "But, what do we do?"

"By the look of things, I'd say you're all going to get some sleep," John predicted, then smiled at David's paled complexion. "Don't worry, David, he's not going to break. I'll come back in about an hour to see how you're doing. And I'm sure Mary will be staying on for a few days to help you adjust."

"Of course, I am," Mary announced. "Somebody has to show these two what happens after the baby arrives!"

"Oh, all right," David answered, feeling relieved. His whole perspective on delivering babies had just done a sudden shift.

Tricia sent them all a tired smile. "Thank you, John, Nancy," she said. "I think I will get some sleep."

***

> *So, there you have it, Leon,* Jack wrote. *They named the little fella Nathanial after Trish's father and Charles, after David's father, so the little guy already has quite a lineage to live up to. Wonder if he'll become a doctor too!*
>
> *I ain't met 'im yet, of course. Plenty of time for introductions later.*

Don't be surprised if you get a letter from David as soon as his head comes down out of the clouds! I have no doubt he will fill in all the details for ya to the point where you'll swear you were there yourself! Something for you to look forward to.

Well, Leon, again, Happy Birthday seems kinda lame considerin', but I wanted ta drop you a line to acknowledge it anyways. Everyone else sends good wishes etc. I'm hopin' ta get in ta see ya in late March, early April, but as usual, it all depends on the weather.

In the meantime, take care of yourself, and I say again: stay outta trouble! It just ain't worth it, gettin' beat up all the time. And even I can tell that Carson is gettin' harder and harder on ya each time you provoke him—so don't do it!

Okay; enough lecturin'. See ya soon,
Jack

***

Leon settled into his pillow and sipped his coffee.

The January blizzard had hit Laramie just as hard as it had Arvada. Everything had gone into lockdown with no one allowed out in the yard even if they'd wanted to.

Wind whistled through the old prison walls, sucking away the heat from the constantly burning fire places at the end of each row of cells. Even the warm sweaters from Jean hadn't been enough to keep the chill out of Leon's bones.

Ten days of everyone, inmates and guards both, being cooped up had frayed a lot of nerves but everyone was too focused on staying warm to start any fights. Dirty looks and rude hand gestures were the best most of them could muster.

When the blizzard did stop, work gangs were organized to clear the roads. There were no fights then either because everyone was so tired at the end of their shifts all they wanted to do was swill down hot chow and curl up in their bunks.

January was a tough month for all concerned.

Then, as things opened up and people began moving around again, word got to the prison of the fate of the large ranches surrounding Laramie.

Just like in Colorado, no one in Wyoming could get out onto the ranges to confirm the devastation. Everyone knew it was going to be bad, but they had no idea how bad.

For once, Leon was glad to have spent those ten days indoors, even if it was in a prison. He worried about Jack. He worried about all of them back home, of course, but he worried about Jack the most. They'd both always avoided ranch work when they could, but now Jack was stuck right in the middle of it. This blizzard would surely have been a test of his nephew's endurance.

Finally, the letter from Jack arrived and Leon stopped worrying about him. But now he felt restless and even a bit homesick.

So, that's that, Leon mused. *Even amongst all that tragedy, life still goes on and here I sit, drinking coffee and staring at these four walls.*

Well, I should be happy for David, I suppose. I can't stop life from continuing around and without me, so I might as well accept it and try to be happy for the good things that are happening back home.

I guess the next grand event will be the arrival of Karma's foal, and I know I'll be receiving a very detailed letter about that occasion.

After that, it'll be Steven and Caroline's wedding, then more letters. More 'wish you could have been here' and 'thinking of you' and 'please take care of yourself'.

Leon sighed.

Another sip of coffee.

The most I have to look forward to is the coming of warm weather, then it'll be too hot, and I'll be looking forward to autumn. Ho hum.

***

February slid away, and March roared in to take its place. Would the snow ever stop falling? The time that Leon did get to spend outside he was usually shoveling snow away from the main gate and along the roadway to allow the provisions wagon access to the yard. By the time he and a few other "lucky" inmates had spent the day doing hard work, they were cold, wet and exhausted. No need to listen to music in his head to fall asleep on those nights.

He was dreaming about Gabi again—a lot. But they were sad dreams, reflecting his own confusion on the matter. They'd start out happy enough, with them together, sharing a home, building a life, just as he had thought would happen, once upon a time. Then, all of a sudden, he'd be inside the cell again. The door would clang shut and, Gabi would drift away.

He could see her disappear down the aisle, and he'd want so much to go with her, but he couldn't. He would call to her to wait for him, but she wouldn't answer and simply waved goodbye, and then was gone in a wisp of mist or smoke or cloud or . . . memory.

He'd wake up lonely and melancholy, feeling like he was never going to get out. Then the morning buzzer would sound, and the cell doors would open, along with the roll call, and he'd be up to face another day.

Gradually, the temperatures began to warm up some, and the snows started to melt away.

Leon sent a quick note off to Jack in acknowledgment of his birthday, and also to send his congratulations to David. Jack had been right; David had written an extended version of Jack's announcement of the new arrival. Though it was old news by then, David's excitement and pleasure were addictive, and Leon even found himself smiling with amusement at some of his friend's descriptive narrative. The good doctor couldn't be any more thrilled about being a new father.

Life, for Leon, carried on, even if it was dull and mundane.

***

Then Leon was hit with another surprise, one more thing that was going to make his life just a little bit better. One more thing that he could add to his list of things to look forward to. Though at first, he found himself feeling anxious about it and even a little resentful at being roped into doing something he really didn't want to do.

Mariam approached Leon in the infirmary, smiling a smile that set off warning bells and caused him to glance around for an escape route.

"Good morning, Napoleon," she greeted him. "It's nice to see you again, and it appears you have come through the winter without any new injuries."

"Yes, ma'am," Leon confirmed, though his brow furrowed

with growing suspicion. Never being one to beat around the bush, he came out and asked her point blank: "Is there something on your mind, Doctor?"

"Well, yes there is," she responded with a big smile and a conspiratorial hand on his arm. "My orphans would like to meet you, Napoleon."

"Ohh, well now. I don't know—"

"Well, why not?" she asked, feigning surprise at his reluctance. "They feel such a connection to you, and it would do you good to talk with them."

"It would do me good?" Leon queried. "How do you figure that?"

"For one thing, you could get out of here for a while," she said, then stopped the teasing and became more serious. "You'd be surprised, Napoleon, how spending some time with children can brighten the heart and lighten the soul."

"I don't think so," Leon wanted to back out. "I'd have nothing to say to them."

"Oh, don't worry about that, they'll do most of the talking." Then it was Mariam's turn to furrow her brow in concern, as she noticed the tightening around his mouth and the hard look in his eyes. "What are you so afraid of?"

Leon smiled. "I'm not afraid," he insisted, as he dropped his gaze from hers. "I mean, I just don't know what I would say to them. They think I'm this romantic hero. How am I supposed to live up to that?"

"You don't," she told him. "Just be yourself."

Leon smirked, but continued to look uncomfortable.

"That would be disappointing," he mumbled. "The dashing, romantic hero being revealed as nothing more than a thief and a conman."

"Napoleon, you know there is a lot more to you than that," she pointed out, taking a hard line. "As I mentioned to you before, you have a shared history with these children, and I know you would have a lot to offer them." She smiled and squeezed his arm again. "C'mon, just come the one time at least, and if you don't want to come back again, then you don't have to."

"I don't think the warden would approve . . ."

"I have already spoken with Warden Mitchell about this," Mariam informed him. "He has given his approval. And Officers

Reece and Pearson have agreed to accompany you."

And this was where Leon began to feel like he had been backed into a corner. All this conspiring going on around and about him, and he was the last one to know.

Well, that was typical.

His shoulders slumped as he submitted to the inevitable, and Mariam smiled, knowing she had won the day.

***

Leon was in a foul mood for the rest of his shift. Again, he had decided that he was going to be cantankerous because he hadn't gotten his way, and everyone else around him was going to pay for it.

"What the hell is your problem?" Palin finally snapped at him. "You're actin' like a bear with a bee up its butt. If you're gonna carry on like this, why don't you just go back to your cell and save me the misery of your company."

"I don't wanna go back to my cell."

"Well, I don't want ya here if you're gonna carry on like this."

"Fine!"

"Fine!"

The two men stood and glared at each other, neither one showing any sign of backing down. Considering how stubborn both men could be, there was no telling how long the stand-off would have continued if Officer Kenny Reece hadn't chosen that moment to drop by the infirmary.

"What's got you two at odds?" Kenny asked as he approached the pair.

"How the hell should I know?" Palin growled. "Nash is the one walkin' around with his hackles up—ask him. But have your billy club ready, Ken; he just might bite." Then the doctor turned and headed toward his office, mumbling. "Son of a bitch . . ."

Kenny couldn't help but smile at the doctor's obvious irritation, but his expression turned serious as he looked at the inmate.

Leon dropped his gaze and relaxed his hostile stance.

Kenny scrutinized him.

"You looking for trouble today, Nash?"

"No sir, Mr. Reece. No trouble."

"Good," Kenny responded, "because I need to ask something of you, and I want you to answer me honestly." Leon continued to stare at the floor. "Has Dr. Mariam spoken to you about the proposed trip to the orphanage?"

"Yes sir."

"Good," Kenny repeated, then took a deep breath and organized his thoughts before expressing them. "I would not normally bother to ask an inmate this question, because most of the inmates here I would not trust to give me an honest answer. On the other hand, I know that you are a man of your word; that once you give it, you will keep it."

A slight frown flashed across Leon's face as he continued to look at the floor. He wondered where this was going.

Kenny continued. "Now, on the trip to the orphanage, you will be transported in the prison wagon and you will be shackled, as usual. But I believe it would be more suitable that once we enter the building and you are presented to the children, that the shackles have been removed. You'll be wearing the boot, of course, but I've seen you haul that thing around, and you manage to get where you want to go. I also expect that if you got your hands on any kind of a lock pick, you could have that boot off in no time at all." Kenny paused and sent the inmate a strong look. "Nash, look at me. Look me in the eye."

Leon raised his gaze from the floor and looked straight and solid into Kenny's gray eyes.

"I need your word that you will not, at any point during this visit, try to escape," Kenny stated. "Do I have your word on this, Mr. Nash?"

Leon blinked and swallowed, feeling strangely honored that Kenny would even ask him this.

"Yessir, Mr. Reece," Leon answered him through a slightly tightened throat. "You have my word."

"Good," Kenny nodded, then a ghost of a smile tugged at his lips. "Because Warden Mitchell has given me strict instructions that he would rather I bring you back dead than not bring you back at all. And I must admit, having to shoot you down in front of the Sisters and a group of orphaned children would ruin my day. Do we understand each other?"

It was Leon's turn to feel the tug of a smile. He nodded. "Yes sir, Mr. Reece. You have my word. I will not try to escape."

"Good. Carry on, Convict. I'll see you in the morning."

CHAPTER TWENTY
A SPECIAL DAY

The next day, Leon was nervous and mad at himself for it.

What's the big deal, anyway? They're just a bunch of children. It's not like I'm on trial again, and my whole future hinges on the outcome! What does it matter? Just relax.

But he couldn't help it. As he pulled on his layers of clothing in preparation for heading outdoors, he couldn't quiet the butterflies in his stomach. Bottom line, he wasn't that comfortable around children. Jack was better. Yeah, Jack should be the one doing this. Maybe he would suggest it to Mariam later.

Yeah, ask Jack to do it.

It would be easier to arrange as well, since he could simply swing by the orphanage on his way to or from visiting with me. No need for guards or transportation, he could just go on his own. Yeah, I like this idea. Too late for now but maybe for the next time . . .

But meanwhile, he still had to get through the day.

Kenny came to collect him shortly after breakfast and took him over near the guards' dormitory to get him ready for transport.

Once Leon was secured in irons, they met Pearson who was waiting for them by the armory. That guard was already toteing a handgun and a rifle, and once Kenny had procured the same items, they were ready for travel.

The three men headed toward the exit to the yard, with Leon feeling like all this was a bit of overkill. He'd already given his word he wouldn't try anything, but he supposed they had to follow orders and be prepared. Who knows? Maybe this was all a set-up, and the Elk Mountain Gang was going to waylay them on the road and abscond with the prisoner.

Leon allowed a pessimistic smirk to escape. *Yeah, like that was going to happen.*

Kenny glanced at him, and Leon gave a shake of his head; he hadn't meant anything by it.

Stepping outside, Leon could feel the damp chilliness in the air and was happy for his toque and sweater. It wasn't raining at the moment, but it was a cold, overcast day, and the melting slush and gray pools of standing water made it feel like January all over again, instead of March. Even with his layers of clothing, Leon shivered in the morning air and found himself hoping it wouldn't take too long to reach their destination, despite what waited for him there.

Pearson opened the back door of the armored coach and stepped up and in, then turned and waited for the inmate to do the same.

Leon remembered his last journey in this coach, even though he had been out cold through most of the trip. He'd also been hurting from his encounter with Deputy Mike, so his memories of this vehicle were not pleasant.

The only times Leon had been transported outside the prison had been during the summer months, when he'd been put on a work gang for some outdoor chore or other. On those occasions, the armored coach wasn't used, since it would have been as hot as an oven for the convicts to be forced to ride in. Instead, they were transported in a converted buckboard that had metal rings embedded in the floorboards, so the prisoners could be secured where they sat along a makeshift bench. Not particularly comfortable, but even Leon could appreciate the difference between riding in an open buckboard and being cooped up inside an iron coach in the summertime.

With an eerie feeling of déjà vu, Leon stepped into the coach, spying the Oregon Boot already on the bench, waiting for him. Kenny came in right behind him, sat down on the side bench and waited. He handed his rifle to Pearson, and, securing the prisoner to the coach floor with the ever-present ankle cuffs, he made sure Leon had nowhere to go. Leon accepted it all as part of his daily routine now.

Kenny retrieved his rifle, sat down on the bench opposite their prisoner, then nodded to Pearson.

"Okay," he said, "let's get this show on the road."

"Yessir," came the response.

Pearson exited. The door closed and Leon heard the ominous

sound of the bolt sliding across and the lock clicking into place. He shivered, only this time it wasn't from the cold. He always hated that sound, and being in prison where he was hearing it on a regular basis hadn't made it any easier to take. He gave a heavy sigh and inadvertently glanced at the guard sitting across from him.

Kenny was smiling at him.

"C'mon, Nash," he said. "Why don't you look at this as a break from the routine? I can think of plenty of other inmates who would jump at a chance like this."

Leon smirked as the coach gave a jolt and started moving toward the gates.

Yeah, a break in the routine, he thought. *So was having the dentist come and pull teeth without any whiskey. Oh, let's just get this day over with so I can get back to my routine. What a nuisance!*

***

As it happened, the school and orphanage were on the other side of Laramie from the prison, so naturally, the fastest route to it was straight through town.

Leon's spirits lifted as they made their way along the busy main street. Even with the chilly weather, the town bustled. Leon shifted against his chains to he could look out the barred window and watch the townsfolk moving about their business.

He couldn't help but envy them. There was a time when he would have thought of their lives as mundane, but now he wished he could be a part of what they had—freedom. Sure, they had worries too; making a living and raising families wasn't always easy, but at least they had freedom of will, they could make choices and didn't have to kowtow to anyone. Unless it was their boss—or their wife!

Funny, Leon mused. *You don't appreciate freedom until it's taken from you. Then there you are, staring at it through the bars of a prison, wishing you could just reach out and touch it. Wishing it could be yours again.*

He smiled at two young boys running down the boardwalk, making pests of themselves wherever they went. And then, that little girl stamping her foot in anger because her mother was saying "no". It kind of reminded him of two other young girls he used to know.

A couple more blocks down were the saloon and bordello, the section of town where the nice people didn't go—and Leon felt right at home. He smiled and yelled a greeting at the pretty little thing in a corset and high heels, who waved at him and showed a bit of leg despite the chill in the air. Oh, what a tease. She knew darn well there was nothing he could do, but she sent him a sweet smile and a kiss anyway.

Leon laughed and shook his head. *Damn. The fun I could have with her. To hell with going to the orphanage and spending time with children. I could stay right here and fill in a few hours quite nicely. Oh well.*

The coach carried on through the far side of town and headed down the road toward their destination. Soon, all the sights and sounds of activity were left behind them.

Leon settled back into position again, then noticed Kenny watching him. He looked away from those gray eyes, feeling slightly embarrassed that he had allowed a natural male lusting to take hold of him like that. But it'd been so long since he'd had anything other than his own imagination to make love to, that the sight of a young lady's bare leg was more than enough to send him over the edge. If nothing else, it at least confirmed once again, that Leon was still quite capable and the only thing putting a damper on his libido was prison life.

Kenny just smiled. He wasn't being judgmental, only observant. He knew that side of a convict's life was extremely hard on the younger inmates, and that sexual frustration was most of what was behind a lot of the aggressive behavior exhibited by the more alpha of the convicts. Still, he didn't have an answer for it. It's not like they could bring women into the prison to fulfill that need—jeez, talk about the makings of a brawl.

The two men sat in silence: Kenny, thankful he had a wife to go home to, and Leon wishing he did, or at least the equivalent.

They continued in that manner, each lost in his own thoughts until they arrived at their destination.

Once the coach stopped, and ole' Bart had come to take charge of the team, Pearson came around to open the back door. He entered the coach to again assist Kenny with the prisoner, then all three disembarked, to land outside on the cold, slushy ground.

Leon found himself looking at a large, white structure that still resembled the hotel it had once been. Not quite so high-class now, but still holding onto past glory. Steps led up to a large, wrap-around veranda, a solid, double-wide front door, and lots of windows with green shutters, now open to let in what little sunlight there was to be had. It felt like a warm, inviting home, and Leon couldn't help but feel a little envious when comparing this place to Blessed Heart.

Pearson removed the chains and tossed them into the wagon, while Kenny brought the boot out with him and made sure it got securely attached.

Then the three men started up the steps, Pearson in front, then Leon with Kenny holding onto his arm; a subtle, but non-threatening reminder to the inmate that he was a prisoner and certain rules still applied.

Just as they reached the landing, Mariam, who had been informed of their arrival, opened the front door and greeted them with her usual friendly smile.

"Gentlemen! How wonderful to see you!" she exclaimed as though it was a huge surprise. She sent Leon a special smile. "Hello, Napoleon."

"Ma'am." He answered her smile with a friendly nod.

"Dr Soames," Reece greeted her. "I'll trust you to lead the way."

"Of course, gentlemen. Do come in."

Stepping into the alcove was like coming into a mansion when compared to what Leon was now accustomed to. The carpeting and hardwood floors were old and had seen better days, but they were clean and well cared for. The walls were adorned with photographs and artwork created by the children of various ages and talent levels. But each one was given its special place, without concern For technique or ability. This went a long way toward making visitors feel welcome.

There was also a big wood stove doing a good job of sending heat throughout the downstairs rooms. Leon smiled as he felt the warmth of it settle into his fingers. The two that had been broken still tended to ache when they got cold, so the heat coming to them was very much appreciated.

"This way, gentlemen," Mariam directed them, as she headed down the hallway. "The children are in class right now, but I'm sure they won't mind this diversion."

Oh boy, here we go. Leon felt the butterflies attack his stomach again. He was going to have to tread carefully here.

What am I going to say to these kids? How should I approach them? This is ridiculous. I wasn't this nervous at my first bank robbery.

He felt certain that if Kenny hadn't had a hold of his arm, encouraging him to keep moving forward, he would have made a break for it and run back to the prison coach, Oregon Boot and all.

They reached the end of the hallway and Mariam smiled back at them, then knocked on the door, opened it, went inside and closed it behind her.

"Okay, Nash," Kenny said. "Remember our agreement and behave yourself, all right?"

"Yeah," Leon croaked.

Kenny smiled as he gave the prisoner a pat on the shoulder.

"Just relax," he suggested. "Try to enjoy yourself. I'm the one with the rifle, not them."

"Hmm."

The door opened again, and Mariam motioned for them to come in.

Kenny checked his rifle to make sure the safety was on, then kept the weapon pointed down, toward the floor. He nodded to Pearson, indicating for him to stand guard outside the door, then gave Leon a push, sending him into no man's land.

Leon thought for sure he was going to throw up. This was just like walking into that courtroom again, knowing that all eyes were upon him.

Mariam smiled at his discomfort and, taking his arm, she pulled him forward to stand by the front desk where she introduced him to the older Sister who had been teaching the class.

"Napoleon, this is Sister Cornelia. She generally teaches the older children, but today we brought all the children into the one room, so they could meet you. Sister Cornelia, this is Napoleon Nash."

"Mr. Nash," the Sister greeted him, "how nice to meet you. I dare say, the children greatly appreciated the letter you sent them at Christmas."

"Ahh, thank you ma'am—Sister," Leon returned the greeting, remembering to remove his toque. "I really appreciated the cookies."

This comment was met by some stifled giggling from the assembly, and Leon turned to survey his audience.

The small classroom was filled with about twenty children, ranging in age from four up to fifteen, and every one of them was looking, with awe and excitement, at their infamous visitor.

Leon took a deep cleansing breath. *Well, if I'm going to do this, I may as well do it right!*

He smiled his wide, charming grin. "Good morning," he greeted them all. "How are you doing today?"

A loud chorus of "Fine Mr. Nash!" came cascading back at him, and he knew from the dropped jaws and admiring looks from all the young ladies—irrespective of age—that his dimples and dark brown eyes had already won them over.

"Now, I was led to believe," he began, his deep voice flowing like warm, melted chocolate, "that all you fine ladies and gentlemen pestered poor Doctor Mariam no end until she agreed to invite me here for this visit."

This statement was met with some embarrassed giggling from the girls, and rolling eyes from the boys. Boys always were harder to impress.

"So," Leon continued, as he leaned back against the front desk. "What made you think I would be willing to leave my tiny, cold, dark cell to come here to this fine, warm and comfortable home to spend my time talking with you lot?"

This was met with some more giggling, then one young man in the back row, raised his hand and stood up.

"We were hopin' you could tell us about how you grew up, Mr. Nash," he stated, matter-of-factly, "considerin' you was raised in an orphanage too."

"Yes, I could do that," Leon agreed, and crossed his arms. "What's your name?"

"Michael, sir."

"Good to meet you, Michael. What would you like to know?"

"Was it much different from what we have here?"

"Ohh yes," Leon was emphatic. "As soon as I stepped into the front foyer here, I knew it was different. As I mentioned in my letter to you, the Civil War was raging, and nobody had time for orphans. Blessed Heart was cold in the winter and hot in the summer, and there was never enough to eat.*" Hmm, much like where I'm living now*. "I had to steal food to keep myself and my nephew from starving. Looking at you lot, I don't think you have that problem here."

"No."

"We get lots to eat."

"That's terrible. No wonder you ran away."

Leon grinned.

Kenny smiled and settled himself against the wall by the classroom door. He wasn't surprised to see Leon rising to the occasion. His vocal dexterity and natural charm had taken over, and now that he was on a roll, chances were good they were going to be here for the rest of the morning.

"Was it fun robbing trains and banks?" came a little voice from the back.

"What's your name?"

"Sally."

"Sally. You asked me that in your letter, didn't you?"

Sally blushed, but smiled, obviously pleased that he had remembered her.

"I don't know if fun is the right word for it," Leon explained. "It was exciting, but dangerous, too. Especially the trains. Trains are like a moving building, and forcing one to stop required precise timing, and just a little bit of crazy." Sadness crossed his features, just for an instant. "I lost more than one man who misjudged his jump and ended up under the wheels."

He looked out at his audience and was met by dropped jaws and wide eyes; everyone was entranced. He smiled again.

"Anyway, that's just one of the reasons me and the Kid decided to get out of the business."

"Why else would you want to quit?" asked another boy. "You were so good at it."

"Why, thank you." Leon was genuinely pleased. "What's your name?"

"Henry."

"Henry." Leon thought about it for a moment. "I didn't get a letter from you, did I?"

Henry looked embarrassed and shuffled around in his chair.

"No sir."

"Well, that's all right, Henry," Leon assured him. "A lot of young men don't like to write letters."

Again, Leon was saying all the right things, and Henry smiled with pride at being referred to as a young man.

"I guess the main reason me and the Kid decided to quit the business was because we began to realize how wrong it was," Leon explained. "We always prided ourselves on the fact that we never hurt anyone, but then we began to realize that there is more than one way to hurt another person.

"We always told ourselves that we were just stealing from the large companies, so that made it all right. But the truth of it is, we were stealing from everyday folk too; people who had to work hard for their money, and that wasn't right. It also wasn't right to hold innocent folk at gunpoint, which we did on a regular basis. That can be frightening for people, and even though we never hurt anyone, we still caused harm."

Leon paused, feeling a little warm with the heat from the wood stove finally seeping into his bones. He automatically began to pull his sweater up over his tunic, but then remembered his situation and sent a quick glance to Kenny, who was now sitting by the door.

Kenny gave him a subtle nod of permission, and Leon completed the task of pulling off the sweater and laying it aside. He turned back to the class and noticed a change in the atmosphere. The smiles were gone from the youthful faces and their glances shifted back and forth between Leon and Kenny.

The casual exchange between prisoner and guard, and its meaning, had not been lost on the assembly.

Leon smiled, taking the opportunity to put in a bit of a tease.

"Oh, don't worry about Officer Reece. I like to let him feel that he's doing his job."

Kenny rolled his eyes, but it broke the mood, and the children giggled and returned their focus to the ex-outlaw.

Another boy stood up then and, having figured out the protocol, began the question with his name.

"My name is Charlie."

"Yes Charlie, what would you like to know?"

"How did you get a funny name like Napoleon?" he asked, with a smirk. "I never heard of such a name before."

Leon grinned. "You've never heard of the great French Emperor, Napoleon Bonaparte, who wasn't actually French at all, but Corsican?"

Charlie shook his head.

"Good!" Leon continued, "because I'm not named after him. But my father's family was originally from France, and Napoleon was a popular name from way back. It was in our family long before Bonaparte came alone and tarnished it. I never understood why, but my father named me after his grandfather. I suppose, back in the old country, it's an honorable name, but here in the West it does pose a challenge."

"Oh," came the unified and sympathetic response from the group.

"What's surprising about bein' named after your grandpa?" asked Charlie. "Lots a people do that."

Leon decided that here and now was not the time to get into his unfortunate family history.

"Nothing's wrong with it," he said. "Nothing at all. Something a little easier on the tongue would have been more appreciated, though."

"But I like that name," came the quiet admission from little Melanie, sitting in the back corner. "It's different. It makes you special."

Leon looked at her and a warm smile settled onto his features. Maybe he should start appreciating his given name a bit more. But then a full grin broke out over his face and a sparkle came to his eye.

"Well, if you like that one, young lady, you're going to love my second name," he told her. "It seems my pa was kind of homesick by the time I came along, because he added the family name, Navarre, to the damage he'd already done."

"Navarre?" came the boisterous reply from most of the boys in the classroom.

"Oh no."

"No wonder you became an outlaw."

"Was that your ma's name before she married your pa?" Beth asked. "That's where my brother got his second name from; it was from our ma's family."

At this point, a certain little boy sent his sister a reproving look, then silently mouthed the decree, *Don't you dare tell him!*

Leon smiled at the sibling conflict. "You're close," he told her, "but it comes from the maternal side of my pa's family. The Kansas Kid is lucky he didn't get stuck with it as well, since his mother was my half-sister."

"Oh yeah."

"That's right, the Kansas Kid is your nephew."

"I forgot about that."

Sally giggled. "That's funny. He's your nephew, but you're both old."

"Hey!" Leon feigned outrage. "We're not that old. Besides, it happens that way sometimes. Large families and all that. My older sister was already married and had her first child before I was born. With all the young'uns that had come before us, I don't know why it was me who got stuck with that handle. But I did."

Most of the boys laughed and hooted over that, but the girls seemed to think there was nothing at all wrong with either of the names. Little Melanie especially thought they were both quite nice names and were very romantic in a heroic sort of way.

After a few minutes of boisterous teasing and joking with one another about various family names, the group settled down again, and then one of the older girls raised her hand and introduced herself.

"Mr. Nash, my name is Gillian."

Leon smiled at her. "Hello Gillian. I remember your letter. Did you have another question for me?"

"Yes sir. Since your name is Napoleon, how come Doctor Mariam sometimes calls you Peter?"

Leon cocked a brow. "She does?"

Gillian shrugged. "Sometimes. I don't think she means to; it just comes out."

"Oh." Leon smiled, oddly pleased with this information. "Well, you see, that was the name I was using when we first met Doctor Mariam," Leon explained. "Even though the Kid and I had gone straight, the law was still looking for us so we had to use aliases in order to stay discreet."

"What's an 'alias'?"

"Oh, well that's a name you use when you don't want people to know who you really are," Leon told her. "So, Doctor Mariam first came to know me as Peter Black, and I suppose it's just habit, and 'Peter" slips out once in a while. I don't mind; I like the name which is why I chose it for my alias in the first place."

"Does everyone else call you Napoleon now that you're not wanted anymore?" came a question from the back of the room.

"Some do. Even some who used to know me as Peter before, have switched over to Napoleon. But some still call me Peter. Most just call me Leon, or Nash." He smiled with a memory. "There was one lady in particular who used to call me Monsieur Nash, even though we've been lov—Ah, I mean good friends for some time."

A couple of the older boys picked up on the slip and smiled

knowingly. But on the most part, this admission was taken at face value and met with giggles and comments about how silly that was. She should appreciate his given name. It was special.

Sally stood up again and raised her hand.

"Yes, Sally?" Leon acknowledged her.

"I read in one of the dime novels that you held up a stagecoach and took all their money," she informed him. "But that's not stealing from the large person, that's stealing from the little people."

"Yes, it is," Leon agreed. "And you can't believe everything you read in those dime novels. Actually," and he smiled, "you can't believe most of what you read in those dime novels. The Kid and I rarely held up stagecoaches, mainly for that very reason. Coaches never carried anything of much value. They might occasionally have a payroll, and we did focus on those, but we never stole from the passengers. It really wasn't worth our while. We focused on trains and banks, cause, well, as another great outlaw once said: that's where the money was kept."

Even Kenny got a chuckle out of that reasoning, but it was drowned out by the hoots and chortles coming from the children.

Then Leon noticed two of the older boys in the back having a silent argument. The one was nudging his friend, trying to get him to ask something, but the other one obviously did not want to. He kept slapping his friend's nudges away and mouthing "no" whenever it came up. Naturally, this piqued Leon's curiosity.

"You fellas got something you want to ask?" he sent back to them.

All heads turned, and suddenly they were the focus of attention. They both looked embarrassed at being found out, but then the one who had been doing the nudging, stood up and introduced himself.

"Ah, yessir, Mr. Nash. My name is William, sir. Ah, we was wonderin', what's it like in prison? If ya don't mind sayin', sir."

Leon leaned back and crossed his arms for a moment while he contemplated the question.

"No, I don't mind saying. It's a good question. Actually, that was one of the things my nephew asked me the first time he came to visit. I mean, we'd always speculated about this. We both had a prison sentence hanging over our heads, so of course you think about it from time to time. You know, what if . . .? That sort of thing. And like I told him, it's worse than anything we had imagined."

A few low groans came from his audience. Leon remained silent for a moment, further contemplating his answer. Everyone in the room, children and adults alike, waited patiently for him to collect his thoughts and voice his opinion.

"It's not that Jack and I didn't have good imaginations, it's just that living the reality of it is worse than any imaginings could possibly have been. It's not just that your freedom is gone. That's obvious. But your freedom of speech is taken from you; your right to have an opinion, your individuality. You're no longer allowed to be a person; you are now a convict and convicts don't have rights or opinions. You do what you're told, and if you don't do it fast enough, you're punished."

The room was silent, and all eyes were on him.

Leon felt an overwhelming sadness come over him as he was once again reminded of his true situation. Then, looking at the wide-eyed audience sitting before him, he decided it would be best not to dwell on his own personal feelings. He needed to focus on the situation as a whole, and how it might relate to these youngsters, who apparently thought anything he had to say was important.

"So," he continued, with a sigh, "my advice to you is to avoid prison at any cost. I've noticed some young fellas here who are just coming of age, and I remember when I was fourteen, fifteen years old, and how I felt about things." Leon's eyes locked onto the older boys in the group. "I know you're feeling restless, like you want to break out of here and go your own way."

The older boys all nodded, silently. They felt naked, having this person whom they respected and admired for his audacity, suddenly turn the tables on them. It was as though he could see into their very souls.

"But as I said in my letter: please don't follow in my footsteps. For one thing, our situation was far different than yours is here. Jack and I were starving, and Blessed Heart had nothing for us. But even then, I often wonder if we made the right choice to leave at that time. We had no skills and very little education to help us get legitimate work. The only choice we had to survive was to steal.

"I would hate to feel that any of you think that because that is the choice we made, it supports you doing the same thing. For one thing, Jack and I both regret the decisions we made. Although, looking back, I don't honestly know what else we could have done, given the circumstances. But you young men, you have choices here.

"This is a good place. You're well fed and you have people here who care about you. You're getting an education. Believe me, nothing is more important than an education. You might be feeling restless, that you want to move on, but I'm standing here, pleading with you to hang on until you have something to move on to. No one out there is going to care about you the way the Sisters here do. No one out there wants to see you succeed because they're all after the same jobs, the same opportunities. They'll be knifing you in the back to get that job for themselves. All you are is someone standing in their way.

"The only way you can succeed out there now is with an education. Officer Reece here knows that," and Leon glanced at a surprised Kenny. Leon smiled, then turned back to his audience. "He works hard at a job that maybe he doesn't always like to do, because he wants to see his children get an education. I admire him for that. He knows the importance of it.

"Now, Officer Reece here came from a good family, so he had more opportunities for an education than I did. But then the Civil War took that away from both of us. But he knows the importance of it, and he works hard to send his children to college.

"So, if I can instill anything in any of you today, it's the importance of staying in school and learning as much as you possibly can. And if a trade is offered to you, then thank your lucky stars and grab it. If any of you are fortunate enough to have an opportunity to go to college, again, grab it!

"You don't want to end up like me and the Kid. There is nothing romantic or honorable about what we did, we were simply thieves. We fell into that way of life out of desperation, just trying to stay alive, but we continued in that way of life because it was easy money and good times.

"But good times earned that way don't last, and eventually, you have to take responsibility and pay your dues. You don't want to do what we did. You don't want to end up in prison."

The room was engulfed in silence again. Everyone was solemn and a little scared. Then another tiny arm was raised, and a little voice came forth.

"Are the guards mean to you?" asked Melanie. "Are they not very nice?"

"Ahh," Leon glanced back at Kenny.

That guard sent him a raised eyebrow. *How are you going to handle this one, Buckwheat*?

Leon smiled. "Well, it depends," he explained to his audience. "Most of them are just doing their jobs and they treat us pretty fairly. Some of them can be a little mean, and I have to watch my back around them." Moans and groans from the audience. "But others, like Officer Reece here," Leon emphasized, "are fair and only hit us when we deserve it."

This statement was met with mixed reviews. Most of the children accepted this statement as fair treatment, but a few of the others creased their brows and sent Officer Reece some suspicious looks.

Leon laughed. "No, no," he assured them. "Officer Reece is one of the good guards. No need for violence. You be nice to him, and he'll be nice to you."

Everyone smiled, and Kenny was accepted into the inner circle.

Another boy raised his hand, and Leon acknowledged him.

"Yes, you have a question?"

"Yessir. My name is Todd."

"Okay Todd, nice to meet you. What would you like to know?"

"Yes sir. How come you got sent to prison and the Kansas Kid didn't? Was he not as good an outlaw as you?"

Leon grinned, then laughed out loud. *Oh, Jack would love this!*

"That's always been my opinion," he joked, then turned serious again and honestly contemplated the question.

How was he supposed to answer that one? He considered just giving a simple pat answer and moving on, but he remembered back to when he was this boy's age, and how much he hated it when adults were condescending toward him. It was a legitimate question; it deserved a legitimate answer.

"No, seriously," Leon emphasized, "Jack Kiefer was and is my equal partner in all ways." Then he pursed his lips and frowned as he contemplated the best way to explain the politics of what had happened.

The children all waited with bated breath for Leon's answer, and Kenny had to admit that he was also curious to hear what Leon had to say on this matter.

Finally, Leon took a deep breath and began to put his thoughts and feelings into words.

"A friend of mine, who used to run with us but changed sides and became a lawman, approached us to say that the Governor of Wyoming wanted to broker a deal that could lead to us being pardoned. At first, we weren't interested, but then, things went bad I began to realize the futility of our lives."

"What does broker mean?" came the question from the group.

"Ah, that means that a third party, in this case, our friend, Sheriff Murphy, sets up or arranges a meeting or agreement between us and the governor. Now, Governor Hoyt was fed up with us disrupting his banks and railroads, so he offered us a deal. If we agreed to not only stop robbing the territory blind, but to do undercover work for him on occasion, then in a year or so, he would consider giving us our pardons.

"Looking back on it now, it does seem like a fool's agreement, but we were desperate. We wanted out, and this seemed like the best deal we were going to get. So, we agreed.

"Time went on and the governors changed, and none of them wanted to risk their political careers by granting us pardons. On top of that, I guess we were just too good at what we did, and the governors found us to be quite useful. Giving us our freedom would be like shooting a gift horse in the foot, as far as they were concerned. So, it never happened.

"Then, one day, the inevitable came about; we were arrested and brought to trial. Now, a good friend of ours told us that if we allowed ourselves to remain in custody and go to trial, then he would stand by us and help in any way he could. So, that's what we decided to do."

Leon stopped again and took a deep breath. He could feel a lot of the anger and resentment over his situation threaten to rise and come forth again. He kept a lid on it though and continued with the narrative without his emotions tainting the words.

"Lots of people got involved then," he explained. "Many were insisting the Governor's Office should honor its agreement and grant us the pardons. After all, we had held up our end of the deal and had shown that we could stay law-abiding, so many people felt we had earned it. But then, on the other hand, all the large corporations were mad at us. They were putting pressure on the

Governor's Office to ignore the pardon agreement and send us to prison.

"So, Governor Warren decided that to try and keep everyone happy, he would play the middle ground. To keep the powerful and wealthy corporations satisfied, he would send one of us to prison, and to keep the common folk, the tax payers, and voters, happy, he would grant to the other the pardon.

"So, it was just through a twist of fate really, that I ended up going to trial first and thereby being the one who was sent to prison, and Jack Kiefer ended up receiving the pardon."

A heavy silence enveloped the classroom. Kenny wondered fleetingly if he was going to have a small riot on his hands. Fortunately, the protests, when they came, were all of the verbal variety.

"That's not fair."

"How could he do that?"

"You both should have got it."

"Yeah. We should let the governor know that he should do something about that."

"We should all go to Cheyenne and let him know."

"Yeah. We can all go."

"Whoa!" Leon held up his hands in mild protest. "Hang on. I don't think the Sisters would be too happy with you all heading off to Cheyenne."

"No, indeed," Sister Cornelia piped in. "Perhaps you could write letters instead. How would that be?"

Leon smiled. "There ya go. I'm sure the governor would love to get a sack full of letters from the orphaned children in Laramie."

The suggestion was met with a loud chorus of approval and instantly all the children were on their feet and chattering amongst themselves about the best way to tackle this new assignment.

Leon was thoroughly enjoying himself as he sat on the desk, watching the loud and animated conversation swirling on around him.

Kenny sighed and shook his head. He should have known that Leon would find a way to get them riled up about something.

Sister Cornelia, who was not as accustomed to prison discipline as Doctor Mariam was, took up the yard stick to bring the children back to order.

"Children! Children! Quiet down!" she insisted, while at the same time, bringing the stick down in three, hard, successive raps against the desk right next to where Leon sat.

The inmate's reaction was instantaneous. He was on his feet in a flash, bringing his arm up to protect that side of his head from an expected blow and nearly losing his balance in his attempt to avoid the assault.

Kenny was also quick to his feet and over to the inmate's side, where he grabbed Leon's other arm to steady him and stop him from over-reacting.

"Easy Nash," Kenny told him. "You're all right. It was nothing."

Leon looked around at him, obviously shaken. "What?"

"You're all right, Nash," Kenny repeated. "Just relax."

"Oh. Yeah." Leon did relax a bit, but he could still feel himself shaking. Then he smiled, a little embarrassed by his reaction. "I'm sorry, Sister, you just startled me."

"Yes, I can see that," Sister Cornelia observed, looking concerned. "I do apologize; I didn't realize . . ."

The door to the classroom opened and Pearson stuck his head in.

"Everything all right in here?" he asked.

"Yes, Mr. Pearson," Kenny assured him. "Everything is fine. We won't be much longer."

"Yes sir," and he disappeared behind the closed door again.

Mariam came around and put a conciliatory hand on her companion's arm.

"It's all right, Sister Cornelia," she said. "No harm done. Children, back to your seats now please."

The whole group of children were standing with their mouths open, and staring at the adults at the head of the classroom. Nobody moved. Then suddenly, little Sally came running up to the front of the room and put her arms around Leon's waist, or at least as close as she could reach.

Leon frowned. *This is unexpected. Now what am I supposed to do?*

She looked up at him with her big brown eyes, all serious and concerned. He looked down at her, feeling Kenny's grip on his arm tighten, just a bit.

"Don't worry, Mr. Nash, we'll get you out," she said, very intently. "We'll all write to the governor and tell him that he has to let you go."

Leon grinned and then knelt, to be on eye level with her. Kenny wasn't going to let him do it at first, but then he released his grip, and Leon went down to her and stroked her auburn hair.

"Thank you, darlin'," he said to her. "I know you'll do your best."

She smiled at him, then quick as a wink she threw her arms around his neck and gave him a kiss on the cheek. Then she turned and ran back to her chair, looking pleased with herself at having accomplished her mission.

Leon felt his throat tighten just a bit, but he swallowed it down and, straightening up again, he smiled at Mariam.

She smiled back.

"Oh Napoleon, thank you for coming," she said to him, and came in and gave him a hug before Kenny could say anything about it. "I hope you'll come back."

"I will if it's permitted," Leon promised.

They both turned and looked at Kenny.

The guard shrugged.

"We'll see," he said. "It's up to the warden, but thank you, Sister, Doctor. I think we should be heading back now."

This set off a chorus of protests from the assembly.

"Aw no! Do you have to?"

"Can't you stay just a while longer?"

"You can't go yet."

"Settle down, children," Sister Cornelia insisted and was just about to tap the desk with the yard stick again when she thought better of it, and simply raised her hand instead. "Settle down please. I'm sure Mr. Nash will come back again."

Good manners prevailed, although there was a certain amount of grumbling to be heard from various undisclosed locations around the room.

Leon smiled at the group.

"Thank you for inviting me to come visit with you," he said to them. "And I will come back again, if I'm able." He flashed his dimples as a thought struck him. "Perhaps next time the Kansas Kid can come as well."

This suggestion was met with a loud chorus of approval. They were all up and talking at once again, much to the dismay of the two women who were trying to keep order in the classroom.

"Oh! The Kansas Kid! That would be great."

"You mean we could talk to both of you?"

"Wow! Maybe he'll show us his fast draw."

"Can we ask him to come? Where is he?"

"Well," Leon saw an opportunity to have some fun. "I'm sure friendly Officer Reece here would be more than happy to ask the Kid if he'd like to join us."

He then sent the devil's smile back to Kenny, as the flood of youthful enthusiasm changed course and washed over that official in total expectation of an answer right then and there.

The look Kenny flashed at Leon said it all: *You bastard.*

But fortunately, Kenny and Leon were both saved from further high energy inquiries when the women finally took back control.

"Children, children, calm down, please," Mariam insisted. "I'm sure Officer Reece will do what he can to arrange that, but in the meantime, why don't you display your good manners and thank these gentlemen for their time, and bid them a good day."

The group quieted and everyone settled into their seats one more time.

"Thank you, Mr. Nash," came all in one response. "Thank you, Officer Reece."

Leon grinned; this was fun.

"Goodbye young ladies and gentlemen," he said. "I hope to see you all again soon." He turned to the two ladies. "Sister, Doctor. Thank you."

"Napoleon."

"Mr. Nash."

Kenny nodded his farewell, then, with just the slightest pressure on Leon's arm, he led the inmate back to the door and out to the hallway.

Pearson stood up to meet them, quickly putting down and hopefully hiding his cup of tea.

"Everything go okay?" he asked. "It was sounding kinda wild in there at times."

Kenny rolled his eyes. "I suppose it went all right. But you pushed it a couple of times in there, Nash. Now what the hell am I supposed to say to Jack next time he comes calling?"

Leon grinned, thinking it served Kenny right for setting him up for this.

"I believe that was a direct question, Convict!"

"Oh! Ahh, don't worry about it. I'll mention it to him. I'm sure he'll be real pleased to help out."

"Uh huh," was Kenny's skeptical response. "Then I'll have two of you to worry about. Still, I doubt the warden will go for that anyway."

Mariam joined them in the hallway to escort them back to the main foyer, and to return Leon's sweater and toque, which he had inadvertently left on the desk.

"Gentlemen, again, thank you so much," she emphasized. "You have no idea how much this means to them. They'll be talking about this for weeks. And you can be sure the governor is going to be getting a stack of letters on his desk soon."

"You're welcome, Doctor," Kenny said. "I'm glad it worked out."

"Ma'am," Leon inquired, "will I see you at the infirmary again next week?"

"I expect so, Napoleon. Yes, the weather is getting better now so I'm not having as much difficulty getting there. Hopefully Mathew will be coming to visit you again soon."

"I certainly hope so," Leon commented. "I know everyone has had a tough winter, but I do miss our visits."

"All right, Nash," Kenny got his attention, "let's go."

"Oh, yeah."

***

As is so often the case, what had begun as something Leon had decided he wasn't going to enjoy, ended up being a highlight of his time at the prison. He would always remember that first visit to the orphanage with pleasure and a sense of accomplishment. If he could stop just one young person from making the same mistakes he had, then the visit had been more than just a fun day out.

***

The ride back to the prison was quiet for the most part. Leon didn't even turn to watch the goings on in the town as they passed through it again. His mind was on other things. His talk with the orphans had revived old emotions and past regrets, and he couldn't help but be contemplative of them during that chilly return journey.

Kenny sat across from the inmate and watched him, knowing that Leon was too deep into his own thoughts to even be aware of the scrutiny. Some of Leon's answers and comments had surprised the guard, and in a way, pleased him. Somehow, Leon had locked into Kenny's personal life and motivations, and had been able to rise above his own situation to appreciate why Kenny Reece was doing what he did.

Again, Kenny had to marvel at the intelligence of the man, the intuitiveness. That he was able, even under these most dire of circumstances, to look beyond the surface and see the true motivation. Then, probably due to the hardships of his own childhood, he could see the sacrifices being made for the benefit of family, and the worthiness of those sacrifices.

It was almost as though Leon had a better understanding of Kenny, than Kenny had of Leon. It made the guard realize he needed to be paying more attention to the inmate. It almost made Kenny angry, not at Leon, but at Carson and now, Thompson. They were two men who had a certain amount of intelligence, but who seemed to be utterly missing the whole picture.

Carson was not an idiot, but he always had that need to squash any indication of intelligence or charisma in an inmate. He had to dominate, degrade and ultimately destroy the stronger personality, and unfortunately, the prison system was a conveniently legal outlet for that obsession.

Now, there was Thompson. A much younger and weaker version of Carson but moving quickly along the same track. Naturally, the two of them would be drawn together.

Kenny sighed to himself, feeling frustrated at his attempts to counter the negative effects of the abusive treatment handed out by his superior. Leon had realized something that Kenny was only now becoming aware of himself. That he was disappointed in his job. He had enjoyed it at first; felt that he was doing something worthwhile, that he could be there to offer some support to the inmates, and life wasn't all billy clubs and harsh orders. That once they found their footing, they could make a place for themselves at the prison, learn something worthwhile and then move on.

But lately, Kenny felt like he was fighting a losing battle. Carson was getting worse in his abusive behavior, and Warden Mitchell didn't seem to care or think that there was anything wrong with this. As long as the prison ran smoothly, that's all that mattered.

Indeed, as Leon had surmised, Kenny was sticking it out at a job that was no longer satisfying, because he had a family to care for. He had three sons who were growing fast and would be looking for an education. Indeed, his eldest, Conner, was already back East and in collage, and the other two were expecting the same opportunities.

Kenny already worried about how he was going to afford it all. Even his youngest, little Evelyn, was making noises about furthering her own education. It used to be a girl was a safe bet to simply get married and provide grandchildren, but things were changing. Slowly, but surely, girls were wanting more from life than that, and Evelyn was definitely one of them.

Kenny sighed again, not knowing where the money for all this was going to come from. Then he came back from his own musings to find that the tables had been turned, and the inmate was scrutinizing him.

Leon instantly dropped his gaze, then looked out the back window just to give himself something else to focus on.

Kenny smiled.

"You did good today, Nash," Reece assured him.

Leon just nodded.

"Do you want to go back again?"

"Yes sir, Mr. Reece," Leon admitted. "If it can be arranged."

Kenny nodded, surprised at the twinge of disappointment he felt. In the classroom, Leon had relaxed a little bit, and had even been teasing the guard, just a touch—but having fun with it. Now, the inmate was back to the old protocol, and it was painfully obvious how he was subjugating his own personality in order to avoid punishment. Kenny might be one of the good guards, but he was still a guard, and rules had to be followed.

"I'll let the warden know that it went well," Kenny informed him, "and perhaps we can set up another visit."

Leon smiled. He met the guard's eyes for the briefest instant, then dropped his gaze again. The rest of the trip back to the prison passed in silence.

CHAPTER TWENTY-ONE
THE GREAT THAW

Arvada, Colorado
April 1887

Finally, the snow on the ranges melted away enough for ranchers to get out and do a check on what remained of their herds.

Jack and Sam bundled up against the still cold temperatures and, with Spike doing duty as a pack horse, they headed out to take a tally of the cattle and the horses, if they could find them, and to get supplies up to Zeke and his crew at the line cabin.

The going was slow as the horses still had to push through wet snow that, in some places, came up to their knees. Sam and Jack took turns breaking trail, but they only made half the distance that day than they normally would at this time of year.

They were lucky to make their way to the sheltered spot for their night camp. Before darkness caught them out in the open. It had been used before for this purpose and most of the hands knew its location. Anyone caught out at night could head for this protected alcove, get a fire going and spend a reasonably comfortable night. There was even a place for the horses to get out of the wind and weather so it was an ideal spot.

On the second day out, Jack noticed a change in the landscape that had him scratching his head.

"I ain't never seen snow drifts like that before." He swept his gloved hand out to encompass the whole section of range before them that was covered in large, white bumps as far as the eye could see.

Sam shaded his eyes against the early spring sun. "Those aren't snow drifts, Mr. Kiefer. Take a closer look."

Jack bit a glove off his hand and pulled his spyglass from the saddlebag. He put the glass up to his eye and focused in on the bumps. What he saw sent ice crystals through his veins.

"Oh, my God."

Horns, as far as he could see, were sticking up out of the snow mounds. On some of those mounds, where the snow had begun to melt away, tawny hide showed through to reveal the first of the herds that had perished.

Jack returned the glass to his bag and felt sick. Again, he was reminded of that first winter spent with the Marshams when he and their hired hand at the time, Ansley Lubbick, had made a similar trek out to check on livestock. The carcasses they had found then had been bad enough, but this was ten-fold the corruption from that year. And yet, then, it had been enough to put Cameron out of business.

Was that samc thing going to happen again, only this time on a much larger scale?

"C'mon," said Sam, as he pushed his mare into the lead for her turn at breaking trail. "We best keep movin'."

All that day and into the next they rode through the never-ending mounds of dead cattle. It became a graveyard with long, curving horns reaching to the sky as symbolic headstones.

Even the horses got jittery walking through this now sacred ground. A small gust of wind got them snorting, and if they accidently trod upon a dead, covered hoof, they'd spring off it as though expecting the creature to come to life and gore them for their insolence.

It was one of the worst things Jack had ever witnessed, but what they came across next put the graveyard to shame.

They knew they were coming up on a fence line, but they weren't able to spot it, not even with the spy glass.

"We didn't get turned around, did we?" Jack asked. "I'm sure we'd a come across that fence by now."

Sam scrutinized the landmarks and decided that the mountain range was right where it was supposed to be.

"No, we're good. It's probably just buried. We'll find it."

Two hours later, Sam's prediction proved correct. Snow drifts, as far along the line as they could see, hid the fence from view until they were right up to it. But as they got closer, they realized again, that it was not snow.

"What the hell?"

"Oh my God."

They knew then, without a doubt, that whole herds had perished. Hundreds of cattle had gotten hung up along fence lines because they didn't have enough sense to turn away from them. The leaders had stopped, but the ones coming up behind continued to walk into them, piling up along the fence, until the whole lot died from being trampled or from exposure.

By the time Jack and Sam had completed their errand and returned to the ranch house, the reality of the devastation was unavoidable.

Many of the larger ranches lost such a high percentage of their cattle that they would never be able to recover from the blow. Oddly enough, it was the smaller ranches that fared better. Tucked up beside mountains and in the woods, the animals found shelter and enough grass to get them through, but only just.

The Rocking M had not escaped the carnage. Later that spring, when it came time for the round-ups, and everyone assessed their losses, Cameron figured that forty percent of his cattle had died over the winter. He felt it was a staggering number, until he looked around at his neighbors. Those who had bought along the same range of hills that he had, did better, but those who were further down on the open plains were done for.

Property that had been considered prime because of the wide-open spaces, with all that room for thousands of cattle, had now turned into death traps. The day of wide-open ranges, with cattle merging together in great herds, not to be separated by ownership until the spring round-ups, were gone. Fencing suddenly became acceptable. Keeping your own herd on your own property, and therefore easier to manage, quickly became the norm.

Nobody was laughing at the Rocking M anymore and many of the local ranchers now turned to Cameron for help. Methods of growing and storing hay then getting it out to the cattle during particularly cold winters were being studied, and the day of the great round-ups and cattle drives was over. The cattle that did survive those devastating ten days in January, limped through until spring, and those that made it to market were in such bad shape, it was hardly worth the effort.

Cameron helped where he could. His own good planning, along with Penny's intuitive grasp of all things financial, had kept the Rocking M in the black. He'd had the time to study this ranch before he bought it, unlike many others who had just been happy to buy a place.

But at the same time, the Marshams had to be careful with their own supplies. The hay that had been cut and baled, then stored for the winter months, wasn't as good or plentiful as usual, but they had enough for their own stock. If they were too generous and gave away their feed, then their own animals would end up starving.

Then, along with the snow thaw, came the thawing of all the cattle carcasses piled up against fence lines or lying out, stretching for miles across the mucky range. For months, the land was blanketed with the acrid stink of decay. There were so many cattle, spread over such great distances that there was nothing to be done about it.

The stench permeated the clothing: the water became so contaminated that it all had to be boiled before it was safe to drink or use for cooking. Food, whether cooked or eaten fresh from the garden tasted of corruption. Even freshly butchered meat tasted rotten since the animals had eaten the grass and drunk the water that was contaminated.

It is not surprising that all of these events put together made that spring another first at being the worst.

To Jack, this whole situation was yet another reminder why he wasn't in any hurry to buy himself a ranch. Even though, right now, he could probably get one just by showing up at the front door. The reality of being so much at the mercy of Mother Nature didn't set well with him at all.

But, despite all of this hardship and back-breaking work, Jack knew he had things good for now, so he sure wasn't going to start complaining.

***

Jack Kiefer rode down the lane toward the ranch house on his way back from town where he had been visiting with David and his new family. He smiled as Karma came up and trotted heavily along the fence line, happy to see her friend returning to keep her company. The two equine buddies nickered at each other, but time for visiting would have to come later.

Jack kept ole Midnight trotting forward and entered the yard to see Jean over by her vegetable garden, cleaning up the weeds to get it ready for spring planting. Everyone had come to accept the constant reek in the air and did their best to get back to some kind of normalcy

Even Eli was all bundled up in warm clothing and sitting in the dirt, playing with some sticks and stones. Only he knew what the full intent of his game was, and he seemed quite focused on it. That was, of course, until he spied his "Unc'a 'ack" come riding into the yard. Then, with a wild screech of delight, the toddler maneuvered himself to his feet and came at a fast waddle toward his friend.

Jean looked up from her weed pulling to watch the exchange between her son and his favorite uncle, and couldn't help but smile at the relationship that had developed between them.

"Hey there, little man," Jack greeted the toddler, as Eli came up to his horse. Jack pulled Midnight to a halt, so as not to step on the little fella.

Midnight felt a hint of irritation. Of course, he wasn't going to step on the miniature human; he knew better than that.

Eli seemed to know it, too, as he promptly wrapped his arms around Midnight's near foreleg and looked up, eyes filled with admiration for the man on the horse.

Midnight brought his muzzle around to blow into the tousled blonde hair. He always tried to be careful with these small creatures and was very patient with them, but he never quite knew what they were going to do.

Jack laughed and gave the big gelding an appreciative pat on the neck. Then he reached down and, grabbing Eli by the suspenders on his pants, pulled him up amidst shrieks of laughter to sit on his lap at the front of the saddle.

Midnight continued to stand still, with his head up and his ears pointed back toward the noisy creature. He knew to be careful with them when they were around his feet, but he wasn't so sure about having one of them sitting on him.

"Giddy!" Eli ordered, and started to swing his legs in an imitation of kicking a horse.

"Hey! Don't you talk to Midnight like that," Jack admonished him gently. "Midnight's a good ole boy. Show him some respect."

"Giddy!" Eli ordered again and laughed.

Jack smiled, and leaning forward just a touch, he pressed his lower leg against Midnight's flanks and the patient horse moved out at a walk. Eli sat there, all smiles and holding onto the saddle horn.

Fast!"

"Ya wanna go faster?"

"Yea. Fast!"

"Okay. But Midnight can go pretty fast, ya know," Jack cautioned him. "He used to be able to keep up with trains and outrun posses, so you better hang on."

Jack touched the gelding with his heel and soon they were into a trot and moving around the yard to the accompaniment of laughter and demands to go faster.

Midnight tucked his head and shook it, not so sure he was appreciating his second passenger, but still trying to make the best of the situation.

Karma watched placidly from her pasture; her only concern was wondering when her friend was going to be turned out to keep her company. Or, better yet, when was she going to be brought in for supper?

After about ten minutes of this new entertainment, Jean got up from her gardening and began brushing the dirt off her clothes and hands.

"Come along, Eli," she called out. "Time for you to get cleaned up for supper."

"Aww, no!"

Jack smiled as he brought Midnight down to a walk, then turned him toward Jean.

"You best listen to your ma," Jack told the youngster. "Besides, Midnight has already had a busy day, and he's gettin' tired."

"Aww."

Jack pulled up in front of Jean and, hoisting Eli out of the saddle, he swung him over and handed him down to his mother's waiting arms. Jean took him and settled him onto the ground, but held onto him long enough for him to get his balance.

She straightened up with a groan.

"Oh my, he's getting heavy," she complained. "I'm getting too old for this."

Jack smiled as he dismounted.

"I thought children were supposed ta keep ya young," he commented.

"Ha!" Jean waved an admonishing finger at him. "Just you wait; your time is coming."

"Uh huh."

"Are you going to visit Peter soon?" she asked him, all teasing aside.

"Yup," Jack answered. "I thought I'd head over there this weekend, if that's all right with Cameron."

"Oh, I'm sure it will be," Jean assured him. "He knows you've been itching to see him and make sure he's okay."

"Yeah," Jack repeated. "I want to see what Kenny has ta say about our plans as well, and just how far he would be willin' ta go along with 'em. A lot of this is gonna hinge on the support from both him and Dr. Palin."

"Yes, I know," Jean agreed. "I just hope we won't need to push it that far. It would be so nice to have Peter here for Caroline's wedding."

"Yeah. Well, we'll see." Jack didn't sound optimistic.

Jean smiled and put a hand on his arm.

"I know," she said. "Well, help Sam get the horses settled in for the evening and then come in for supper. Penny should have it ready here pretty soon."

"Yes ma'am."

***

Laramie, Wyoming

The weekend was upon them and though the temperatures were chilly, and patches of snow still covered the ground, it was gradually melting away. The roads and the rail lines were all clear and the risk of blizzards had become very low to totally unlikely.

Leon anticipated a visit from his nephew. For one thing, he couldn't wait to see the look on his face when he discovered that he had been volunteered to put in a visit at the orphanage. But when Jack hadn't shown up as expected, the anticipation turned to disappointment, and then to worry.

It was odd that there had been no sign of him, since the last letter Jack had written suggesting an impatience on his own part to get out for a visit.

Oh well, something may have come up and he hasn't been able to get away from the ranch.

Despite his disappointment, Leon hoped everything was all right, then tried to settle in to read his afternoon away.

On Monday after supper, when Leon returned to his cell with his customary cup of coffee, he spotted a telegram lying on his cot. What was this about? Picking it up, he read the short message;

KR. Tell NN next week. JK.

Oh, okay. Obviously, there had been a delay of some sort, and Jack would be coming the following weekend. Well, that's fine. At least he let me know. Now, all I have to do is get through yet another mundane week without getting into any trouble.

***

The following Saturday, Jack Kiefer walked into the foyer of the prison and knocked on the door to the processing room. He appeared strained; not at all like a man who was anticipating a happy reunion with his partner. It was obvious that something was on his mind.

Officer Davis opened the door and Jack handed over his gun, holster and coat, then plastered on a polite smile when asked the usual questions.

You'd think by now they would know who I am, and who I'm comin' ta see. This is beyond getting old.

"All right, Mr. Kiefer," Davis announced once the search had been completed, "if you would just take a seat for a few minutes. Officer Reece wants to talk to you before you go in for your visit."

"Hmm, yeah, okay," came Jack's non-committal response. Indeed, the fact that Kenny wanted to speak with him was hardly a surprise. Probably wanted to know what his intentions were.

Jack went to the bench in the hallway and sat down to wait. About fifteen minutes later, Kenny appeared and, joining the ex-outlaw, sat down beside him. The two men contemplated each other, until Kenny finally sighed and asked the inevitable question.

"So—are you planning on telling him?"

"Yeah. I think I should," Jack responded.

Kenny looked disappointed. "You sure?" he asked, even though he knew Jack was probably right. "It's just that he has been doing so well all winter, and news like this could be all it takes to send him spiraling down again."

Jack nodded sadly, looking at his hands for a moment.

"I know," he conceded. "But he's gonna find out about it sooner or later, you know that. I think it best if he hears it from me first."

"True enough," Kenny agreed, but he didn't look any happier about it than Jack did.

"I'm surprised that Officer Carson hasn't already told him," Jack commented. "This is exactly the kind of news I expect he would love to throw in Leon's face."

"Yeah," Kenny sighed. "I think the warden has told Mr. Carson to lay off Nash for a while. Too many outsiders paying attention to what goes on here."

"Oh," Jack nodded. "Well, at least that's one good thing. For now, anyway; I hope it don't blow up in our faces later."

"Time will tell," said Kenny. He took a deep breath, and the two men stood up. "I'll keep an eye on him over the next few days, try and stop him from doing anything stupid."

Jack smiled and nodded. "Yeah, okay. Thank you."

"All right. In the meantime, we need to discuss that other thing," Kenny pointed out. "You're going to be in town tonight, aren't you?"

"Yeah. I'll be at the hotel and catch the train in the morning."

"Why don't you come over for supper?" Kenny invited him. "I have to admit, the kids would love to meet you, and it would also give us a chance to talk with more privacy."

"Oh." Jack was taken by surprise. "Well, if it's all right with your wife—"

"I already asked her," Kenny admitted, then smiled. "Apparently, she would like to meet you, too."

"Okay," Jack accepted with a nod. "That'd be nice."

"Good," Kenny said. "Around seven would be fine. You can ask Officer Davis over there for the directions when you're done here. I have a feeling we're going to have a lot to talk about."

The two men parted company, and Kenny went to carry on with his duties. Officer Davis motioned to Kiefer that Leon was ready to see him now, so Jack headed to the door to the processing room. He stopped there for a moment, his hand on the knob, feeling like he didn't want to do this, but knowing that he had to. He took a deep breath, opened the door and went in.

Leon sat at his usual place on the other side of the table, and a huge grin spread across his face when he saw his nephew step into the room. But by the time Jack sat down, Leon's smile was gone, and a look of concern crept across his features.

"Jack?" he asked, suddenly worried. "What is it? What's wrong?"

"Leon, I . . ." but then Jack's throat tightened on him, and he had to clench his jaw to keep the emotion from rising up and taking control. He looked away from his uncle's worried eyes, suddenly unable to meet them.

"Aww Jack, now you're scaring me," Leon admitted, a slight tremor in his voice. "Just spit it out—just tell me, will you?"

Jack took a deep breath and told himself, *Yeah, just spit it out—just say it.* He forced himself to raise his eyes and look directly at his uncle. He swallowed and then, spit it out.

"Leon, I'm sorry. The Elk Mountain Gang is gone."

Coming soon

Volume Four: Departures

Jack was just about to his feet when the whole train car exploded with the reports from numerous Winchester rifles discharging at once. Glass windows exploded with deadly shards, and the air was filled with smoke. Jack, along with the other non-combatants, was instantly on the floor and covering this head.

Then all hell broke loose.

Armed men took positions on both sides of the car, ducking down beneath the shattered windows and firing at will at any target that presented itself. Bullets crashed into the car, sending more glass flying through the air and chipping away at the wooden interior, causing lethal missiles to shoot out and embed themselves in anything that got in their way.

Jack was on the floor beneath the seats, knowing it was too late to give warning; too late to help any of his friends out there in no man's land. He rolled himself into a ball, covering his head with his arms as the world exploded around him. He could feel the glass and wood splinters hitting him, but his adrenaline was pumping so hard, he wouldn't notice that they were embedding themselves into his hands.

Right then, all he knew was the chaos, with the acrid smell of gun powder burning his nostrils, and the wild yells of men, both inside the car and outside, caught up in the frenzy of battle. Jeez. How long could this go on for? How many of his friends were dying out there? And here he was, lying on the floor, unable to move; unable to help. Even in the shock of this assault, he knew if he pulled his gun and started shooting the ambushers, he'd be dead in seconds.

Oh, God. If Morrison was behind this, those fellas out there didn't stand a chance.

List of Characters

- Ames: Inmate. Young. In for arson
- Bart: Handyman at the orphanage
- Baxter, George: Governor of Wyoming, 1886
- Baxter, Mary: Tricia's mother
- Billings: Young inmate that died while in Leon's care
- Charlie: Mable's son
- Cleveland, Grover: U.S. President. 1885 – 1889, 1893 – 1897
- Daa'za (Summer): Leon's maternal grandmother
- Dale: Guard
- Davis: Guard
- Gibson, Nathanial Charles: Son of David and Tricia
- Ginger: Sam's horse, sorrel mare
- Hamilton, John: Doctor in Arvada before David took over
- Hamilton, Nancy: John's wife, mid-wife.
- Harry: Young sharp-shooter who challenges Jack to a fast-draw in Arvada.
- Hicks: A guard who had been attacked and killed by an inmate
- Jenkins, Martha: Widow woman and Taggard's friend, Medicine Bow, Wyoming
- Johnston: Inmate
- Huittsuu-a (Butterfly): Leon's mother
- Kwinaa (Eagle): Leon's childhood Shoshoni name
- Lucille: Suzie's daughter
- Mable: Jean's friend
- MacIntosh: Inmate
- Michael: Eligible young man, living at the Twin Star Ranch
- Millicent (Millie): Jean's friend, and Tricia's neighbor
- Moonlight, Thomas: Governor of Wyoming Territory, 1887 - 1889
- Morgan, Elliot: Secretary of the Territory and acting governor of Wyoming, 1886 – 1887

- Mukua (Spirit): A holy man and Leon's maternal uncle, and member of The Elk Mountain Gang
- Napai'aishe (Two At The Same Time): Leon's adult Shoshoni name
- Nat-soo-gant (Medicine Man): Leon's maternal grandfather
- Netuá (my son): Leon's pet name
- Orphan children: Beth, Charlie, Gillian, Henry, Ben, Joshua, Melanie, Michael, Sally, Todd and William
- Philip: Engaged to Sharon Wilson
- Reece, Alexander: Youngest son of Kenny and Sarah
- Reece, Charlie: Middle son of Kenny and Sarah
- Reece, Conner: Eldest son of Kenny and Sarah
- Reece, Evelyn: Daughter and youngest child of Kenny and Sarah
- Reece, Sarah: Kenny's wife
- Robbie: Deputy, Arvada, Colorado
- Robertson, Caleb: Infant son of Wendy and Floyd, died at birth
- Robertson, Floyd: Small rancher outside of Arvada, Colorado
- Robertson, Wendy: Floyd's wife, died in childbirth
- Sister Cornelia: A nun at the orphanage. Laramie, Wyoming
- Soames, Mariam, Doctor of Theology, conducts sermons at the Wyoming Territorial Prison, a friend of Leon and Jack
- Suzie: Jean's friend
- Thomas, Theodore: Lucille's betrothed
- Thompson: Young guard, bully, Carson's right-hand man
- Wilson, Sharon: engaged to Philip, due to unexpected pregnancy

WYOMING GOVERNORS

In order of term

- Hoyt, John Wesley: 1878 – 1882
- Hale, William: 1882 – 1885
- Morgan, Elliot: 1885.
- Warren, Frances: 1885 – 1886
- Baxter, George: 1886
- Morgan, Elliot: 1886 – 1887
- Moonlight, Thomas: 1887 – 1889
- Warren, Frances: 1889 – 1890
- Barber, Amos: 1890 – 1893
- Osborn, John: 1893 – 1895
- Richards, William: 1895 - 1899
- Richards, DeForrest: 1899 – 1903

ABOUT THE AUTHOR

I have always been a cowgirl at heart even though I have lived my whole life on the West Coast of Canada and the USA., but our road trips always draw us east and south. Montana, Wyoming, Colorado; these are places where my imagination runs wild.

I've been an artist/writer all my life, painting and writing about my first passion, the West. I also found a niche with painting pet portraits and animal studies. Now that I am retired, I can indulge in the things I love the most: my husband, my animals, my art and my writing. I'm busier now than I have ever been before, and I wouldn't have it any other way.

www.twoblazesartworks.com

Made in the USA
Columbia, SC
19 February 2023

12530206R00240